Praise

"This book may be called *In Ruins* but the only thing it will ruin is giving you a good night's sleep as you won't be able to put this book down!"

—Cheryl's Book Nook

"A fantastic read! I would recommend this to anyone that enjoys love/hate relationships!"

—The Book Enthusiast on *In Ruins*

"*In Ruins* was jammed packed with GOODNESS! This book reminds me and gave me all the feels *Beautiful Disaster* by Jamie McGuire did. For all you Travis Maddox lovers out there, you will love Tucker Green just as much."

—PunchDrunkLibrary

In Pieces

DANIELLE PEARL

FOREVER

New York   Boston

Copyright © 2017 by Danielle Pearl

Cover design by Elizabeth Turner

Cover images © istock/Getty Images, Shutterstock

Cover copyright © 2017 by Hachette Book Group, Inc.

Forever

Hachette Book Group

1290 Avenue of the Americas, New York, NY 10104

forever-romance.com

twitter.com/foreverromance

First Edition: October 2017

Forever is an imprint of Grand Central Publishing. The Forever name and logo are trademarks of Hachette Book Group, Inc.

The publisher is not responsible for websites (or their content) that are not owned by the publisher.

The Hachette Speakers Bureau provides a wide range of authors for speaking events. To find out more, go to www.hachettespeakersbureau.com or call (866) 376-6591.

Library of Congress Cataloging-in-Publication Data has been applied for.

ISBNs: 978-1-4555-6831-4 (trade paperback), 978-1-4555-6832-1 (ebook)

Printed in the United States of America

LSC-C

10 9 8 7 6 5 4 3 2 1

For my mom, the woman who set fate into motion with my name, and who has never stopped encouraging my writing. I wouldn't be here without you, figuratively, and, of course, literally. Because, moms.

Prologue

Beth

Age 15

The front door slams shut, the sound echoing through the house, underscoring its emptiness.

It's nothing new. I'm used to it—the emptiness. It lives inside me, and I feel most at home when my world reflects it.

When there's no one around, there's no one to pretend for.

My brother's car engine starts, idles, and then off he drives, the faint crunch of gravel fading into quiet. Then…nothing but the crickets.

I like the silence. It matches the emptiness. It fits, and I let it blanket me, wondering what ever appealed to me about things like conversation and laughter.

A soft crack reverberates off my bedroom window and my pulse takes off like a rocket ship.

Is he here?

I move to the window that overlooks my backyard, violently wrestling the heavy drapery out of the way to search for him in his usual spot.

Or what used to be his usual spot.

The emptiness burgeons and billows. *There's no one there.*

I curl my fingers into a fist and grind it into my sternum. It doesn't relieve the build up of pressure. The emptiness is more palpable than any tangible substance, and it's finally stretching the bars of its cage, seeking new territory to conquer.

It's nothing if not determined.

I make my way over to my vast walk-in closet and kneel in the back right corner, reaching into the old duffel I'd used for my two-summer stint at sleepaway camp. I dig around until I find my stash, pull out a tiny bottle of Jack Daniel's, and down it in two swallows. I don't even taste it. I repeat the action with a second mini-whiskey, then stow the drained bottles in an otherwise empty Tory Burch shoebox hidden in plain sight on my shoe rack.

But my olfactory senses aren't as lucky as my taste buds, and the ominous, pungent scent of alcohol—one I recognized by the time I was five, that used to warn me the switch inside my father was in danger of flipping—overtakes me. Memories flash, unbidden: the esteemed, professional façade he wore for the world shattering in a flash—shouting and shoving, my mother's shrieks, my brother's cries. Their bruises…even blood. And me, cowering in a corner somewhere, waiting for a reprieve that would only ever be temporary.

But still…I never wanted him to leave.

Too bad my brother felt differently; he kicked our father out of our house and our lives the minute he was big enough to hit back. And too bad my father didn't care enough to come back for us. *For me.*

After he left, I started to suspect that mine wasn't the normal kind of sadness other kids felt. That not everyone experienced the lost, hopeless sense of emptiness that, at times, threatened to crush me like a boa constrictor strangling its prey. I was just barely eleven.

The emptiness has only grown more and more persistent since then, and while I used to be able to find temporary refuge in simple things, like friendship and family and fun, losing Brian changed everything. Just like when my father left, my break up fed the emptiness like some kind of magic fertilizer, sending its thorny brambles climbing and twisting, until it resembled something out of *Little Shop of Horrors*—a monstrous weed intent on consuming even the most fledgling buds of happiness in my life.

The emptiness is a greedy bastard.

I used to wonder how far it would spread, what it would do when I had nothing left for it to feed on. I'd imagine it bursting free of my body, escaping the confines of its own wreckage. I picture the familiar image now—a torrent of melancholic colors, dark and murky, finally too much for the body that created it, exploding and escaping, destroying its shell. *Free*. And I imagine the relief. It's positively palpable.

Because I know how close it is.

I startle when my phone buzzes with a text. It's my brother.

> Just got to Coop's. People asking for you. Let me know if you want me to come back and get you, ok? 9:36 PM

I sigh, but don't send a reply. Sammy tried everything to get me to come out with him tonight. To *show Brian I'm over it*.

It's ironic, really. A year ago my brother had scoffed at my suggestion he take me to a party with him.

But it's been weeks since I've been to a party. In fact, it's been weeks since I've done any socializing at all, and I don't even miss it. I only miss *him*. Still, the last place on earth I want to be is the home of Brian's friend, at a party he is almost certainly attending, pretending to be indifferent when he acts like I don't exist.

And, anyway, I have my own plans tonight.

The look my big brother gave me before he left—the hurt, sad bloodhound eyes, the concern and the love—it gave me the resolve I need to move forward. Because I can't see him look like that anymore. I can't be the cause of everyone's pain. I won't.

A muffled crack reaches my ears and I freeze. *It's not him*, I tell myself. It's never him anymore.

But I tentatively make my way back to the window, anyway. Just in case.

And there, past the flagstone patio, in the shadows of the white cedar gazebo, is a dark form.

He's here.

My heart skips and hops all over the place, stumbling to gain its footing.

He's really here!

I check myself in the full-length mirror and I'm taken aback by my ghastly appearance. I look like utter shit. My hair is disheveled, unwashed and limp, and I'm not wearing an ounce of makeup. My once bright, flawless skin is marred by blemishes from every day I've been too tired to wash my face, and the sweats I haven't changed in days are wrinkled and dirty.

Yep—shit.

I should change. I should put on makeup. Really I should shower, but surely by then he'd be gone, and then he might never come back.

I check my phone to see if he called or texted to say he was coming, but all I find are the last several texts from our year-long chat—all from me, all unanswered.

He must have wanted to surprise me. To tell me he was wrong, that we can make it work long distance, that he misses me. I don't care what he tells me at this point, just as long as he speaks to me.

Like the first warm spring breeze after a long, frosty winter, my frigid heart thaws the slightest bit, and I recognize a feeling he stole from me when he broke my heart. *Hope.*

But a blast of cold grips my chest before it even can fully take shape—the thought of looking Brian in the eye faltering my steps. My belly rolls with nausea as unbearable regret lances through me, and I nearly double over. *Could he ever forgive me?*

I force it out of my mind. I have to get to him before he changes his mind about wanting to see me.

I rush down the stairs and through our foyer, nearly slipping on the marble tile. I take the quickest route outside—through the great room and out the French doors—only mildly aware that I'm barefoot. I hurry across the patio and around the pool, and down the two stone steps until my soles meet the dewy grass. And still, I run. I make a beeline for the gazebo—*our gazebo*.

"Bri?" I call out.

He doesn't respond.

"Bri, are you here?"

Silence.

"Brian?"

I search through the shadows, seeking out his familiar form. But it's too dark. We always leave the lights off in the gazebo. He may or may not know Sammy is at his friend Cooper's party, but he doesn't know my mother is in the city for the weekend, so surely he's sticking to our protocol for sneaking around. Brian is closer to my brother's age than mine, a grade above him, in fact, and only weeks shy of eighteen. Sammy was less than thrilled about us from the start, so we've always taken caution to keep our private life private.

Brian isn't in the gazebo, a fact I realize before I step onto the wood-planked floor, so I sit on the bench that lines the walls, waiting for him to reveal himself. But when he still doesn't emerge from the trees a minute later, I know.

He isn't here.

He was never here.

I've become so desperate that even my mind has begun to betray me, conjuring visions of things that were never real, not even when they were real. Maybe tangibly, but not truly. Or I wouldn't be alone in this gazebo right now.

The emptiness swells, the hopelessness surges, and I'm finally ready to set it free. There's no other choice.

I slowly make my way back into the house. I'm in no rush—I've timed it perfectly. Sammy is staying at his best friend Tucker's tonight, and my mother won't be home until Sunday evening. I can't let anyone mess things up, or make me second-guess something I'm sure of.

My feet track dew-damp spots through the house, but they'll be long dry before anyone comes home to find them. I step back into my bedroom, and I pause to really take it in. The memories are suffocating.

Smiles and giggles as my mother painted my toenails right there on my stark white eyelet bedspread. My dad's tickle attacks and dramatic readings of Harry Potter—awful British accent and all—but only on weekends, if he happened to be home for my bedtime. Sammy and his friends Tucker and David unapologetically manipulated by their six-year-old hostess into the tea parties and dance parties I loved so much.

But although those happier memories are greater in number, it's the other, more potent memories that monopolize thoughts of my childhood.

I slip my hand between my mattress and box spring, to the small cardboard box that will fix everything.

I remember the moment my father handed it to me on my eighth birthday—how my eyes lit up as I opened the white box with the gold-lettered logo from the popular, local jewelry shop, to reveal a second, black velvet case. I reach unconsciously for the chain dangling from my neck, fingering the hand-shaped white-gold charm with the diamond eye in the center. A "hamsa," traditional to his Jewish heritage, meant to keep away the evil eye. To bring luck.

Worthless piece of shit.

I tear it from my neck, not bothering with the clasp, and empty the current contents of the box into my palm, slipping the necklace back into its original home. I replace the cover, and slide it back under my mattress, pushing it deep, where no one will find it.

I close my hand around the forty or so small, football-shaped white pills I've pilfered from my mother's medicine cabinet over the past two months, always fearful she'd notice. She never did.

I sit on the edge of my bed, and grab the water bottle off of my nightstand.

Should I leave a note? Maybe text my brother and mother that I love them? But I don't want them to know something's up—to give them time to thwart me. I pick up my phone. Maybe I can leave an unsent email for them to find later…

I jump as it buzzes in my hand, as if it knows what I'm planning.

Or whoever's texting me does.

I know I shouldn't look—that it's probably Sammy again, worrying as usual lately. But against my better judgment, I click on the home-screen and open the text.

My heart leaps into my throat.

It's Sammy's friend David.

Hey kid. Thought you'd finally be out tonight. 9:51 pm

I shouldn't respond. David is a wildcard. He makes me feel things. He always has. Things even Brian never did. But Brian returned my affections; David never could. He's my brother's oldest friend, after all.

Not feeling up to it I guess. 9:54 pm

I shoot back the quick reply and stare idly at the phone in my palm for a few beats, before my other hand squeezes its contents, reminding me that this is not a moment for chatting with my childhood crush. Even if once, for one fleeting moment, I thought maybe, someday, he could possibly be something more. Because I'm holding a handful of guarantees that that'll never happen.

Buzz.

I startle again.

Again I look, despite warning myself not to. Because just the fact that he gives half a shit has me acting like a stupid, boy-crazy schoolgirl again.

Fuck that. Fuck HIM. Let me come get you. You need to roll up
in here and show him you don't give a fuck. 9:55 pm

But I do give a fuck. I give all of them.

Come on, Bea. You've always been too good for that dipshit. We
can go somewhere else if you want. Just get out of that fucking
house, okay? 9:57 pm

Bea, not *kid*. My chest swells and my heart races. My lips almost
twist into some semblance of a smile, but I catch myself.

Because I've put too much thought into this to be swayed by some
false hope and a pet name that once meant the world to me, and nothing to him. *Story of my life.*

Maybe tomorrow. 9:58

The lie comes easily enough in its digital form. Because there will
be no more tomorrows. Not for me.

Another buzz from my phone, but this time I just power it off.

David. He's the one thing causing that whisper of doubt I really
don't need right now.

I sit on the edge of my bed, and I down the pills. Every last one.

I wait for that moment of panic, of regret, but it doesn't come. Only
certainty and relief.

I lie back on my bed, wondering how long they will take to work.

And then, I cry. Not for myself, but for the few people in this world
who love me. Because I know that tomorrow they will be hurting beyond measure, but I also know that in the long run, they will be far,
far better off.

Chapter One

Beth

Present Day (Three years later)

I take my seat in the enormous lecture hall, settling in for an hour of tedium. If you thought Psych 101 would be interesting, you'd be wrong. Or at least, the lectures aren't especially interesting, but I suppose that's more the fault of Professor Fawning than the actual subject matter.

The class itself is a mixed bag. Freshman and sophomore psych majors, like me, sit in the first few rows, intent on succeeding in a course that will be the foundation of our studies here at Rill Rock University. But there are also plenty of upperclassmen just looking to get an elective out of the way—something they'd hoped would offer easy credits. Which it probably will. It's only the third class of the semester, but so far it doesn't seem especially difficult.

My eyelids droop, threatening to lead me into an inconvenient nap, so I straighten my spine, abandoning the comfort of my seat-back.

I was up late. Not partying, like most of the other students half-asleep right now, but manically trying to finish the first assignment for my Shakespeare class.

I peek at my watch. Professor Fawning will cut off his droning any minute now, and it can't come soon enough. I need to get my legs moving to ward off this late-morning lethargy.

"There he is, like fucking clockwork," my roommate, Elana, murmurs from beside me, never one to miss an opportunity for a well-placed expletive. "Your sexy-as-fuck bodyguard."

But I already knew he was there. I've always had an inexplicable kind of sixth sense for his proximity, and I glance over to the doorway, where he casts a towering shadow into the room.

I can't help but roll my eyes. David isn't here out of his own interest, or even concern. He cares about me, sure, in his own big-brotherly way, but that isn't the reason he's here. My brother's oldest friend is outside my psych class, waiting for me like he did on Tuesday and last Thursday before that, because he promised Sammy he'd look out for me. And, it would appear, he's taken that to mean babysitting.

But I don't need a damned babysitter. Or *bodyguard*, as Lani put it.

Fawning dismisses us, and I dutifully march over to my de facto on-campus big brother, Lani keeping step beside me. I barely meet David's eyes as he hands me an iced coffee. They're too disarming, and they still affect me in ways no big-brother type should.

"You don't have to keep checking up on me," I grumble.

I don't know if Sammy actually asked him to look after me outright—though I suspect he did—or if David just took it upon himself as his implied duty, but I've survived freshman orientation and the first week of classes intact, so I'm hoping he'll back off soon. There's something about the luster of his company that's always been dulled by knowing that it's only out of obligation.

"You can check up on *me*, anytime," Lani suggests, her lashes batting dramatically.

That's her. No poise, no guile. She thinks David is hot, and she wants him to know it. Not that he could miss it.

"No sweat, kid," he replies, ignoring Lani's comment as he slings a friendly arm around my shoulders, and we fall into step toward the building's exit, sipping our coffees as we head in the direction of the student union—or Stu-U, as David calls it.

"You know, *I* like coffee," Lani interjects, refusing to be ignored. "I like toned and inked-up arms around me, too."

I can't help my laugh. David does have fantastic arms. The tattoos are mostly new—a few older than the rest—an array of religious symbols, admired figures, and quotes.

"Don't you have your own friends, gnat?" David murmurs absently to Lani.

I wince inwardly. I don't like that he's given her a pet name. Even one that implies she's annoying and unwanted. Because she's the kind of girl guys *want*. She's freaking beautiful. All deep red waves and chocolate eyes, curvy in all the right places…Yeah, she knows what guys see when they look at her, which is why she takes David's teasing in stride.

"*Friends*, yes. My own personal bodyguard? Not since I ditched my last mistake, but I'm in the market for my next one," she says cheekily.

I let out another laugh. She really is something else. Fortunately for me, though, David ignores her.

I probably should have said something to her about him earlier, back when I first noticed her interest. Or maybe I should have anticipated it. David is the kind of guy who attracts crushes—he always has been. But now, he's something different. Something more.

I didn't follow David to school here, and I'm glad no one has ever noticed my crush enough to presume otherwise. RRU is a state school here on Long Island, where we all grew up, and though it isn't big, it is renowned for its School of Arts and Sciences, which includes the psychology and social work program that brought me here. After everything I've endured in my short lifetime, I know what saved me, and I want to be that—to do that—for other kids someday.

David, on the other hand, is here for the creative writing program. Words have always been his thing, though he'd always kept his passion mostly to himself. In fact, I doubt even his closest friends—my brother included—knew all that much about his interest or talent before he won that national short story competition their sophomore year of high school.

But I knew. I knew a long time ago. Because he told me, and I can't help but wonder if he even remembers. I wouldn't blame him if he didn't. It feels like a lifetime ago. Back before the world got so complicated—when the worst kind of heartache was a schoolyard crush, the angsty sting of unrequited love. Turns out, love gets far more dangerous when it's actually returned.

I try not to be so affected by David's arm around me, reminding myself of my place with him—which is his best friend's kid sister at least, and a friend at best—but when you've carried a torch this long, it doesn't take much to spark its flame.

"So, kid, no morning classes tomorrow, right?" he asks.

I narrow my eyes, wondering where he's going with this. "Not until noon," I confirm warily.

"Perfect. BEG's hosting its first party of the year, and you're my guest of honor."

"What in the actual fuck are you talking about, David?" *Looks like a week of living with Lani has started to rub off on me.*

David startles vaguely at my colorful response, and I barely catch the amused smirk that tugs at his mouth. Before he can answer me, however, Lani's enthusiasm bubbles over.

"Uh, *yes*. Yes, yes, yes! We accept your generous invitation to be your *guests* of honor!" She emphasizes the plural, and again I laugh. This time David also cracks a smile, and deep in my belly the vicious snake of jealousy lifts its ugly head.

I urge it back to sleep. "A frat party? Really, David?" I arch a skeptical brow. David's in Beta Epsilon Gamma, a fraternity notoriously filled with athletes—and decidedly different kinds of *players*. But he doesn't live in the house—*not his style*, he told me.

He hooks his arm further around me so he can turn me to face him, and we all stop walking. "Bea…Come." His eyes—a green-

and-honey hazel that have fascinated me for years—grab hold of me, seducing and imploring.

"Why?" I breathe.

David sighs. "You need a fun night out, where you don't have to worry about anything, or anyone."

"And you think a frat house is the place to do that?" My skepticism returns. I'm not naïve. I know what goes on in places like that. And David knows me well enough to know my social anxiety gives me more than just the usual reasons to be leery of a frat party.

"*My* frat house, kid. With *my* brothers. And more importantly, *me*." He looks at me meaningfully.

I look away, my eyes inadvertently landing on his defined bicep, and I notice ink I haven't seen before peeking out from beneath the hem of his short sleeve. My fingers reach out to stroke it before I can stop myself. A quote in beautiful black script, matching the others.

There are more things in heaven and earth than are dreamt of in your philosophy.

"*Hamlet*." It's one of my favorite quotes from one of my favorite plays—more words from the master to add to David's collection.

"Shakespeare, really?" Lani says.

He cocks an eyebrow. "You got a problem with the Bard?" he retorts, but he's looking at me. They're the exact words he said to me after he got that first quote inked into his skin—also from *the Bard*, back in high school.

My eyes automatically shoot to his T-shirt, envisioning the ink over his left pectoral muscle, engraved into his skin back when he was legally too young to even get one. It made him seem like a real badass, even though it was a quote from Shakespeare.

But it's this new one that's got me thinking. Because there *is* more to life than I can learn in a classroom; I know that.

"Beth's taking a Shakespeare elective this semester—maybe she can study off of your body," Lani smirks. We both ignore her.

"Look, Bea, college isn't only about academics, okay?"

Bea. Not *kid*.

"And I'm not saying you need to make up for lost time all in one night. Just to try and keep an open mind and have some fun. You trust me, don't you?"

"Of course I do." My answer is instant and honest.

And the thing is, part of me knows David is right. I missed out on a normal high school experience in part because I never knew how to find any balance. When I wasn't surrendering to social anxiety—or the debilitating emptiness that flared more and more—I was diving into a relationship I was ill-prepared for, experiencing too much, too early on. I can't pretend I haven't wondered what it would have been like to feel young and carefree like everyone else my age. To drink a little too much, smoke an occasional joint, or engage in a hookup that had no greater meaning. I've still only ever slept with one guy, and that was over three years ago.

"Great. Show up at nine."

And I will. Because David called me *Bea*, and even if it was just a slip of the tongue to him, it is a magic word to me, and I wonder if he even remembers when he first called me that.

* * *

Abnormal Psych is in a smaller lecture hall. Professor Bowman is a practicing social worker, and she also runs the student help line in the mental health offices of the on-campus health center, where I stopped by during orientation to look into volunteering.

I don't want to wait until I have a degree and a license to help people. I know better than most how empty life can feel—how despairingly hopeless—and the difference it can make just to have someone to talk to.

If there's anything I've learned over the years, it's that there's no getting used to having your thoughts and emotions hijacked by the chemicals inside your own brain—having your life sabotaged by an invisible rogue force inside your own body.

It was thanks to my mother and Sammy, and not least of all to Dr. Schall, that I found a treatment that works for me. And it's still a struggle some days, but while I've accepted that it will always be a part of me, I've also learned how to embrace it—how to channel it into something positive. In fact, David actually helped with that, even if he doesn't know it.

It's only the third class, but it's already obvious that Professor Bowman is a great teacher, and I don't have to feign my interest in her lecture, or fight to stay awake. Bowman is knowledgeable and engaging, and the class flies by.

But despite my interest, I find myself distracted by an inexplicable sense of unease.

I feel strangely unsettled. Like someone is watching me.

A vague shiver creeps down my spine and I'm struck with the urge to turn around.

So I do. I peek over my shoulder from my seat in the first row, and my gaze automatically lands on the culprit.

My stomach flips as I try to place the stranger.

He isn't even watching me—he's *glaring* at me. Aren't you supposed to look away when someone catches you staring?

Glaring.

A beat passes. Two. A third, and then he looks away with irritation, as if he doesn't feel particularly compelled to submit to this social demand, and only does so reluctantly. I return my eyes to the front of the room.

What the fuck was that?

Who *the fuck was that?*

If I've ever seen him before, I have no memory of it.

I decide to sneak another peek.

He has the grace to look away faster this time, but his eyes were most definitely on me a split second ago.

And what eyes they are. Completely foreign, and yet somehow unfathomably familiar. Deep blue, similar to mine in shade, but different in every other way. His are like the ocean. Not the translucent aquamarine of the Caribbean, but a dark ocean. A stormy, turbulent one. An ocean hiding secrets below its depths, its murky waters concealing the dangers beneath.

The kind of ocean that will drown you if you're not careful.

But I have no intention of getting caught in a riptide, by him or any other man. I've been there, done that, been drowned and reborn, and I'll stick to the safety of swimming pools, thank you very much.

But then, this guy didn't seem to be staring at me in the usual way a boy stares at a girl, which is all the more off-putting. He wants something from me, I've no doubt, but I don't think it's what most guys want, and that frightens me.

I take advantage of his attention being elsewhere, even if he's faking it, and take a moment to study him.

I hadn't noticed him before today, which is strange. Not because I've taken note of each of the fifty or so students in the room—I haven't—but because he's the kind of guy a girl notices.

Even seated, his stature is unmistakable. He's got to be at least six feet, probably a few inches over. He's bulky in a way that makes it obvious he's committed to his fitness, but I doubt it's out of vanity. He seems intense—the kind of guy who works out to release hostile energy, and his sculpted muscles are simply a happy by-product. His face is all sharp lines and hard planes, his dark, prominent, masculine brow furrowed in what seems to be perpetual agitation. He positively radiates disquiet.

It raises my hackles even more.

I'm about to look away when he resettles his glare right on mine, brazenly meeting my eyes. It's shameless, but instead of averting my gaze, I find myself returning his glare dead-on.

And why should *I* back down? *He's* the one challenging me with his inappropriate fucking staring.

A lightning bolt of familiarity strikes in my gut like a wave of *déjà vu*, and it makes no sense. He must remind me of someone. David, maybe. Or my brother, who definitely has his intense moments.

And then, so subtly I almost miss it, the corner of the stranger's mouth twitches, as if it wants to smile, but barely knows how.

I narrow my eyes, refusing to surrender, because regardless of what he thinks I look like, I am *not* some weak little girl.

I am a *survivor*. And he will not intimidate me with a fucking *glare*.

"Okay, guys. See you Tuesday." Professor Bowman dismisses us, and glarey asshole looks away first—*victory!*—grabs his notebook, and pushes his way down the aisle, students scampering out of his path as he moves. Yeah, he has that kind of presence.

I'm done wasting my time on him, so I approach Bowman to ask her about volunteer hours. She offers to meet me tomorrow morning, which is perfect since I don't have a class until noon.

Glarey stranger is gone when I leave the room, much to my relief, and I head to my last class of the day wondering if there's any way of getting out of the BEG party tonight. But considering how adamant David seemed this morning, he would probably show up at my dorm and drag me there by my hair.

I blush at the prospect. It doesn't sound all that terrible.

Chapter Two

David

"Tonight will be mostly upperclassmen, but a few brothers mentioned they invited some exceptionally hot freshmen, so go easy, please. These girls don't need to be traumatized their first week on campus, and definitely not at our house," Steven Bogart, our fraternity's president, announces about tonight's party. "Last thing we need is to blacken our rep even more."

"Wait. Fresh girls are off limits? Even for us?" Rectum Ralph asks. Most of the pledges are freshmen, and he's obviously not happy at the thought of being limited to older girls who aren't likely to give him the time of day. Or so he assumes. Clearly he has yet to learn what it means to be in BEG, even if only as a pledge.

But he will. Probably tonight, for that matter. Hell, I bagged a junior at my first frat party. I'd been on campus all of four days.

"No one's off limits," I correct him for Bogart. "But I wouldn't recommend trying to move in on another brother's territory, and since any freshmen here tonight would have been invited by someone…"

"Got it. Me and my hand tonight," Rectum grumbles.

There's a chorus of laughter and some name calling.

"Brother March, I move to revoke Rectum's pledge bid and toss him the fuck out of BEG!" Trevor calls out, but his eyes glint with

humor and his smirk tells me he's just busting the pledge's balls—
one of our favorite pastimes. *Hey, we've all been there.*

"Violation?" I ask, playing along, suppressing my chuckle as Rectum's eyes go wide as flying fucking saucers.

"Quoting fucking Pink."

The room fills with another round of laughter, as well as Rectum's
palpable relief as he realizes he's just being fucked with. Yeah, no one
wants to get tossed from BEG. They're all still counting their lucky
fucking stars they even got tapped in the first place.

"Noted. We'll put it up for a vote at the next meeting." More
laughter. "Anyway, to answer your question, Rectum, since you're
still technically a pledge—*for now*—you'll learn sooner than later that
every chick on campus wants a Beta. You don't need to stick to freshmen," Bogart explains.

"Beta Epsilon Gamma, makes all the bitches B-E-G!" A random
brother jokingly chants a well-known phrase about our frat—if not
one I'm particularly proud of.

"Sweet," Rectum exclaims.

Yeah. *Sweet, in-fucking-deed*. He has no idea, but he will.

Rex assigns the pledges their duties and instructions for setup
tonight, as Reeve—who's probably my closest friend here at RRU, and
definitely in BEG—sucks down his second beer, openly bored as fuck.
He rarely bothers to emerge from his basement bedroom to discuss
things like pledge duties or chapter meetings, so no one takes his disinterest personally.

But before Bogart dismisses the pledges, I add one more thing—
the most important.

"There will be one freshman girl here tonight who *is* off limits. My
boy's kid sister, Beth Caplan. She's fucking family and she is not to be
fucked with, under any circumstances. If you see anyone even thinking about fucking with her, you intervene, and you send someone to
inform me, immediately and in that order," I command.

"How do we know who she is?" Dicknose asks, looking a little anxious.

"Easy," I reply. "When the girl who looks like a fucking angel walks through that door, and every head turns her way and every dick turns to stone—that's Beth. But remember. Off. Fucking. Limits. She's the Hope fucking diamond. Stunning, too good for any of you, and she carries the curse of death for anyone who tries to get their nasty, unworthy paws on her." I mean every word. "We fucking clear?"

Chapter Three

Beth

There are throngs of people outside of the frat house, a small crowd slowly but surely funneling its way up the walkway and into the party David finally convinced me to come to.

But the more I think about it—and his new tattoo—the more I think he's right. Part of why I chose to go away to school despite my parents all but begging me to commute was to prove to them and Sammy—and maybe even to myself—that I'm not the same broken girl I was three years ago. That I'm ready for this. Adulthood. Independence. All of it. And like David said—like his bicep will forever say—*there are more things in heaven and earth…*

It takes a full five minutes before Lani and I are even on the steps of the front porch.

"Ten dollars each," some faceless frat boy tells the group in front of us. He's a walking cliché, with his jeans, polo shirt, and RRU baseball cap.

"I can't believe we have to pay to get in here," I murmur to Lani, and we both hastily rummage through our bags and pull together twenty dollars. Lucky, since I don't often carry cash, it being 2017 and all.

The group in front of us is allowed through the door and we walk up next. Faceless frat boy does in fact have a face, it turns out. And it's actually a pretty handsome face. He is the epitome of *All-American* with his blond hair and blue eyes, but he reminds me of Brian, and I find it a little irksome.

"Well hello there, beautiful girls," Frat Boy smiles wryly.

Okay, *flirting*. I remember how to do this, right? "Uh…hi." *Apparently not.*

"Hi handsome, this your house?" *Thank God for Lani.*

His smirk widens. "Sure is. Are you freshmen or transfers? Because I definitely would have remembered seeing you before."

"Freshmen," we say in unison, and I wince.

But Frat Boy chuckles. "Welcome to Rill Rock. Hope to see more of you." He looks between the two of us like he hasn't decided which one he finds more interesting, but I doubt he cares. It's early days, and we are fresh meat.

"Um, it's ten dollars, right?" I murmur.

Another chuckle. "For some people, yeah. Not for beautiful girls, though. Put your money away." His stare slithers down my body in a way that makes me shudder, and I peek over at Lani. But her smile is pleased and inviting, and directed squarely at Frat Boy.

"I'm Drew." His gaze lands on me as he holds out his hand.

I shakily slip mine in for a shake, but he kisses my knuckles instead. "Beth Caplan."

He drops my hand like it's on fire and I startle. He abandons the flirtation, his smirk rebounding into a cordial smile. "Go on in. Nice to meet you."

I roll my eyes and start in through the open door.

"Your bodyguard is really starting to cramp my style," Lani grumbles.

I wonder if David warned the entire party about hitting on me, or just his frat brothers. It's irrational—I know I should probably be grateful, considering I have zero interest in dating right now—but still, it bugs me. Because it isn't my disinterest that motivated him. It's that he still sees me as a child. Imagine if he knew about my suicide attempt? He'd probably cover me in freaking bubble wrap and write "delicate" across my ass in black Sharpie.

The party is packed, and people toss drinks down their throats faster than they can refill their cups. Everyone seems to know each other, and I start to gather that we may be two of the only freshmen here. Some guy offers Lani and me drinks, but I stop her before she can accept. I know better than to take a drink from a stranger, and I tell him that we'll make our way to the keg ourselves.

"There she is," David's voice drawls from behind me.

I turn to face him and he falters for a strange moment. Of course, this has got to be weird for him, too—seeing me here, in his frat house, all done up and in a dress.

"Let me get you guys drinks," he says, recovering.

Minutes later we're being introduced to crowd after crowd, drinks in hand, but I do note the guys are exceptionally disinterested. Lani grows increasingly discouraged as the night wears on, and eventually she gets tired of her boy-repellant roommate, and excuses herself to see what kind of trouble she can find.

While the guys work hard to discredit every frat-boy stereotype ever portrayed, at least every time they get within five feet of me—an act that would be far more encouraging if it were earnest and not, in fact, an act—the girls, on the other hand, are walking clichés. They don't seem remotely daunted by the fact that David has a girl on his arm, ostensibly at least. I mean, they don't know me. They don't know I'm not his date, right?

Of course, it's possible that they know David, or know his reputation well enough to assume that even if I were his date, it wouldn't make him any less available. It irritates me, and I shrug his arm from around my shoulders, masking it by stepping the few feet back to the keg to refill my cup.

It takes less than a minute, and by the time I turn around to make my way back to him, another lioness has moved in on my territory.

Not your territory, Beth, I reluctantly remind myself. It's a familiar message, and you'd think that all these years of repetition might actually get it through my head.

I hang back, watching her overt flirting, watching David fall so naturally into his role in this little game. He was made for it. Hitting on girls, getting laid. My chest echoes with a timeworn ache.

Well, I don't have to watch him in action.

I'm about to turn around and go find Lani when he spots me, and before I can make my escape, his huge palm closes around my shoulder, as if he knows I'm about to flee.

"Beth, come meet Liz. She's in SDG, our sister sorority."

Liz's smile stretches wide, revealing a mouth full of unnaturally whitened teeth, framed by scarlet lips that match her nails. "Nice to meet you," she sings, but I suspect she's less than thrilled about adding another girl to the equation.

I murmur a cursory greeting. I'm not great at conversation, especially small talk with strangers. It doesn't help that David's hand hasn't left my shoulder, and I try to focus on the tail end of whatever this girl who wants to sleep with him is saying, instead of the way his contact sears my skin.

"I don't think that's really Beth's thing," David murmurs, and I blink at him, mortified that I have no idea what was even said.

But David rescues me. "Sororities aren't for everyone," he says. "Rush starts next week," he explains.

"Oh—uh, yeah," I agree.

Liz doesn't respond. The way she looks at me has unease rising in my belly—like she's sizing up the competition or something. Well, the joke's on her, because that's the last thing I am. I am the girl-next-door to her vixen, the kid sister to her one-night stand. But that's fine. In all of my fantasies of David, I never once imagined myself as some one-night stand. No, I wanted to be more than that, and that's something this girl will never be.

"So, Beth," she says, "is that your full name? Or is it Elizabeth?"

"Oh. Um, it's Elizabeth. But no one ever calls me that." It's not that I didn't know Liz is short for Elizabeth; it's just that I haven't enough interest in her to care.

"How funny," she coos, though I don't know why. It's not exactly an uncommon name.

My smile is forced and, I suspect, only marginally convincing.

David's hand squeezes my shoulder in encouragement, or camaraderie. He may want to fuck her—hell, for all I know he already has—but he doesn't think much more of her than I do. I know him well enough to know that.

"You know, my mom once told me they'd considered calling me Beth. You know, as a nickname. But she said it was too..." Liz searches for the word, waving her hand in practiced nonchalance. "You know—like for a little girl. *Childish*. And she knew it would stick, so she went with *Lizzie*, knowing that as I grew up it could easily be shortened to *Liz*." She laughs dismissively, flipping her long, black hair, as if it's all just good fun. Like she didn't just insult my name. It's calculated, and I see right through it.

Yeah, this is why I don't like people.

"Beth isn't childish," David interrupts before I can even work my way up to a response.

Liz's eyes go wide—*fake*—as if she's been misunderstood. *Bullshit*. "Oh, no. I didn't mean *she's* childish. I was talking about nicknames and—"

"No. The name. *Beth*. It isn't childish." David's voice strengthens as he loses his patience.

Liz waves her hand again. "Of course not. I was just saying my mother—well, you know, it doesn't really matter. She just preferred the name *Liz*. It was her hang-up. She went to school with some girl they nicknamed *Bad-Breath Beth*, and I guess—"

"That's so funny," David cuts her off. "My mom went to school with some bitch named Liz they nicknamed *Lizard*. On account of her reptilian personality."

Liz's mouth gapes and her eyes narrow. I chew on my bottom lip to fight a smile, clamping down the giggle trying to burrow its way out.

Liz pretends she doesn't realize David's dig was personal. Instead, she changes the subject, but if David was open to her advances before, he obviously wants nothing to do with her now. That's one thing about these boys—my brother and his *brothers*. They like their fun, but fuck with one of their own and they close ranks like SEAL Team Six.

And I am one of their own.

* * *

Eventually, David's frat brother Reeve emerges from the basement door like he's only even mildly aware there's a party going on at his frat house, and he gives exactly no fucks about it one way or the other. He's David's closest friend here at school, and idly I wonder how you become close to someone who seems so unapologetically closed off. Reeve forgoes the keg, retrieving a bottle of Scotch from some cabinet in the kitchen island, and drinks from it straight.

I've met him a couple of times before, but I can never quite get a read on him, and it's a little unnerving. There's something dark about him, and even when he's partying with his friends—his *brothers*—he never seems sincerely happy. He doesn't talk much, and I've never seen him flirt with girls, or do *anything* really, other than drink a hell of a lot of whiskey and keep to himself. But he's been nice enough to me so far, so I suppose I should probably just mind my own business when it comes to him. And other than my small smile to acknowledge his nod—the extent of his greeting as he passes—that's exactly what I do.

I sip drink after drink, slowly at first, until I lose count of how many I've had. The guys continue to treat me like I'm contagious or something, and David barely leaves my side all night, which I find both appealing and frustrating.

"You don't have to babysit me, you know."

His eyebrows raise. "Is that what you think I'm doing?"

"Isn't it?" I accuse.

He doesn't respond, and I follow him as he heads toward the kitchen.

"I invited you, Bea. Did it ever occur to you that it's not babysitting if I enjoy your company?" He elbows me playfully and I struggle not to succumb to his charm.

"You warned all of your friends to stay away from me, and you haven't taken your damned eyes off me all night."

I vaguely catch him muttering "no fucking kidding" under his breath.

"What?"

He glares at me for a beat, his expression inscrutable, before he sighs and gestures around the room. "Neither has any other guy here."

I roll my eyes. Here we go with the paranoid, overprotective bullshit…

"And I didn't tell anyone to stay away from you."

I shoot him a skeptical look.

"I told them to respect you. There's a difference."

"Yeah, I'm sure," I grumble.

"Come on, kid, these guys are looking for a hookup. 'The fuck do you need some guy trying to get you drunk and drag you to his bedroom for? 'The fuck do *I* need that for? To get into a fight with my frat brothers? Nah. It's better that they're warned."

Frustration mixes with alcohol, surging through my inebriated body. "I'm not a kid!" I growl. "And you know what? It's not about what I need or don't need. And it's definitely not about *you*, David. The point is I can handle myself without a fake fucking big brother making sure there's nothing to handle!"

I stomp off, much like the kid I just swore I wasn't. But *what the actual hell*? He wanted me to have some fun—to experience the so-cial side of college, right? So here I am, and he's put me in a figurative fucking bubble.

I hear him call after me, and even though he's calling me *Bea* and not *kid*—even though it makes me want to turn back, I don't. I head around a bend and spot Lani talking closely with a tall, dark, and very good-looking guy in a David Wright jersey. *My kind of guy.*

I wouldn't interrupt them, but some other guy does it first, joining in on their conversation, so I do the same. Lani introduces me to her new friend Derek, who's about two full heads taller than her and plays on our school's baseball team. His skin is a deep mahogany that makes his unusual honey eyes stand out even more. The friend who inter-rupted them is Sal. He's a more average height, but also pretty damned handsome, and I start to wonder if exceptional good looks are a pre-requisite to pledge BEG.

"I'm Lani." She introduces herself to Sal. "And this is my roommate—"

"Bea."

Sal rakes me purposefully—almost predatorily—with his gaze. I don't appreciate it, but it doesn't especially bother me, either. Like I told David, I can handle it. Guys flirting blatantly in search of a one-night stand are not the danger. At least not to me. The danger lies in those who promise more.

"Bea." Sal purposefully smoothes his voice. "That's a pretty name."

I fight an eye roll. *Original.* "Uh, thanks."

"So, you're a freshman?"

"Yep."

"If you ever need someone to show you around campus—"

"She already has a fucking tour guide, Salvatore, *thanks*. And her name is *Beth*," David interrupts from behind me. Sal's face registers instant recognition. *Great.*

I huff and start walking away, but David grabs my elbow. "Bea, what the fuck?"

Oh, so *he* can call me *Bea*. "What?" I snap.

"*What?* How about Salvatore Tinelli is a fucking douche bag who likes to sleep with girls and then hide articles of their clothing just to make them endure public walks of shame."

My stomach rolls with revulsion. What an *asshat*. But again—not the point. "I'm not a kid. I can take care of myself," I remind David. *As if I would sleep with that guy even if he weren't a douche bag. I don't even* know *him. We were just talking, for God fucking sake!*

"Yeah, Bea, I know that."

That shuts me up.

David shoves his hand through his hair and sighs. "I'm not underestimating you, okay? I know you can take care of yourself. Any girl worth shit can. But you know what? Any *guy* worth shit looks out for her anyway," he growls.

I drop my gaze. How can I argue with that?

Suddenly David's eyes dart over my shoulder, and he tenses, his face going pale in an instant. I try to turn to see what's irked him, but he grabs my shoulders and tugs me back around the bend, angling me so he's effectively blocking my line of sight.

What the fuck?

"Beth, I need you to do me a favor. I need you to stay here for a few minutes, in this exact spot."

"What—"

"Please. I'm asking you to do this for me." His hazel eyes implore me desperately, and it's deeply out of character. "Bea, please?"

My mouth gapes open, and I think I'm more stunned by his plea than his reaction to whatever's got him all worked up. But before I can even respond, he squeezes my shoulders to emphasize his request— *stay*—and then he's gone.

I look around from my time-out corner, infinitely puzzled. What the hell is going on? Is David in trouble?

My heart races in concern. I don't really know him in this world, but back when they were in high school, he and his friends, including my brother—*especially* my brother—definitely threw their share of fists. I wince when I remember David walking into our house with Sammy and Tucker hot on his heels, six pairs of knuckles swollen and bloody just days after Brian broke up with me.

Brian didn't show up to school for over a week.

I shift in place, tapping my fingers on my opposite elbow with impatience. It's not like me to hang back on the sidelines, or to do what I'm told without challenge. But the way he asked me to stay here…

Suddenly there's shouting in the distance.

I hesitate briefly, but even David's desperate plea can't change my nature, and I abandon my corner in search of the commotion.

I find it by the back door.

David shoves someone into two of his frat brothers, who grab the guy and start pulling him outside. "I didn't fucking know it was your frat," the guy sneers.

I freeze. That voice is unmistakably familiar, but of course, it's impossible.

David wipes off his hands like he's just handled trash. "Now you fucking know. Don't come back here." He turns his back on—

Holy shit—Brian.

Brian is here. "Brian?" His name falls from my lips like I'm in a dream, and all eyes turn to me. "Bethy—" Brian starts to say something, but David gestures to his buddies and they quite literally throw him out.

I stand, frozen, in the middle of the back hallway, still not entirely convinced this is reality.

"Beth." David gets my attention, and I blink at him.

"What is he doing here?"

He rubs his palm down his face in frustration. "He transferred here."

"What? Why?" That makes no sense. "He's at Dartmouth."

David grits his teeth, grinding them together in that way he does when he's trying to hold in his frustration. "Not anymore. There was an open position on our soccer team. He got recruited."

I rub at my head, trying to relieve the tension pooling in my temples.

And I don't even know *why*. It shouldn't even matter. He's just an ex-boyfriend. It's been three years. We were only kids…or at least I was.

But no matter how much time has passed, how much pain endured, you never forget your first heartbreak. And no matter how much you heal, you never fully recover.

But then something else strikes me, and I fix my glare on David. "You knew?"

He rubs the back of his neck, looking decidedly sheepish. "Yeah, kid."

And I explode. "I'm. Not. A. Fucking. Kid!" I don't care that heads turn our way, or that David frowns so hard his brow seems to swallow his eyes. "Damn it, David! You don't have to barge into my conversations, or warn guys away from me like I'm your helpless little sister! You're *not* my brother! You're just my brother's friend, and you barely even know me." It isn't true, and we both know it, but I have a point to make. David doesn't know what's best for me, and he doesn't get to control my life. "I'm not a child that needs to be coddled or lied to!"

He recoils like I've slapped him. *Well, good!* "Beth—"

I turn and walk away from him. I'm a little drunk, and a lot aggravated, and I just want to get the hell out of here. I let my anger feed me, consuming my thoughts, mentally cursing David. I have to. Because if I don't overreact, if there's room beyond the anger, then I will have to process Brian's presence, and I really don't want to do that right now.

I storm through the crowded house and out the front door. I text Lani that I'm leaving, and get about three feet off the front porch before I'm snatched back by a huge hand on my arm. "Where the hell do you think you're going?" David practically snarls.

"Back to my dorm!" I wrench from his grip.

He jumps in my way and gets in my face. "You don't walk home alone. *Ever*."

"I can take care of myself!" We square off. Rationally I know he's right, but I've dug my heels in so deep I'm afraid I'm stuck.

"Dicknose!" David shouts.

Huh?

Some kid appears by his side as if summoned by royalty. He looks attentively up at David, who's casually lighting a cigarette.

"Pledge task—walk Beth home. Keep your fucking hands to yourself and your eyes off her ass," David orders.

"For God's sake." I turn on my heel and leave.

Great. Now my babysitter has assigned a pledge to do his duty *for* him.

He shuffles up to me. "Hi. I'm—"

"Dicknose. I got it."

His steps falter. "Well, that's my pledge name. But my actual name is Grant."

"Well I don't need a babysitter, *Grant*, so why don't you scurry on back to the frat house," I spit.

He hesitates. "Uh…I can't really do that."

I suspected as much. I increase my pace, and, thankfully, he doesn't try to catch up, but I'm continuously aware of his footsteps echoing about five feet behind me the whole way home.

It's less than a ten-minute walk, and while there are a few other students around, Thursday is a notorious party night, and most people are out, not hanging around the dorm. I have to reluctantly admit I'm glad I didn't leave alone, after all. Well, to myself anyway. To Dicknose, I only turn and glare, silently dismissing him. He does have kind of a long nose, and I have to suppress a giggle at the image my mind conjures up.

"I uh—should probably walk you to your door," he mumbles uncertainly.

Not going to happen. I'm perfectly capable of walking the fifty yards through the small quad at Standman Hall. "I'm not going inside yet. I want to have a cigarette," I lie.

He shuffles from foot to foot. "That's okay. I'll wait."

I sigh in exasperation. I don't even actually *have* a cigarette. "Look, I just want to be alone, okay?"

He doesn't move, and every moment that passes, I grow more and more irritated.

"Okay, Dicknose. You have three seconds to leave. After that, I'm going to start screaming, and well, people are going to assume what they're going to assume, and then—"

He splays his palms in surrender. "All right, *Jeez.*" He scowls at me like I'm more trouble than I'm worth, which was, of course, my intention. "But if Brother March asks, I walked you to your door, okay?"

"Totally," I agree, and off Dicknose goes.

I blow out a long breath. I'm used to overprotection, and I usually accept it in stride. But not here, and not from David. There's a reason I left home for college, and I'm done being the depressed girl that everyone has to keep an extra eye on. How will I ever assert my independence with David watching over me like some kind of misguided security detail?

And now *Brian* is here.

Here, of all places. But why?

Certainly he hasn't sought me out, or I'm sure he would have just called or texted at the very least. But he had to know I'm here, right?

Three years ago the thought would have thrilled me. Now it's just confusing and disconcerting. And actually kind of annoying.

I make my way along the walkway that bisects the courtyard at the center of Standman that passes for a quad. The five red brick buildings set in a U sit quietly in the lamplight. I don't pass a single soul on my way to the door.

But I'm wrong, and I startle when I spot someone in the shadows of one of the narrow alleyways that separate each building. Well, I spot the glowing cherry of his cigarette hanging in his hand by his side anyway, and it's only when I'm reaching in my purse for my security key fob that he takes a pull, the small light source illuminating his features just enough to make out the face of that glarey stranger from my abnormal psych class.

Why is he lurking in alleyways like a freaking serial killer? And why is he still glaring at me? A shiver of unease rolls through me, and suddenly I wonder if he's more than just strange—if he's actually dangerous.

I rush through the door and make sure it closes securely behind me. At least he can't get in here—dorm security and all. I'll never admit it to David but, for the first time, I consider that maybe having a *bodyguard* on campus isn't the end of the world, after all.

Chapter Four

Beth

Age twelve

I hurry down the steps of our synagogue, rushing around the corner, and behind the nook where the kids who think they're too cool for Hebrew school smoke cigarettes during the one break we get during class. I kick the few littered snack bags and cigarette butts out of the way, clearing myself a spot before sliding down along the brick façade and hugging my knees to my chest.

I choke back a sob. I've been coming here almost every Sunday since kindergarten, but the class is half empty now, kids dropping like flies as soon as their bar or bat mitzvah passes. We're all supposed to be here for the Jewish education, but it's the worst kept secret in Port Woodmere that nine times out of ten, our parents only send us because Temple Chaverim requires it to hold the coming-of-age ceremony here.

Most of the girls have already stopped showing up, having had their bat mitzvahs at twelve, as per tradition. But I stopped coming for a while after my dad left, leaving me with well over a year to make up before the rabbi would agree to schedule my official foray into womanhood. It was my father, after all, who'd pushed our religious education, considering my mother was raised calling herself

Protestant but practicing nothing. Which happens to be the exact reason I just ran out of our Hebrew lesson nearly half an hour early: if my mother had been born Jewish, Ira Traeger wouldn't have just called me a *shiksa*, and told the whole class that, as a non-Jew, I shouldn't be allowed to be bat mitzvahed at all.

I swipe at my flushed cheeks with my knuckles, resenting my tears as much as the words that caused them. I wish I was tougher. The kind of girl immune to the sting of words. My best friend, Darcy, who stopped coming last May after her mildly inappropriate *Game of Thrones* themed bat mitzvah—the one that had half the town calling her parents' judgment into question—would have simply laughed it off if Ira Traeger had insulted her, or perhaps rolled her eyes and slung a far wittier insult right back. Under no circumstances would she have fled the classroom, slamming her knee on the doorframe on her way thanks to her tear-blurred sight.

I rub my palm just under the hem of my denim shorts, where the bright red, vertical ellipse promises a telltale bruise by morning. It really hurts, but it's not the physical pain that crushes me.

I sniffle. I wouldn't even *be* in that class with that jerk if it weren't for my father's choice to run away rather than face his mistakes.

I'm so lost in my own self-pity that I don't recognize the waft of cigarette smoke until it's too close to run or hide, and I sit here, frozen, as the figure too tall to be another thirteen-year-old emerges from around the corner.

My stomach flips as he comes into view, his cocky swagger viscerally familiar. Even backlit and hidden in shadow, I recognize David.

"B?"

I should get up. I should dry my cheeks. *I should, I should, I should . . .* I don't. "Hi," I croak.

David's brow furrows, and he drops his cigarette and stubs it beneath his sneaker. I expect him to help me up, but he crouches down instead, bringing himself to my level. "Who do I have to kill?" he asks, only half kidding, and magically, a small laugh bubbles its way up from my chest. That's where David lives. Right inside my chest, bouncing around the four chambers of my heart, where he made himself at home the very first time I laid eyes on him at one of Sammy's soccer games.

I avert my gaze and shake my head, not wanting him to see my vulnerability, even if rationally I realize it's too late for that. Another rogue tear slides down my nose, but he gets to it before I do. "You could tell me why you're upset, kid. Or I can go in there"—he nods to the building—"and interrogate your little classmates until someone talks."

I crack a smile, but I keep my eyes trained on my Uggs.

David nudges my chin so that I meet his gaze. He raises his brows. "I'm not above enhanced interrogation techniques. Or flat-out fucking torture, for that matter."

I shrug. "I'm just being stupid," I admit.

His mouth twists into a lopsided smirk, but it's a sad smirk—a skeptical one. "I find that hard to believe."

I finally really look at him, taking in his sweat-damp T-shirt and loose basketball shorts. "What are you doing here?" I don't think I've seen him at temple since his own bar mitzvah, save the rare high holiday he might be guilted into escorting his mother to.

"Picking you up, kid," he says like it should be obvious. "I was playing ball with Cap and your mom was giving us a ride back to your house. We told her we'd wait here until you're done so she didn't have to make two trips. I just told her I needed to take a piss so I could sneak in a smoke." He nods to the forgotten cigarette on the ground. "So, now that I am here, are you going to tell me what has you in tears at fucking Hebrew school?"

I sigh, pushing down the nerves that roll my stomach at admitting my real concerns. "Did you know I'm not really Jewish?" I ask David. Has Sammy ever talked about this? Does he even know it?

David cocks a brow. "Of course you are."

I shake my head. "I thought we were, but…Ira Traeger said it goes by your mother. That if your dad isn't Jewish, but your mom is, then you're Jewish. But if your mom isn't, even if your dad is…"

"That's motherfucking bullshit." David is adamant. I love his fierceness, and I love his expletives. I need them right now.

"But I asked Morah Biederman, and she said—"

"Who gives a fuck what that mean old hag said? Who gives a fuck what Ira fucking Traeger said, for that matter? You were raised Jewish, you want to be Jewish, so you're Jewish," he shrugs. *Simple as that.*

But it isn't.

"But technically, you know, I'm not."

David watches me thoughtfully, and it's unnerving. "B, what's this really about?"

I swallow. *What is this about?* It's about me thinking I was something my whole life, only to learn I don't know *what* I am.

I sigh. "I don't know. I guess…It used to be so important to my dad, you know? The whole Hebrew school thing. He was so excited at Sammy's bar mitzvah, so proud…" I trail off. He was—at first. Until he drank himself angry and shoved my mother into the wall in the bridal suite of the Port Woodmere Country Club.

David tucks the curtain of hair that's fallen over my cheek—the one I'm hiding under—behind my ear. "Your dad didn't leave because of you. And you don't need to get bat mitzvahed to try and impress him. If he's not already proud of you then he's a fucking idiot."

I stare at the cracked concrete under my heels, imagining the crack growing and widening until it's too big to cross. Until I'm completely isolated. It's an appropriate metaphor. The more time that passes without contact from my father, the further away he feels. Even if I know he's just across the river in Manhattan. But every day he's not a part of my life makes it that much less likely he ever will be again. And maybe part of me did want to pursue a bat mitzvah to please him.

Maybe subconsciously I thought he might actually show up. That I'd get him back.

My eyes well with tears and I focus on keeping them leveed. The last thing I want is to cry in front of David. David is toughness and fight, profanity and crude comments. David is rebellion. David is not tears. And I don't want to be the weepy little girl to his badassery.

"Want to see something?" he says cryptically.

The knowing smirk stretched across his face gets my heart beating faster. I nod.

David reaches up over his shoulders and grabs his T-shirt by the back of the neckline before yanking the whole thing up over his head. My heart rate skyrockets. Where David was once lanky and trim, he is filling out in a very grown-up kind of way. Light hair adorns his chest and lean muscles bulge as he moves. He sits back on his haunches and twists around to show me his back, and my eyes zero in on a white piece of bandage over his right shoulder.

I gasp. "You got another one?" David is only fourteen. He shouldn't be getting tattoos that will decorate his skin for the rest of his life. Fourteen is no age to make permanent decisions. It's not even legal! And beyond that, it's against our religion. *His* religion.

"Peel back the tape," he whispers.

My stomach flutters. I swallow down my nerves as my fingers touch his hot skin, slipping beneath the sticky adhesive until I can slide down the gauze.

It's absolutely beautiful.

His skin has already healed over the intricate black Hebrew letters. חי

My fingers automatically glide over the ink. *Chai. Life.* "You're not supposed to get tattoos, *nice Jewish boy*," I whisper. "They won't bury you in a Jewish cemetery." I repeat the warning we've been told all our lives to ward us away from the horrible sin of tattoos.

But why does something so wrong look so freaking beautiful?

His mouth quirks up. "But I'm not that *nice*—you know that, B. And I'm not actually a *Jewish boy*, either."

I blink at him.

David sighs. "It's ironic, yeah? Tribute to a religion that bans them. Like it does me. And you—if you buy into Ira Traeger's bullshit."

"But your mom's Jewish," I remind him.

David's Adam's apple rolls with his swallow, and it surprises me. David is rarely ever nervous. "My parents are both Jewish," he agrees. "But, they're not really my parents."

"What?"

"Well, they are. But they're not my birth parents."

Huh? "You're adopted?" I've known David most of my life, have vacationed with his family, and this is the first I'm hearing of this.

David nods.

I frown. "I never knew that." Disappointment sinks my heart into my stomach. Not because he's adopted, but because I didn't know. Because I don't know him as well as I thought I did.

David's broad shoulders shrug, the *chai* dancing on his skin. "Neither did I. I only found out a few months ago."

Wow. "Does my brother know?"

The small shake of his head means the world to me.

David just confided something to me he hasn't even told his best friend.

"So, you know, I'm just as Jewish, or *not Jewish*, as you."

"Have you met your birth parents?" I ask him, suddenly less interested in Ira Traeger's bullshit.

David scoffs. "Nah. No thanks, right? They got rid of me as fast as they could, so why would I want to meet them now?"

I don't respond to that. I'm not sure I agree with him, but I do know there's something all wrong about not wanting David, even if rationally I know they might've had good reason for their choices.

"But…I know her name." I know he means his birth mother.

"You do?"

"I asked my mom." He averts his gaze and starts to slip his shirt back on.

"Well, who is she?" I ask. Where did David come from? Whose genes combined to make this impossible, perfectly imperfect boy?

"I don't really want to get into it, B, but I'll tell you this—she's not Jewish. So *I'm* not. I'm not actually *anything*, technically. So if I could have a stupid bar mitzvah, then you can, too. But if you want to do it, do it for you, not for your dad, okay? That's a fuck of a lot of time to put into something for someone who doesn't put any time into you."

I stare at David. Reality is sharp and bitter, but that doesn't make it any less true, and if anyone knows the truth about my father, it's David. "Yeah, you're right."

"Always am, kid," David smiles. "But I still think this Ira Traeger could use a good ass-kicking."

I giggle. "It wouldn't be a fair fight." I picture scrawny, pimply Ira. David would crush him with nothing more than a look.

"No such thing as a fair fight, B. Someone always has the advantage."

I suppose he's right.

David stands and holds out his hand to help me up. "Come on, let's blow this joint."

I let him lead me to our car, where Sammy and my mom don't ask questions. There's only a few minutes left of class now, and my tears have long dried.

David hasn't made me feel any more or less Jewish than Ira Traeger said. But he has made me realize the technicalities don't really matter. I can be what I want. I can forge my own identity.

Chapter Five

David

I lean against the red brick wall of Building D of Standman Hall, sipping my black iced coffee, and waiting impatiently. Beth still won't return my texts, and it's pissing me off. I get that she's mad, and I don't actually blame her, but it's not like I can take it back, right? It's not like I can go back in time and tell her about Falco before the douche bag showed up at last night's party—unin-fucking-vited, by the way. And to be honest, even if I could, I probably still wouldn't. In fact, the only thing I'd do differently is make sure he knew better than to show up at my goddamned frat house.

I glance at my phone again. Neither of the texts I've received are from Beth, so I don't bother reading them. Not even the one from the hot senior I used to mess around with last year.

Lani waltzes out of the Hall, swaying her considerable curves with no conscious effort whatsoever—but I barely even look.

"Hey there, bodyguard," she greets through her permanent smirk. "Lose your client?"

"Yeah, actually. I thought she'd be leaving for class now." I hold up the second iced coffee, the one I brought for Beth, light and sweet, and currently watered down by the ice that did not survive the past forty-five minutes in the midday late summer sun.

Lani's smirk actually shifts into a sympathetic smile. "You missed her by about three hours."

Huh? "I thought her first class was at noon."

"It is. But she headed over to the student health center around nine this morning to talk to them about volunteering."

I nod, equally disappointed and impressed. But not remotely surprised.

"She pissed at me?" I ask, against my better judgment.

"Shouldn't she be?" Lani counters.

"'The fuck was I supposed to do? Ruin her first few weeks of college? Give her a reason to stay holed up in her fucking dorm room? She was already looking for excuses not to go out," I remind her. She seems to care about Beth, but girls can be shitty as hell to each other, and my jury is still out on Lani. Beth needs a real friend. Besides me, I mean.

Lani sighs. "I know that, Dave. But she found out anyway, didn't she? And in a much more fucked-up way than hearing it from someone who cares about her. Lying to her, or keeping something from her that you knew would affect her..." She shakes her head reproachfully, and I really don't appreciate being admonished like some wayward fucking kid.

But Lani's right. I should have told Beth. My stomach twists with guilt—an ironically familiar and unfamiliar sensation. Because I've never given enough fucks to feel guilty over shit. Except with Beth, and when it comes to her, the shit I've done to deserve that guilt—how I contributed to one of the lowest points of her life...It cuts me into fucking pieces, even to this day.

I sigh. "Get her to text me back, will you?" I mutter, and push off the wall to head to class.

I toss the wasted iced coffee in the trash bin. I need a better fucking peace offering.

* * *

I finish the day the same way I started it, waiting outside Beth's dorm.

The girl still refuses to text me back, and I oscillate between guilt and anger. Because what the fuck? I didn't kill her fucking dog.

I text my mom to check in while I wait. My dad can go fuck himself. If he had his way, I wouldn't even be here. I'd be at some top business school—not studying to "waste my life as a starving writer." But I'd rather be a "worthless loser who could never support a family" than a rich asshole like him.

I get the eerie feeling I'm being watched, and out of the corner of my eye, I glimpse some unfamiliar guy who's been hanging around out here as long as I have.

Actually, scratch that. He's not exactly unfamiliar. I realize I've seen him around over the past week, but never before this semester. But he's definitely not a freshman—there's no way that guy is only eighteen.

And yet it's more than that, too—the familiarity. But I can't put my finger on it either. He takes a drag on his cigarette and I look away so he doesn't catch me watching him.

But I'm good at looking at someone in just my peripheral, so when he thinks I'm staring out at the road, he takes another opportunity to watch me, and I confirm that I'm not paranoid.

Shit. Did I bag this guy's girlfriend or something? Sister?

Mother?

I haven't even hooked up with anyone since we all got back to campus.

Then I catch a flash of blond hopping up the steps that lead to the quad from the Washington Avenue entrance. I toss my cigarette on the ground and stub it out with my shoe before making my way toward her.

Beth startles when she notices me, and she stops walking, so I make up the distance still between us. She looks adorable as all hell in those tight jeans and loose racerback tank top. Her bra shows at her sides and I'm equally turned on and annoyed by it. She never did have any kind of self-awareness. At least not when it comes to how goddamned attractive she is. And it bugs me that every guy that's passed her today has caught a glimpse of that black lace.

I shove my hand through my hair. "Beth," I sigh.

I wait for her to go off on me again, but she doesn't. She just kind of looks up at me, her resentment a palpable thing. I can't stand to see her look at me like that. But what makes my lungs burn is knowing that I deserve her resentment. She has no idea how much. Fuck, I hope to God she never will. Especially not now that she's come so far—that she's doing so well. Well enough to tell me off in public, at my own party, anyway.

But not tonight, it seems, and when she still doesn't say anything at all, I make my attempt. "Look, I'm sorry, okay? I thought I was protecting you."

"I don't need protection," she counters.

I nod. "I know. I just thought…Falco being around would give you an excuse to hide away in your dorm, and I wanted you to experience…"

"Experience *what*, David?"

I shrug. "I don't know. Fucking life, I guess."

Beth looks down at her shoes. I hate that she won't even look at me. "Okay, whatever," she murmurs.

"*Whatever?*" I repeat incredulously. Here I am, *apologizing*— something I'm not exactly fucking known for—and all she has to say is *whatever?*

"Yeah. *Whatever*. I get it. It just sucks, you know?"

I take a much-needed deep breath. "I know, Bea."

At last her eyes meet mine, hostility finally gone. I take the opportunity to retrieve my new peace offering from my back pocket. Well, not *new*. My worn and weathered copy of *Hamlet*, riddled with years' worth of my own highlights and notes, its pages filled with more of my own words than those of the author himself. I hope it will help in her Shakespeare class. If nothing else, it will give her an invasive insight into who I am and how I think, just like all the other books I've given her over the years, and I wonder if she realizes just how personal it is.

She takes it, her thin brows pinched together in confused awe. "This is your copy," she breathes.

Suddenly I feel too vulnerable, uncomfortably exposed. "Thought it could help in your class," I half-lie. Because it's more than that, and I suspect she knows it.

Her pretty pink lips twist into a small smile, her cheeks going even rounder than usual, and it hits me right in the chest. Not for the first time I tell myself the affection I feel for her is strictly familial. *More lies.*

"Thanks."

I smile. "You eat dinner yet?"

She shrugs. "I was gonna heat a cup of noodles and study."

Cup of fucking noodles? "Fuck that. Come to the Stu-U. Let's get some real food."

Beth rolls her eyes. "Fine. But just some quick food, okay? I really need to study."

"*There are more things in heaven and earth*, Bea," I smirk at her, and she sets free a short giggle. *There it is.*

I take her girly-ass backpack and slip it over my shoulder, giving her no choice but to follow me. But as soon as I turn around, my eyes catch on that same guy, just as he's averting his gaze. Only this time he wasn't looking at me. He was looking at *Beth*; I'm sure of it. Rage rushes through my veins, and I grit my teeth. I don't know who the fuck this guy is, but there's something off about him, and there's absolutely nothing good about Beth drawing his attention.

My jaw clenches. I slip my arm protectively around her shoulders, despite just having been scolded for being *overprotective*. "Beth, in two seconds, I want you to subtly glance to your left, between buildings B and C, okay?"

Her brows pinch together again. She looks so damned cute when she does that. She doesn't wait the two seconds, and her "subtle glance" is more of a full-on stare. "*Glance*," I whisper-growl. I wait until she's facing forward again, and then start leading her from the quad. "Did you see that guy?" I ask her.

She nods hesitantly.

"Do you know him?"

"Yeah. I mean, no. He's in my Abnormal Psych class. And I saw him last night."

"Saw him doing what?"

"The same thing. Standing around smoking cigarettes like a fucking creep."

"I think he was looking at you," I admit.

"And that."

So this isn't the first time that guy's been staring at Beth. Unease swirls in my gut. "Stay away from him," I warn her.

"Do you know him?" she asks uncertainly.

"No. But I don't like the way he was looking at you."

Of course, I've never liked the way any guys have looked at her.

Chapter Six

Beth

David's copy of *Hamlet*, it turns out, has been infinitely more helpful than I ever could have imagined. David knew this of course, since it turns out he took the same class his freshman year. *Hamlet* is the first of three plays we'll study in depth this semester, aside from *King Lear* and *Macbeth*, and after Professor London's first lecture on Act I, I start to suspect that David would do a better job teaching the course himself.

I finish my hours at the student health center and stop in to see Professor Bowman. I'll see her in an hour in Abnormal Psych, but I have a few ideas I wanted to discuss with her.

"Hi Beth. How are things?" she asks.

I smile. "Good. I like my classes. Well, most of them. I like yours, anyway," I amend.

Professor Bowman chuckles lightly. "That's good to hear, I suppose. And how has volunteering been? I know it can be daunting sometimes."

It can. I volunteer at the help line, answering random anonymous calls, talking to strangers about their problems, never admitting the irony of them getting advice from a girl who has no answers for herself. "It's been okay. But I was just thinking…a lot of the people who call—or more, the people who don't call even though they might need to talk to someone…they might not really feel comfortable talking, you know, to strangers. Like, a lot of people who suffer from depression, or other issues, are more introverted, you know?"

Bowman offers me a sympathetic smile, exhaling a long-winded sigh. "You're absolutely right, Beth. Of course, it's the catch-22 of the program, isn't it? That those who need help the most are the least likely to reach out for it." Her eyes swim with empathy and I suspect she's good enough at her profession to know my thoughts come from experience.

"So, I was thinking. What if they didn't have to call at all?"

"I'm listening…"

"What if they could text a number? Either to say what they're upset or worried about, or even just the word 'help,' or that they want to talk. What if they could just text a number and say 'hi'? Just starting a conversation, having someone to talk to with complete anonymity, it could go a really long way." I think of the night I tried to kill myself. I think of the one thing that made me hesitate. The texts from David urging me to go out, offering to pick me up. The ones that, with just a few words, reminded me that there were people out there who cared.

It wasn't enough to save me. Only fate did that when my brother happened to come home early. But it could save someone else.

Bowman rubs her chin contemplatively. "Beth, that is very smart. Frankly, I'm a bit ashamed I haven't considered it before. I'm going to look into the logistics of something like that tonight. There must be software available to facilitate it."

My cheeks color themselves pink, and I grin proudly. I thank her for listening to my idea, and head out to the student union to get lunch before Abnormal Psych.

A wave of unease settles over me as I walk through the rotunda. It's been following me around ever since Brian showed up at the Beta party. Now I understand why David didn't want me knowing he's here. But so far, mercifully, I haven't run into him.

There's still that small piece of me that wonders if Brian ever worries about us crossing paths. But deep down, I know he probably doesn't much care, either way. I'm just an ex he dated for less than a year, back in high school, after all.

I meet Lani and chat over subpar pizza, my eyes anxiously scanning the dining hall every few minutes. She notices, and offers a sympathetic smile.

"Total dick move, huh? Your ex, I mean."

I frown at her. "What do you mean?"

Lani's eyes roll with impatience. "Uh, showing up at your college? Trying to reinsert himself into your world just when you're starting to build your own life."

"Well, he's not really reinserting himself into my life. He's not here for me. It doesn't surprise me that he'd transfer for a spot on a Division One soccer team like RRU's. It's just a shitty coincidence, that's all."

Lani stares at me like I'm missing something. "Do you really believe that?"

I blink at her for a beat. "Well, yeah. Look, Lan, it's a romantic thought. A guy transferring schools to win back his ex. But that's just not Brian, okay? I mean, he was sweet, for a time. But then he cast me aside like an old-model iPhone after a new release. He didn't have regrets. He didn't ever talk to me again, actually. So the idea that he moved across three states, left all his friends, to do his senior year at another school *for me*—it's just a fantasy, okay? And not even *my* fantasy."

It's true. It's been a long time since I pined over Brian. I won't pretend he doesn't still cross my mind now and again—that I don't wonder why it was so easy for him to just discard me so suddenly and completely. How he could have just sat there and watched his phone announce incoming text after text, never compelled to reply, or even acknowledge that I continued to exist.

My family kept my suicide attempt close to the vest—something I've always appreciated—but there's yet another piece of me that has always wondered what Brian would have done had he known. If he would have shown up at the hospital, or just continued on with his life—like my father did, at the time.

What would Brian have done if he'd known that taking those pills wasn't even the toughest choice I'd had to make since he'd dumped me?

But I know better than to harp on *what-ifs*.

If I could forgive this new, sober version of my father, accept him back into our lives and our family when he and my mother got back together a few years ago—if *Sammy* could…eventually, anyway—then who the hell is *Brian*? If there's one thing I can do, it's let go of the past. I love my dad, I can move on from an old, schoolgirl crush on David, and Brian Falco is just an ex—someone I dated back in high school. *No big deal.*

Lani sighs, long and dramatic. "Oh, B, sometimes you really are naïve."

Truer words were never spoken. And they make me question myself. Is it possible that Lani is right? Could Brian really be here for me?

And more importantly, do I want him to be?

* * *

Abnormal Psych passes in a rush. That's the thing about things that actually hold your interest. But despite my focus on the lecture, it's impossible not to be distracted when eyes bore into the back of your head.

From five minutes in, I can feel them. It's less eerie this time—that sense of being watched. Now that I know where it's coming from, I'm more exasperated than unnerved.

I glance back and my stalker looks away. I roll my eyes, allowing him to see that he's not frightening me. He is a nuisance, and I want him to know it.

When the feeling doesn't go away, I turn and stare at him. My gaze issues a challenge. Subtlety abandoned, I narrow my eyes, warning him that I am not some little girl to be fucked with.

But instead of backing down, his murky blue eyes glow with amusement, and the corner of his mouth lifts into an unmistakable smile. But only for a beat. His gaze never leaves mine, and when I have no choice but to break eye contact first to return my attention to Professor Bowman, it feels like a devastating defeat.

My anger only builds through the remainder of the class, and when Bowman dismisses us, I fly from the room before the rest of the students are even out of their seats. But once in the corridor, I pause.

Why the hell am I running away? *He's* the one acting like a total psycho.

So I don't run. I wait.

I wait as my classmates file out of the lecture hall and disperse in their respective directions. And I wait for my stalker.

As soon as I see him, I pounce.

I charge forward, ignoring his shocked expression as I back him against the wall. "What the fuck is your problem?" I growl.

His eyes go even wider.

"Who are you?" I demand.

"Uh, a student?" he phrases it like a question—like *I'm* the crazy one, attacking him for no apparent reason.

My hostility rolls off me in waves, but while the creepy stranger still looks surprised, his deep blue eyes dance with mirth, and I'm afraid I'm falling short of the desired effect.

Yeah, he's far from intimidated. In fact, he seems to be battling a *smile*.

And why *should* he be intimidated? I doubt he'd be put off by a fucking biker gang. He's all tall and looming, arms and neck covered in ink, muscles bulging so prominently they stretch his T-shirt, precariously taunting its seams. His scruff is obviously the result of not giving a single fuck what anyone thinks of him, and he practically screams *bad boy*.

It hits me again that he could actually be dangerous, and I wonder what in the hell I was thinking coming at him like this.

I huff out my anger, sinking slowly back into defeat. "Look, I don't know who the fuck you are, but you need to stop staring at me all the goddamned time like a fucking stalker."

His eyes bore into mine, just as strange and strangely familiar as they first appeared. "And what if I don't want to?" His lips quirk and a small dimple peeks out. Not only is he not intimidated by me, but apparently he finds me to be a complete joke.

My shoulders deflate, and my gaze drops to the floor. "Who are you?"

When he doesn't respond, I meet his eyes again, and for the first time, they're missing that amused glint. He actually looks concerned. "My name's Brody," he murmurs.

Brody. I don't know a *Brody*. "Why do you keep staring at me?"

He quirks an eyebrow, as if to say the answer is obvious, but it's a lie.

"You're making me uncomfortable," I admit. I should just ask him nicely to stop doing it. "You need to cut it the fuck out," I say instead.

Another twitch of a smile, another flash of his dimple. An unsettling wave of *déjà vu* surges in my gut, but I can't place it. "I can try," he offers.

At least it's something. "Okay," I breathe, and I start my retreat, releasing him from my invisible hold against the wall. The one, I suddenly realize, I never had any power to hold him to at all. The one he'd willingly submitted to. To indulge me? For his own entertainment?

I feel increasingly pathetic, and I turn to escape this inexplicable encounter.

"Hey. Tell me your name," he calls out.

I face him. "Something tells me you already know it," I counter. His interest is too obvious, so why wouldn't he have sought out that most basic piece of information, especially when it's been readily available in class?

Another twitch-smile. It's like his face can't hold the expression for long. "Still would like to hear you say it."

Ah, so he wants to go from creepy stalker to casual introductions. "Beth," I murmur for no reason I can fathom.

Brody takes a few long strides, eating up the space I'd purposely put between us. "It's nice to meet you, Beth." For the first time, his lips stretch into a genuine smile. It's almost shy, and it actually holds, as if it's true and earnest. Brody holds out his hand as if for a shake, and wordlessly and robotically, I slip my small hand into his massive one. His fingers close around it, dwarfing my hand so it practically disappears.

I tug my hand back. I'm so confused by this guy. What the hell is he *about*?

Brody nods, as if to acknowledge that he deserves my distrust. His palm lands on the back of his neck, which he proceeds to rub. "All right. I'm sorry, okay? Look, I'm not like, one of those overly friendly frat pretty boys. I'm not good at just, you know, coming up to people and making conversation. I tend to intimidate people. I'm more of a hang-around-in-the-background-and-observe kinda guy. And you just caught my eye, and then instead of being intimidated, you got all challenge-y on me." He shrugs. "Which just made me more interested."

"And you couldn't just say 'hi' and introduce yourself?" I grumble. It would have saved me a serious amount of aggravation. But he's already explained that introductions aren't his thing, and how can I judge him? They're not mine, either. I don't think I've ever walked up to a stranger and started a conversation in my life, and even when someone else makes the introductions for me, I either get all awkward and mumbly, or I freeze.

Brody smiles kind of sadly, and it squeezes my chest. "Wish I could have, kiddo. But…" He just kind of trails off, but then, he's already explained himself.

Social anxiety can range from annoying to utterly debilitating, and looking like he does can't help matters.

I smile at my stalker—Brody—for the first time. "Right. You needed an ice-breaker. Good thing I'm the queen of those." I gesture between the two of us. "Confronting a guy twice your size and accusing him of stalking you is a total classic, you know."

A deep, rumbling chuckle echoes from his throat, and it makes my smile widen even more. "I'll have to try that one in the future," he jokes.

"Yeah, good luck finding a guy twice *your* size," I tease. For some reason, knowing he's not a social guy has made me braver. It's taken the pressure off somehow, and made me feel comfortable enough to just be myself. *How strange.*

Another chuckle. I like his chuckles, I realize. They're a glimmer of sunlight in a guy who's mostly darkness. "So, Beth, do you have another class now? Or can I buy you a coffee to apologize for my stalker-ish ways? You can give me some more ice-breaker ideas so I don't freak out the next person I find interesting."

I consider him. I notice his jaw is clenched and he's chewing the inside of his cheek, something my brother does when he's anxious. I realize the nerve he must have worked up just to see if I'd have coffee with him and I'm struck with a deep sense of empathy—a kindred connection, and it's unexpected. It's not romantic or sexual. It's simply…I don't know what it is, actually. But it's real.

"You owe me at least, like, six coffees. But whatever, we can start with one."

* * *

"So I took off two years after high school to work and save up. I didn't want to take too many student loans if I didn't have to, you know?" Brody murmurs before looking to his coffee to take a sip.

I take the opportunity to study him, seated in the booth across from me in the busy coffee shop, and offer a cursory nod. But I don't *know*, really. I've never had to worry about money, and while I've always known I was privileged, knowing it and feeling it are two different things.

"So I did my first two years at NYU, but then my mom got sick. So I transferred here so I could be closer to help out with doctor appointments and shit, you know?" He runs his fingers through his hair. "I grew up in Suffolk county. Southampton. But not the rich part. We had a small bungalow, but it was enough for just the two of us."

"What about your dad?" I ask.

"Never really had one of those."

"Oh," I breathe, embarrassed to have pried.

"What about you?" he asks. "Are you close with your parents?"

"Uh, yeah, actually. My mom is my best friend. And not in the way girls say that when they want to make their mom look cool. She's literally my best friend…For a while she was my only friend," I add quietly. I don't know why. Maybe it's because Brody is being so open with me.

"What about your dad?" he asks.

What about my dad, indeed. "We're closer now, I guess. But he was kind of…out of my life for a while. He only started coming back around a couple of years ago, and he's been great, really. But, I don't know…it's complicated."

Brody looks like he wants to ask more, but he bites his tongue. I think he's afraid I might become skittish. I'm afraid he's probably right.

But for some reason, because he doesn't press me, the words just slip right out. "He used to drink."

Brody's eyes narrow.

"Not often. But when he did, he would change. He was…violent. When I was ten, he got drunk and he—uh…he hit my mom. He'd done it before. To my brother, too. But this time, Sammy, he hit him back. He was only thirteen, but he made our dad leave.

"And, well, he *did*. He left, and never looked back. I didn't hear from him for years. And then, two years ago, suddenly I find out he's in AA, five years sober, and he and my mom are secretly dating behind my back like freaking teenagers." The bitterness in my tone surprises me. I was nothing but thrilled to get my dad back, and I thought I'd moved on…So why do I feel resentful now?

"Did he hit you?" Brody asks, deathly quiet.

"Never." It's the truth.

Brody nods once, contemplatively. He seems deeply connected to my history for someone I just met, and I wonder at his own. He said he never really knew his dad, but I wonder if he had a stepdad or some other relative who suffered from similar issues. But I don't ask. Because I don't want to talk about my father anymore.

"Do you have any siblings?" I ask.

He hesitates. "Only child. Well, actually that's not true, but not in the normal sense. I didn't, like, grow up with brothers or sisters or anything like that. But I did start to get to know my half-brother recently."

I can't help but think of Sammy, and how lonely it would have been growing up without him.

"What about your brother? Are you close with him?" Brody asks hastily, like he'd rather get off the topic of himself and change the subject back to me.

I nod. "We've been close since we were kids. He kind of took over the protective role after my dad left. Actually he was pretty overprotective of me before, too. It's kind of who he is," I shrug. "We never really did that brother-sister fighting thing. He's always kind of indulged me."

Brody's smile turns wistful. "Well, then you're lucky. He sounds like a good guy."

I nod emphatically. "He really is the best. And he has this group of close friends he grew up with. They kind of became de facto big brothers, too. You know, looking out for me, threatening boys not to bother me. Of course, they and I had different definitions of what was a 'bother'," I admit.

Brody laughs. "I bet."

I sigh. "But they mean well," I concede. The waitress brings over my second cup of coffee, and I tear open three sugars and add them to my milky latte. "So do you go home to see your mom a lot?" I ask.

Brody looks down at the table and takes another sip of coffee. *Black, one sugar.* "That was the plan." He sets his mug back on the table. "I moved half my shit back home, the other half in the dorm, planning to spend enough time here to keep up with my course work, but to be there for her as much as possible. The doctors said it would be a long road, you know?"

Another cursory nod. I don't know anyone who's been sick like that.

"Anyway, the cancer progressed faster than they expected. Multiple myeloma. In the bone marrow." He swallows thickly. "She was gone before summer was out."

My lip trembles as I try to think of what to say. "That's fucked up," I breathe. God, and *he's* the one with social problems?

But his eyes flash to mine, and he doesn't seem offended. He seems…impressed. "That's exactly what it is," he agrees.

Suddenly I understand Brody a little more, and my heart aches for him. I guess that tends to happen after you spend—I glance at the clock—holy shit, two plus hours talking to someone.

He must feel so lost. "I'm glad you stalked me, Brody," I whisper. "Otherwise we might never have been friends."

* * *

Chapter Seven

David

When I pushed Beth to come out to the bar tonight, I expected more of a fight, especially since the last party I pressured her into ended with her storming off pissed. But when she not only agreed, but told me she was inviting a new friend, I felt relieved. Lani's cool and all, but Beth needs more than one fucking friend.

Toolies is the bar close to campus known for being lax with IDs. It's one of the few freshmen and sophomores can drink at without having to worry, and a girl who looks like Beth? They probably won't even card her.

I walk in around ten-thirty with a few of my boys. The place is already crowded with sweaty bodies swaying drunkenly to the music. The girls move suggestively, some teasing, some seeking, and the guys all stalk their prey, only ever vaguely aware that they're being stalked just as surely.

I learned early on that girls are as likely to be looking for a hookup as guys. High school taught me that. And I indulged, I'll admit. But in recent years I've learned the value of selection, in letting them come to me.

But right now, I'm not looking for a hookup. I'm looking for Beth.

The bar isn't huge, but it's stuffed with students, and I don't spot her for a good fifteen minutes. In fact, it's Beth who spots me. Or, rather, it's Lani.

"Not exactly winning any awards tonight, bodyguard. Where have you been?"

My eyes roll, like they often do in response to her comments, and they skip right over her and land on Beth.

Fuck me she looks gorgeous. Her long blond hair is styled in loose waves and she wears dark eye makeup and a pale lip color. It's a sultry effect, and if there's one thing I really don't need my best friend's kid sister being, it's fucking *sultry*.

"Hey, kid," I greet her, if only to remind myself that she's still that tow-headed little girl who used to tantrum me into tea parties and watching *The Little Mermaid*. But it doesn't really work, because even the nickname, *kid*, has become a term of endearment, and it only highlights the fact that she is most definitely all grown up. As does her form-fitting top and equally tight jeans.

Beth stares a minute, and I watch her take in my very boring black T-shirt and dark jeans. It's not the first time I've caught her checking me out, and it doesn't please me any less than it has before. A soft blush paints her pretty round cheeks, and I think about other things I could say to her or do to her that would make her blush.

Fuck, I need to stop.

"Do you want a beer?" I ask her.

"Sure."

I look to Lani and raise my eyebrows, offering her one as well.

"Yes, please," Lani says, and I order them two Amstel Lights.

Derek is on Lani in seconds, and I'm not surprised. He's been asking about her practically nonstop since our first party at the house, and his interest is no secret. And I can't blame him either. She is definitely an attractive girl.

It's impossible not to compare her to Beth, being as they're almost always side by side these days. And, as I've always found when I've compared a girl to Beth, she's just lacking in the ways that actually matter.

Because Beth is so unique that it's hard to believe she's real. How does a girl possess equal parts naivety and badassery? Confidence and that sweet, quiet humility? Deep blue eyes that both widen in innocence and narrow in ferocity. She thinks she's awkward. But it's the world that's awkward. She's fucking perfect.

"So where's this friend you invited?" I ask Beth.

Beth turns toward the entrance, her pretty features falling into a frown. "I don't know. I thought he'd be here by now."

He? My gut clenches. *Why*, I don't know. I'm friends with plenty of girls, and there's no reason why Beth can't befriend a dude…except that she looks like a seductive fucking angel, and any guy cozying up to her is surely looking for something else. "You said you met him in your psych class?"

But she's still searching the entrance, brows pinched together as if it will help her see better, as if it will make this guy appear, and then suddenly I'm pissed. Who the *fuck* is this guy to make her wait? Or worse—stand her up? Irrationally my arms tighten and tense, itching to throw a punch. And it makes no sense, because whoever this guy is, I don't want him hanging out with Beth, anyway.

This is the juxtaposition of us. It has been for years. She is family and a little sister and someone to protect, and at the same time, deep in my gut, despite a lifetime of denial…I know I want her for myself.

But that doesn't mean I can act on my feelings. I tried once, and I almost destroyed something that means everything to me.

Just then, I spot that guy. The one who was staring at me outside of Standman. The one who was staring at *Beth*. I automatically look to my left, to my right, taking stock of my brothers, my back-up.

"There he is," Beth murmurs, and I turn to her, stunned.

"That guy? Are you fucking serious?"

Beth's eyes go wide and she blinks at me. "Oh, right, I forgot you saw him that time."

What the actual fuck?

"Look, David, I know he's a little different. But he's really nice, and we're friends now, and I really need you to stand down."

Stand down? It's then that I realize my arms are flexing and my chest is puffed out.

I am a walking fucking cliché. But I don't really care. There's something not right about this guy, and friends or not, Beth shouldn't trust him.

God, she's always so fucking naïve when it comes to guys. Falco, this guy…*me*.

"Please, David," she breathes one last time as the fucking creep approaches.

I don't *stand down* as she asked, but I don't pounce on the guy, either. I just fucking stand here like a sentinel, like the goddamned bodyguard Lani is always accusing me of being.

The creep slows his steps as he meets us and takes me in, looking uncertainly between me and Beth. But Beth smiles that warm Beth smile, and his tension eases marginally. He leans down, that same uncertainty practically rushing from his pores, and presses a small, chaste kiss to her cheek.

"Hey," he breathes. There's something unsettlingly familiar about him, but then I've known a lot of fucking creeps.

"Hi, Brody. This is David. David, Brody." Beth introduces us like everything is completely normal.

We size each other up like the testosterone-filled guys we obviously both are. And I'm irritated to find that he's looking at me like *I'm* the one not to be trusted. He looks between me and Beth, like he's the fucking protective one and I'm the one trying to get in her pants, and it stuns me silent.

Beth shifts from foot to foot, waiting for the tension to dissipate, but it doesn't. "David is one of Sammy's best friends, one of the ones I was telling you about," Beth murmurs.

Sammy? Telling him about? Just what the fuck has she told this guy in the five minutes they've supposedly been friends?

"Brody is in my Abnormal Psych class," Beth tells me. "He just transferred here this semester to...be closer to family. He doesn't really know anyone." Beth tries hard to make things right, but as much as I want to appease her, it isn't enough of an explanation for me.

"Is that why you stalk girls from alleyways?" I accuse.

Brody doesn't even flinch. He just glares at me.

Beth pinches my bicep—not too subtly, either. "He was just nervous to introduce himself. Like I said, he doesn't know anyone."

"Do you want a beer?" Brody seems over this conversation.

"She already has one," I point out, but it doesn't seem to daunt him, and he orders one for himself.

Despite my hostility, Brody and Beth fall into easy conversation, and I have no choice but to participate, since I'm not about to leave her alone with this guy. He doesn't really talk to anyone else, and when social graces force me to introduce him to a few people, he doesn't do much more than offer a cursory nod or a tip of his beer.

"Hi, David," coos the voice that now sounds like nails on a chalkboard, and I turn to find Liz—*Lizard*—smiling at me like that whole exchange at last week's party never happened. "Hi, Beth."

Beth's eyes flash with incredulity. She doesn't do fake, and she doesn't understand it, either. "Um, hi," she replies uncertainly.

"What's up, Liz?" My tone makes it clear I'm not asking how she's doing, I'm asking her what the fuck she wants.

"I just wanted to apologize for, you know, at the party." She looks between Beth and me. "I really didn't mean it to come out like that. Sometimes I say bitchy things and I don't even realize it until after, and then it's too late."

I'm not buying it. Because that wasn't the first bitchy thing I've heard her say. It was just the first time it was aimed at someone I care about. And I know full well she doesn't show remorse unless there are consequences, and apparently she considers my attitude just that. Our houses take the brother frat–sister sorority thing seriously, and we're supposed to look out for them. We've roughed up many an asshole that got too forward with one of our "sisters."

But Beth's eyes soften with sympathy, and I grit my teeth. *So damn naïve.* Because that's the thing about people. We never get to live inside someone else's head. The only real frame of reference we have is our own, and Beth would never hurt someone on purpose, so it's easy for her to believe that this girl wouldn't either. But I know better.

"It's okay," Beth murmurs.

It's not, though, and I don't pretend it is.

"So are you going to introduce me to your friend?" Liz purrs.

Ah, the real reason for her apology. Our Lizard has taken an interest in Creepy Stalker. Well, *perfect.* I bet they fucking deserve each other. "Liz, this is Brody. He just transferred. Brody, Liz," I dismissively introduce them.

Liz starts making conversation with Brody. Or as much of a conversation you can get out of a guy who mostly just nods and grunts. I watch him look her over. He makes absolutely no effort to disguise the fact that his interest—which appears marginal at best—is in what's beneath her clothing, and not what's coming out of her mouth. Incidentally, I happen to know from experience that Lizard's mouth is one of her best features. But not when it's talking.

Frankly, I'm just relieved Brody isn't looking at Beth like that, and while he's reluctantly distracted I take the opportunity to drag her a few feet away. But I do notice Brody's eyes subtly follow her, and it pisses me off.

"What the fuck?" I chide when they're out of earshot. "Days ago he's stalking you and now you're best fucking friends?"

Beth rolls her eyes. "We're not 'best friends.' He noticed me in class and he wanted to introduce himself, but he's shy, and he couldn't bring himself to do it. Hence the staring."

Again, not buying it. "He was standing outside your fucking dorm."

"You don't know that's why he was there. He could have been visiting someone else and just stopped to smoke a cigarette. He could live at Standman, for all I know. Look, I know he's a little awkward, but you know what? So am I, David."

"You're only awkward in the best possible ways," I tell her honestly.

Her pink little bow of a mouth stretches into a small, sweet smile. "Please give him a chance," she pleads. She peeks over her shoulder, satisfied that Brody at least seems to be feigning interest in whatever the fuck Liz is going on about. "His mom was sick and he transferred to be closer to home to take care of her. But she died over the summer. He's all alone." Beth's voice cracks and her eyes shine, and it tugs at my chest.

And at the same time my stomach rolls with nausea. It hits too close to home.

Yet I don't let Brody's history sway my opinion of him. Because his story may be true, or it could be a fabricated tale concocted to play on Beth's considerable sympathies. But either way, experiencing tragedy doesn't make you a good person.

I sigh. "I still don't trust him, Bea."

"I know. But just give him a chance. Okay, David? Please?"

Fuck this girl and her angelic, pleading eyes. Fuck the way she says my name—the only person alive who calls me *David* instead of *Dave*. She will be the end of me. "Fucking fine," I mutter with blatant reluctance.

A few of my boys join us at the bar, and Lani and Derek start sucking face in a booth. I elbow Beth until she notices and lets out a sharp giggle. I smirk. "I'm going to the bathroom. Stay with my boys, okay?"

Beth nods her agreement, but I still whisper to Drew to look after her until I get back, careful she doesn't overhear. I don't need another argument about how she's not a kid. I couldn't be more aware of the fucking fact. That's the whole problem. Because this isn't a crowd where you have to worry about kids, but gorgeous, naïve girls with big open hearts—they're another story.

I push past the line to the girl's bathroom, into the mostly empty men's room. On my way back, I stop by the quieter end of the bar and order two more beers. But when I get eyes back on Beth, and I catch her deer-in-headlights expression, I stop short.

The fuck?

Drew stands beside her, looking confused—obviously not doing his goddamned job. I didn't order him to just stand the fuck around. I catch sight of the fucking dipshit who broke her heart, and immediately start pushing my way back through the crowd to get to her.

"…Come on, Bethy, I just want to talk. You owe me that, at least."

Drew just fucking stands there, but Brody steps in. "Look, man, I don't know who the fuck you are, but I'll tell you one thing—not a single girl here owes you a damned thing, *least* of all Beth. So I suggest you back the fuck off." His arms flex in warning.

Well at least he's good for something.

Falco swallows anxiously, but ignores Brody. "Bethy—"

I make it to them before he can finish whatever pathetic bullshit he can spew, and I grab his elbow and spin him around.

"Back. The fuck. Off." My threat isn't loud, but it is fervent. I've been struggling with pent-up aggression all night, and Falco is my ideal target. It's been too long since I've felt the satisfaction of my fist slamming into his jaw.

The bastard takes a step back from Beth. "I just wanted to talk to her."

"You had years to do that, asshole. Time's fucking up."

He shoots me a contemptuous glare. Yeah, he hates me, but he knows he's the bad guy in this situation, even if my hands aren't exactly clean. And suddenly my gut rolls with the fear that he *could* talk to her at some point—he could tell her everything. And then what? Would she ever forgive me?

Beth watches silently as Brian retreats. The look on her face makes my chest ache. She looks...lost.

I wait for her to register some reaction. For those eyes to narrow in anger, or dampen with tears—for an outburst...*anything*.

But she just stands there, frozen, her full lower lip trembling as if she's seen a ghost. And I guess, in a way, she has. She knew Falco was here at school with us, but does knowing a ghost is real make seeing it any less fucking fucked up? And Beth has already had her share of fucked up.

Lani is asking Beth what happened, Lani who has retracted her tongue from Derek's throat long enough to make her way over to her friend. "Are you okay?" she asks.

"Are you okay?" Brody asks.

Are you okay, are you okay, are you okay. What a stupid fucking question. Because I don't know what Beth is right now, but *okay* isn't it.

I need to get her the hell out of here.

I grab her hand. "We're leaving," I tell her, and Lani, and fucking creepy ass Brody, and whoever the hell else is listening. No one tries to stop me.

Beth is complacent, and I think she would walk out with a stranger if one was willing to remove her from the situation.

Fucking Falco.

"Come on, Bea," I breathe into her ear, and I lead her out of the crowded bar.

She doesn't say anything. She just follows me.

I don't want to take her back to her dorm, because I don't want her to be alone yet. She needs to talk to someone, and I'm more than prepared to wait until she's ready to do it.

I cross Lincoln Avenue and lead her to the far corner of Veteran's Park, where it's a little less crowded and easier to get a cab. I raise my hand and one stops for me instantly. I open the back door and gesture for Beth to get in. She doesn't ask where we're going. She doesn't say anything at all.

I tell the driver to take us to Smithy's Diner. It's still early enough that it shouldn't be too busy yet, but once the bars close around two a.m., the drunk coeds start stumbling in to order late-night junk food.

I lead Beth to a booth in the back, where no one will bother us, just in case. I order two cups of coffee, and add milk and two sugars to hers, the way she likes it. She takes the mug, but doesn't sip. She just kind of stares at it.

"I'm gonna need you to say something, kid," I tell her. The silence is freaking me out.

"I'm sorry," she mouths.

I shake my head. "No. You're not fucking sorry. You have nothing to be *sorry* about, Bea. But you're upset, and I need you to talk to me, okay?"

Her gaze finally abandons the coffee to meet mine. "I was just surprised, I guess," she murmurs.

"I get it. But you know he's here. And you saw him when he showed up at the BEG party," I remind her. Why was this time so shocking?

I watch her long, delicate neck move with her anxious swallow. "But, he wasn't there for me."

"What do you mean?"

"He's here for his spot on the soccer team. And he showed up at BEG because…well, I don't know why. He probably just heard about a cool party and decided to go. But tonight…"

I resist the urge to interrupt her. Because she's wrong. She's so damned wrong. She has no idea what she's worth and it's all that fucker's fault. I don't care if it took him this long to wake the fuck up; Beth's ex wouldn't show up at her school, at the first party and bar she's gone out to, unless he's here for more than fucking soccer, an excuse I didn't really buy for a moment.

"I saw him walk in, and right away he was looking for something. And then he saw me, and just marched right over, and I realized he'd been looking for *me*. Which made no sense. But then he started asking me to talk."

"So you were shocked silent because your ex wanted to talk to you?" How does she not understand that *of course* Falco would want to talk to her. He didn't want to give her up in the first place—he just also didn't want to give up his shot at bagging a bunch of girls in college. And when faced with the ultimatum, he chose the latter. But three years later, he's no doubt been there and done that, and now he's here, and if he had half a brain, he'd be bending over backward for even the slightest chance at winning her back. Of course, if he had half a brain, he wouldn't have let her go in the first place, a fact I suspect he's finally realized.

"David, you don't get it. He dumped me. You know that. But he didn't just break up with me—he cut me off completely. He stopped taking my calls, ignored my texts. It was like I stopped existing."

Guilt crushes my chest until I find it hard to breathe, and I have to close my eyes for a moment to get my bearings.

"Why would he want to talk *now*?" She's confused, but she's also scared and unsure. Which unnerves me deeply. Falco nearly destroyed her once, and she can't give him the power to hurt her again. I won't let her.

"I don't know, Bea. But whatever his motivation, he doesn't deserve you, okay? In any capacity. He didn't then, and he doesn't now."

"I know that," she says automatically, but already I know she doesn't believe it.

"Your creepy stalker was right about one thing, Bea. You don't owe Falco a goddamned thing."

* * *

We move on from the topic of Falco, and Beth gradually cheers up, eventually deciding that she's hungry. I take her appetite as a victory.

She can't decide between pancakes and french toast, so we order both and share.

I take a bite and my eyes roll back in pleasure. "Fuck, Bea, you've got to try this strawberry syrup. They make it here; it's fucking heaven."

She frowns, her nose scrunching adorably. "I don't think I like flavored syrup."

"Oh, shut up." Beth always thinks never having tried something and not liking it are the same thing. I cut her a piece of french toast and dip it in the euphoria-inducing syrup. "Open," I order her, and her lips part for my fork.

Her eyes close as she chews, a soft moan dancing in her throat. My dick twitches and I shift in my seat, subtly adjusting my jeans with my free hand. It's impossible not to imagine slipping something else between those perfect lips, listening to that gorgeous fucking moan, feeling it vibrate through me.

Best friend's kid sister, best friend's kid sister, best friend's kid sister. It's a familiar fucking mantra.

Beth can only make it through half of her share of the food, so when she declares she's done, I leave cash on the table and we start walking. Smithy's is just off campus and less than half a mile from Standman, and the night is bright and mild. You can see the stars clearly here; fewer than fifty miles from the city, yet an entire universe away.

I walk Beth through the quad and right up to the front door of her building, texting the sober pledge to come pick me up. One is assigned every night, so we don't have to worry about rides or drinking and driving. I hated it when I pledged, but considering the kind of hazing that used to go on at these schools a decade ago, we've all gotten off pretty damned easy.

"Thanks, David. I'm sorry I let Brian bug me out. He just gets in my head, you know?" Beth murmurs.

"No *sorries*, remember? And I get it. But he doesn't deserve to get in your head, Bea. He doesn't deserve to get inside any part of you. He never fucking did." I know I shouldn't have brought that up, but I couldn't fucking help it. Fuck him for sleeping with her. Fuck her for letting him—for not knowing she was too good for him. And fuck me for being jealous.

"I know," she whispers. And she does. But she also doesn't, and it's what tears me up.

I sling my arm around her slim shoulders and haul her in for a hug. "You're too good for all of us, kid. Don't forget that," I tell her honestly.

She huffs out a shallow laugh. "You're always so good to me, David. Even when I act like an idiot."

"*Especially* when you act like an idiot," I correct her.

She smiles a closed-mouthed smile. "Sammy's lucky to have you as a friend. I'm lucky," she whispers.

I shake my head. "Cap's not here, Bea. And he's not the reason I am, either. I think you know that." Beth and I have had our own friendship for a long time, and I'm sick of pretending it's only because of her brother.

"That means a lot to me," she says.

"Good." I press a soft kiss to her forehead. "Night, Bea. Get some sleep."

She smiles up at me from under her long lashes. Not for the first time, I wish she was less beautiful.

"Night." And she disappears inside.

I lean back against the wall of her building and stare up at the sky, cursing the joke that is my life. I pull my pack of Parliaments from my pocket and light one up, sucking the nicotine into my lungs, letting it calm my senses—letting the poison blacken my insides until they match the way I feel. I smoke the thing down to the filter before stubbing it out on the brick wall and tossing it into the trash can.

Mangina texts that he's parked on the north side of the quad, so I head down the steps and along the pathway. A tiny orange light flashes in the dark of my peripheral, and I turn. The creep—Brody—is there, in his alleyway, watching me. My eyes narrow, and I'm about to cross over to confront him, but he turns and leaves.

I don't chase after him. After all, Beth is safe in her dorm room, and Brody can't get in there without a security key fob.

But what the fuck? Why is he still spying on her? There's something off about him, and I silently vow to get to the bottom of it before whatever the fuck it is can hurt her.

Chapter Eight

Beth

I woke up to a text from Brian. Even after Friday night, it was the last thing I was expecting. He's still just begging to talk, but I can't imagine what could be left to talk about. So, I pack my bag for the day and tell myself it's *my* turn to ignore *his* texts.

But I guess I'm not quite as good at it as he was, because as I go through my Monday classes, I get four more, and by the time I'm leaving my shift at the student health and guidance center, I'm texting him back, agreeing to meet him for coffee like a damned fool. I even blow off the call from my mom—something I never do—telling her I have to study, fearful she'd hear the uncertainty in my voice, sure she'd more than disapprove if she knew what I was up to.

And I wouldn't blame her. *I* disapprove.

I can't help but think of the last time Brian and I actually spoke.

If you'd have told me then that it would *be* the last time, I wouldn't have believed you. Not then. Not after he'd spent nearly a year slowly and methodically stamping out my many insecurities and doubts, even as I sensed that my anxiety had begun to burden our relationship—had begun to burden *him*. But that night…that night had been special.

Brian had taken me out to dinner at our favorite restaurant before he planned to go to yet another party at his friend Cooper's. I didn't want to go, feeling more and more that Brian was starting to get annoyed when I'd inevitably wind up in a corner somewhere, reading on my phone or otherwise avoiding the crowd. So, when his halfhearted invitation came, sandwiched between comments about needing to "put in time with the boys," I took the hint. He was leaving for Dartmouth in just a few months, after all, and while I knew I'd be missing him more than I could even imagine, he had all kinds of people he'd be missing—his family, his friends—and it didn't occur to me that I should have been his first priority. That night more than ever.

His parents had been away, and we decided to go back to his house to fool around, which went pretty much as usual, at first. But much like Brian's patience with my flaws and quirks had been waning, his patience with the progression of our physical relationship was, too, and as much as he tried to hide it, his frustration had more than begun to show.

And I didn't even blame him for it. He was almost eighteen, and we'd been together long enough by most high school relationship standards, but a part of me was still holding out for something I didn't understand. And I still don't, even now. Brian loved me—he said he loved me. I loved him. Or I thought I did.

But, that night—*that* night, his talk of Dartmouth and leaving…it got to me. It ignited old fears and insecurities. Brian kept telling me how much he loved me, and how badly he wanted to prove that to me—physically. "The only thing I know right now, Bethy, is that nobody will ever love anyone as much as I do, right now, in this moment." And what's a puppy love-struck fifteen-year-old girl to do?

Like I said, I thought I *loved* him. I *did* love him. I…don't know anymore.

Brian took my virginity in his childhood bedroom, between his dinner date with me and his appearance at Cooper's party. It had been painful but it was over fairly quickly, and I'd been scared but Brian said all the right things.

He'd promised to meet me in our gazebo after the party—the one in my family's backyard where Brian and I used to meet in secret the summer before, with blankets and wine coolers for slightly more innocent sleepovers, back before Sammy had become more tolerant of our relationship. But it turned out Sammy had been right about Brian all along. I never should have trusted him.

I fell asleep that night still waiting for Brian, hours after he said he'd come. I awoke in that gazebo early the next morning, wrapped in the blankets from his truck, but I was utterly alone. In Brian's place was a note—one that appeared to have been hastily written on a piece of paper presumably torn from the notebook he kept in his backseat—both swearing his love for me, and breaking up with me.

He was doing it for *me*, his note said. It wouldn't have been fair to *trap me in a long-distance relationship, to hold me back from living my life*, and he *loved me enough to let me go, and make a clean break before it's too late*.

But it was already too late for me.

I was in denial at first, sure it had to be some incomprehensible, exceptionally un-funny joke, or something. But Brian didn't take my calls, or return my texts, and I started to unravel.

Then he changed his relationship status on Facebook, and I could actually feel my heart shatter into pieces, the wreckage sinking into my stomach and making me sick.

It was all a misunderstanding—it had to be. I didn't feel *held back* by our relationship, or want him to let me go, and I was pitifully certain that if Brian would just give me the chance to explain, that I could sort everything out between us.

It was when I saw him at school on Monday—when he looked right through me as if I were a ghost, refusing to even acknowledge that I still existed—that I finally understood. There was nothing *to* sort out. Brian was done with me. He'd finally slept with me, and now he was moving on to the next conquest. That's when the rest of me shattered, too.

Brian was out of school for over a week after that, rumors and the sight of Sammy's, David's, and Tucker's knuckles making sure I knew that Brian had been punished—whether for fucking me, or breaking my heart, or dating me in the first place, I never really knew.

But he never spoke to me again.

Even when I continued to call and text, even when I begged him for just a single minute of his time.

Even when I told him it was life or death.

But Brian couldn't be bothered with me then, so what could he possibly have to say to me now that three years have passed?

I sigh out loud. I guess I'm about to find out.

My phone is close to dying, so I power it off, saving the last of the battery for my walk home. I make my way to Jazzy Java, the coffee shop just off campus where I've agreed to meet Brian, fully aware that David prefers the more straightforward Coffee House. The last thing I need is another confrontation between him and Brian. I agreed to meet him, after all—his excessive persistence notwithstanding. Even if it's only to tell him to leave me alone.

I walk briskly, gathering courage, squaring my shoulders and straightening my spine to feign what I can't muster. I enter the shop with an artful portrayal of confidence, surprised and pleased to realize the majority of it is earnest.

My heart—though still not fully healed and permanently scarred—continues to beat, despite Brian so expertly coaxing me to hand it over, only to toss it in a Dumpster. But my heart is my own again. It hasn't belonged to him in quite some time, and whether that's because he threw it away like he never wanted it in the first place, or because I finally gathered the strength to pick it up off the floor, the fact remains—I'm over Brian.

I push through the crowded entryway, unconsciously reaching into my bag for my phone, absently scrolling or checking for messages—a tool I often use to distract myself—not expecting to see Brian yet, as he's never been punctual for anything in his life.

But I'm wrong, because he's there, perched anxiously on a royal purple, tufted velvet sofa in the corner, with two large cups of coffee. He looks handsome—he always has—and his obvious anxiety does nothing to mitigate his all-American good looks. His hair is still buzzed short on the sides, but kept longer on top, and his blond streaks are lighter at the ends. He runs his fingers nervously through it. My confidence drains with the color in my cheeks, and my stomach rolls with anxiety.

This was a mistake.

I've spent the past three plus years growing and healing, and I thought I was strong enough for this. But it only takes one moment for me to realize I'm just the same naïve little girl I always was. Vulnerable. And I need to get out of here. I'm just about to turn and flee when his eyes land on me.

Shit.

Brian's hand shoots up, but he thinks twice and retracts it halfway, waving uncertainly, his face contorted with a grimace of a smile. He's beyond anxious—he's completely frazzled. And surprisingly, it eases my own nerves marginally.

I take a hesitant step toward him, and then another, until I'm approaching the purple couch in the back of the shop. Brian stands to greet me and when he leans in to kiss my cheek, I let him. His lips feel as unsure as the rest of him.

"Bethy."

I gulp. I wish he wouldn't call me that. "H-hi," I stammer.

His eyes skate over the two coffees, the couch, and he gestures jerkily. "Do you want to sit?"

What I want is to run away and hide until he graduates in May. But I sit instead, because I am not a coward—not anymore. Brian hands me the coffee he obviously ordered for me. There's milk and artificial sweetener on the table.

"Didn't remember how you take it," he murmurs.

"Um, milk and sugar." As Brian gets up to replace the sweeteners with real, diabetes-inducing, pure cane white sugar, I think idly to myself that David always remembers exactly how I take my coffee.

Brian lets a few minutes pass while I fix my coffee and take a few sips. He quietly sips his own, watching me cautiously as if I might run at any moment. And I might.

"You look really pretty, Bethy," he murmurs.

I look down at my faded boyfriend jeans and loose white T-shirt, a navy blue scarf covering any cleavage that might have shown.

"Thanks," I say back. "Look—"

"Look—" he says at the exact same time.

We both laugh nervously, and each gesture for the other to go first. "You asked to meet me," I remind him.

Brian nods. He's about to begin again, but I cut him off.

"But look, Bri. *Brian*. I'm not interested in rehashing the past. You're here now, for better or worse, and I get that we're going to run into each other. I'm sorry I didn't respond to you when you showed up at the bar. And the party. I was just kind of in shock, you know? I didn't know you were here, and then I—I just wasn't expecting to see you, I guess. But the past is the past, and I don't have hard feelings, okay?"

Brian stares at me. I guess he's not used to so many words falling from my mouth so quickly. But he doesn't know me anymore.

"Well that makes things kinda difficult for me, to be honest."

I frown at him.

His eyes widen. "No. I didn't mean…Not that you don't have hard feelings; that's a big relief, actually. But I did kinda want to talk about the past."

I swallow audibly. "I don't see what good that'll do," I admit. "It's over."

"But what if it isn't?"

What?

Brian sighs. "Okay, I don't want to upset you. That's not why I'm here. I just want to tell you that I'm sorry. I'm really so fucking sorry, Bethy." His voice cracks.

"I forgave you a long time ago, Bri."

Brian nods, but I know him well enough to know he's not satisfied. "Well, that's good," he mutters, nodding vaguely to himself. He stares at me, indecisive, as if he doesn't know what to say—whether or not to say something.

And I hope he doesn't. Whatever it is, it can do no good. The only good that can come from this conversation is for us to shake hands and go our separate ways.

But Brian won't give me that, I can see it even before he rubs his palm over his face and huffs out a frustrated exhale. "Fuck, no, it's not *good*, Bethy. I don't deserve your forgiveness. I never deserved you at all. But I need you to know I'm sorry. I've spent three years being sorry. And I'll spend the rest of my life being it, too. I never should have ended us. I was just scared, and I was going away to school, and I thought I wanted different things. You know, freedom. New experiences. But I was young, and stupid, and listening to the wrong people, and it's the biggest regret of my life."

My heart races, and I subtly pinch the sensitive skin on the inside of my elbow to make sure I'm not dreaming.

Ow.

Nope, definitely wide awake.

It's just that I'd imagined this scene so many times—a contrite, sorrowful Brian, full of apologies and regret. But now that it's sitting before me, I realize it's just far too little, three years too late. My love for him, if it was ever real in the first place, burned itself out long ago.

"But you didn't just break up with me, Brian. You took everything from me, and then you ghosted me. You killed me." I don't let myself dwell on how literal that metaphor can be taken. Part of me wants to scream and shout, to tell him everything, to make him understand just how much I'd needed him—how alone I'd been, how scared…but it won't change the past. And there's no point in blaming him for what he couldn't know, for what he'll never know. He made his choices, and I made mine.

Brian's eyes shine with actual tears. I've never seen them before, and they strike me silent. He nods. "I know. I had to."

"You *had* to?" *Don't get emotional*, I remind myself. He doesn't deserve any more of my tears.

"I loved you, Bethy. But I thought I was doing what was right for us. Or what was right for me, anyway. It was stupid, and selfish, but I knew that if I saw you, spoke to you, I would beg you to take me back, and I was convinced that wasn't the right thing." He seems like he wants to say more, but stops himself.

I look down at my lap, picking at my cuticles. "Like I said, I forgive you." But my voice is no longer sure.

"I just want to start over," Brian pleads.

"*Start over?* Are you serious?"

Brian blanches. "Or not *start over*. But start again, maybe? Or just—I don't know. I just want another chance, Bethy."

"No." The word is firm and resolute, and Brian blinks in surprise. But I don't care, because *is he fucking kidding me?* "There's no such thing as *starting over*, Brian. Our histories—they make us who we are. And I'm not the same naïve little girl who fell in love with an older boy who broke her heart. You left me. That was your choice. And I'm sorry if you wish you could take it back. I really am. I know what it feels like to wonder what I could have done differently to change things. To blame myself for our breakup. But you know what the difference is, Brian?" I wait a beat. "You *are* to blame. I never was."

I stand up. If I'd known this was what he was planning, I honestly wouldn't have come.

Brian stands, too, eyes frantic, hands reaching. "No. Please don't go. I'm sorry. Please just stay and finish your coffee."

I swallow my frustration and sit back down, wrapping both hands around my mug. I should leave. I know. But I'm not good about doing what's best for myself when other people are hurting, even people who have hurt me, apparently. "I don't want to talk about starting over or second chances. There's no such thing," I tell him. "I just wanted to tell you that I forgive you, and I want to move forward. That's all I can offer you."

Brian nods, but he's just placating me. "Okay, Bethy."

"Beth," I correct him.

He glares at me a moment, wounded, and it twists my chest even though I know it shouldn't. "Beth," he finally agrees. "No starting over. I got it. Moving forward." He nods to himself. "But I can't pretend you're not here. I think about you every minute."

"Brian—"

"Right. I'm sorry. What I meant was—" He sighs in frustration. "I meant, you're here. I'm here. We're having coffee, and the world didn't end, right?"

I narrow my eyes at him, wondering where he's going with this.

He licks his lips, calculating. "I mean, we can do this again, right? Just get coffee. Be friends?"

"Brian—"

"Just hear me out, Bethy—*Beth*. We were never friends, right? I fell for you the moment I saw you, and we…well, you were there." He laughs nervously.

"I was there," I agree timidly. I don't want to think of that perfect summer. Before the rest of the world got in the way, as I'd always feared it would.

"Can't we just try to be friends?" His eyes beg and implore, and I succumb to the inevitable masochism.

"I guess we can try," I concede.

Brian breathes deeply, fighting a triumphant grin, and it's a little contagious. I've never had someone so excited about my friendship.

"But *just* friends, Brian. I'm not looking to date. Not you, or any-one. I need to focus on school and just, you know, having a good time."

"Right. I get it."

I'm not sure he does, but I suppose I have no choice but to give him the benefit of the doubt.

* * *

It's dark when I get back to campus, but students are out and about, chatting and smoking in clusters around the student union. It isn't un-usual for early evening, but the excitable atmosphere is. People talk closely, gesturing wildly, whispering with wide eyes. Anxiety flows from student to student, and it's palpable.

What the hell is going on?

I reach into my bag and power on my phone.

It buzzes and buzzes, indicating missed calls and texts—way more than I would have expected. I turn onto Washington, toward the Standman quad, about to read one of the several missed texts from David and Lani when I bump into a slim body.

Torrence, a girl from my Shakespeare class, starts apologizing at the same time as I do.

"I wasn't watching where I was going," I admit.

She's talking with a girl I don't know, and she introduces her as her roommate, Asia.

"Nice to meet you," I murmur, but it's obvious I've interrupted some serious conversation. I'm about to get on my way when Torrence raises her eyebrows expectantly.

"Did you hear?" she asks cryptically.

I blink at her. "Hear what?"

The two girls exchange a glance. My stomach drops. Something is up.

"There was an assault this weekend. On campus!" To their credit, they don't seem to be gossiping; they appear sincerely horrified, and I mirror their sentiment.

"W-what kind of assault?" Though already I suspect.

"A girl from SDG was almost raped," Asia says with appropriate somberness.

My throat tightens. "Do you know who?"

"Liz Poletti."

Oh my God. *Liz.* I just saw her. Friday night at Toolies bar. "Is she…is she okay?" I ask shakily.

"I don't really know how to answer that," Torrence admits.

"Right. Of course not."

"All I heard was that she came home to the sorority house when most of the girls were still out, but Kari Marx—she's in my women's studies class—was home studying or something and saw her. She came in all messed up and disheveled, or whatever, and Kari kept asking her what happened, and finally she admitted a guy attacked her."

I shiver. I know the news I've just heard is probably making me paranoid, but I still have that feeling that I'm being watched. Of course, that's probably because of Brody's stalky behavior before we became friends.

"Do you know who it was?" I ask.

They both shrug. "Yeah. She knew the guy. He's a senior, but new on campus. I don't know his name."

The hairs on the back of my neck stand at attention, my subconscious whispering the name that only just floated through my mind. *Brody*. But I know better. I may not know him all that well, and I may be naïve when it comes to guys, but I know he wouldn't do something like that.

Still, even as I assure myself that there are hundreds, maybe thousands of transferred seniors on campus, I recall Liz flirting with Brody at Toolies Friday night…

What if they met up the next night? What if they went out, and

Brody…*No*. I halt my train of thought. I told him we were friends, and I owe a friend the benefit of the doubt. Especially with something as abhorrent as *this*.

I mutter some cursory platitudes about how awful it all is, and make my way onto the deserted quad, the shadows of the ancient maples setting my already jittery nerves on edge. I swipe open my phone, but before I can open one of the many unread texts, it buzzes in my hand. *David calling*.

"Hey," I answer. I've already figured that he's been trying to reach me to tell me about Liz, and probably to use her as a cautionary tale to be more careful around campus. But how careful can one really be? If Liz knew the guy, chances are he didn't just assault her on the street, right? Are we never supposed to trust anyone at all?

"Bea? Where in the actual motherfucking fuck have you mother-fucking been?"

Jesus. His hysterics make me giggle, and I hear him huff through the phone, unamused. "I was…just having coffee." *With Brian*. But David doesn't need to know that yet. Not while he's in such a state. "My battery was low. I turned my phone off so I'd have it for the walk home."

David's excitable breathing is audible through the phone. "Good. That was smart. Good," he says almost to himself.

"David, are you okay?" I know he's probably upset about Liz. They are friends, after all.

I spot Brody between Standman C and D, smoking with his head down, so I guess the quad isn't completely empty, after all. I throw him a wave, and he gives an uncertain one back. I wonder who he's visiting when he comes here, or if he lives in one of the other buildings, and I make a note to ask him. He looks agitated, and he takes a step like he wants to speak to me, but right now I need to get to my dorm to charge my damned phone, before it shuts down mid-conversation and David really loses it.

"Bea, did you hear what happened Saturday? To Liz?"

"I just heard from a girl in my Shakespeare class. I can't believe it."

"Well I fucking can," David growls, stopping me in my tracks. "I told you, Bea!" He says furiously. He's angry with me, but I don't understand why, or what he's even talking about.

"W-what did you tell me?" I ask hesitantly.

David senses my reaction and sucks in a deep, calming breath. "Your fucking stalker. *Brody*," he spits.

The phone shakes in my trembling hand and my throat tightens until it's hard to breathe. My instinct is denial. Because Brody wouldn't do that, *would he?*

But of course I don't know what he would or wouldn't do. I don't really know him *at all*. All I know is some sob story about his mom—a story, I now realize, he could have easily made up.

"Where are you?" David asks frantically.

"In the quad," I croak.

And then I remember he's here—Brody—smoking in the alley between the two buildings, and I glance over my shoulder to where I'd seen him.

But he's not there anymore. No, he's marching toward me, in obvious agitation, and it takes too long for my brain to get the message to my feet to fucking *move*.

By the time I'm running toward the door to my building, fumbling for the security key fob, Brody has nearly caught up to me. Fear surges in my gut, constricting my chest until I'm gasping for each breath, my heart racing for its life.

Why is he chasing me? What does he want?

And why is he not locked up?

I try to rationalize and tell myself if he was going to do something to me, he'd have done it already. But then, he's never had me alone, and right now there's no one around. I peek back and find him only fifteen feet behind me, his features held in a glower that sends chills down my spine and churns my stomach with dread.

Tears blur my vision as I hold the fob up to the sensor, and I trip over my own feet, barely righting myself as the door buzzes open.

"Beth!" Brody calls.

But I'm through the door in a heartbeat, pulling it closed tightly behind me. Brody can't get in here without a key fob, and even though rationally I know I'm safe, I don't feel it with his frustrated glare shooting daggers at me through the wall of glass—all that separates us.

I suck in deep breaths, only vaguely aware of David's muffled voice shouting frenziedly from the phone I dropped into my bag when I got my keys.

And then my heart stops beating as Brody slowly reaches into his pocket and retrieves his own key fob.

I know they're all identical no matter where on campus you live, but as he holds it out toward the sensor, I stop breathing entirely. Idly I wonder why I've never considered that he might live in my own building, especially after seeing him around here those times. But by the time the door buzzes its access I'm already flying toward the elevator, slamming my palm on the call button.

In a rare bit of luck, the elevator is already idling in the lobby, and the doors slide open immediately. I throw myself into the car and desperately hit the button for the fourth floor, watching in horror as Brody's long, purposeful strides cover the distance too quickly, still glaring at me with unfathomable intent.

Terror is a living, breathing thing, crushing my lungs and roiling my stomach. But God must be watching over me tonight, because the doors close just before Brody can get a hand between them, and he's calling my name as I'm lifted to safety.

The stairs.

The realization strikes me in the gut. Four flights. But with his size and physique, it isn't the obstacle it would be for someone like me.

Does he know what floor I live on? If he's the stalker David accused him of being, then he probably does, and my heart skips dangerously as I struggle with the key to my room.

"Lani?" I call as my shaking fingers try to jam my key into the lock. But I'm greeted with silence, and I know she isn't home.

The familiar loud creak of the oil-deprived stairwell door resonates down the hall, and I know it's him without even turning to check. But I'm through my door and locking it before I even hear him call my name.

Brody continues calling for me through the door I've slid down, hugging my knees to my chest, trying to catch my breath and staunch my tears. Violent knocking rattles the door and vibrates down my spine, and I jump farther into the room, putting as much distance between Brody and myself as possible.

"Go away!" I sob.

His voice is muffled through the door, but I can make out, "…just want to talk…please, Beth…"

I wonder if he'd told Liz he *just wanted to talk*. Nausea rises in my gut and I fall into a chant, begging him to "go away, go away, go away!"

I'm still chanting when I realize my voice is the only one filling the room. That Brody's voice is gone, and his knocking has ceased.

I quiet.

I listen carefully, not daring to take so much as a step toward the door. And then I hear the distant sound of a voice that reminds me I'm not alone.

I hurry to the bag I dropped when I stumbled through the door, and grab my phone. The screen displays David's name and his Facebook photo, a particularly handsome shot of him wearing his trademark lopsided, roguish smirk. The timer on the screen indicates that the call has lasted only twelve minutes.

How? How can only twelve minutes have passed since I answered his call?

The phone shakes in my hand. "H-hello," I rasp. I don't know why.

I don't know why I don't tell him what happened. Why I don't beg him to help me.

Maybe because, deep down, I know he's already on his way.

"Bea? *Bea*? What the fuck! Where are you? I'm on my way to Standman," he confirms.

"M-my dorm."

"Fuck, Bea, I'm losing my mind over here! Are you okay? Who was shouting?"

"It was him."

"I fucking knew it! Damn it, Beth, he's dangerous!"

"I know!" I cry. "He followed me! I didn't—"

"How did he get into Standman?"

I pause, my voice tiny when I say, "He lives here. In my building. I didn't know."

David rattles off a string of colorful expletives, their familiarity in his deep tenor calming my nerves. He sucks in a settling breath. "Is he gone?" he asks.

"I think."

"Look through your peephole."

I approach my door warily, as if the moment I reach it, the shouting and banging will start up again. But when I look through my peephole, no one is there. "He's gone," I confirm.

David sighs. "I'm gonna hang up—"

"No!" I cry. It's irrational, but having him on the phone makes me feel safe, like more than his voice is here with me, ready to take up for me like always.

"Bea, he's gone, and your door is locked, right?"

"Yeah."

"I'm going to hang up, and you're going to call campus security, and report him. Right now, okay?" He talks slowly and carefully, as if to an hysterical child—I suppose that's what Brody has reduced me to, and the thought has resentment brewing in my chest.

It morphs into anger, and then resolve.

I am *not* a helpless little girl, and I will not be victimized by someone I've shown nothing but kindness.

"Why is he even free? Shouldn't he be in jail?" I ask.

David sighs again. "Yeah, he motherfucking should. Supposedly they brought him in for questioning, but released him 'pending investigation'," he spits bitterly.

"He denied it?" I gasp.

"Well would *you* fucking admit it?" he says harshly. "Look, I'm sorry. I don't know all the details. I only spoke to Kari—she's one of Liz's sorority sisters. But you know how these things go. He said–she said and all that shit. He denies he was even with her, so they're investigating, I guess. I texted Liz, but she's not responding to me. Not that I can fucking blame her, considering I'm the one who introduced her to that piece of shit."

I swallow down my guilt. Because, actually, that was me. I'm the one who befriended him, who invited him to the bar Friday night.

"This isn't your fault, Bea." David reads my mind. "It's not. But you need to be a little less trusting, okay? Not everyone deserves your friendship."

"Yeah," I breathe.

But the fact remains, if I'd been smarter, more vigilant, Liz would never have been attacked. Brody's behavior was alarming, and I so easily dismissed it and accepted his explanation.

Did he read me? Realize I was awkward and shy, and use it against me? Am I that easy to manipulate?

I feel stupid. The self-worth I've spent three years trying to rebuild into something tangible slowly starts to chip away again. I hate that I've given Brody that power, and it makes me resent myself even more.

"Look, I'm almost at your dorm. Hang up, and call security," David says softly, kid gloves on tight. I don't even blame him.

"I need to sign you in," I say almost robotically.

"No."

"But—"

"Do not leave your room for any reason, Bea. Do you understand?"

David's order reminds me that the danger remains, and that it is very real. "Okay."

"I'll have Shitface sign me in. He lives in your building."

"Good to have pledges," I murmur.

David huffs out a breath. "I'll see you in a minute." He hangs up.

I stare at my phone. But instead of calling campus security, my first call is to Lani. She's jumpy and nervous and confirms she's been trying to reach me to tell me about the assault. She's in Campus West, another freshman dorm, studying with Elise, a girl in her statistics class she's become friends with.

I tell her what happened with Brody. She had no idea he lived in our building, either.

"Which is weird, right?" she says. "A guy who looks like that…I mean, you notice him, you know? Although he seems kinda lurky, like he's trying to blend into the shadows."

She has no idea. Again, I'm reminded that the red flags were all there, and that I chose to ignore them.

"Yeah," I tell her. "Look, I gotta go. But maybe you should ask Elise if you could stay there tonight?" Lani has mentioned that Elise's roommate is a townie who rarely stays in the dorm, so I know there's probably an empty bed for her.

"I'm not going to leave you alone tonight, Beth," Lani asserts. Because she's that kind of friend.

"I'm already in the room, door locked tight. And anyway, David is on his way up."

I hear the smirk in her voice when she says, "Of course he is. Well, you know, maybe he should stay the night. Just to make sure everything's kosher, right? He can sleep in my bed. I wouldn't mind coming home to my pillow smelling of that man."

Lani elicits an impossible giggle despite my mood, if a vaguely jealous one. I don't want David in her bed, even alone.

"Or, actually, my bed is super uncomfortable. I totally forgot. He should probably just bunk up with you. You can both fit; you just need to cuddle real close—"

"Oh, shh, Lani!"

"Hashtag, *just saying*."

"Don't say *hashtag*," I admonish her, not for the first time, but I'm sure she can hear my smile.

"Hashtag, *sorry, not sorry*," she says just to be annoying.

It has the opposite effect, and I exhale some of my residual anxiety. "Okay, I have to call campus security before David gets up here and scolds me about it."

"*Or*, you could let yourself get in trouble with your bodyguard. Maybe tell him you need to be punished. A nice spank—"

"Good-bye!" I squeal, and hang up the phone.

I'm only just calling campus security—a number we were all instructed to program into our speed dial at orientation—when David knocks fervently on the door. I check the peephole before I let him in.

His presence is enormous in the shoebox of a room. Not just because of his height and build, but because of his energy. He chews his bottom lip when he realizes I'm on the phone, and that he'll have to hold his questions, or lecture, for now. Campus security tells me they're sending an officer to talk to me, and others to sweep the building and quad, but there's no point, since Brody lives here.

I hang up the phone and sit on my small twin bed, sagging in defeat.

"What'd they say?" David asks, brows raised expectantly.

"They're sending someone to talk to me. And officers to look around campus, but…"

"But?"

I sigh. "You heard me when I told them what happened. It just sounded like some guy went into his own dorm and came by my room to talk to me."

"Some guy who attacked a girl less than two days ago!" David growls.

"I know that. But that hasn't been proven yet, as far as they're concerned. It's not like they're going to arrest him for knocking on my door."

David stews in place, realizing the truth of my words, radiating frustrated energy. I can feel his aggravation—it's there in his tense muscles, the clench of his sharp, rugged jaw.

I feel like an errant child, and I study my fingernails with practiced fascination, scratching absently at my cuticles. Eventually he sits beside me, his heavy arm settling comfortingly around my shoulders.

"It's going to be fine, kid. Okay?"

I don't reply. I don't even remember what *fine* is anymore.

We wait in silence for campus security, and an officer arrives no more than five minutes later. As I predicted, my account of Brody's chase and my narrow escape sounds a lot less sinister than it felt.

"Did he say anything other than that he wanted to talk to you?" the officer asks.

I shake my head in defeat.

"All right, Miss Caplan, we'll have a talk with him and let him know that he should keep his distance from you."

"Thanks," I murmur. I wonder how effective that will be.

David asks to speak to the officer in private, and they go into the hall. I don't bother trying to listen. I already know David is expressing his outrage, demanding that they do more to protect me.

But what can they do? Brody is innocent until proven otherwise, and he had every right to be in his own dorm building, and to knock on my door, apparently.

David bursts back through my door, visibly pissed off. I don't bother asking why.

He stands there, staring at me, and then he whirls into motion. He opens my closet, then looks under my bed, and pulls out my overnight bag. He tosses it at me. "Pack your shit," he orders.

I stare at him blankly.

David starts pulling clothing out of my closet and, still, I blink at him in confusion. When he opens the top drawer of my dresser, he freezes and rakes his fingers through his hair, and I remember that it's my underwear drawer. I rush in front of him and slam it shut. "What are you doing?" I demand.

"You're staying at my place," he deadpans.

"I don't need all this for one night, David." I gesture to the pile he's laid out on my bed.

He stops short. "*One night?*" He shakes his head. "Beth, you're staying with me *indefinitely*."

I frown at him. "I can't do that."

He takes a step forward until I have to crane my neck just to meet his gaze. "Well I can't leave you alone here, with him free, having full access to the building you live in."

I swallow audibly at the implication.

"So you can either come stay with me, in my nice, big apartment, with plenty of room for the both of us, or I can stay here, sleep on the floor, and wait for Lani to take advantage of me while I sleep." His lip twitches and I huff out a short laugh.

But the fact is, he's right. I don't know if Brody's intention tonight was really just to talk or something more nefarious, but I do know I can't be putting myself in the position to find out every time I come home from fucking class.

"Just until he's arrested for real, okay?" David placates.

I nod. "Yeah, okay."

Chapter Nine

David

Beth looks around my place as if she's seeing it for the first time. She's been here a few times since school started, of course, but she never had to consider it as her home. Her temporary home, anyway.

I grab the towel I carelessly left on the floor just outside the bathroom, and toss it into the hamper just as Beth steps into the living room. I knock the empty Gatorade bottles from the kitchen counter into the trash, and place this morning's cereal bowl into the sink. If I knew I'd be bringing her back here, I'd have straightened up. It's not like I'm a slob, but I'm a single twenty-year-old guy who lives alone, and one thing I've never been accused of is being a neat freak. I make a mental note to make more of an effort. My mother is the only chick I've ever lived with, and what can I say? She always picked up after me.

But I've shared a space with Beth before, so it shouldn't be too weird. Of course, we were younger then. Vacations where the parents would throw us kids all together in our own room so they could screw in peace.

"Well?" I ask, waiting for her verdict on my place. I've only just moved in a matter of weeks ago and the apartment is pretty basic. One bedroom, one bathroom, a living room adjacent to an open kitchen full of rarely used appliances, and a small breakfast area. It's furnished exactly how you'd expect a single male student to furnish an apartment—in boring black leather and glass, and not a single thing that can be referred to as *decor*.

As Beth runs her delicate fingers over the black leather of my new sofa, I'm glad I haven't brought any girls here. When it comes to hooking up, I've always avoided bringing anyone home—easier to make a quick getaway at their place—but as Beth's skin touches the soft fabric, I know it would have been wrong to let her come into contact with a couch I fucked some one-night stand on. I cringe at the thought. She is better than that. She is better than everything.

She is better than me.

"It's…nice," she murmurs.

I bark out a laugh. "Nice? You think?" I goad her. She's so full of shit.

Beth reluctantly smiles. "Well you haven't exactly put much thought into the design, have you." It isn't a question.

I quirk an eyebrow.

"No, you wouldn't." She answers her own non-question. "I could help if you want."

"Help?"

"Yeah. You know. A few throw pillows, some picture frames…It wouldn't take much to make it look less like a…"

"A…"

She shrugs. "Well, a temporary CIA safe house, or some other place no one actually means to live in."

I burst into laughter and Beth grins. She's right, of course. That's exactly what the place looks like. But that's what it is. A temporary lodging, not a home. I'll be here for one school year—two at the most. But if Beth wants some throw pillows, then I'll buy some fucking throw pillows. Whatever makes her feel comfortable at my place. She could be here for a couple of nights, or for the rest of the year for all I know. Because if Brody stays free, then Beth stays with me. No way will I let him get his dirty, depraved fucking hands on her.

She runs her palms over the seat cushions. "Do you have extra sheets? A blanket? So I can make it up?" She nods down at the sofa.

"I'll do that," I tell her. "Don't worry your pretty little head, kid." I start to lead her to the kitchen, but she doesn't move.

"I don't want to be a bug, David. I can make up my own bed."

I stop short. "Your own bed?" I laugh again. She thinks I'd let her sleep on a fucking *couch*?

"I know I can be a thoughtless asshole, but you're family, Bea. And anyway, I basically kidnapped you; I'm not making you crash on the fucking couch. Your bed is in there." I gesture to the bedroom door. "I'll make up the couch for myself later." I turn my back on her and head around the island into the kitchen, and grab a beer from the fridge. "Want one?" I offer.

Should I be offering her a beer? She's only eighteen, but we all drank whenever we wanted as freshmen. Who am I kidding, we did it in high school, too. But Beth is still Beth. She's still Cap's little sister, even if the more time I spend with her away from him, the easier it is to forget why she's off limits.

"No thanks," she murmurs, and proceeds to grab herself a water bottle from the fridge. "If I'm going to stay here, I'm not going to be waited on like some guest."

Ooh, my assertive little rebel has a point to make. I chew the inside of my cheek to fight my smirk.

"And I can't steal your bed, David. If I were Sammy—"

I hold up my hand. "If you were your brother, there wouldn't be some sicko fucking stalking you." Or there might, because Cap has definitely had his share of overzealous chicks. We all have. But the difference is Cap, me—we can take care of ourselves.

But I know Beth well enough not to articulate my silent elaboration. The dumbest thing I could do right now is to make her feel inferior because of her age or gender. But what she doesn't understand is that it isn't about inferiority. It's about value. It's not just that she needs protecting, it's that she's *worth* protecting.

Beth's lips lift into a small smile. "They wouldn't dare fuck with Sammy. Rory would kick their skinny asses."

I smile. Also true. Cap's girl, the one who suddenly showed up halfway through our senior year and converted him from infamous teenaged playboy into love-struck, doting boyfriend, is a fucking badass.

Beth takes a swig of her water bottle, her eyes skating into the living room, back onto that damned couch. And I get it. She wouldn't be Beth if she wasn't reluctant to kick a man out of his own bed. If she wasn't ready and willing to forgo her own comfort for that of someone she cares about.

My chest swells with warmth. I know she cares about me, and owning the affection, sisterly or not, of someone like Beth…it's not something I take for granted.

"You have dinner?" I ask, partly to get her attention off the damned sofa, and partly because I'm fucking hungry.

Her cheeks heat with a telltale blush, and I wonder what it's about. "No, I just had coffee."

Well, that explains nothing. "I'll order from Mama Nona's. You want to see the menu?"

Beth shrugs. "I'll just eat whatever you get."

I tell her I'm just going to have some pizza, and, predictably, she asks for extra cheese. I tell her to make herself at home and ask her to give me a minute, which I use to straighten up the bedroom and change the sheets for her. When I emerge, Beth is sitting on the floor of my living room, books sprawled out on my coffee table, furiously jotting down notes.

I smile. I want her to feel like it's her home, too. The more comfortable she is, the less awkward it will be.

I sit on the corner of the sofa—my new bed—and pick up my copy of *Angels In America*, delving back into "Millennium Approaches" both for my playwright class and because Tony Kushner is a fucking genius.

The buzzer rings, announcing our pizza's arrival, and I realize that the last half hour passed by in what feels like a single breath. I glance at Beth. I've never experienced such comfortable quiet with another girl, and I wonder if it's another sisterly thing, or it it's simply a Beth thing.

I buzz the delivery guy in, and he's at our door a minute later.

Beth asks if I mind if she studies while we eat. I don't, and I down three slices while I read ahead of my assignment—something I've done my whole life, but never would have admitted to in high school.

Beth finally closes and packs up her books around ten, and I close *Angels* and set it back on the side table. I take a peek inside the pizza box to check how much she ate, and she glares at me in accusation. I grimace, caught. She hates being checked after, and I make a mental note to be more subtle about it in the future.

Because I can't just let it go. I will never forget the version of her destroyed by that scumbag, Brian Falco. How much weight she lost when she was already barely a hundred pounds soaking wet, how she stopped changing out of sweats, or washing her hair, for that matter. But it was more than the obvious physical changes. It was her spirit. It was like the light drained from her eyes just as surely as the color from her cheeks.

I tried to help her. Even if it wasn't really my place. Especially not after my role in the whole clusterfuck. But I couldn't bear to see her that way. Still, no matter how many words of encouragement I offered, how many books I dropped off for her when she wasn't feeling well enough to even come down from her bedroom, or how many texts I sent, she just seemed to spiral further and further into an abyss of misery until she wasn't even *her* anymore.

I don't even know what happened in the end. Supposedly her mom and Cap finally just had enough, and they intervened and got her help. I suspect there's something I haven't been told, some detail too personal to discuss in front of someone considered *like* family, but not *actually* family. Someone who, when all is said and done, isn't bound to Beth by anything more than a lifelong friendship with her brother and the friendship of our parents.

"I ate two slices." She lets the sarcasm drip from her tone. "Happy?"

I ignore her snark. "So who did you have coffee with tonight?" I ask.

She composes her startle quickly, but I don't miss it. Her eyes flit from mine to her books, deliberating between truth and lies. But when her gaze meets mine again, and her deep blue eyes gleam guileless and anxious, I know before she speaks I'm about to get a truth I'm not going to like.

"Look, don't be mad, okay?"

My eyes roll toward the popcorn ceiling. "I fucking hate when people start sentences like that."

Beth blows out a deep exhale. "I had coffee with Brian."

She is right—I don't fucking like it, and I am definitely mad. *"The fuck,* Bea?" I try not to growl.

Beth launches into her mile-a-minute ramblings about Falco just wanting to talk, and his supposed apologies. She says he invoked the age-old excuse of youthful stupidity, and swore his unending regret for making such a monumental mistake.

But it wasn't a mistake. It was *his* mistake. And he doesn't *get* to take it back. He doesn't *get* another chance. We all have to make choices, and I made mine years ago, and accepted what that meant, but in the end Falco made his, too. And yeah, I had my part in it, but I was looking out for her.

I *thought* I was looking out for her.

But even as I think it, my gut rolls with dread at the old fear that

Falco could blow up my spot. He has no real reason not to, and Beth may not see things from my perspective. Not for the first time, I think I should just tell her myself. But I am a fucking coward.

"David, please don't be mad," Beth pleads, her eyes lined in worry.

She cares what I think. I need to remember that. Because there's power in it, and I've learned my lesson when it comes to influencing the lives of others.

"I don't want you seeing him." *Or not.*

Beth's eyes narrow. "It's not your choice to make, David."

Well, fuck.

I grit my teeth, swallowing down all the things I know better than to say. I have to trust she already knows them all—remind myself she isn't a kid anymore. "You're giving him another chance?" My voice is low and toneless.

Surprise widens her eyes and her mouth gapes slightly. "What?"

I don't speak. She heard the question, and her hesitation makes me take whatever her response is with a grain of wound-stinging salt.

"No, David. I'm not interested in him like that anymore. He burned that bridge a long time ago."

My eyebrow arches all on its own.

"Okay, fine," she concedes. "He strung it up with dynamite, lit the fuse, and walked away without a backward glance. Happy?"

I exhale the tension coiling my muscles, glancing down at my socked feet for a moment to compose myself. Beth waits for me to meet her gaze again, eyes wide and expectant. "I just don't want to see you hurt again," I admit.

There's that small smile. "I know."

I nod reluctantly. "Are you gonna see him again?"

Beth shrugs, her oversized v-neck slipping off her pale, delicate shoulder. I don't know why I find it so goddamned sexy, and I hold my breath until she unconsciously fixes it. "I told him I would consider a friendship."

I bite my tongue. I literally hold it between my teeth to keep the words in.

"I know," she says. "He doesn't deserve my friendship."

Damn fucking straight.

"But I don't want to punish him, David. It took me a long time to get over Brian, but I did get over him. The love, if that's really what it ever was—it's gone. But so is the hate, the resentment…all of it, you know? And now? Honestly? I'm kind of indifferent." She shrugs. "I wouldn't have pursued a friendship with him. But he's here, and I'm not going to pretend I don't know him." Another shrug. "It is what it is."

With a sigh of surrender, I let it go. I don't want to think about Brian-fucking-Falco. I don't want him here with us, in my god-damned apartment.

Beth says she's tired, so I show her where the towels are, but she waves me off. She uses the bathroom while I make up the couch.

"Are you sure about this, David? I'm really fine sleeping on the couch."

I snort. *Like that's fucking happening.* "Bea, I pass out watching TV on this thing most nights anyway. It's comfortable. It's no big fucking deal."

Her eyes narrow subtly, and I remind myself she knows me well, too. Enough to know I definitely don't watch TV nightly, or much at all besides sports. But she doesn't call me out on it.

Our first awkward moment announces itself with deafening silence. We say good night, facing each other uncertainly across the room. It feels like I should do something. If she were leaving, and we were saying "good-bye" and not "good night," I'd give her a hug, or maybe playfully muss her hair. But she's staying. So, like an idiot, I give her a halfhearted salute, and she lets out a hiccup of a giggle, and gives me one back before heading to bed.

I curl up on my couch and grab *Angels* from the side table, planning to read until my eyes close of their own accord. Because this couch is uncomfortable as fuck to sleep on.

Chapter Ten

Beth

I scroll through my emails and check my assignment for my Shakespeare class, glancing at the clock yet again. *Fifteen minutes more.* On Wednesday evenings I'm the only one who mans the new student chatline—the anonymous messaging guidance program Professor Bowman recently implemented. It's usually all but radio silence, save for your random bored prankster, and, once, an exceptionally unimpressive dick pic.

But there have been a few students using it sincerely, and slowly but surely it's been gaining popularity. Well, as popular as a student mental health outreach tool can be expected to become, anyway. But this particular shift tends to be especially quiet, and aside from getting a good amount of studying done, I'm all but bored to tears.

And as much as I care about volunteering, I'm anxious to get home to David's—to banter and bullshit and talk about our day.

I text Lani to check in. She's still staying with Elise—who I've become pretty friendly with—but even if Brody hasn't been on campus since the attack, we'd both rather be safe than sorry.

Ping.

I'm so surprised by the chime of the incoming message that I actually jump in my chair.

Hi, the message says.

Hi, my name is Beth. How are you doing today? I reply with the standard greeting. It's up to us whether we use our real names or not. I couldn't think of a reason not to. I'm not ashamed of who I am.

I've been better.

My attention focuses and I sit straighter in my chair as I realize this is not, in fact, a prank. Rough day? I prompt.

Ha.

I wait for a follow-up, and it comes a second later.

Rough life.

I swallow hard. I can empathize. But I also know there's a way back from the emptiness. What should I call you? I reply. It's a non-pressure tactic, but I already doubt I'll get an actual name from this one.

You? Fucking trash, probably.

My heart aches for this stranger. That isn't true, I assure the person who thought I would refer to him as *fucking trash*.

You sure about that, Beth?

The response sets my anxiety alarm off hard. Even though I know I gave him my name, something about his using it now, in this context, makes me uneasy. I don't even actually know that it's a *him* at all, and I don't know why the few messages he—or she—has sent have given me that impression. But they have. That I wouldn't call you trash? Yes. I'm sure, I reply. When two minutes pass without a response, I add, No one deserves to be treated that way.

The application lets me know he's typing, and I wait. And wait. But when the next message comes, all it says is, No. They fucking don't, Beth.

My pulse accelerates and my palms dampen with nervous sweat as I type. Do you know me? *So much for the script.*

You sure as fuck don't know me.

I'm trying to craft a response that doesn't violate half of Bowman's guidelines when whoever it was abruptly ends the conversation. But part of the appeal of the software—beyond the expected anonymity—

is that it only keeps record of the last exchange. So I can't even go back and re-read the strange conversation. I can't even be sure that it *was* a strange conversation. Especially considering some of the exchanges I've seen or heard about since I started volunteering here.

But I can't escape the unsettling feeling that there was something uncomfortably intimate about the way he used my name—in the way he didn't answer whether he knew me or not, but instead said it was me who didn't know him.

Did it mean something?

And then vaguely I remember telling Brody about my volunteering that first time we went out for coffee, and we were talking about schedules, and I can't fucking remember if I mentioned that I manned the chatline alone on Wednesday nights…

But then, this is also a symptom of my anxiety. This kind of paranoia.

The truth is I don't even know what made me think of Brody. According to David, who spoke to the local detective, the investigation is still ongoing, but if Liz said he assaulted her then I have to believe he did, right? Why would anyone lie about something like that?

But why would Brody contact me at all, let alone anonymously like this?

David's accusations of Brody being a "creepy stalker"—my own accusations—ring through my mind, and despite logic telling me it was more than likely just a stranger using the program for exactly the purpose it was intended, I can't escape the gut feeling that there was something personal about it. Maybe even something sinister.

* * *

"Honey, I'm home!" I call out.

The sweet and sour aroma of delicious, greasy Chinese food fills the apartment, and my mouth waters. I haven't eaten since breakfast.

I find David at the breakfast bar, book in hand, the counter topped with unopened cardboard containers. "You didn't have to wait for me."

David closes the book and sets it down. "Food just got here a few minutes ago."

He'd have waited anyway, and we both know it. David, for all his zero-fucks-given attitude, can be thoughtful when he wants to be.

His phone starts buzzing a moment before Jay-Z's "Big Pimpin'" starts blaring from its speaker, and David silences it without so much as glancing at the screen, or acknowledging it, for that matter. He doesn't even meet my gaze until I start laughing out loud, raising his eyebrows in question until he notices my attention on his phone.

"Was that your pimp?" I tease. "Do you have to go to work?"

David rolls his eyes, but his mouth twitches, and I don't miss it. "Bogart programmed his own ringtone," he explains. "Don't ask."

"You could change it, you know." I try unsuccessfully to suppress my amused smile.

David's eyes spark with mirth. "I did, actually. He changed it back. And technically he gets to—BEG rules, and he's chapter president..." His full lips quirk up. "Why, Bea? Are you going to pretend like you still hate hip-hop?"

My cheeks burn with the strength of my grin but still, I shrug, messing with him. "It's all right, I guess." But my expression gives me away easily, and, of course, David knows the truth.

And the truth is I did hate hip-hop. I *loathed* it. I was a daddy's girl, after all—the daddy he was when he hadn't been drinking, anyway—and *my* dad had had me addicted to his favorite classic rock albums since before conscious memory. Literally, in fact, since my mother always swore he played them for me in utero.

The Stones, The Doors, The Who—they were the bands I fell in love with, the songs I learned to move to—to dance to. Music always had magical properties for me, and dancing is—*was*—one of the very few things in my life that has ever come naturally to me. And as I got a little older and found myself shying away from my classmates, struggling more and more to connect to kids my own age, I would increasingly turn to music instead. Because when my body moved to a song almost on impulse, all of the obsessive thoughts and worries that somehow seemed to both plague me constantly and attack at random were notably quiet. It was almost as if they, too, wanted to hear the music.

Music freed my soul, and dance, my body.

That is, until my father left.

But I couldn't help what my subconscious had connected to that music—music that, no matter their melody or lyrics, would do nothing but slice open festering, unhealed wounds. My loyalty to my father's classic rock bands disappeared with the man himself, so in the years after he left, with years still to go before he'd come back into our lives, I'd lost not only my father and the music I grew up loving, but the freedom of dancing to it—dancing at all—as well.

It wasn't a conscious decision. It just happened. When you have a pain response to a stimulus, you avoid it at all costs. You burn your hand on the stove, and you don't touch the stove the next time. A song gut-punches you until you can't breathe, you turn off the damned radio app. And you don't turn it back on. By the time I realized I'd been avoiding music altogether, I'd already stopped my dance lessons and quietly quit the team.

I don't know if David even knew that when he reintroduced me to hip-hop, a genre I'd thought I couldn't stand.

He gets up and starts opening the Chinese food containers before handing me a pair of chopsticks.

"All right, huh?" David nonchalantly clicks around on his phone until Jay-Z's *Hard Knock Life* album starts playing, and he bursts into laughter as, after no more than a minute max, my shoulders start bobbing of their own volition as the song demands, *bounce with me, bounce with me…*

I concede with a smile, and get us each a bottle of water from the fridge. I wonder just how much he remembers about that night. If he ever realized just what he'd given back to me in offering me music that sounded nothing like my father's favorites.

"Do you remember that club you snuck me into in Puerto Rico?" I ask him. We'd continued our shared family vacations after my dad left, and one night, on a trip to Puerto Rico, Sammy had met a girl, leaving me alone with David. I hadn't complained.

David's smirk stretches wider. "You mean the *hip-hop* club?"

"Ha." But I take a massive bite of my egg roll just to give my mouth something to do other than grin like an idiot. It was only months before I met Brian, and I was schoolgirl-crushing on David hard. The resort we were staying in had a couple of nightclubs, including a teen club, and a few of the other kids had invited us—well, really just David—to join them there that night. I'd been upset because there was a minimum age requirement of fifteen, and I was still several months shy, so when David declined, I stayed quiet.

"How did you know?" I ask him suddenly, and he cocks his head in confusion. "That I wanted to go to that club?" Because I hadn't said anything. I hadn't done anything except follow him around like a loyal puppy dog as he walked along the beach and drank tiny bottles of Jack Daniel's he'd stolen from a stranger's minibar.

David's shoulder lifts in a half shrug. "I saw your face when that girl reminded you how old you had to be to get into that cheesy teenie club."

I keep my gaze trained on the broccoli in my chopsticks. "But you didn't take me to that *cheesy teenie club* . . ." I remind him. No, David snuck me into the eighteen and over club, by tricking a busboy into letting us in through the back.

David scoffs. "Fuck that. I heard that bullshit techno music coming from that place. No way was I going to subject you to that shit." He practically oozes self-satisfaction.

"Oh yeah? And how were you so sure we wouldn't get caught, huh?"

David shakes his head in mock reproach. "She has the nerve to doubt me. *Tsk, tsk, tsk...*"

I meet his laughing gaze. "Maybe you have a little too much confidence. Has anyone ever told you that?" It's utter bullshit, and I suspect he knows it.

"I seem to remember you calling me *the bravest person you know*." David's self-satisfaction grows to epic proportions before imploding in on itself, and I know he's recalling the rest of that conversation as vividly as I am, because it's written all over his handsome, bemused face.

David had led me past the teen club and around to the back of the one we were supposed to have needed ID to get into. He hadn't let me in on his plan, but I'd gone along with him implicitly—excitedly. He'd angled me away from the door, pulling me too close, as if he'd brought me back there not to sneak into a dance club, but for something else entirely. It had sent my heart racing to match the hip-hop beat emanating from the venue.

"Just stand like this," he'd whispered. "Pretend we came out here for—you know—privacy."

Pretend. Right. Duh.

"Good girl," David had praised quietly. "Just relax."

I'd blown out a long breath. "How do you never get nervous?" I'd whispered a little resentfully.

David had stared down at me. "Not never, Bea," he'd rumbled. His voice had begun to grow deeper in those days, and it would strike me every time.

"Please," I'd scoffed, "you're the bravest person I know." I remember wincing inwardly. *'You're the bravest person I know'? What am I— his groupie?*

But David's brow had furrowed. "Like I said," he'd breathed, "not always." The back of the building hadn't been as brightly lit as the rest of the resort's pavilion, but David's hazel eyes had seemed to be struggling with an uncertainty that seemed like it couldn't possibly belong to him.

"I find that hard to believe," I'd admitted softly.

"Believe it."

I'd frowned up at him, and his brow creased even more.

"Remember what I told you outside the temple that time? About my parents?"

I'd blinked at him for a moment, stunned not only that he was bringing up telling me about his adoption—which hadn't been spoken about since—but equally stunned at the suggestion I might not remember.

Was he freaking insane?

"Of course," I'd breathed.

David had nodded, satisfied. "Not brave enough to meet them," he'd murmured, as if to prove his point.

"I thought you said you didn't want to?"

David had stared a beat, as if surprised I'd remembered that, too, before shrugging.

"Then meet them," I'd said matter-of-factly. But *hadn't* it been a matter of fact for David? Hadn't it been as simple as doing what he wanted, because he wanted to? That's what he'd always told me.

The corner of his mouth had twitched and his forehead smoothed. "Maybe I'm nervous, Bea." He'd given me a small, halfhearted smirk, teasing me, not unlike he'd been doing just seconds ago. "Maybe I'm not *brave* enough."

"Then maybe you should be." It'd just slipped out, and I hadn't meant to sound insensitive—I just couldn't reconcile the idea that David March could not find the courage to do something he wanted to. "Unless you don't really want to."

I swallow anxiously. I hadn't meant to come off so callous, and I can't help but wonder if David is thinking about those words, too.

I watch him cautiously over the cartons of food. We haven't spoken about his birth parents or his adoption since, and it takes every ounce of courage I can muster to bring it up now.

My voice is small and hesitant. "Have you thought about it at all since? You know…meeting them…?" Nothing he's said indicates he even remembers the details of that conversation, but I know David well enough to read him, and he's gone from teasing to sober in a heartbeat.

But David acts like he doesn't even hear me, let alone know what I'm talking about. He changes the subject to the egg rolls, and I take the hint, and let it go.

I consider telling him about the strange conversation on the student chatline this evening, but the more I think about it, the more I'm convinced I'm just being paranoid, and the last thing I need is to give David yet another reason to be overprotective.

I catch sight of a sliver of tanned, perfectly carved abs peeking out from beneath the hem of his T-shirt as he rolls his shoulders like he's trying to loosen them up. He's been doing that all week—since the second day I was here. I've asked him if it's because of the couch, and he swore he just overdid it at the gym. But I've been here over a week now and it doesn't seem to be easing up.

I come up behind him and rub his shoulders, digging in my thumbs to feel his traps.

He's caught off guard and he winces. "Shit," he barks.

"This isn't from lifting weights. Your back is all knotted up!"

He turns and shrugs me off, but I reach around to feel the back of his neck. This time he holds in his reaction, but the stiffness doesn't lie. I retract my hand. "It's the couch—"

"It's not the fucking couch!" He cuts me off.

I glare at him. "Fine. If the couch is so comfortable, then I'll sleep on it tonight. You take the bed." I grab another piece of broccoli with my chopsticks and pop it into my mouth.

David watches me carefully. "Not happening."

I shrug. "But it's so *comfy*. And I'm the guest. I want to experience this incredible, *comfy* couch." I dig into the veggie lo mein, unperturbed by his resistance.

"I didn't say it was more *comfortable* than the bed. And I never fucking used the word '*comfy*,' for the record," he adds.

"Which is why you should take the bed, at least until you recover from your *weight-lifting injuries*," I snark.

David grinds his teeth, his jaw tight with frustration. "No."

"Why—"

But he's had enough of my snarky sarcasm and he blows up. "Because it's the least comfortable fucking couch in the history of couches! Because its cushions are filled with fucking rocks and the bones of the men it's killed before me!"

Finally. I keep my composure, casually invading the sweet and sour chicken carton he's holding and grabbing a piece. "Then you shouldn't be sleeping on it. I'll be okay. We can take turns, or at least until you feel bet—"

"I'm not letting you sleep on that fucking sofa from hell." He is adamant.

I lift my gaze to meet his. I know my next suggestion is stupid, but it's also perfectly reasonable. I am like a sister to him, after all, right? "Your bed is big enough, David. We can share it." I may be contending with a serious crush, but it's not like I can't sleep beside him without controlling myself.

David glares at me like I'm insane.

I shrug. "We've shared a bed before." I remind him of the time our families went skiing and Sammy slept with Tucker and I shared with him.

"You were five."

True. "So? It was a full. Now you have a king."

"It's not happening."

But it is. And after we finish eating and doing our schoolwork in the comfortable quiet I've grown accustomed to over the past week, I let him make up the couch like usual. Only this time, when he's in the bathroom washing up, I climb between the sheets and close my eyes. I twist and turn over and over again, trying to find a comfortable position, but David was right; it does seem to be impossible. There's no way I can let him sleep here. Especially since there's no telling how long I'll be staying.

Brody hasn't been in class and I haven't seen him lurking around campus, but I also know he hasn't been arrested as the investigation is still "ongoing." Even Lani is still staying in Campus West. David might be willing to spend the foreseeable future wincing in pain, but I'm not willing to watch it, not when I can do something about it.

"'The fuck are you doing, Bea?"

"Sleeping." I roll from my back to my side, trying to get comfortable.

"The fuck you are."

"*The fuck, fuck, fuck.* I can curse, too. And I can sleep on a sofa. And you can take a night to get your back straight."

"So you can barely turn your head tomorrow?" he snarls. "Fuck that! Get up!"

I don't move. He's not angry with me. He's just being stubborn and he knows I'm right. But still, his shouting renders my voice soft and unsure. "I can't watch you wince in pain every time you move your neck, David."

He blows out a long-winded exhale. "You're not sleeping there."

"Then I'll go back to my dorm." It's an empty threat, but he won't take that chance.

His eyes close and he huffs in deep, exasperated breaths. "Fucking *fine,*" he practically growls, and then stomps off to his bedroom in defeat.

* * *

I wake up to the shirtless form of an Adonis. David is tucked along the opposite edge of the bed, lying on his back, his muscular arm thrown over his head as he breathes softly in his sleep. More than a week of waking up to this exact image has done nothing to desensitize me to it. My heart short-circuits at the first sight of him, just like it did yesterday and the day before that, and I struggle to swallow down the familiar wave of longing that surges in my chest, and lower in my body.

There's at least a foot of space between us, and I've once again stolen the entire comforter in the night and hoarded it for myself, my new modus operandi, apparently. The white bed sheet covers David only up to his lean waist, the defined grid of his abs rising and falling with his relaxed breathing.

I take in his muscular chest, the lines of muscle and sinew in his shoulders, his bicep curled around his mess of mahogany bed-head. I flush with heat. I am not five anymore. And then my gaze shoots to the bed sheet, to the massive tent his body creates, and I swallow again.

I am not naïve enough to think there's anything personal about his body's reaction. I know about morning wood; I grew up with a brother, after all. But my own body's reaction to the sight of it—that is entirely new, and very personal to its owner. It is also the perfect example of why this arrangement might not be the best idea. But neither David nor I have come up with a better one, so I guess we'll have to suck it up.

Oh, God. I hate puns.

I jump out of bed and into the shower, purposely keeping the water on the cool side to douse visions of David and their aftereffects.

I wash my hair and shave my legs, and it hits me that I left my phone on the charger in his bedroom. I usually take it with me. It's not that I think he'd look through it, but I also know that on the off chance he did, he wouldn't be pleased. Because if David looked through my texts, he'd see the ones from Brian. Or, more specifically, he'd see my replies, and I don't want him to know that I met Brian for coffee again the other night, even though I'm not exactly clear on why I kept it from him in the first place.

Sure, David has made his thoughts on the matter abundantly clear, but that's only because he's worried I might do something stupid, like get back together with Brian. But there's no chance of that happening, and I told Brian as much—*again*—and considering his less than agreeable reaction, I doubt another coffee date is even in the cards for us. Which is fine with me.

I sigh and turn off the shower, and it's when I'm wrapping one of David's navy blue towels around my body that I realize that in my haste to get to the shower, my phone wasn't the only thing I forgot—I forgot my change of clothes as well, apparently.

On weekdays I usually shower before David even wakes up, and then get dressed in the bathroom—a habit I picked up back when he was still sleeping on the couch. I started doing it to give him the chance to get to his clothing in the morning, so we wouldn't get in each other's way.

But now, here I am, stranded in a towel.

Fucking wonderful.

I tighten the knot at my chest, wishing the towel were a bit bigger, but as it is my ass is barely covered. I let out another sigh. Maybe David is still asleep. I jump onto that hope and slowly open the bathroom door, careful not to make a sound as I creep back toward the bedroom. The door is open just a crack, which is how I must have left it in my rush out of the room. I'm about to push it open when I hear a sound.

A groan.

I freeze, listening, waiting for evidence either that I imagined it or that David is indeed awake.

"Yes…" It's barely a whisper. More like a low rasp, actually, and its husky tone undoes all the good of my shower, flushing my skin and heating my belly.

I stand there, swallowing down my anxiety, wondering what to do.

The more my ears adjust to the quiet, the more clearly his heavy breaths echo through the crack. "Fuuuck," he grates hoarsely, and even before I look, I know exactly what he's doing.

I know I should give him privacy—go back into the bathroom and let him finish in peace. Or I should at least knock on his door to let him know he's not alone. What I absolutely should *not* do is take a step to my left so I can see through the small gap between door and frame. I shouldn't find his form on the bed, the sheet now bunched at his muscular thighs, the waistband of his flannel pajama pants shoved down to reveal the one part of him I've never seen before—fantasies notwithstanding. The part he holds in his huge hand, palm and fingers wrapped so tightly that his forearm appears to turn to stone with his effort.

I tell myself how wrong it is to watch this. How selfish. That it's a violation of David's trust, and I know how I would feel if the situation were reversed—mortified…betrayed. So no, I absolutely should not stand here and watch him with rapt attention.

But that is what I do.

David's hand moves slowly at first, up and down, and then twisting around, over and over, in no particular rhythm. It's positively riveting.

I have no control over my gaze as it travels upward, along the abs that just twenty minutes ago were enough to fuel my blush. I watch them ripple with each of his harsh breaths, and I wonder what it would be like to trace my fingers along the masterpiece that is his body. It is utterly breathtaking—all sharp lines where muscle meets in shadow, and intricately designed symbols and swirls where rich, dark ink adorns his skin.

My eyes move greedily up his firm chest, his defined pecs rising and falling sharply as his rib cage expands and deflates, and continue over the strained cords of his neck. His head hangs back onto his pillow, the hard edges of his jaw shadowed by stubble, his mouth parted in not-so-silent gasps.

Each guttural sound clambers from deep within him, gruff and thick, as if fighting past the need constricting his throat. His eyes are squeezed shut, his brow furrowed in what could just as easily be mistaken for pain or devastation if I didn't already know what held those gorgeous features hostage.

Pure, primal lust.

I don't dare so much as shift my weight for fear of being caught spying as David's hand finds a tempo, sliding up and down to music only he can hear. Faster and faster he moves, his bicep flexed tight, the muscles in his arm a seductive tapestry of ink as they do their job to bring him closer and closer to the edge.

The expanse of his hand does nothing to mask the sheer size of his arousal, so impossibly hard and thick that I can't imagine it performing as nature intended with anything other than a very experienced female counterpart. It's just another way David and I don't fit, figuratively, and now, literally.

No wonder he's so cocky. I cringe internally, because *puns*. But any man walking around with *that* between his legs has every right to David's trademark sexual confidence, and I can't help but idly wonder if I exude my inexperience and self-doubt just as surely.

A muffled moan rips through his gritted teeth, reminding me that this isn't the time for self-pity. Not when David is unknowingly treating me to the most erotic moment of my life, and that includes sex with Brian.

David's fist tightens even more, his face contorting in some kind of agony as he worships himself with an almost violent vigor. "Fuck, yes," he breathes.

Instantly I imagine that deep timbre whispered into my ear, and my breath catches, my heart threatening to pound its way out of my chest.

"Spread those sweet thighs for me." I can only just make out the mumbled words he growls to some invisible woman. Surely one who's been in his bed in a decidedly different way than I have.

"You fucking love having me inside you, don't you, beautiful girl…" It's not a question, it's a taunt, and whether the woman he's picturing is real or imagined, I have no doubt she absolutely does love it.

But my envy of his invisible partner is overshadowed by the effects of his dirty words, and heat consumes my lower belly, the ache between my legs flaring almost painfully.

I stare, unblinking, in rapt fascination as his movements grow more frenzied, chasing release like he's in some kind of race to disarm a bomb before it explodes.

But the explosion is what he's after, of course, and I've never been so eager to witness something in my life. I am immoral and indecent and wanton.

But I can worry about that later.

My thighs press together again and again in search of some relief, my hips rocking subtly to the same music guiding David's hand. His pelvis joins the dance, thrusting savagely into his fist as if it's a girl above him instead of his own hand. Instantly I picture myself in the role, straddling him as his fingers grip my hips, urging me over him the way he needs.

The image invokes a visceral, physical reaction, and I have to forcibly resist the urge to slip my fingers beneath my towel.

David's rhythm changes again, growing desperate and erratic. He growls muffled words I mostly can't make out as his back arches and his hips rut toward the ceiling. "Ride it…" Words I can't decipher…"beautiful girl…" *Unintelligible*…"Yes, baby…take it all…"

His face contorts in a perfect mask of ecstasy and he goes off in a symphony of gasps and groans. And then a word I'm sure I've imagined—

"*Bea.*"

I freeze. For a split second I allow myself to get lost in the fantasy—that it's me inside his head.

But it's a fast trip back to reality. Because of course he didn't say my fucking name. He wasn't thinking of me as he furiously pleasured himself. "*Bea,*" can be a part of so many words, including ba-*by*, which is clearly in his dirty little repertoire of vocabulary.

David sighs a sound of pure satisfaction, sagging back onto the bed, still half on another planet.

He catches his breath, and his lids dazedly flutter open after just a few moments. It's all the time he allows himself to bask in the afterglow before returning to earth with a crash landing. His eyes are anxious and his movements suddenly hastened. He grabs a handful of tissues from the dispenser on his nightstand, and expertly cleans his mess. He shoots a nervous glance in my direction, and though my brain knows full well there's no way he could see me from where I stand, it doesn't stop me from flinching.

David frowns, his head tilting in a way that makes me think he's straining to hear if the shower's still running. I guess he was too distracted to notice when it turned off several minutes ago. He tucks himself back into his pants and casts another nervous look toward the door, and I finally snap out of my lustful, David-induced trance.

I am a perfect little mouse as I tiptoe across the hall and back into the bathroom, careful not to make a sound. I wait no more than ten seconds before I leave again, closing the door hard enough that David will hear it and think I've just now finished my shower.

I knock tentatively on his bedroom door, pulling my towel a little higher and tightening the knot.

"Bea? Uh, come in," he calls.

I do. He's still in just his pajama pants, but he's sitting on the edge of the mattress, his handsome face arranged in its usual easy aloofness.

I catch his gaze sliding up my bare legs, and he rakes his fingers through his bed-mussed mahogany locks. It takes me until now to re-alize that my state of undress is making him uncomfortable, and my cheeks heat. "I, uh—forgot to bring my clothes to the bathroom," I murmur.

David blinks. "Oh. Yeah. It's cool." He stands up. "Just change in here. I'm gonna grab my shower now, anyway."

I nod. But I can't stop replaying the vision of him laid back on the bed, or imagining myself above him, watching him come apart under-neath me. My eyes automatically slide down to his ass as he heads to the door, and I barely look away fast enough when he turns back to face me.

He taps his palm nonchalantly against the doorframe. "Your last class is at four today, right?" he asks.

I nod my confirmation, and David mimics it back to me, nodding slowly like he's working something out.

"Good," he says finally, "we're going out tonight."

Chapter Eleven

Beth

I'm ready at nine as David asked.

I texted him this afternoon to ask where we were going tonight, and all I got back was, "dress up a little."

Big freaking help.

Like, fancy?

I'd texted back.

Yeah, Bea. It's a black fucking tie affair.

His sarcasm was even less helpful, so, naturally, I returned the favor.

Okay. I only have one evening gown at school, though, so I'll stop by my dorm after class to get it.

I nearly bit right through my lip trying to stifle the grin that threatened.

All I got back, though, was,

behave.

I call my mom while I wait for him. She's the only person in my life besides Sammy who won't settle for texting, and she gets worried if I don't call at least every other day. Of course, she's one of the few people I really don't mind talking to, and I know we're closer than most mothers and daughters, but still, it bugs me that she feels like she needs to keep tabs on me. But I know I've given her ample reason for concern in the past, and without me home for her to see for herself that I have my anxiety and depression in check, these phone calls are probably the only thing keeping *her* sane.

I tell her about Abnormal Psych, which is even more interesting now that I'm not distracted by the glare of a stalker—no, *attempted rapist,* I inwardly correct myself. I shudder at the thought, grateful to my mom when she changes she subject. There's no reason to tell her about Brody, just like there was no reason to tell her about Brian being here. It would only give her more to worry over, and I've already caused her more than my allotted quota of grief.

"Have you seen much of Dave on campus? Is he still acting like a 'bodyguard'?" my mom asks with an adoring laugh. She's always had a soft spot for David. *Like mother, like daughter.*

"Not as bad as the first couple of weeks, but, you know, I'm sure Sammy has him under strict orders. Plus, he's helping me with my Shakespeare class," I half-lie.

Another affectionate laugh. "Of course he is." My mom sighs. "I hope he's keeping out of trouble."

"We're going out tonight," I tease, "I'm not sure where, but he said something about a crack house—or was it an opium den…?"

"*Hilarious*, Bits," my mom volleys my sarcasm right back to me—she's where I learned it, after all. "Well, have fun at your meth lab."

I hang up with her barely moments before I hear David's key in the lock.

He pauses in the small entrance hall when he sees me standing in the kitchen, self-consciously flattening the short, flouncy skirt of my black-and-white-striped, two-piece dress, which is basically just a skirt and a crop-top that meet about a half-inch above my naval. His eyes trail me from head to toe and back again, seeming to linger on my blood-red lips before finally landing on my gaze. I anxiously twirl the tendril of fine hair that's fallen from the golden knot on top of my head, waiting for his assessment. My experience with makeup is decidedly limited, and suddenly I wonder what I was thinking attempting a smokey-eye, red-lipped look like I'm some kind of fashion model or Insta-celeb or something.

David is freshly showered and dressed in dark jeans and a fitted John Varvatos charcoal gray T-shirt. The material stretches to accommodate his defined biceps, his broad shoulders and chest filling it out in a way they didn't even just a year ago.

When he still doesn't say anything I start shifting from foot to foot, and if he were any other guy I'd probably run and hide right now. I have to consciously remind myself that this is *David*—the guy who can sleep beside me in his bed entirely unaffected. But that sound I swore I heard as I spied on him this morning—*Bea*—in that seductive, guttural tone…It's been sneaking into my thoughts all day, and there's still that pathetic, hopeful little part of me that wonders…*Is* he entirely unaffected?

"I really don't have anything fancier here," I explain.

David blinks, like it takes him a second to figure out what I'm even saying. He gives his head a subtle shake, and then he's back. His shoulders relax and his lips default into their unapologetic, vaguely amused smirk. "What about your gown?" he teases, his smirk growing exponentially, its familiarity relaxing me instantly.

"Thought I'd save it to wear to class tomorrow instead."

David laughs. "Good idea, Bea. You look perfect, anyway."

It's a throwaway comment, but it heats my cheeks and warms my insides. "So do you," I admit.

"I try."

I'm exceptionally aware of David's body heat as I skate around him so he can lock the front door behind us, and I'm almost positive I hear him mutter something to himself that sounds suspiciously like "Fuck. Me."

* * *

"Are you guys having a party tonight?" I ask when we pull up in front of David's frat house. There aren't that many cars here, and I'm not sure why he'd have me dress up just to hang out at the BEG house.

"Nope." No elaboration.

He grips my shoulder to stop me when I reach for the door handle, but before I can ask him why, the door behind me opens and Reeve and Steven Bogart climb into the backseat.

"Hey, kid," Reeve's low, perpetually expressionless voice greets me as he slides behind David. I still can't quite get a read on him, but he seems earnest—if still a little dark, somehow. But he appears to be a loyal friend to David, and he's been nothing but kind to me, so I should probably cut him some slack.

"Hi…" I murmur back, drawing out the word as I look to David for answers.

"Damn, girl," Steven vaguely slurs. He perches himself on the edge of the middle seat so he can lean forward over the console, taking up way too much space in the process. "You look good enough to eat. You sure clean up nice, but I bet you'd look even better—"

David grabs Steven's face with an open palm, shoving him away from me, and Steven bellows his laughter as his back hits leather. The sharp scent of vodka assails my senses. It's faint, but the all-too-familiar scent is enough to summon memories of my father at his worst, and my pulse takes off in fight or flight—my response conditioned, having been beaten, quite literally, not into *me,* but into my loved ones during my formative years.

"I see you got started early," David says dryly, giving me the time to take a few deep breaths and sort myself out.

"Been pre-gaming since six, homie!" Steven replies in his corny *bro*-voice.

David ignores him and pulls away from the house, heading toward town.

"Will someone tell me where we're going?" I try an old move that has never worked on David, but that Steven seems to be the perfect mark for. "Because if you guys are taking me somewhere lame…"

"*Hot Box* isn't fucking lame!" Steven feigns shock and I grin with self-satisfaction.

David shakes his head at his friend's easy, unwitting slipup, the corner of his mouth pulling into the rogue smirk that never fails to make my insides somersault, and he shoots me a sideways glance before returning his eyes to the road.

Steven grips my shoulder and starts rubbing like he's soothing away my idiocy for suggesting that *Hot Box*—whatever the hell that is—might be lame. "Don't worry, kid. You're still new. It's not your fault," he teases, barely pausing to chuckle when David's right hand flies from the steering wheel to slap Steven's from my shoulder. "Don't worry, we're almost there. Then we'll see how *lame* you think the hottest club outside Manhattan is."

My gaze swings to David's, but he keeps his eyes trained carefully on the road ahead. His smirk is gone, in favor of his rare earnest smile.

He's taking me dancing.

* * *

According to my phone—or, more accurately, Google—Hot Box is the only popular nightclub in town. Which would explain the long line of trendy clothes and pushed-up cleavage snaking its way from the parking lot.

David leads us right up to the velvet rope, ignoring the line altogether, like he knows his place and a line isn't it.

And it appears he's right. The bouncer greets him like an old friend with that handshake-half-hug thing men do, and Steven starts questioning the guy about the girls that have already showed up tonight and the ones he's still expecting, as if they're on the drink menu or something.

I linger just behind them, zoning right out of their conversation. My brain is already inside the club, losing myself to the music, and I practically bounce on my heels with impatience as they continue to stand around and chat like a bunch of old *yentas*.

I pick at my nail polish to distract from my own impatience, focusing on the music instead. Even from the sidewalk, I can make out the hook from the new Rihanna song blaring on a loop as the DJ beat-matches a classic hip-hop record I've no doubt David could tell me the name, artist, and release year of.

I'm already so lost to the beat that I don't immediately realize our group has finally stopped yapping about the *something Delta something* party that apparently got cancelled, and is actually moving past the coveted velvet ropes, until the crowd's envious shouts break through my trance.

"Your girl?" the bouncer asks David as I pass, his eyes sliding purposefully down my body.

"N—" I start to answer, but David shifts his stance to block me from the bouncer's view, and suddenly I'm staring at the strained, broad muscles of David's back through his fitted T-shirt. "Sorry, brother," he murmurs nonchalantly, his tone completely at odds with the tension in his back. "She's a nun. Married to God, you know."

David sets his hand on the small of my back, and I try not to be so affected by his touch as he guides me around him and urges me inside.

The bass-line punches the floorboards beneath my feet the moment we're through the heavy aluminum doors, and David's comment and the bouncer are hastily forgotten as it reverberates in my bones.

The music fills the room like a tangible force, grabbing every single body to move to its will, and even those who don't dance are under its control. They bob their heads or tap their feet as they wait for their drink orders, or stare down at their phones, waiting for a text. Always *waiting*. But those people—they're missing out. They're missing the *entire point*.

But not the people on the dance floor. The ones who don't fight the music at all—who know how to surrender to it. No, they're not missing anything…*they* are *free*.

My hips start swaying on their own as we walk the length of the long bar that runs along the south wall of the venue. The place is completely packed with chic, attractive people who don't look all that much like college students to me, but then I probably look at least a few years older tonight, too.

David and the guys stop to talk to no fewer than three groups of girls, all of whom seem to know them well enough. Reeve, as usual, has very little to say, and communicates mostly with nods and grunts, more concerned with sipping his Guinness, which magically appeared in his hand moments after we got inside.

I could ask David how he knows so many people, but I already know the answer. A guy like him, especially surrounded with friends who look like his, is going to get attention no matter where he goes. How we got in so easily without waiting on line is another question, but I'm not going to look that gift horse in the mouth right now.

We finally arrive at the far end of the bar, and Reeve takes a seat on one of the only empty bar stools, making himself comfortable—well, as comfortable as he ever seems, anyway—like he plans to park there for a while. I'm practically jumping out of my skin, eager to get on the dance floor, and when the DJ mixes in the refrain from Jay-Z's "99 Problems," I burst into a grin.

David catches my gaze instantly—he's the one who turned me on to hip-hop, after all—and his laughter at my excitement echoes right in my chest. I don't even mind the smug, *told ya so* look on his face right now.

Steven orders a round of shots, and I down mine before David can say anything. But he just raises his eyebrows, and, without a word, tosses back his own. Of course, I don't know why I expected anything else. His recent overprotective behavior must be throwing me off, because my brother is the one who would give me shit about drinking, not David.

Steven hands out another round, and I drink mine quickly, if only to get closer to the part when we actually get to *dance*.

By the time he orders a third round, I'm all out of patience.

I tap David on the bicep. "I want to dance," I tell him, but it's too loud, and I don't want to shout over the music.

The way David's mouth twitches makes me think he heard me anyway, either by reading my lips, or just by virtue of knowing me so freaking well. But he points to his ear like he didn't hear at all, and then he's moving closer—close enough to lean down to me—and it takes me a second to realize that he just means to hear me better. His chest comes precariously close to mine, and when his rough jaw grazes my cheek, I have to physically refrain from turning into his warmth.

God. David has always affected me in all the wrong ways. *Or the right ones.*

His breath caresses the sensitive skin of my neck in small, heated gusts, a sharp exhale stroking me so surely I'd swear it was his hand.

What did I want to say again?

"I…" *Holy freaking shit,* my brain is short-circuiting… or maybe it's my subconscious trying to draw this moment out as long as possible.

"You…" David breathes against me and I almost sigh. *Out loud.*

I…what?

Christ, I need to pull it together. *Logic* … This is *David*— Sammy's best friend, practically my *family* … My *roommate*. My *fucking* bed-*mate*.

My truncated internal pep-talk does its thing—*miraculously*—and my brain suddenly reboots.

"I want to dance," I force out.

David pulls back enough to look down at me, his lips pulling into a smirk. "Thought you might." He arches a sarcastic brow and I respond with a playful-but-impatient scowl.

David half-turns back to the bar to grab his third shot, and tosses it down. He gestures with the empty glass toward the busy dance floor, which is separated from the bar by a row of art-deco style columns. "Go for it, kid."

Kid.

Steven slams his glass down on the bar, which is somehow loud—or sudden—enough to make me jump. He announces he's going "hunting," before unceremoniously making his way into the crowd.

I roll my eyes and grab the glass from David's fingers to set it down for him. "Come with me," I ask. I want to dance, but I'm not sure I'm brave enough to just march out there on my own.

"I don't think so, Bea," he says simply, and I hate the way my heart sinks into my stomach at his rejection, even as David's lips twitch in amusement.

"But *they* might be up for it." David nods behind me, and I spin around to find Lani, Elise, and Toni—a girl from David's building we've all become friendly with—grinning with mischief.

I jump and squeal and hug them, positively thrilled by the surprise. I've seen Lani during class and lunch, and I've gotten to know Elise—who Lani is still staying with—pretty well, too. But none of us have gone out much since the weekend Liz was attacked, and I think we all need to blow off some steam.

"Come on!" Lani shouts to be heard over the music. I smirk as I catch Reeve's eyes rake her from head to toe as she grabs my hand to take me exactly where I want to go. I toss a small, grateful smile over my shoulder at David, whose self-satisfaction is written all over his face.

"I can't believe he got us in here!" Lani gushes. I don't ask who she means. I don't have to ask to know that David did this. He got my friends here. He gave me a night out doing my favorite thing with my girls.

"I didn't know you were into dancing," Toni says excitedly. "You should come to my contemporary dance class at the rec center. The instructor dances backup for Lady Gaga!"

Really? But I automatically dismiss the thought. It's been years since I took any kind of dance class. Still, even as I tell Toni I'm not interested, I wonder if it's true.

The dance floor is packed tight with strangers, who in any other circumstance would make my head spin and my stomach turn. But they're not real. They're just bodies, moving to the same beat that's had me in its clutches since I walked through the doors.

So after a few minutes of trying to scream a conversation over the music, Lani, Elise, Toni, and I surrender to its power instead. My eyes close, my hips sway, and my feet move in rhythm with each song.

A half-naked girl with enormous, fake breasts and more collagen than human flesh in her Kylie-Jenner-lips comes around with candy-flavored shots every now and again, and we take turns buying rounds.

Freedom. It rushes through my veins and fills my chest. It's utterly palpable, and even if I still wish David would come out here and experience it with me—share it with me—I'm still more grateful to him than he knows.

I turn to search through the blinking lights and tangle of undulating bodies to try and find David by the bar, but I don't see him.

I consider asking the girls if any of them saw where he went, but they're all dancing with guys, and I don't want to interrupt. I scan the length of the bar, and even though it's basically a mob scene, I know there's no way I would miss that dark head of hair towering over the crowd. I scour the adjacent areas next, and I spot him just a minute later, off to the side where the booths are—the mostly *empty* booths—

with a girl in a barely-there black dress. She's practically on top of him, writhing her body in what can only very loosely be referred to as *dancing*, while David sways halfheartedly behind her.

So he does dance, after all.

He just doesn't dance *with me*.

The way the girl barely catches the floor with each step leaves no mystery as to just how drunk she is, and though I'm far from sober myself, even I can tell she's in no condition to consent to any kind of hookup. There aren't many reasons a guy like David would suddenly start dancing, and I fiercely hope he isn't planning to pick her up in that state. I don't doubt the girl would jump at the chance to be with him if she was stone sober, too, but that's not the point.

My stomach rolls. I want to believe I know David better than that. That he wouldn't do something like that. But his vague irritation coupled with the bored look on his face makes it clear he isn't in it for the dancing. In fact, he seems downright resentful at having to suffer through it at all. But it would explain his refusal to dance with me, since he only dances with girls he wants to fuck, apparently, and that certainly doesn't include *Cap's little sister*.

I glance back at Lani to see if she's seeing what I am, but she's still too caught up with her cute dancing partner to be aware of anything else.

David grabs the girl's hips, like he's trying to turn her to face him, but she ignores him, and seductively wiggles her ass against him instead. I still don't see her face, and when her hand slips behind her to grope his thigh, a feeling too awful to name rushes violently through me, blurring my vision and clogging my throat. I can't even describe what happens inside my chest. The effect isn't unfamiliar when it comes to David, but it is sharper than I can ever remember, and I have no doubt that our current living arrangements—and *sleeping* arrangements—are the culprits. They seem to be convincing my subconscious that I have some kind of claim on him. And that's a dangerous thing.

Because I don't, no matter how much it might sometimes feel like I do—or, at least, like I *should*. But the reality is David owes me nothing—he never has. Unfortunately, *reality* has never made any of this any easier, or made witnessing him with girls cut any less.

And that's the worst part. That I don't actually have *a right* to these feelings. Not the brutal jealousy or the inexplicable sense of betrayal. *Or* of inadequacy—that one less inexplicable. They all start shouting inside me at once, an emotional mutiny staged by my own defective mind.

The vast room is suddenly too small, the dance floor so cramped it's hard to breathe. I close my eyes as the impulse to flee fires from each synapse in my brain to every nerve in my body.

But I don't.

Instead, I suck in a choppy gulp of air, and silently count the beats to the music the way Dr. Schall taught me when he first started treating me. It's a coping method that had me skeptical at first—doubtful that something as elementary as counting could help—but as I subtly nod my head to keep time, letting the bass-line guide and soothe me, I manage to get my heart rate back in check. It isn't always enough, but counting musical beats is only one in an arsenal of mental health tools and strategies I've spent the better part of three years of therapy cultivating, and *coping* has become almost second nature to me. And so has managing my demons.

Anxiety and depression aren't like cancer. You don't get to fight the good fight, and, if you're lucky, beat the disease that tried to destroy you back into submission—or *remission*. My disease is ingrained not just into my body, but into *me*. Into the person I am, and everything I feel—everything I've *ever* felt, in some respect or another. And, for that matter, everything I *will* ever feel, until the day I die.

So how do you defeat demons that are a part of your very soul?

The simple answer—you don't.

So, instead, I manage them. And it took a long time for me to learn how to do even that. My meds help, too, of course, but considering the time and work I've put into my recovery since the night I almost let those demons defeat *me* for good, I'd say I've earned enough of the damned credit for myself. Because the truth is it's still a constant battle. They still whisper to me. They lurk in the shadows of my mind, lying in wait to exploit my weakest moments.

Moments like seeing the boy I've crushed on for years doing his own cocky-yet-detached version of some mating dance with some drunk stranger, who may very well end up sleeping in my bed tonight.

David's bed, I silently correct myself.

But even the thought of having to ask Elise if I can crash at her dorm tonight doesn't rock my resolve. I don't freak out, or run away. And I don't go borderline catatonic like I did after Brian approached me at the bar a few weeks ago. No; instead, I keep my composure tight and my head level. Because it may not always come easily, but I'm stronger than I was, and that's not nothing.

I suck in one last settling breath and gingerly open my eyes, desperately trying to retain one modicum of self-respect and not to look in David's direction.

I fail, immediately and epically, because my eyes go straight to the booths, now *completely* empty, and if the sight of him alone with that girl gutted me before, the sight of their abandoned foreplay-site—and that it means they've likely found someplace more private to *play*—threatens to send those last two sugary shots of liquor back up my throat.

So I take another deep, calming breath.

And then something happens.

A lifetime of longing and unrequited love evolves into something else entirely. Something new…

Anger.

My hands curl into fists at my sides and my eyes narrow at no one in particular. Because this isn't even *unrequited love*. I don't *love* David.

I've *never* loved him. I *loved* Brian...I think—or used to think. And I survived losing him. I survived the devastating aftermath, even if only barely. But I did—I survived. All of it. The rejection and despair, the secrets and the fear...and the truth I alone couldn't hide from. And this—this pathetic fucking jealousy, induced by the remnants of a childhood crush I should have outgrown years ago? This is fucking *nothing*.

A massive pair of fake boobs passes lazily by, and just below them, another tray of shots. I catch the pair of eyes attached to their owner, and gesture for two, handing her the cash I'd had tucked under my bra strap. I down the shots in quick succession, ignoring her judging eyes as I set the empty glasses back on her tray.

I turn my back on her and spot Elise making out with some guy, who, as it happens, is not the one she was grinding all over just minutes ago. Lani is dancing and scream-talking with a group of girls she appears to have befriended.

Normally this is when I would take a bathroom break, whether or not I actually had to use the bathroom. I'd make my escape, take my refuge, and then use it to decide whether to try and stick it out or flee.

But I'm here to dance. So that's what I do.

I let the music soothe and lift me, giving my body over to it, leaving room for nothing else—no demons, no whispers. I see Steven approach through the figures on the dance floor, and I catch his gaze just as the judgey shot-girl reaches him. He raises his eyebrows to ask if I want one and *judgey* follows his line of sight. I grin sweetly, defiantly, and nod. Steven's googly-eyed amusement reflects each of the many drinks he's consumed tonight, and I doubt he has any idea what he even finds amusing right now.

Steven brings me my shot, we take them in unison, and I'm lost in the music again. I wonder if David sent him over to babysit me while he gets himself some action in a dark corner somewhere.

David may have refused to dance with me, but that doesn't mean

I can't find a guy to dance with, and if Steven is going to babysit me, I might as well get something out of it. I eye him up and down. Sure, he's cute, but he does nothing for me. I shrug inwardly. I'm only here to dance, after all.

I start moving a little more seductively, meeting his eyes as I move gradually closer to him. He's drunker than I realized, and it takes him an extra beat to process my wordless invitation—*dance with me*.

His response is also delayed, and I laugh at his brief show of surprise followed immediately by an almost predatory smile. *Men*.

His arm comes around my waist and he pulls me into his body, bending at the knees and moving sloppily and a little off-beat. I don't even care. I ignore his rhythm, close my eyes, and let the music lead us.

The heavy scent of vodka invades my nostrils, and my stomach rolls. I open my eyes to find Steven's face too close, looking down at me a little too intently. Those candy shots we just took definitely weren't vodka-based, or I wouldn't have gone anywhere near them, and I wonder just how much he's drunk tonight.

I take a half-step back and place my palm on his chest, which Steven seems to like. He pouts when I deny his attempt to turn me around, and the music swallows my laughter. Steven is kind of adorable—in a drunken, foolish, self-deprecating sort of way. But I'm still not about to turn around so he can grind himself into my ass and call it dancing. Fortunately he takes the rejection in stride, but it doesn't stop him from trying again thirty seconds later.

I pull back and smile apologetically, shaking my head again. The room spins suddenly, and I don't even realize I've stumbled until Steven's hands are catching me around my waist and he's asking if I'm all right—which is surprisingly considerate of him. I insist that I am, even as, inwardly, I think I probably shouldn't have taken that last shot. Or the two before it.

But screw it. I'm out, and drunk, and dancing, and I can deal with the consequences tomorrow.

We're barely halfway into the third song when I stumble again, nearly falling this time before I'm saved by Steven's grip on my elbow.

No—*not* Steven, actually. Because *Steven* is about four feet in front of me, ass-down on the stained-concrete dance floor, his wide, glazed eyes blinking in consternation.

My gaze swings to David, who seems to have appeared from out of nowhere. I stare up at him in shock as he squeezes my elbow once, in some silent message that goes right over my head. He spares me a glance to make sure I'm steady before releasing me, but mostly his glare is fixated on the spot where his friend is splayed out on the floor, surrounded by strange, gaping faces.

It takes my inebriated and stunned brain another moment to realize that David just shoved his own fraternity president down to the ground, in the middle of the crowded dance floor of the town's most popular club.

When he steps in front of me, toward Steven, my heart stops. For a second I think he might attack him or something—though I'm completely lost as to what the hell David's problem even is, especially if he sent Steven over to babysit me in the first place. And even if he didn't, it's not like Steven was touching me inappropriately or anything—or not for a guy dancing with a girl in a club, anyway.

I'm just about ready to launch myself between them when David leans down and holds his hand out to his friend. Idly I'm aware of Reeve in the not-so-distant background, intently observing the situation unfold, as if prepared to jump in at any moment—whether to break it up or back up David, I'm not sure.

Steven warily eyes David's hand for one tense moment before he takes it. He lets David help him to his feet, their glares locked in some silent standoff until, finally, Steven apologizes.

Steven apologizes. Even though David is the one who basically just assaulted *him*.

One moment Steven was dancing with me, the next he's been

tossed to the ground by his own boy, and seconds later he's telling David, "my bad."

"Hope. Diamond." David growls cryptically, but his words don't make sense, and I wonder if I even heard him right over the music.

Steven splays his palms in surrender. "Curse of death. Got it."

What the actual fuck?

Chapter Twelve

David

I keep my glare trained on Bogart as he leaves the dance floor and makes his way to the bar, not that he needs any more fucking alcohol. Though I guess I shouldn't really be talking, considering I'm just this side of shit-faced, myself.

I blow out a long-winded exhale, ignoring Reeve's knowing smirk. *Glad he's fucking entertained.* Fortunately, with the threat of violence dissipated, he turns and heads back to his lonely bar stool, probably disappointed at the lost opportunity to throw a few punches, even if it would have been at his own frat brother. But the idiot fucking deserved it.

The small cluster of people who stopped to watch the show fades back into the crowd, and even though the music never actually missed a beat, it feels like it's only now returning to full volume.

I take one more second to gather myself before I meet Beth's gaze, wishing I was even drunker right now.

Her deep blue eyes meet my mine dead-on, for once giving nothing away. I expected to find confusion or anger, or even accusation—*something* to prompt me on what to say next. I don't know how to explain away my behavior if I don't know what the fuck is going through her head.

But instead of some kind of judgment, Beth's eyes hold only

questions, demanding to know what's going on—what the hell I was thinking.

"David…" I see the word on her lips, even if she says it too softly to hear over the music. But instead of knocking me from my trance, it just diverts my attention to her mouth.

Fuck, *that mouth*.

She was wearing some reddish lipstick or gloss or whatever-the-fuck when we left the apartment, but the night has worn it off, and they're back to that perfect natural pink that always makes me think of that strawberry lava cake I had on vacation in Miami once—the one I could never find anywhere else. I bet those lips would taste just as fucking sweet.

And just as unobtainable.

I swallow hard, prying my eyes away from Beth's mouth. My pulse is too fast, and I'm out of options. I don't have any answers for her. I don't even have answers for myself. At this point I'm so thrown off by the alcohol, or her fucking mouth, or both, that I barely even remember what got us here. But the fact remains that I don't know what the fuck to say to her, so I don't say anything at all.

I take a step forward, and then another, until I'm close enough that, if we were different people, if it were a different life, I could kiss her. And then I take one more.

Fuck it.

I hook my arm around her waist and haul her against me, enjoying her small gasp of surprise as I start moving to the beat. She unfreezes a half-moment later, her body melting into mine as my hips and hands—which I painstakingly keep in safe zones—guide her motion. I'm careful to leave a one-inch buffer between our lower bodies.

We're too close for eye contact, my cheek brushing her temple with each movement, and it's so much better than *talking*—especially about stupid fucking assholes who want to get their hands on her.

Stupid fucking assholes *like me*.

But while I may not be the guy for Beth, I'm certainly not the worst of them. I would never hurt her. Not intentionally, at least, and never physically. But there are others who would, and when I think about that piece of shit Brody, my arms tighten around her, my gut a familiar battleground for both the urge to keep her safe, and the one that wants to just keep her *for myself*.

Beth has called me overprotective lately, a complaint she used to reserve for Cap, and maybe she's right...but he's not here to look out for her.

Maybe if Liz had someone being a little overprotective of *her*, that motherfucking stalker wouldn't have gotten her in such a vulnerable position. Maybe she wouldn't be such a fucking mess right now. She definitely wouldn't be out at a club with new "friends" she barely knows, wearing a dress that's too skimpy even for my taste. And I have a soft spot for slutty dresses.

I was so surprised to see her here that I did a double take. I'd been so captivated by the way Beth's body moved to the music, the way her face lit up with pure exhilaration when she really let herself go, that I didn't even notice Liz walk right by me at first. But there she was, out for the first time since she was almost raped, dressed to the fucking nines like a night out on the town is her only worldly concern.

I'd tried texting Liz a couple of times over the past few weeks, but she'd never replied, and I took her showing up tonight as my chance to talk to her. So I told Reeve to pry his eyes from Lani's ass and keep watch over Beth, and then made my way over to Liz.

I admit I felt guilty. Not just for my role in introducing her to Brody in the first place, but because while I do want to check on how she's holding up, I also had an ulterior motive. Because I haven't been entirely truthful with Beth about the status of the investigation.

My jaw clenches with frustration and my hands close around Beth's waist, as if to remind me just what's at stake if Brody stays free. Because the investigation *is* still "ongoing," according to Detective

Blunt—who finally started returning my calls when he realized that not doing so just led to me showing up to the precinct in person. But Brody is no closer to being arrested. Getting information about a campus rape investigation is like pulling fucking teeth, but I've managed to learn that the case is essentially at a standstill because "a witness isn't cooperating." It didn't take a genius to figure out what that meant in a he-said/she-said sexual assault case. There are only two real witnesses, and I doubt they were counting on the fucking rapist's cooperation to make the charges stick. Which means Liz is the *uncooperative* one.

It makes no fucking sense, and I need to get to the bottom of it. Liz is the only one who can get Brody off the goddamned streets.

She wasn't interested in talking, however. I may not exactly be sober, but it took me about two seconds to realize that Liz was completely hammered, and she seemed intent on getting even *more* hammered. I tried to caution her, but she reacted about as well as I would, and, instead, I found myself downing shot after shot just to keep up, still hoping to get some answers.

I got nothing, and when Liz insisted on dancing, I led her over to the slightly quieter lounge area, in hopes of getting a few words in while she did. But she wasn't hearing a damned word.

And she wasn't really *dancing*, either; at least not in any way I've seen her dance before. Or in a way I've seen *anybody* dance without a metal pole between their legs, for that fucking matter. Instead Liz took teasing and seduction to a whole other level, and I started to wonder if she was going to try and fuck me right there on one of the empty booths. It was damned uncomfortable for me, but as she relaxed and loosened up, I tried one more time to get her to talk.

All I got back was her barely covered ass grinding against my uninterested dick, which was still semi-hard from watching Beth dance. When Liz grabbed for it right through my jeans, I finally lost my shit.

I pushed her hand away and put some distance between us. But just as I was about to snap at her, a strobe light flashed on her unfocused eyes, betraying a fresh coat of moisture she obviously didn't want me to see.

Tears. Nothing makes me more uncomfortable than a girl crying. It would have been enough to back me off, but Liz turned on her heel and stomped away before I even had the chance, and I stood there gaping after her, wondering what the fuck had just happened. But it was clear I wasn't getting through to Liz tonight, and I realized I probably wasn't in the best state to keep trying, anyway, since I've been told I'm not the most patient drunk. So I sent a text to one of the bouncers working tonight, a BEG alum, to make sure she gets home safely, offering him my car if necessary—not much of a sacrifice considering I was already planning to Uber it home.

That was when I noticed the text from Reeve from a few minutes earlier, directing my attention to the dance floor.

I drop my hands a little lower on Beth's waist, to where I found Steven's hands on her body, and I rub my open palms just a little, as if they can wipe away his touch. The sight of her in his arms set me into immediate action, too consumed with rage and alcohol to pause for rational thought.

And Bogart is lucky for that. *Rational thought* wouldn't have let me stop at just shoving him away from her.

He's lucky I let it end where it did. He's lucky he's a brother. But that doesn't mean this is over. He crossed a line, which he knows full-well—knew even as he was fucking doing it. My fingers tighten without conscious thought, gently digging into Beth's skin, and I blow out a harsh breath, trying to release some of my aggravation along with it. I run my hands down to her hips, careful not to go out of bounds as I guide her to the music. Not that she needs any help—this is her element, and she owns it with a confidence that makes me grin with pride. That inch is still there between our hips, and the more we move, the more desperate I am to close it.

Vaguely I know this is fucked up. That I'm doing exactly what Steven just did, and thinking about worse.

But, *God*, her body was fucking *made* for this.

Tension coils in my belly and my dick desperately needs adjusting in my jeans, but I'm not sure there's any hiding the situation she's caused. If Beth has noticed, she doesn't seem to care. She must be drunk. *I'm* fucking drunk.

She moves her hands to my biceps and slides them up toward my shoulders. It sends a shiver of heat through my whole body, and makes my jeans feel even tighter.

I suck in another deep breath, the tension coiling tighter and tighter…and then something inside me—something that's been hanging on by a thread for *years*—finally breaks.

Fuck it.

If any man is going to get his hands on Beth, why *shouldn't* it be me? Just because I'm—as one ex fuck-buddy once put it—*not boyfriend material*, doesn't mean I'm some kind of fucking scumbag. I'm straight with girls. They know what—and what not—to expect from me. I may not be the kind of guy to look for a commitment, at least not at twenty-fucking-one, but I'm not like some of these other guys, who play girls and spit lies. I may have been accused of breaking a heart or two, but no one can say I break promises.

The pads of Beth's fingers brush my chest, and I think she means to control the distance between us, but after the briefest hesitation, like she tried and failed to resist an impulse, they bunch into my T-shirt and draw me even closer.

I lean down on instinct, wanting not only our bodies closer, but our faces, too. I want to feel the heat of her breath, the smoothness of her soft cheek. *Fuck*, she smells good.

My hands slide back to her waist and around to her lower back, my palms spreading until my thumbs can feel her racing heartbeat through her rib cage. My pinky fingers are so close to her ass that, if they wanted to, they could easily cop a small feel. And *fuck* how they want to.

My cock is so hard I think it forgot it can't have her, and she gasps when she inadvertently presses up against it. Part of me remembers why this isn't okay, but most of me can't help my satisfaction when she flushes from her cheeks down to her perfect cleavage.

My pulse is off the charts and every inch of me pangs with hunger—with a lifetime of *starvation* for this one fucking girl. My palm slides up her back until my fingers thread through the blond locks at her nape, my thumb stroking her delicate jaw.

I don't know who stops dancing first, but neither of us does anything to unlock our bodies from each other as the mass of faceless strangers continues to grind and sway around us. I tug her hair gently and angle her face up to mine, my body losing a long-fought battle of restraint as I stare down at deep blue eyes that are fucking *screaming* with desire.

Fuck. That look.

My eyes drop to her mouth, and all I can think about is strawberry lava cake. Suddenly I think I'll die if I don't have at least one taste.

Beth swallows hard, her eyes reflecting a mixture of need and fear as I slowly lean down, unable to stop myself even if I wanted to. But I *don't* fucking want to.

"So this is the reason you're blowing me off?" A familiar, slimy voice rips me from my trance—and my mouth from its trajectory.

Beth flinches, her eyes going wide as they fix on a spot right over my shoulder, and I turn, careful to keep her shielded behind me.

"'The fuck are you doing here, Falco?" I growl at the last fucking person I want in my face right now. I'm drunk, and irritable, and horny, and confused as fuck.

But Falco looks right through me to Beth. "Not interested in dating *anyone*, huh?" he spits.

Beside me, Beth takes a step forward, and I'm startled by the look of shock on her face. Unease settles over me all at once, the abundance of alcohol I've ingested tonight turning sour in my veins.

"Brian, I told you—"

"You told me *what*? You can keep having coffee with me, but *what*? You're fucking *March* now?"

"No!" Beth denies it, and I don't know why it pisses me off—of course she isn't *fucking me*. But she's not fucking supposed to be seeing Falco, either.

She starts to say something else, but I cut her off. "*Keep* having coffee with him?"

She swallows down her obvious anxiety, and my instinct is to soothe her somehow, but I also want to know what the fuck he's talking about.

"You had coffee with him once. Like a month ago."

Falco smirks in my peripheral vision, and I feel like a total fucking schmuck. Beth doesn't say a word.

"I guess she's been lying to both of us." Falco's voice slithers through my ears like a venomous snake, and I grit my teeth to keep from spitting in his fucking face. Because *what the actual fuck?* Why would she be going on fucking *coffee dates* with him? Does she want to get back together with fucking *Falco? After everything he put her through?* My hands clench into fists.

"So, what? You're just a fucking *slut* now?" Falco's words go too far, and I swing.

My vision fires red in an instant, all the sexual tension in my body suddenly rewired for violence, and it's only when Reeve and Bogart are holding my arms and talking me down that I even realize I didn't stop at one punch.

I look around in a post-homicidal daze—or a *less* homicidal one— heaving in deep breaths until I start to calm.

"Bea." *Where the fuck is she?*

And then I catch her in my sideview, kneeling at Falco's side as he recoils away from her like *she's* the villain in all this.

It's like a pickaxe to my gut. She ran to *his* aid? The scumbag who broke her heart and left her in motherfucking *pieces*, and then had the balls to say what he just did to her?

Well, *fuck that.*

But at least Beth doesn't take any *more* shit from him—way too small a consolation right now. At his rejection, she simply shakes her head in disapproval and abandons him, making her way back to the solace of her girlfriends, who seem to have gathered for the show along with half the fucking club.

Beth's arms hug around her middle as she fixes me with her glare. I reflect it right the fuck back at her. This is her fault, too. She's the one who's been seeing her piece-of-shit ex.

She's the one who lied to me about it.

I march over and she meets my gaze with open defiance. "We're leaving." My words come out like an order, and I'm not sure I've ever used that tone with her before. I'm not sure I've used it, period.

But she doesn't wait for me to lead us toward the exit. Instead, she lifts her chin, walks around me, and heads right out the door.

Chapter Thirteen

David

Age Sixteen

"'Night, kid," I call out to Beth, who huffs past Cap and me and stomps into the house, no less pissed than she was when we left Cooper's party fifteen minutes ago. I pretend it doesn't sting when she ignores me, and instead light up the joint I expertly rolled on the car ride home. Well, not *home*—to the Caplans's, but same thing.

I live a couple of blocks around the way, but if I cut through backyards and hop a fence or two, it's barely even a football field to my house, so I usually just get out with Cap when we get a ride from somewhere. Sometimes I stay over—it isn't like they don't have the fucking room—but most of the time we end up chilling, or smoking, or both, and then I'm on my way.

"We're going to have to do something about Falco," I remind Cap. I already told him I caught him flirting with Beth at the party we just left, but we haven't discussed how we're going to stop it from happening again.

Cap's lip curls in disgust at the mention of it. "Weren't you watching her?" he asks, only mildly accusatory. I'm the one who convinced him to let her tag along tonight, after all. It was her first high school party, and she hasn't even technically started high school yet. But I took no issue with Cap's demand that I babysit, and Cap knows I'd barely left Beth's side all night. We were having a pretty damned good time, actually... until Falco fucking showed up.

"She went to the bathroom, man, and I was waiting for her at the end of the hall. He had to have come around the other way on purpose." I lock eyes with Cap. I know I might sound paranoid to anyone else, but I don't believe for a second that Falco *bumping into* Beth was any kind of accident.

I pass Cap the joint. If it was football season, he wouldn't risk touching the stuff, but it's summer, and he's free to do whatever the fuck he wants, just like me.

Except I'm not. Not really.

I think about Beth's flushed cheeks as she stormed out of the party, as I caught up to her outside. I think about the way she accused me of treating her like a child by ordering her away from Falco, and how much more selfish my true motivations actually were. And then I think about what he'd said to her—how he'd called her "pretty."

Fucking *pretty*.

But Bea isn't just fucking *pretty*, she's more than than, and any guy who can't see the fucking difference doesn't deserve so much as a chance with her—least of all Brian-fucking-Falco, who, as it happens, I never really had a problem with before tonight. But now—*now*, I can see him for the slimeball he fucking is, even if Beth can't.

"We can pay him a little visit tomorrow. Explain the situation," Cap says calmly. But under the calm lies a storm I know well, one I've been known to both feed and feed on, in turn. Cap and me, Tuck and rest of the boys—we've always had one another's backs.

The glance I toss Cap makes sure he knows I'm up for whatever is necessary. I always have been, when it comes to the Caplans, especially. There have been times when they've felt more like family to me than my own, and I may have my jackass moments, but I'm loyal as fuck above all else, and Cap fucking knows it.

I picture the way Beth blushed for Falco and bile rises in my throat.

But I'm not an idiot. I know why this is fucking me up so badly, and it isn't overprotectiveness—that's Cap's thing, after all. What's got my stomach rolled tighter than this goddamned joint is what happened *after* I caught her outside that party. It's the way she looked up at me from under those fucking lashes, how she reacted when I told her the truth. That Falco was wrong. That she *wasn't* pretty—that she was motherfucking *beautiful*.

It's the way my eyes fell to those strawberry fucking lips, and, for the first time, actually considered stealing a taste.

Thank fucking God Cap announced himself by calling after Beth. That would not have been a good sight for him to walk in on.

"It isn't going to stop, you know," I murmur, and Cap's brow furrows. "Guys are going to want her," I explain. "She's…" I trail off. Beth is his kid sister, but Cap has fucking eyes. And it's more than that. It's always been more than that. Beth is just…different. More.

Deep inside my chest, an ember glows, warm and familiar, slowly igniting the ones around it, spreading, until my mouth twitches into a smile. Beth does it to me every damned time.

"Fuck if that's going to happen," Cap says yet again—the same line anytime somebody brings up the possibility of Beth dating anyone at all. But he's got to know that's not realistic. Not for a girl who looks like her. I mean, fuck, she came to one party and she's already got an incoming senior hot on her tail.

"But it *is* going to happen, Cap," I say bluntly.

He turns to face me, handing me back the joint, which I take a deep pull from. "As long as we can help it, it *isn't*," he says adamantly.

I shake my head at him. Not because I don't think we can handle the guys at our school, but because I'm not sure he's even considered Beth herself in this equation at all. "How long you think she's going to let us get away with that shit, huh?" I ask him. "Weeks? Months if we're lucky?" I bark out a humorless laugh. "She'll start dating some douche bag just to prove she can."

Cap swallows nervously. He knows I'm right. "Fucking shit," he mutters to himself.

"What if—" I shut my mouth tight just as fast as the words are out. But it's too late. I can't shove them back down my throat any more than I can bury the idea back into the depths of my mind.

"What if *what*?" Cap asks.

I take an even longer, deeper pull, holding the smoke in my lungs before blowing out a slow, calming exhale. I pass what's left of the joint back to Cap, checking to make sure the cherry is still lit. Now I'm the one with the anxious swallow. "You know...Beth and me...we've always been...close. Right?"

Cap shrugs, hitting the joint. "You think you can talk some sense into her?" he guesses.

Wrong. So wrong. "Sense? As in, not dating in high school at all?"

Cap clenches his eyes shut. He knows we aren't going to get away with that shit, and anything else isn't a picture he wants to see. Beth will always be his baby sister, after all, and he will always be her protector first and foremost.

"I meant..." I try starting again, and Cap's eyes open, hopeful, desperate, and that ember in my chest glows with hope as well. "What if...I mean—"

"You're stuttering now, Dave?" Cap busts my balls, and he should.

I don't stammer over words, because I don't give a fuck. But this...this is one of the few things in this world I *do* give a fuck about. So I just come right out and say it. "I want to take her out."

Cap blinks at me. "Out where?"

"Like, on a date...?" I don't mean for it to come out like a question, but it is. Because I don't take girls on fucking dates—neither of us do. We hook up.

"Who?" Cap asks, like his mind can't seem to wrap itself around the idea of what I'm suggesting, and I don't blame him. It's hard for me to get there myself, to be honest.

But those strawberry fucking lips...

"Beth," I say clearly. "Fuck Falco. And fuck the rest of the guys that will want her. I care about her. You know that."

Cap stops blinking in confusion. He stops blinking altogether, actually, his eyes intensifying until his glare leaves no question as to whether or not he still doesn't get my meaning. The small clip that was once our joint unceremoniously falls from his hand, and he doesn't even bother to stomp it out, or kick it under a bush so his mom doesn't find it. "You..." He takes a step toward me, but I don't retreat. "You want to *date* my sister?"

I nod once, firm, true.

Cap catches me off guard, taking a full-on swing at my left eye. And then he's on me.

We wrestle around on his gravel driveway until I get one up on him and land a solid punch to his jaw. I take advantage of his disorientation and shove him off of me, putting some distance between us, huffing out hostile energy, clenching my fists to keep from throwing them back at my best fucking friend.

"You don't *date*, Dave," Cap pants out, catching his breath. "You hook up, and you bounce."

"Like you should be talking," I retort.

"I'm not the one suggesting I'm good enough to date fucking *Beth*!"

Cap steps closer to me, but I stand tall. If he wants to hit me again, I'm ready. I may even deserve it, but at least I'm ready. But he doesn't swing. Instead, he lets his words do the pummeling. "You—" He points his finger in my fucking face. "You think you and Bits are 'close'? That you have some special bond? Well, I call *bullshit*."

But his words don't pummel, they *cut*—they slice me right open. They're not true.

"You do the same shit with every fucking girl, Dave. Get what you want and then lose interest. And then what? You think you can just break my baby sister's heart and then come over to play ball the next day? You and Beth would be done, and you and me—*we'd* be done, too."

I gulp at the implication. My dad and I don't get along, and my mom—well, she rarely acts like anything more than an extension of her husband. The Caplans, my boys…they're all I've really got, and if we fell out…

"It would be different with her." It's my only defense. Because most of me knows Cap is right. My history with girls isn't something to be proud of outside of a locker room. But I'm sixteen, and I haven't met a girl worth more than the time I gave her, so what the fuck was I supposed to do? Get married or stay celibate? And Cap is the biggest fucking player of us all, so for this judgment to come from him…It pisses me the hell off.

He takes one more step forward until we are almost nose to nose. "You are not good enough for Bits, Dave. Don't you fucking get it? You don't know *how* to give a fuck."

My mouth opens, but the retort doesn't come. Already I can feel my left eye swelling, pounding painfully with each heartbeat. I thought it could be different with Beth. That *I* could be different for her. But Cap is the person—other than my parents, of course—who has known me longer than anyone. My oldest friend. And if *he* thinks I'm the piece of shit he's describing—which, incidentally, sounds an awful lot like my dad's assessment—well then maybe they're both fucking right.

"Yeah, *brother*," I spit. "You're right." I turn my back on him. "This is me—not giving a fuck." And I start slowly down his long, circular driveway. I don't feel like hopping fences tonight. A nice, long walk in the cool, early summer midnight air and about half a pack of cigarettes sound a hell of a lot better right about now.

"Stay the fuck away from here, March," Cap calls after me. "Until you get your fucking head straight."

I ignore him.

"And if you so much as suggest this bullshit again, you won't be welcomed back here at all!"

I keep walking.

"You fucking got me, Dave?" Cap shouts desperately. If the thought of me taking Beth on a date has him this riled up, he must think even less of me than I realized. He wasn't half this agitated over the thought of Falco dating her—Falco, the clean-cut soccer star.

I throw one hand in the air in a halfhearted wave of my middle finger, both indicating that Cap's been heard, and that I resent the fuck out of it.

Because I do hear him, loud and fucking clear.

Chapter Fourteen

David

Present Day

Beth slams the door of the Uber and runs barefoot into the building, her heels dangling from her hand by their straps. I give her a thirty-second head start, clenching my jaw shut to resist calling after her with something I might regret, knowing my temper and the still-potent buzz of alcohol have the potential to create the perfect storm right now.

Beth bypasses the small elevator bank and veers left toward the stairwell, heaving the door open and making sure to slam it loudly behind her.

I shake my head in disapproval, wanting to berate her for even that—taking the stairs alone at night when she knows the elevators are safer. Even if the small part of my brain that's still somewhat rational admits that my building is relatively safe in general. But it's her *mentality* that's making me crazy. With everything going on right now, and everything she knows about this fucked-up world, why would she take risks with her safety *at all*? Because Brian fucking Falco isn't the only danger out there, which Beth very well knows.

So what the *hell* is she thinking sneaking around behind the back of the one fucking guy on campus who actually *gives a shit* about her? Like I'm just some kind of paranoid, overprotective asshole, out to cramp her goddamned style. Or keep her apart from her worth-less ex—the jerk-off who tossed her away like fucking garbage, who just called her a *slut* in the middle of a club—like they're star-crossed lovers or some shit. It's completely ass-fucking-backward, and I can't help the resentment tearing through my chest.

I continue to pace myself through the lobby, measuring each step carefully so as not eat up too much of Beth's lead, but the turbulent anger she leaves in her wake is so damned palpable I slow on instinct anyway, as if to physically trudge through it.

Barney, our doorman, stops me to comment on Sunday's football game, and I'm equal parts grateful and irritated. I know Beth and I would probably both benefit from some space after this confusing-as-fuck night—especially with all the time we've been spending together—but right now, the more alone time I have with my thoughts, the more agitated I become.

By the time I enter the stairwell to the echo of small feet padding passive-aggressively above me, my blood is practically begging for a nicotine fix. Beth has always hated smoking, and though she didn't actually ask me to, I've cut down substantially since she moved in. I don't even think it was a conscious choice. But right now, I fuck-ing need one—*bad*—before I get up to that apartment. I light up a cigarette right in the fucking stairwell, just as another door slams two stories overhead to announce Beth reaching our floor. Well, *good*. I'll feel at least marginally better once she's back in my apartment, safely tucked away from the Falcos and Brodys and even the Steven-fucking-Bogarts of the world.

I close my eyes and suck in a long drag, letting the tobacco fill my lungs, waiting for its magic to circulate through my system. I need to calm the fuck down and get my head straight, and *fast*.

It's no use, though. I can't stop picturing Falco's infuriating, smug smirk when he realized Beth had kept me in the dark. But he's got another fucking thing coming if he thinks I'm going to let him set her up for more pain in this lifetime. Or the fucking next, for that matter. I backed down once before, and that was the only damned shot with her he's going to get.

Because *fuck* that motherfucker. And even more aggravating—I can't figure out what the hell Beth was thinking having coffee with him yet again. To what fucking *end*?

And what the *double* fuck is she doing *lying* to me about it?

My gut clenches with those feelings from four years ago—from when they first met, and I understood even then that he could be things to her I never would. Just the thought had sent me instantly reeling, consuming me with emotions I didn't understand...

Jealousy of someone I didn't even fucking like. *Possessiveness* over someone I had no business even *thinking* about in a way that—according to Cap—would be akin to fucking incest, despite not actually being related. *Regret* for something that was never even mine—that *could* never have been mine.

But *Falco* wasn't her brother's oldest friend. He didn't have my reputation or my reckless streak. No, what *he* had was a chance with Beth.

And he used it to fucking *hurt* her.

I shove my hand through my hair and slam my foot into the doorjamb. I just can't fucking believe her right now! And she has the balls to stomp away from *me* as if *I'm* the fucking bad guy? For *what*? Hitting her asshat ex? What the hell did either of them *expect* me to do after he said that shit to her? And then she went to his side like she fucking owed *him* something!

I haven't had much occasion for indignation in my life, but right now it's making me grind my teeth into fucking dust. Because the reality is Beth could get hurt again. She could get hurt *worse*. Look at what happened to Liz! Beth could get...*fuck*.

My brain gets caught on that last thought, and I can't get past it no matter how hard I try. It rages through me until my blood boils over, the buzz of alcohol feeding the flames like gasoline as they fire me back into motion. I crush what's left of my cigarette under my shoe, and march up the rest of the steps and down our hallway. I'm already reaching for the door with my keys when I realize it's fucking ajar, and the sight of it incenses me even more.

Could she possibly be any more cavalier with her goddamned safety?

It's after one in the motherfucking morning! Who the hell leaves their front door open in the middle of the night like an invitation for trouble? Especially someone who, on top of everything else, just spent the entire fucking night drinking. She once told me she thought *I* was trouble. She has no idea what trouble even is.

I barge through the door, all out of patience and ready to tell her off, but the apartment is dark, the only light glowing from the crack beneath the bedroom door. Beth's presence would be impossible to miss, though, what with the sound of her tramping around the room, violently yanking and slamming drawers like she wants the whole damned building to feel her wrath.

Well, at least that's one feeling that is definitely fucking mutual.

I throw the bedroom door open with more force than I intend, and Beth jumps at the reverberating *bang* as it smacks against the wall. But she catches herself without even glancing my way, continuing about her business like I don't even fucking exist.

My outrage dissipates as I take her in. Her long blond hair is haphazardly piled on top of her head, and she's already changed into a T-shirt and yoga pants. My eyes get stuck on her ass for several seconds before I even process the fact that she's shoving her shit into her duffel bag.

She yanks open another drawer—the one I'd cleared for her bras and underwear—and panic rolls through me. It doesn't mix well with the indignation. Or the booze.

Somehow I manage to force enough patience to keep from unloading my every grievance on her at once, and I just stand here glowering, biting back every word I couldn't wait to get out just moments ago—those words now lodged uncomfortably in my throat, held hostage by that fucking duffel. And suddenly I resent that, too. The fact that Beth has the nerve to vilify me for looking out for her. For taking her out to do something she fucking loves. But more than anything, I resent that I fucking *care*. That the sight of her packing her things *affects* me. Not just my feelings—my motherfucking *feelings*—but my actions, too.

It gives her a kind of control—power. It's not a dynamic I'm used to with women, and it's left me a little lost and a lot confused. And even more pissed the fuck off. It's enough to demolish even my pretense of patience, my composure shattering in one fell swoop, and I spring into action, thrusting myself in front of her in challenge.

"'The *fuck* are you doing?" I demand.

Beth's jaw locks, but she just sidesteps around me.

"Beth," I warn.

She snatches handfuls of panties from her drawer—*my drawer*—with enough hostility that I worry for the integrity of the delicate lace, and my inebriated mind actually pities them until I remember it's *me* she's fucking pissed at. The appearance of her underwear doesn't help my focus, either. But watching her shove them purposefully into her bag snaps me back to reality. Or it snaps me the fuck out of my Beth-panty-coma, at least.

"What the *fucking* hell are you doing?" I repeat as calmly as I can manage—which, it turns out, isn't calm at all. But where the hell does she think she's going in the middle of the goddamned night?

"Taking my stuff and going back to my dorm," Beth deadpans, and it takes me a second to realize she's not actually kidding.

I shake my head and grab her upper arms. "The fuck you are!"

Beth wrenches from my grip, and I have to release her or risk hurting her, which is *not* a fucking option. "*The fuck I am*, is right!" she shouts, skirting back around me to stuff more clothes into her bag.

And, finally, I lose it.

I grab the offending duffel and flop it upside-down, shaking it violently until all of her shit falls onto my bed in an unceremonious pile of all things *Beth*.

"What the hell are you doing!" she hisses, climbing onto the bed to regather her clothes.

I don't even think. I take hold of her calves and jerk her knees straight, and she squeals with surprise, falling facedown onto the bed, right atop the heap of clothing. But I don't back off. I grab her hips and flip her onto her back in one not-so-smooth movement, bending over her and planting my palms on either side of her face in a makeshift cage. Beth's lips part in a small *o* of shock, but she can't escape my gaze, trapped beneath me like she is.

But that goes both ways, and I force myself to close my eyes, and inhale a choppy rush of air before meeting hers.

Something changes when I reopen my eyes. Beth's temper seems to have dissipated, her dark blond brows pulled together in helpless bemusement. Her eyes are deep blue oceans, and they draw me in like an undertow, luring me into their shallows before drowning me in their depths.

But somehow, they calm me, and the anger is drained right out of me as something tugs inside my chest. For a moment I forget how we even got here. All I register are her sharp, shallow breaths as they whisper against my lips in soft gusts.

Somewhere in the back of my mind I know this is dangerous—her lying beneath me like this. It calls to that reckless part of me. The same part that risked dancing with her tonight…that wants to just say *fuck it,* again and again and again. The part that can't remember the reasons to stay away.

Beth's tongue darts out to lick her bottom lip, and my dick jumps in my jeans, still swollen and aching, which it has been all night on some level or another. I suck in an uneven breath, the air hissing between my teeth, and I know I need to either get off of her or inside her in the next sixty seconds or I'm going to fucking implode.

My fingers fist the comforter on either side of her, and I close my eyes again to regain my bearings, refusing to look at her until I've backed up off of her and put a few yards of sense between us.

Beth doesn't get up. She just pulls her knees up and plants her small bare feet on the bedspread, blinking slowly at the ceiling as if emerging from some kind of daze.

Yeah, I know the feeling.

But her flushed skin and heavy breathing catch me off guard. It's not that I didn't think Beth was attracted to me. I know it sounds cocky, but from my experience, *most* girls are probably more or less attracted to me. But her reaction makes me wonder, for the first time, if she might actually want to *act* on it. My already throbbing cock jerks at the thought, my pulse going haywire at the chaos it invokes. Because that's what it would be if Beth and I ever happened—utter fucking *chaos*.

I have to consciously resist the urge to drop my palm to my raging hard-on just to ease the ache, and I run it through my hair instead, if only to occupy it elsewhere.

I lean back against the wall and cross my arms over my chest. Beth sits up and scoots to the edge of the bed, her shoulders sagging in unexpected defeat.

"You've been seeing Falco." I mean it to be a question, but it doesn't come out like one.

Beth shakes her head. "I met him for coffee. Twice."

"And lied to me about it..." I grit my teeth.

Beth meets my gaze from under her long, thick lashes, her mask of innocence belying the deceit I didn't think her capable of before tonight. What the fuck *else* has she been lying about?

Was it really just *twice*? Was it even *just coffee*?

Did she let him fucking touch her? The thought makes my hands ball into fists, and I cross my arms more tightly to hide them behind my biceps.

Beth doesn't say a word, and her silence just leaves a clear, smooth path for my anger to snowball out of control.

My slow, liquored-up brain suddenly recalls her slinking in just before ten on Monday night, when I'd thought she'd been at the library with Toni, a girl from her Psych 101 class who lives in my building. They've been walking home together when I'm not around, and I took it for granted that Beth knew better than to walk that far alone, especially at night. You know, being as there's a fucking *rapist* on the loose who just so happens to have a history of *stalking* her.

Not for the first time I think I might have fucked up in downplaying the whole situation to Cap—in corroborating Beth's story that she's staying with me for every reason but the truth. *It's closer to her classes, it's nicer than the dorms, to give Lani privacy with her fictitious boyfriend...* My stomach rolls at the reminder that I lied—continue to lie—to my oldest friend, and my eyes narrow at the reason for my uncharacteristic betrayal.

"Monday?" I demand.

Beth's nod is tentative, even as she meets my hostile glare with unapologetic defiance. "It was just coffee, David."

"Just coffee with motherfucking *Falco*, who you're sneaking around to see!"

Beth jumps to her feet. "I didn't—"

"You didn't walk around alone at night? Without telling anyone where you were going or who with?" I accuse. Images of all the terrible things that could have happened hit me all at once, but my jealous, riled up, intoxicated mind fixates on the one of Falco's hands on her above all. Because I didn't have *enough* to fucking worry about before her piece-of-shit ex weaseled his way back into the picture.

And I'm not a fucking *worrier*. This shit isn't *me*.

Beth's eyes narrow to match mine, but she has no comeback. She knows I'm fucking right.

I huff out what resembles a growl. "Damn it, Beth!" I gesture pointedly to the pile on my bed. "'The fuck is the point of *this* then, huh?" More heat rolls through me, the alcohol in my system acting as a dangerous accelerant, and between my fury and my hard-on there's a good chance I might spontaneously combust. "I don't know why you're even fucking *staying* here if you're just going to walk around like you're challenging the goddamned universe! Next time just send a fucking email blast to the whole student motherfucking body! That way any random piece of shit looking for a hot young coed to take advantage of can find you and do whatever the fuck they want!" But I'm assaulted by that image of Steven Bogart pawing at her in the damned club, and I'm not even sure what I'm talking about anymore—if my heart's practically beating out of my chest over Brody's threat to her safety, or fucking Falco's threat to her sanity, or Bogart's threat to...*what? Take her from me?*

"Goddamn it!" I roar, shoving another hand through my hair and forcibly averting my gaze to escape the sight of her in those tight fucking pants. Because somehow she looks even sexier now than she did in that hot-as-fuck little number she had on at the club tonight.

But my temper ignites something violent in Beth, and suddenly she's rushing me like a defensive tackle, her teeth practically bared as she unleashes her own torrent of swear words, her palms shoving hard at my chest.

If I wasn't so pissed I might smirk. *I* taught her those words, over a decade ago, though I don't remember them sounding so goddamned hot coming from her mouth. But there's no question how they affect me now, and for a moment I just stand here and let her release her obvious frustration, even as my back is thrust repeatedly into the wall with more force than I'd expect from her small, slim body. It isn't enough to hurt me, though, and I wonder if she's actually trying to.

"Whose idea what *that*, huh?" she seethes. "*I* don't know why I'm fucking staying here, *either*!" she adds with another shove at my chest, and I try to ignore the way her touch burns my skin even through my shirt, or how it travels straight to my dick like she alone holds some kind of map of secret paths through my body, ones that seem to exist only for her. "I'm not a little fucking kid anymore, David!"

I've heard it before, but my patience was running on empty when I got here, and right now, after this crazy, amazing, shitty fucking night, all I've got left is feeling and instinct. I snatch her wrists and yank her into me to stop her aggression. "So you keep fucking telling me!"

Beth tries to pull free but I hold her wrists more firmly to my chest, hauling her harder against me to make my point...whatever the fucking fuck that may be. But she doesn't just get to go off on me without hearing me say my piece. But I'm not sure what that is anymore, and before I manage to figure it out, Beth is back on the offensive.

She's given up on breaking free, so she pushes me instead, this time with her entire body. "Fuck *you*!" she spits—words I've never heard her say before—not directed at *me*.

"Fuck *me*?"

"Yes! *Ugh*!" Another shove. "You don't have to stop guys from *dancing* with me—"

If she was looking to push me over the edge, it fucking worked. I spin us around so it's *her* back against the wall, effectively cutting her off. My hand slides to the nape of her neck, guiding her gaze where it belongs; I don't release her wrists, either. Instead, I steal the half-step between us, crowding her until I loom over her almost threateningly.

But I wouldn't hurt her—I know that, she knows that. So what the hell am I threatening? The truth is I'm not exactly sure, but this whole night feels precarious, like it's hanging on by a thread—or I am—and it's getting closer and closer to snapping by the second.

"Dancing with you? Or fucking *groping* you?" I grit out. My volume may have plummeted, but my tone more than makes up for it.

Beth jerks her restrained wrists. "I'm not a child," she huffs, "and you're not my fucking brother." She lets out a sharp, exasperated exhale. "I lost the chance to have a normal high school experience because of a guy. I won't miss out on college, too… not even for you." She glares up at me with a scrappy determination, and it's obvious she's preparing for a fight.

But what the fuck is *that* supposed to mean? *Not even for me?* Why would *I* suddenly fucking matter?

"You either need to accept that I'm an adult, or I can't stay here. I'm nineteen years old, for God's sake!"

Don't I fucking know it! But the last thing she should want is for me to *accept that she's an adult.* Because if I were to stop the constant internal reminders that she's still the same *Bits*—the same little girl who got us to dance to Britney Spears and sip fake tea—well, the version in front of me is all I'd have left. And, like she said, that version is a nineteen-year-old woman. A gorgeous nineteen-year-old woman with a tight ass, full, perky tits, and legs that would look way too fucking perfect wrapped around my waist.

It's only when I catch her lower lip trembling in a flicker of uncertainty that I realize how hard I'm breathing, how tense my muscles are, how firm my grasp is on the back of her neck. My fingers spread further, expanding my claim, even if somewhere, buried deep beneath the layers of alcohol, anger, and arousal, I know I should be doing the opposite.

Beth doesn't waver, though. "You have friends who are girls, David. There's no reason why you can't just treat me like anyone else," she says impassively.

And finally, with one final epic *fuck it*, I crack.

My hand tightens around her nape, my fingers thrusting into her hair barely a second before they're pulling her head back, offering her mouth up at the perfect angle. I take full and immediate advantage, giving my brain a much-needed break as I surrender instead to the instructions coming from the rest of my body, all of which are currently consumed by a single thought—tasting those fucking lips.

So I do.

Chapter Fifteen

David

My mouth takes Beth's like a car crash—a fiery disaster we can't turn away from even as it's happening—with two things that have no business coming together doing exactly fucking that.

And the result is just as explosive.

After one brief moment of either hesitation or surprise, Beth responds in earnest, unassuming but sure, as if she's letting me lead her in yet another dance. And, in a way, she is. An untamed, reckless, chaotic dance.

The alcohol is still there in our blood, fueling an entirely different kind of fire than the fury and outrage of just moments ago. But if anything could blaze hotter than my temper, it's my attraction to this fucking girl, and my lips are firm and punishing from the start.

Beth's mouth opens to let out a gasp, and I advance again, my tongue leading the assault. She whimpers into my mouth and I swallow it down greedily.

Fuck, she tastes like whiskey, and fruity shots, and mint gum, and pure fucking *heaven*.

It's *nothing* like the strawberry lava cake I've imagined.

It's so much fucking *better*.

My cock doesn't know what to do with itself, cruelly imprisoned in my jeans, and I'd feel bad for it if not for the distraction of my tongue, which licks and slides against Beth's like it's got a point to prove. And with her soft moans, the way she reciprocates, I can't help but feel like I've proven it in motherfucking *spades*. But whether she realizes it or not, Beth is also making a point of her own. Because with each stroke of her lush lips against mine, with every last taste of her I get, the more intoxicated I become.

Her familiar scent invades my senses, and I respond like an addict, bingeing on everything all at once, like it's my last chance to ever experience any of it. My mouth, my hands, even the way my hips pin hers to the wall—it's all shamefully coarse and rushed, like I've suddenly regressed into a virgin or something, choking under the pressure of the impossible choice between tits and ass. Except the body I'm currently running my hands all over is the one I've lusted over for fucking *ever*, and it's not just any ass or pair of tits driving me goddamned insane, but fucking *Bea's*.

But she doesn't seem to mind the rough exploration of my hands anymore than my frenzied claiming of her mouth. In fact, she gives it all right back to me in equal measure, her fingers—though tentative at first—burning a path from my biceps up and along the lines of my shoulders. When they slide into my hair and tug, I groan right into her mouth, feasting on her responding sharp, surprised exhale. I love that she's as out of control as I am right now.

Her swell of cleavage rises and falls dramatically with every harsh breath, pressing against my chest in a teasing parody of what it would feel like to have her beneath me. My palms zero in on her tight ass, pulling her into my throbbing erection without a conscious thought, and I have never been more desperate for anything in my life. Suddenly her tongue against mine is no longer a distraction from the steel fucking pipe wedged between us. Because, *fuck*, all it's doing is making me think about *more*.

Her mouth—soft, hot, wet…my tongue thrusting inside it…

And then all I can think about is being inside *her*.

My dick swells to unfathomable proportions. My brain sends a faint, distant message that I vaguely register as a warning, but it's lost behind the sound of her soft moan.

That fucking sound.

I grab the backs of her thighs and guide her long legs around my waist, never disconnecting from her mouth as she sucks in yet another gasp. I drop Beth on the bed and climb over her, one hand tangled in her hair, the other cupping her flushed cheek.

"*Fuck*, Bea," I rasp.

Her hair is a wild mess of fine, gold silk, and I absently stroke its softness against the pads of my fingers, savoring the sensation.

I hold achingly still above her, reveling in the way her body's delicate curves embrace me, yielding to the firm planes of my own as if they were built for just this purpose. Her plump, pink, slightly parted lips taunt me from mere inches away, reddened and swollen from my possession, tempting me to take another taste of the only fucking thing in existence that puts strawberry lava cake to shame.

But by some miracle I manage to hang on to a few more moments of self-restraint. I rest my forehead against hers, waiting to catch my breath before I pull back to look at her.

Her eyes fucking slay me, my chest swelling with an uncomfortable ache—something that, strangely, resembles a longing for something I don't even fucking *want*.

I ignore it. Beth is too goddamned beautiful. She always has been. It isn't fucking fair.

She stares up at me with eyes so wide it's like she's looking to me for some kind of answer. But I'm not the guy with the answers for once. No, for once I'm as confused as she is.

But I can't let her see that—and I don't. I mask emotion like a pro, and hiding how Beth gets to me is one act I mastered long ago. But for some reason, even as I slip on a smirk, I find it harder than usual to look unaffected.

"You win, Bea." My voice comes out low and hoarse, strained by desire just as conspicuously as my jeans are. "Definitely not a *little kid*," I concede, though I never argued that point in the first place.

Beth breathes out a short laugh. "That's what I've been trying to tell you," she whines, adorable as all fuck. But I highly doubt *this* is what she's been trying to tell me.

Her T-shirt has fallen off her shoulder, and her bare skin teases me, making it hard to focus despite being such an innocuous part of her body. But it's *her* body, and every part of it is new, and forbidden, and motherfucking *perfect*.

Beth licks her lips and my dick jumps in my jeans. "You taste like whiskey," she smiles tentatively.

I tuck a loose blond wave behind her ear. "I meant what I said," I say pointedly. "If you're going to lie and put yourself at risk—"

But I don't get through a full sentence. "If you weren't so overprotective, I wouldn't have had to lie," she says defensively.

"Well, if you weren't so fucking reckless I wouldn't have to be so protective!" I exhale harshly, aware I'm getting heated again in all the wrong ways, but too on edge to stop it. "You *know* Brody is out there—"

"This isn't about Brody and you know it," Beth spits.

My heart stops. *Where the fuck is she going with this?*

"This is about *Brian*. It's about me seeing him, just like it's about me dancing with Steven…This isn't about Brody. It's not even about *me*! This is about *you*, David."

All the blood drains from my face at once.

"Because you're full of shit, David! You still see me as a child and you know it. You may get drunk and act like every other fucking guy alive—shoving your tongue down the throat of the first willing girl you find—but you don't trust me with Brian because you think I'm still the weak kid I was at fifteen!" she hisses right up into my face. "And you don't trust me dancing with Steven for the same reason.

What? Are my silly little girl senses no match for his masculine prowess?"

My hand tightens in her hair, cutting off her rant, and all I want to do is shut her up with my mouth on hers. To prove her wrong, and right, and more right than she even knows by consuming every last word she has left, straight from her lips to mine. But I don't.

Instead I release her, and push off the mattress and back away, glaring my resentment as if I could shoot each reply currently lodged in my throat like arrows straight into her heart.

"Contrary to your fucking belief, I *don't* want to get in your way, or to ruin your *college fucking experience*. And I didn't want to have to take extreme measures to deal with shit I thought I could handle on my own. But apparently I was fucking mistaken, because that counted on being able to fucking trust you!"

Beth's gaze fires right back at me, and if I wasn't so damned mad right now, it might shrink me down a size or two. "So I'm just *shit you thought you could handle?*"

"That's not—"

"And your next move is to threaten to 'take extreme measures'? What does that even *mean?* And this is supposed to prove that you *don't* treat me like a kid?"

"I have you living in my fucking apartment! I took you out to an over-twenty-one club tonight!" I remind her.

"So you could keep your eye on me!"

Now it's my turn to glare again. I'm starting to lose track of whose move it even is in our little eye-war, and I liked it better when hers were filled with desire instead of anger and indignation.

"You still see me as Cap's kid sister—whatever regrets your dick got you into tonight—and we both know it. You'd still be calling me *Bits* if I hadn't asked you not to."

Definitely still my move. "Ironic that you fault me for treating you like a kid, considering we wouldn't even be having this conversation if you weren't acting like a little fucking brat!" I can't even get through the sentence without losing my temper all over again.

"I'm fucking nineteen!" Beth launches back.

"Then fucking act like it!" I roar. "Stop sneaking around behind my back like a hormonal brat with an overbearing father!"

"Then stop acting like the overbearing father!"

Fuck this!

"I can handle Steven, and Brian, for that matter!" Beth asserts.

And like an uppercut to the jaw, Beth hits me with the name I just can't fucking stand hearing from her mouth right now—the mouth I just tasted every last inch of. Fucking *Brian*.

"So fucking *handle* them, then," I murmur, low and bitter. And then I turn and walk the fuck out.

Chapter Sixteen

David

Three Years ago

Cooper's party is even more packed than usual. With the school year winding down, the energy is growing restless. Us juniors are ready to be seniors and the seniors are ready to get the fuck out of here, run away to college, and chase a future that will probably be a letdown for all but a few.

And then Falco is in the distance, high-five-ing Cooper, presumably over something stupid, and my gaze does a quick survey to confirm that Beth didn't change her mind and come to the party after all.

But he's alone, which means Beth is home. Probably still in those tiny white shorts and that tight tank top she usually wears to bed—the one she's almost always still wearing when I manage to fight a hangover enough to come over and lift with Cap on weekend mornings.

Falco leads Cooper and two of their friends around to the side of the pool house, presumably to spark up a joint—*stingy pricks*. But when the familiar scent doesn't start wafting over a couple of minutes later, I become curious.

My boys are engaged in a competitive round of beer pong, and they don't miss me when I slink off toward the empty pool house. I catch

Cooper's voice from around the bend, and keep myself tucked along the wall so as not to give myself away.

"I call bullshit, man," Cooper says with a ball-busting chuckle. "You're telling me she held out for ten fucking months, only to give it up after a date at fucking *Matteo's*?" He laughs even harder.

My gut rolls at the implication, my hands tightening into fists at my sides. Matteo's is Beth's favorite restaurant, and I know Falco took her there for dinner earlier tonight.

"Ow!" Cooper whine-laughs, like someone halfheartedly hit him.

"Fuck off," Falco says smugly. "Believe it, don't believe it. Like I give a shit. I finally got between those perfect thighs tonight, and you know fucking what? Even right now she's waiting for me at home to leave this party and come give it to her *again*."

I can hear the smirk in his voice as my fingernails draw blood from my palms. My own dinner turns precariously in my stomach, mixing with the alcohol and threatening to come back up. Because as much as I want to deny what Falco's words mean, I can't, and as much as I want to write them off as bullshit male bragging, something tells me he isn't making it up.

And something inside me breaks. The barriers I've built around the jealousy that's done nothing but grow since the night they first met, all crumble in an instant, and I get the fuck away from that damned pool house before I do something crazy, like strangle the fucker.

The overcast sky begins a light drizzle, and everyone relocates inside, but I take cover under the vine-swathed pergola and light a much-needed cigarette. I turn around, and there in the corner is the only other person still outside, and of course it's my least fucking favorite person alive.

Falco nods to me, taking a puff on his own smoke.

I tap some ash onto the ground and watch him. I lift my chin at his cigarette. "Didn't you quit? Or did you just tell your girlfriend that?"

I almost choke on the taste of the word. *Girlfriend*. It's a word that has never appealed to me, but it tastes exponentially more sour in this particular context.

Falco drops the cigarette on the damp flagstone, crushing it under his shoe. He splays his palms in a show of pacifism. "I did quit. It wasn't mine. Just bummed one from Ty."

I raise my eyebrows. "You know quitting doesn't mean just not buying your own pack, right? It means not smoking."

Falco shrugs. "That's the first one I've had in weeks."

I snort. He's supposed to have quit for good months ago.

Falco shifts nervously in place, frowning. "Look, man. Please don't tell her, okay?"

I take another puff and look away from him. I should fucking tell her. But then she'd be upset, and I won't be the reason Beth is upset. I won't give him peace of mind by telling him that, though.

I wish to God Falco would just fucking leave, but he doesn't. He slips his hands in his pockets, rocking on his heels as he watches me pretend to enjoy my smoke. I am his girlfriend's family friend, and I know it serves him to get along with me. Even if I haven't been openly hostile to him in a while, he's always felt my dislike, and after what I've just overheard, I'm sure even that would be favorable to whatever vibes I must be giving off right now. Because I *never* trusted him—not for a fucking minute. He may even genuinely love Beth—*now*—but what happens when there's a thousand miles between them? When there are hot college chicks drunk and available? What are the chances Falco doesn't fuck Beth over?

I mean, the writing is already on the fucking wall. He's already avoiding bringing her to parties, making her less and less of a priority. And if what he told his boys was true, and he's really taken that from her...*Fuck*. Contemptuous jealousy surges through my veins, tensing my muscles and clenching my jaw. Is he really going to put Beth through months—even years—of a long-distance "relationship" when he's already treating her like an inconvenience, talking about her to his friends like she's just some sexual conquest?

"March…" Falco's still scared I'll snitch on him for smoking.

"So, Dartmouth, huh?" I change the subject instead.

He blows out a deep breath, relieved to move on from the subject of his little transgression. "Yeah, man."

"That's a good school. Congrats."

"Thanks."

I stomp out my cigarette, and then immediately take out another and light it. I hold out the pack to Falco—a test—and he takes one—*asshole*—and lights on up. "So what does Beth think about it?" I ask, looking out over the pool, at the steam rising from the heated water. It's a scene out of Stephen King, or Hitchcock, and I imagine myself drowning Falco in the pool and taking Beth for myself. It's a morbid fantasy, but like most of the good in my life, it's still just fantasy.

"About Dartmouth?" Falco asks.

"About you *going away* to Dartmouth," I press.

Falco sighs. "She's supportive. But you know Beth. She's scared."

"It's kind of selfish, don't you think?" I keep my tone light, *just making conversation.*

Falco flinches. "That's the last thing Beth is."

I turn to face him. "Not her. You."

He frowns.

"I'm just saying, it's a lot to put her through, right? All that long-distance shit. Seems to me if you really loved her you'd go somewhere closer," I shrug. In the horror film in my mind, he steps too close to the pool, slips in the rain, and—*oh, shit*—hits his head on the side going down. Liquid crimson dances through the water as he sinks, and I glance around to confirm there are no witnesses—no one to know I had a chance to try and save him.

In reality Falco just stands and glares at me. He wants to tell me to go fuck myself, but he's got more tact than that. "I wanted to play soccer, but that didn't work out. Dartmouth is the best school I got into by a long shot."

I nod like I understand.

I *don't* understand. School is important, but so is Beth. Would it have been that big a deal to go to a slightly less impressive school to be near the girl he claims to fucking *love*? Of course the school he chooses will affect his future, but the same can be said about Beth. So the only conclusion I can draw is that he's not sure *she's* his future. At least not enough to make her a priority. And yet, according to him, that didn't stop him from taking her motherfucking *virginity*.

"So what's the plan for next year then?" I ask him, all still waters on the surface.

He frowns. "Plan?"

Is this guy for real? "To see Beth." *Dipshit.* "You gonna drive home every other weekend? Still got over a year before she gets her license," I remind him.

He blinks at me. Has he not considered any of this? "I guess we'll figure it out as it happens, you know?"

I let out a short laugh. "*As it happens?* As *what* happens? As hot, drunk, freshman girls throw themselves at you? As Beth sits home instead of making new friends because she's being loyal to her boyfriend?"

"She won't sit home," he argues halfheartedly.

"She's sitting home right now," I remind him.

Falco swallows audibly.

"Look man, you and me, we don't know each other. Not really. But you know Beth is like a sister to me, right?"

He snorts. "You remind me every chance you get." *Fair enough.*

"Beth is a good girl." I tell him what he already knows. "If you stay together, she's going to wait for you. She's going to sit home on weekends, waiting to FaceTime with you, missing her high school experience altogether, and then she'll do the same thing in college."

Falco stares at me, unblinking, warily following the strokes of my words as they paint him a portrait we both know to be spot-fucking-on.

I shift my tone, and I don't even have to feign the envy it holds as I go in for the kill. "But I guess that's pretty cool, right? You know...to, like, know who you're gonna end up with and everything at eighteen. While we're all fucking around with random chicks, and whatever." I let out a short laugh. "I mean, most of us frogs have to screw a fuck of a lot of princesses before we turn into a prince. Some of us aren't prince material at all." I gesture to myself.

Falco continues to stare, and I can practically see his mind spin like the predictable asshat he is. It's fucking pathetic. This guy is nowhere near good enough for Beth, and even though a part of me really does hope he does right by her for her heart's sake, there's also the part of me that can't stomach the thought of the two of them ending up together. And, of course, there's the fact that he in no way deserves her. It's infuriating, and I blow out a slow breath before I let the fucked-upness of it all rile me up and show my hand.

Instead, I stay cool as a motherfucking cucumber on the outside, and I finish him. "I can't imagine being with only one girl from the time I'm eighteen. Good for you." I keep my tone calm and casual, looking back out over the pool. After all, I'm not trying to scare him—I'm trying to test him. If he's sure about Beth, then my words won't bug him out. But if he's not, then he can't steal this time from her. He's either got to man up and figure out how he's going to make this work, or let her go. And before he leaves for school. Anything else is selfish and fucked up on his part.

Because we all know how that goes—we've seen it happen over and over to the girls in our grade who had older boyfriends who weren't all-in when they went to college. It would just lead to a year or more of fighting and tears until Falco finally cheated on her and broke her sweet, trusting heart. And then I'd have to kill him for real. I want to go to college next year, not prison.

"Seventeen." His voice is so low I barely make it out.

"Huh?"

"I'm not eighteen for another couple months."

I shrug. Even better. I don't know a lot of guys who wouldn't lose their shit over the thought of being with the same girl from the time he is seventeen until the day he dies, and if he's one of those guys, then he shouldn't be stringing Beth along.

"Whatever," I murmur. "It's not like she's holding you back, right? You can focus on your classes and shit."

"Yeah."

"At least you'll have your shit together. While the rest of us are wasting our time with one-night stands and meaningless hookups, you get to skip all that reckless shit. I mean take in Luce over there," I gesture through the closed sliding glass doors, where we can see our mutual female acquaintance—one I happen to know Falco was particularly interested in before meeting Beth—lifting the hem of her top to flash some of the guys her bra. "Luce with her whole *free-love*, sexual exploration mission…" I roll my eyes. "Imagine how many chicks like that there will be in college." My laugh is convincing enough.

I toss my cigarette into the remnants of someone's drink and head inside. Falco stays outside with the rain and his thoughts, no protection against either, battered by both. He's going to man up and commit to the girl he claims to love with eyes wide open, or he's going to self-destruct. But it's not his destruction I'm worried about. It's Beth's. And if Falco isn't the guy for her, she'll be much better off in the long run if she finds that out now. And if I can help that along, then all the fucking better.

About half an hour later, when the rain has cleared and most of the party has moved back outside, I find Luce alone in Cooper's kitchen. "Hey there, Dave," she smiles suggestively, swaying her hips as she approaches.

"Hi there, honey." I flash her a smile, but when her fingers brush my thigh, I skirt the contact. "You know who needs a little attention?" I tell her. "Falco."

Luce frowns. "Isn't he still dating Beth Caplan?"

I shrug casually. "Is anyone really dating anyone, Luce? Come on." I use her own lines against her. "What happened to *love should be open and free*?"

Luce smirks.

"Anyway, if he's really still dating her, then he won't be interested in you, and if he *is* interested in you..."

Her smirk stretches wider. Luce has always loved a challenge—especially a sexual one.

I pour and hand her two shots of absinthe, nodding in Falco's direction. "May the best woman win," I joke. But I mean every word. Because the best woman has always been Beth and she *will* win here, one way or the other. She will either know for sure that she's wasting her time with a piece of shit who never deserved her, or that piece of shit will man the fuck up. But as I watch Luce approach Beth's boyfriend with the two shots I handed her, I can't help but wonder who the *piece of shit* really is, and I toss back a double shot of my own.

Chapter Seventeen

Beth

Present Day

Hours pass, but still I don't fall asleep.

I didn't bother to draw the shades before I finally gave up on waiting up for David just before three in the morning, and the nearly full moon casts soft, pale light through the otherwise darkened bedroom.

It's just as well. There's no chance for sleep, anyway. Not with my mind racing like it is.

It isn't the first time my brain has refused to shut down at night—demanding instead that I fixate on some seemingly innocuous moment and analyze it half to death—but tonight my usual demons are off the hook. My current thoughts aren't fueled by irrational anxiety. I'm not lying in bed cringing over something I said, or trying to figure out the hidden meaning behind someone else's casual comment. No, tonight my thoughts echo my heartbeat, which pounds to a rhythm as familiar as those demons.

Da-vid—Da-vid—Da-vid.

The events of the night replay on a loop in my head like a series of gifs in a *Buzzfeed* article.

David…Dancing…David dancing with a girl…Steven—David

shoving Steven…David dancing with me. *Brian—David hitting Brian…Arguing with David.*

David pinning me to the bed.

Arguing again.

David kissing *me…*

Kissing him back.

Years of almost-moments and delusionally hopeful *maybe-somedays* all culminating in a whirlwind of passion I was lost to the moment his lips touched mine. One that, even now, I can't be one hundred percent sure was even real.

But the evidence is there in my telltale swollen lips as they silently beg for an encore, and I wonder if it was really just the alcohol, or if there's even the smallest possibility that David is finally seeing me for the woman I am and not the girl I was.

Still, as much as my stupid, naïve heart would love to read more into it, I'm deferring to my brain these days, and rationally I know there's no point in searching for greater meaning when a drunk, horny guy hooks up with the girl he finds in his bedroom.

It would just be so much easier to dismiss if it hadn't been so…so…*explosive.*

I sigh out loud as the memory of his kiss alone sends a rush of wildfire through my veins, my thighs pressing together to try and ease the ache between them. And my heart twists with regret, even as my stomach refills with righteous indignation, when I once again reach the part of how the night ended.

More arguing. And David storming out.

I don't do well with yelling and shouting. Especially not from men, and certainly not from six plus feet of lean muscle I happen to know has plenty of experience throwing punches. Theoretically, at least. Because I may shrink away out of habit when David raises his voice sometimes, but I hold my own with him when it counts, and perhaps most telling—never has he once made me feel an ounce of fear.

But there is something that's far worse than yelling to me. Something, incidentally, I have my father to thank for as well—but not *only* him. Because if there's anything that traumatized my formative years more than my father's rare but brutal alcoholic outbursts, it was when he walked out our front door, and didn't come back for six years. It was when Brian took my virginity, and disappeared from my life the very next morning. *Abandonment issues, indeed.*

The view of David's back as he disappeared out the door—even in memory form—hits me in the gut like a sucker punch, knocking the air from my lungs without fail, no matter how many times I see it in my mind. But that doesn't stop me from hitting replay, again and again and again.

More than an hour after I went to bed, I'm still staring at the shadows on the far wall when a muffled bang travels through the apartment, and I startle. But I don't move.

My body registers it before my mind does—the too-loud slam of the door, the aggressive movements around the kitchen, and the harsh footfalls that sound so unlike David's. My pulse takes off like a rocket and by the time my brain catches up, I'm already covered in a cool sheen of sweat.

He's still angry.

He may even be *more* angry.

And I've been conditioned since childhood to react to a man's anger in only one way—cowering in terror.

But my father isn't the only man in my life with a track record. David has one, too, and even as my hands start to tremble, I remind myself that I am safe. That no matter how out of character he's behaved tonight, or how angry he might be, David would never hurt me.

Not physically, I silently amend. Because Brian never physically hurt me either, and look how well that worked out.

I suck in a deep breath and shake the thought away. This is *David*. Sammy's oldest friend, *my* friend, and he's never been anything but good to me—tonight's argument notwithstanding.

By the time his heavy, stomping steps start to grow louder a couple of short minutes later, I've mostly reined in my irrational fear. But I remain still, keeping my eyes shut tight, feigning sleep. David and I definitely need to talk, about so many things, but I don't want to do that when he's still angry, or when we're both probably still a little drunk.

The bedroom door swings open too hard, and it hits the wall with a thump only muffled by the hoodies hanging on the back of it. It resonates through the dim, quiet room, and I wonder if David noticed my startle.

"Fuck. Me," David mutters in a hushed tone that surprises me in its softness. He doesn't sound angry at all. Just frustrated—and it's all out of synch with his bullish presence.

There's another loud bump just as I'm thinking it, this one followed by several lesser ones, and a string of slurred curses.

I crack open one eye. And then it hits me. David isn't enraged…He's just completely hammered.

I don't know where he went when he left me tonight, but wherever it was definitely served alcohol.

"Fuck," he slurs again, and then a bang and a resounding, "shit!" and I can't hold in my giggle. I turn in bed and spot his massive shadow right away, his hand gripping the closet door for balance as his feet shuffle to catch their footing.

He tries to kick off a sneaker and stumbles again, and I hastily crawl across the bed to help him. The movement catches his attention, and even in the dark, his deep, hazel gaze has the power to halt me in my tracks. And it does, and suddenly I'm sitting here on his bed, waiting for something—anything—to give away his current mood.

Slowly, David's lips stretch at both corners, spreading into a lopsided smirk. "I've had this dream before," he mumbles clumsily.

I frown at him. *Just how drunk is he?*

David squints at me. "There are two—no, four…there's a bunch of you."

I cock my head at him. I don't think I've ever seen him this intoxicated—and I've seen him plenty drunk…and high, for that matter. I get up from the bed and approach him warily. "It's just me," I murmur.

David's grin is almost goofy, and it melts something in me. "You're not *me*. You're *Bea*."

I smile. At least he's not so drunk that he doesn't know who I am.

David wavers on his feet, and stubs his toe into the wall. "Shit!"

"Come on," I say, shaking my head and biting my lip to stifle my own goofy grin. I let him lean on my shoulder and help him to the bed, his unbalanced bulk harder to maneuver than I anticipated. We take a bit of a zigzag path, but I finally get him close enough that he can flop himself down, which he does, on his back, his legs hanging off the bed, feet planted on the floor. His eyes are closed before he hits the mattress.

I push his jacket off his shoulders, holding out each sleeve and guiding his arms through them, and leave it bunched under his heavy back. His leg jerks and it takes me a second to realize he's trying to kick off his shoes again.

I shake his shoulder. "David."

A whiney groan.

"David," I whisper more loudly, shoving at him to try and sit him up. It kind of works, in that he opens one eye and inches up onto his elbows. I climb off the bed to undo his shoelaces and hold his sneaker so he can get it off. "Pull it out," I prompt.

David sits up further, squinting at me under a furrowed brow, and I'm caught off guard by his sudden intensity as I stare up at him from the floor.

I bite back a smile. "I meant *your foot*," I clarify. I wiggle his shoe to urge him to remove it, and he frowns before slipping out of his shoes, one at a time. I startle at the sudden sensation of his hand on my jaw. He huffs in a heavy rush of air, and then he's grabbing me under my arms and yanking me to my feet in front of him.

He nods to himself, satisfied, and then promptly pulls his legs onto the bed, and plops down onto the pillow.

"David, your clothes," I remind him.

"Hmm…" He doesn't even open an eye.

I nudge David's knee with mine. "Your jeans, David."

Nothing.

I could just leave them, but he can't be comfortable—drunk or not—and he sleeps in his underwear half the time anyway. I undo his belt buckle, my fingers hesitantly hovering over his fly. I'm no less aware of his hard-on than I have been all night, and his zipper lays right over the culprit. I swallow hard and undo the button, then slowly and carefully slide down the zipper pull.

David sucks in a sharp breath, but his eyes still don't open, even as I battle his jeans down his hips without the benefit of him lifting his weight to help me. I'm nearly out of breath by the time he's in just his T-shirt and boxer briefs, and if David hadn't told me how much he hates sleeping in a shirt, I would just let it be.

I blow out a long-winded sigh and grab the hem, trying not to gawk as I carefully peel it up inch by inch to reveal abs carved to perfection. I'm wondering how to get the material over his broad shoulders when he sits up suddenly, hooking his arm around my waist, and I yelp in surprise as he hauls me onto his lap, our bodies completely flush. Need flares instantly, burning me everywhere his skin touches mine. His eyes lazily flutter open, dazed and confused, as if trying to deduce between dream and reality.

I can do nothing but sit here like a fool, rendered useless by the shock of desire as David's free arm reaches for the material at his nape. He yanks his whole shirt off in one not-so-smooth motion, its pass up and over his face seeming to uncloud his eyes from that dreamlike glaze.

David doesn't say anything, and I couldn't if I wanted to. We both just stare.

He licks his lip, and I swallow audibly.

And then he's casually and calmly laying back down, except he doesn't release my waist. He pulls me right with him, urging me to curl into him, and my body complies automatically before my brain can even process what's happening.

I don't dare even look up at David to see if his eyes are open or closed, and when I try to shift to give us a little space, his arm tightens around me to keep me in place.

So I give in.

I rest my head on his shoulder, my arm on his chest, and for the first time in my life, after all these nights in his bed, I sleep in David's arms.

* * *

I'm startled awake from a familiar dream, featuring David and me doing things no quasi-siblings should ever do. My body is still on edge from my own fantasy, and it takes me a minute to realize David's clean scent mixed with about a barrel and a half of whiskey isn't actually my imagination.

We're in bed, but we're not sleeping on opposite sides. And then last night comes crashing back, and my heart rate takes off at warp speed.

David may have fallen asleep on his back, but he's rolled onto his side to face me, and I seem to have burrowed into his chest like it's my own personal pillow. His arm is wrapped tight around my waist, ensuring our bodies are as close as possible, and I've hooked my leg around his in my sleep. And the worst part is, I don't have it in me to untangle myself from him.

His lips are so close to my forehead that his breath heats my skin, and it isn't until I finally look up that I even notice he's not asleep, either.

Somehow, in the dark, in the cocoon of his body, everything feels different. Less real. More real.

He can't be fully sober yet—I don't think I even am—but there's something present in his gaze that wasn't there a couple of hours ago.

"What happened?" he rasps, his voice gravelly from sleep.

What happened? Does he not remember wrapping me in his arms? Or worse—kissing me?

I pull back an inch and start to straighten my leg, but his hand shoots down to my thigh to stop me.

"Don't," he says, low and hoarse, and I stop breathing as he slowly guides my thigh further and higher, until we are even closer than before. He doesn't stop until I can feel his impossible hardness against the most sensitive part of me—the part that's positively aching for him—and my hands fly to his shoulders to brace myself.

David's eyes search mine for a reaction, but I'm completely helpless. His touch is my kryptonite and I surrender to it willingly.

"You kissed me," I blurt in a whisper. I know we're both already awake, but there's something surreal and intimate about this strange hour between night and day, like it's casting some kind of spell, and all I know is I don't want to break it.

David frowns.

"You asked what happened. Last night. You—"

"I know that, Bea."

Bea.

I swallow anxiously, excitedly, and my hips rock gently against him all on their own.

"Fuck," David grates out, his fingers tensing on my thigh, digging into my skin as if to still me, or encourage me. The deep furrow of his brow makes me think even he doesn't know for sure. He seems to be grappling with some profound ambivalence, and it keeps me still and silent until his eyes fall to my lips.

One of David's hands threads into the mess of blond tangles at my nape, the other releases my thigh to brush his knuckles along my cheek. He runs the pad of his thumb over my bottom lip. "You think I could forget kissing this mouth?"

I don't reply. I did think that. I *do* think it, and I can't help the flutter of shame that even after all that hard-worked therapy, my self-esteem with guys is still utterly pitiful.

But David doesn't need a reply. He's known me too long—too well. He shakes his head and lets out a short, soft ironic laugh. "You do, don't you?"

I force a halfhearted shrug, admitting nothing, but his eyes are too close—too piercing—and they miss nothing, too.

David frowns, considering something. "You know, Bea…for all the confusing-ass shit you cause in my fucked-up head, none of it has made me *blind*—you realize that, right?"

I blink at him. *What the hell is any of that supposed to mean?*

Another head shake. "You're…" He swallows down some unknown thought, and then blows out an exasperated sigh. "You're fucking *slamming*, Bea."

It's such an out of character thing to say that I don't immediately register his meaning, which, with even more exasperation, he seems to realize.

"Hot as fuck, Beth." He rolls his eyes. "You're goddamned hot as fuck."

I breathe out a small giggle at his choice of words. But my humor is cut short by the reality of them. David has never called me *hot*.

I murmur a cursory *thanks*.

But David isn't satisfied. His mouth slips into a roguish smirk, familiar but laced with something he's never directed at me before—*lust*. "You are, Bea. You've been driving me crazy all fucking night." He gently rolls his hips as if to punctuate his statement, and I gasp as he presses against my center in a way that has me raising my thigh even higher.

David's lips inch closer to mine. "Do you believe me, beautiful girl?" he breathes, with another taunting roll of his hips, and this time, I whimper.

David's eyes slam closed like it's too much for him. "This is so fucked up," he mutters to himself. But when his eyes reopen, all that's left in them is pure, primal hunger.

No one has *ever* looked at me like that.

His look alone sets my blood on fire, and I push into his hardness with shameless need.

David's hand tightens in my hair almost to the point of pain, like some kind of warning. But it's one I have no intention of heeding, and when I rock into him again and raise my mouth toward his, he doesn't wait to see if I'll have the nerve to kiss him—he just attacks.

His lips roughly capture mine, his tongue invading my mouth, his stubble burning my skin. His hands are everywhere all at once, yet it's not nearly enough. His weight shifts, and he rolls us so suddenly that I'm pinned beneath him before I can even steal a full breath, my legs folding around him, holding him between them like some wanton creature I don't even recognize.

God it feels amazing.

I don't even know if this is *real* right now. I could be dreaming, or it could just be that spell of the in-between hour before dawn breaks in earnest. All I know is, whatever it is, I'm grateful for it, and as David utterly consumes me, kiss by kiss, I know this isn't going to stop short like earlier. I can feel it in every desperate slide of his tongue, every urgent roll of his hips.

He finds the hem of my shirt, my arms lifting and our lips parting at just the right moments—and for *only* those moments—to get rid of the offending layer. It's as if every move is choreographed, coordinated in a perfect dance, like we've done it all a thousand times before.

His bare chest comes down on mine with finality. *There's no going back now.* And how could there be? The sensation of his smooth skin, the light spattering of hair against my sensitive breasts, his weight covering my body…It's all too much, and he swallows down my moan like he's starving for it. For *me*.

We don't stop for air until we're gasping for it, David resting his forehead against mine like that's how we belong. Face to face. Skin to skin. Breath to breath. It's so unfathomably intimate, and I think I like it almost as much as his kiss.

Almost.

He pulls back to look at me, his teeth practically bared in an expression of pure carnal intent. Between my legs, he's straining so hard against his boxers that I wonder how the cotton doesn't give. And I *want* it to give. I want it gone. I want to feel him against me…*inside me*.

"Bea," David says huskily. "If we do this…"

But I already know the end of the sentence. Maybe not the exact words, but the point. If we do this, *it can't happen again. Sammy can't find out. It can't change anything.*

"I know," I breathe.

I know all of it. And right now, I don't fucking care. All I care about is experiencing what this feels like when I'm not some frightened virgin, unsure about doing it in the first place. When it isn't all logistics and pain. I deserve to feel this with David—someone who knows what he's doing. Who will make me feel good. Who already makes me ache for him in ways I never felt with Brian.

I nod fervently, agreeing, reassuring, *begging*.

It's enough for David. His mouth is back on mine without another word, speaking instead with his almost brutal kisses, in a language I've never known, but am fast learning.

He rests his weight on one elbow, slipping his opposite hand between us to claim more of me. I don't tell him he already owns me in ways he'll never know. My fingers itch to launch an expedition of their own, and they trace the lines of muscle in his strong back.

His lips finally, reluctantly release mine to taste my skin, working a torturous path down my neck and along my collarbone, and when his palm closes over my breast, I arch up into him.

My heart races, but the rhythm of its beat never wavers—*Da-vid, Da-vid, Da-vid.*

His hand moves over my hip and my body aches so badly for him I fear I might implode. His answering need burns me through the thin layers of cotton that separate skin from skin, and I don't immediately realize his lips have even paused their sweet torment as my gaze drops to his boxer briefs. I want more than anything to tear them from him. David follows my line of sight, his lips quirking into a self-satisfied smirk. "See something you like?" he rumbles.

I blush, but instead of retreating, I nod.

His mirth fades instantly, and his mouth is back on mine. He starts to whisper how much he wants me, his voice low and gravelly, his words utterly surreal, and then he's got the waist of both my pajama shorts and panties in his grasp. He starts to peel them down, and my pulse takes off like wildfire with every inch of progress.

I hold my breath, not daring to watch him as he takes in my nakedness. But I don't miss his sharp exhale or his muttered curse. "This is so fucked up," he repeats, and I want to argue, but I can't. Because he's right. This is fucked up. But that doesn't make me want him any less.

And David appears to be in agreement as he comes back down over me, kissing me, tasting my skin, until I'm so wound up I can hardly breathe. I'm vaguely aware of a rustle of clothing before David's underwear follows mine over the side of the bed, and suddenly I'm staring at David March, naked. And it's glorious.

As if he knows I need a moment to take him in, he pauses above me, letting me shamelessly gawk. But he doesn't call me out on it. Because he's doing the very same thing.

But a moment is all either of us is willing to concede, because we crash back together almost violently, touching, tasting, teasing.

"*God*, Bea," David grits out between kisses. "You are so fucking sweet." His hand slides between my legs, and he begins to stroke me.

My eyes fall closed. It's been so long since I've been touched, and it was so different with Brian. I was so young. So nervous. I sigh, long and strangled, and then David's hand is gone, and he's leaning over me to grab what must be a condom from the nightstand. *A condom.*

This is really happening.

My heart stops as David positions himself, and he meets my eyes with a question that is entirely unnecessary. Because I'm more than *sure*—I'm positively *desperate* for him.

He mutters something to himself through clenched teeth that sounds vaguely like, "fuck it," and then, finally, David gives in.

He pushes inside me in one hard thrust, and I'm surprised by the shock of pain as his groan vibrates against my throat. I thought it was only supposed to hurt the first time, and I don't want David to know just how inexperienced I truly am. But as he starts to move inside me, surging and withdrawing again and again, his hips grinding boldly against mine, the pain begins to melt into something else.

Something *incredible*.

"*Fuck*, you feel *amazing*," David rasps, his words resonating in every part of me—even the one place it really shouldn't—and I silently scold my heart and demand it make itself scarce. "So fucking tight," he marvels. "So *wet. Goddamn,* beautiful girl…" He groans again, and it's the sexiest sound I've ever heard.

Unfathomable pleasure both sates and stokes my desire, and it's maddening. Because the better he feels, the more I need, and I shamelessly meet him thrust for thrust, my legs wrapped tightly around him like I can somehow trap him here with me.

On me.

In me.

The otherwise quiet room fills with the soundtrack of our recklessness—with every creak of the mattress and thump of the headboard, with our heavily labored breaths and collision of flesh—all of it growing in volume and intensity at a pace set by David's expert hips.

I try to keep my mind as present as possible, not wanting to miss a single detail, trying to etch it all permanently onto my brain. But there's too much sensation, too much *David*, and he's just *everywhere*.

My hands rove over each hill and valley of muscle in his strong, broad back, relishing the way they flex and roll, as if to memorize them for some sort of sensual topographic map. Because even as I surrender to his rhythm, even as I lose myself to every rock of his hips, every swipe of his hands, and every last claiming kiss, the awareness that I'll probably never experience this again is ever-present.

"Mother*fuck*, Bea," David growls, and just his nickname for me in that gruff, sexy tone sends waves of mind-numbing pleasure crashing through me like a tidal wave. It's unbelievable. The feeling of him so deep inside my most intimate place, not just moving, but positively *owning*.

"Oh God," I gasp, and it prompts David on.

Faster.

Harder.

Deeper.

And then his name rips from my throat as I shatter into nothing and everything, exploding in all directions, from the heights of the most sinful heaven to the depths of the sweetest hell. Excruciating pleasure seizes every cell in my body, and I clench madly around him, my limbs clamping down on him like I can somehow pull him deeper into not just my body, but my very soul.

"*Fuck*, Bea," David growls. "Motherfucking *Christ*." He never stops, and it's only as I start to come out the other end that I'm aware of his erratic rhythm, his smooth, tanned skin glistening with sweat as he chases release with a savage intensity that almost sends my body into an encore.

I come back to reality just in time to watch as he soars over the edge, his gorgeous features twisted in ecstasy or agony or both, as he drives himself as deep as he possibly can.

I am positively riveted.

"Oh, fuck, *Bea*!" he cries out. "*Fuck*." And then he stills, burying his face in my neck as he takes from my body everything he just gave it, clinging to me just as fiercely, as if he can somehow weld us together.

And if only he could. Because the minutes he takes to recover are pure bliss. Even his crushing weight feels like heaven. The afterglow of mind-blowing sex fills every empty place inside me—including my exiled heart—but it's the knowledge of the pleasure David just derived from *my* body that injects me with euphoria like a syringe filled with one of those drugs I've heard of but would never try. And this is exactly why.

Because even more than the incredible sex, this feeling—*this* is what is most dangerous. Because I could become addicted to this. And somewhere, in the darkest shadows of my mind, where my demons lie in wait, I'm afraid I already have.

Chapter Eighteen

Beth

My mind jolts awake, even as my body silently whines for five more minutes of sleep. My head pounds with the consequences of last night's drinking, and, brushing the tangle of blond out of my eyes, I roll onto my back and stretch my legs.

A sudden twinge of soreness between them snaps me back in focus. *David*.

Oh. My. God.

My skin flushes and my pulse skyrockets as every incredible sight, sound, and sensation comes flooding back. It takes me a moment to convince myself that it wasn't a dream. Because, *my God*, I never knew it could be like that.

But as I rub my thighs together to feel the evidence of last night— or this morning—more sharply, I realize I'm alone. I'm still fully naked, covered only by a white bedsheet, which David appears to have pulled up to my chin. I wrap it around my chest and sit up in bed. I notice his backpack isn't on its usual chair, and I frown as I see his jacket isn't slung over it, either.

My heart sinks slowly into my stomach, and I don't know why. Even mostly drunk, I knew exactly what last night was, and what it wasn't. David was perfectly clear, even if he didn't use so many words. I didn't expect anything to be different this morning…but that's just it. I didn't expect *anything* to be different this morning, and David's absence—waking up alone...that's different.

Old demons of insecurity and apprehension rear their ugly heads, reminding me that I'm now two-for-two. Both times I've had sex, I've managed to send the guy running. At least Brian left a note.

I laugh openly at myself as I swipe a nonsensical tear from my cheek. Everything is fine, and nothing has changed, so why won't this feeling of emptiness subside?

"Ugh," I whine, frustrated with myself. I push off the mattress and pad to the bathroom, determined to go about my normal routine.

Because why wouldn't I? Everything *is* normal.

It doesn't mean anything that David doesn't even have class until later this afternoon. Or that he didn't send me a text, or wake me to let me know where he was going.

I shake my head at the thought. Of *course* he didn't, because he doesn't owe me anything. That's not something we do. But as I apply my lip gloss, I squint at my reflection in the mirror, trying to remember if he's ever left the apartment before I woke up before, and I don't think he has.

The demons grow louder, and I try to shush them by telling myself he must have gone to the gym after all. Even though he hates going in the morning. And even though he's probably still half-drunk.

But as more details from last night gradually return, it becomes harder and harder to rationalize anything about this morning. Not David's leaving me alone in bed—without a word—just hours after having been inside me, and not my overzealous feelings.

Ugh. I *hate* feeling like this. I hate not knowing which emotions are reasonable, which concerns are justified. I make a mental note to schedule another video therapy session with Dr. Schall.

I just wish this morning didn't emulate that terrible one so vividly. The one that saw me wake up in my family's backyard gazebo, scared and sore and utterly alone, except for the handwritten note—the only one Brian ever wrote me—both swearing his love, and saying good-bye. I didn't know then just how final it was. That he would blow off my calls and texts, and ignore me in the halls at school, treating me as if I was invisible until I started to wish it were true. Until I had no choice but to face the consequences of our relationship utterly alone.

No wonder I feel so bleak. I'm completely off balance, and I have Brian to blame—so I do. Because as pissed as I was at David last night, it wasn't his hitting Brian that upset me. It was the babying—the over-protective treatment and distrust. Though in the cold light of day, I can admit that I may have earned the latter by lying.

But that punch? Brian deserved that punch, if perhaps not the ones that followed. *Perhaps*. He *did* call me a *slut* in the middle of a club, after all.

I meet my friend Toni, who lives on the first floor, in the lobby, and we make our way to campus, walking briskly in the crisp autumn sun. I can't escape the feeling that I'm being watched, and I look over my shoulder as an eerie chill creeps down my spine.

Instantly Brian and his selfish bullshit are far from my mind, and even David takes a backseat. Because he was right—Brody is still out there.

I scan the block of school buildings behind me. It's not especially busy, but students come and go, walking at varied paces, some with purpose, some lazily. Some even look familiar. But fortunately, none of them are Brody, so I keep up with Toni, pretending to listen to her story about rush week, stealing intermittent glances over my shoulder all the while.

When we come up to Standman quad, where we usually part ways to go to our respective classes, my hackles go up. But Brody isn't skulking in his alley, and I appear to be developing an entirely new kind of paranoia.

Great. Add it to the fucking list.

"Want to meet me in the library at, like, six? I want to get a head start studying for the midterm," Toni says.

And so do I. But not tonight. I want to be home just in case David does want to talk about what happened last night—this morning. At the very least I'm sure he could use some reassurances that everything is still the same between us. I certainly could.

"Monday instead? Tonight, I...I just—"

"Bethy."

Toni and I both turn, but I'm the only one who tenses so tightly I'm practically in rigor mortis.

Brian's brow is pulled low and his expression is guilty and contrite, but hopeful. And all I've got is anger.

"Bethy—"

"*Beth*." My short tone startles him, and I'm ashamed by the satisfaction it gives me.

"Are you okay, Beth?" Toni asks, eyeing Brian dubiously. She *should* be dubious of him—a man who can go from lover to ghost in a matter of hours.

I realize it isn't just last night I'm angry with Brian about, and I wonder if I ever really forgave him at all. "Yeah, Tone. I'm fine. This is just my *ex*." I don't know why I say the word *ex* so scathingly. Maybe I *want* to scathe him. Maybe I want him to feel a microscopic fraction of what I did for so damned long.

Brian visibly bristles at my tone, and instead of unsettling me, it gratifies me. *Who am I turning into?*

"You're sure?" Toni doesn't seem to be, but I assure her I'm fine, and air-kiss her cheek so she can get on to her class.

"What do you want, Brian?" I ask when she's gone. People keep moving around us, but Brian seems in no rush. He stares at me with that puppy-dog look and I want to slap it right off his face.

"You're mad." He states the obvious.

I glare at him.

Brian's frown deepens. "Bethy. *Beth*," he corrects himself before I do it for him. He takes a step forward, but I stand my ground. "I was drunk last night."

"So?" So was I. I didn't treat him like complete garbage.

Brian sighs. "I'm sorry, okay?" He takes another step forward but pauses halfway when I hold out my palm to stop him.

"*You're sorry…*" I breathe incredulously.

"I am, Beth—" Brian looks away for a beat, and when his gaze returns, the contrite puppy appears to have run off. His jaw clenches. "I saw you. Dancing with *March*. And I…" His nostrils flare as he sucks in a deep breath. "He was *all over you*, Bethy—*Bethy*!" he insists when I open my mouth to correct him this time, and I flinch. Brian doesn't notice. "You want to pretend we're fucking strangers? Fine. But *I* can't! I can't just stand around and watch David-fucking-March put his filthy fucking hands on you—"

"Who the hell asked you to stand anywhere?" I cut him off.

Brian's mouth drops subtly in surprise. I don't blame him. The *Bethy* he remembers wouldn't often speak her mind. But that girl died over three years ago when she swallowed a handful of pills.

"I didn't ask you to come here. I didn't ask to be friends. And I definitely didn't invite you to the club last night. What were you doing there anyway?" I demand.

Brian's eyes narrow slightly. "I went out with some guys from the team," he says defensively. "I wasn't expecting to see you there, you know, since you were so determined to focus on school that you don't have time to date and all."

"I'm *not* dating! I went out *dancing*—"

"With *March*!"

"So fucking *what*?" I snap back. "What if I *was* dating him? You're not my fucking boyfriend! And *you* did that. *You* walked away. After—" I slam my mouth shut, my eyes widening as my brain catches up with it, horrified that my eyes just refuse to stay dry. But that feeling of waking up alone—it's just too raw right now.

"You're not my boyfriend," I say more calmly. "You don't get to judge who I spend my time with or how I spend it. David was in my life long before you, and he's the one who stuck around, Brian. Not you," I remind him. I notice the strain grow around his eyes, but I ignore it. "If I want to dance with David—"

"*Dance?*" Brian scoffs, his eyes narrowed in derision. "If you weren't wearing clothing he would have been *inside you!*"

"Because I'm such a fucking *slut?*" I say slowly.

Brian glares at me, his jaw tight like its holding in a cutting retort. And I don't know why. He didn't bother to hold back last night.

"Is that it, Brian?"

He huffs out a sharp breath, shaking his head. "No! *No*, that's not fucking *it*! Goddamn it!" He shakes his head.

Suddenly some guy is wedging himself between us, and I recognize him as someone I'd noticed while Toni and I were walking from our building. Actually he looks familiar from before then, too. "Is there a problem here?" he demands of Brian, who looks dumbfounded.

"And who the fuck are you?" he spits.

"Who the fuck are *you?*" the stranger counters.

Brian takes a step toward him in challenge, but the guy seems all too ready for a fight, and for a moment I wonder if I really come off so goddamned helpless that random men feel the need to come to my rescue. But then my brain makes the connection.

"*Rectum?*"

The guy throws me a look over his shoulder, and I realize he doesn't appreciate my using his pledge name just now. I bite back a very small smile.

What was his real name again? Or his full pledge name at least?

Rectum Ralph, I recall.

Lovely.

"What are you doing, Ralph?" I ask.

"Who the fuck is this, Beth?" Brian demands. *Demands*—like I owe him fucking *anything*.

Ralph blanches. "Uh…I just…" He forces a sheepish smile. "I was just doing a pledge task."

My fingers come up to rub my temples, my head practically vibrating with the consequences of last night's indulgences. "And what pledge task would that be?" I ask dryly.

But I've already deduced the short of it, and I'm already furiously telling David off in my mind. Because *seriously? This* is his response to my complaining about him babying me? Enlisting his fraternity pledge to do it *for* him?

"Christ, Ralph, you don't have to follow me around." I roll my eyes. "Don't you have class or something?"

He shrugs. "Not for an hour."

I struggle to keep my patience. "Ralph, I'm fine. I can handle Brian." My eyes hold his over Ralph's shoulder. I want Brian to know he doesn't intimidate me. "You can go now, Rectum."

Ralph shifts uncertainly on his feet. "I can't really—"

Oh for God's sake! "Ralph, you can risk your BEG bid or I can report you to campus security for stalking."

His eyes go wide.

"What the fuck?" Brian murmurs, pissed off for sure, but not actually doing anything about it, I note.

Ralph holds up his palms in surrender.

"And you can tell whoever assigned you this task," I add, not wanting to say too much in front of Brian, "to leave me the hell out of your stupid frat bullshit."

Ralph forces a smile, but I know he plans to tell David no such thing, just as I suspect he doesn't plan to go very far at all. He won't disobey David. *Stupid frat bullshit*, indeed. But I don't really care, to be honest, as long as he stays out of sight and out of my way.

I wait until he's out of earshot to turn back to Brian, who looks about ready to explode. But I don't care about *that*, either, and I don't give him the opportunity.

"Don't," I say sternly, my palm splayed for effect.

I take a step back, glaring at Brian. My head shakes all on its own. *Why am I discussing this with him at all?* "You wanted to be friends," I remind him. "I gave it a shot." And I did.

Brian's eyes widen and his brows pinch together anxiously. "Bethy—"

"Beth!" I shout. It shuts him up. "It's *Beth*. And you know what, Brian? I'm done."

He opens his mouth to say something, but thinks better of it.

"You should be glad I had the nerve to tell you in person. A lesser person might just leave a note."

I walk away.

* * *

As if this morning with David and my confrontation with Brian weren't enough, Brody is back in abnormal psych, and I spend the entirety of the hour painstakingly staring ahead. Fortunately, like he did on the first day of class, he pushes his way out the moment we're dismissed, and I take the fact that he didn't try to approach me as a good sign.

By the time I walk home, I'm so mentally exhausted I wouldn't even be able to argue with Dicknose—who follows about fifteen feet behind me at all times—even if I wasn't secretly grateful for his presence now that Brody is apparently back on campus.

So much for moving back to Standman any time soon.

I've resisted texting David all day, but I at least thought he'd be waiting at the student union to walk me home. Our schedules finish around the same time on Fridays, and I can't recall one where he wasn't waiting to the left of those double doors, leaning against the building, smoking a cigarette like he had zero fucks to give. Until I showed up, and then his face would break out into that rogue, lopsided grin.

My heart flips and spins like an Olympic diver, before crashing into the cold water below. It's a sensation I've been experiencing all day—every time I remember that stolen pre-dawn hour with David, and then the reality of waking alone. Again.

I consider he might have gone home early, maybe hoping I'd do the same, so that we might have some time to talk. David will be gone most of the weekend for some big pledge event they're planning, coming home only to sleep—and who knows how much of that he'll even be doing.

I glance at my phone one last time before I head upstairs, but David hasn't texted me, either, and while that isn't weird for us, for some reason it still unsettles me.

Part of me expects to find him in the apartment, but it's unnervingly quiet. So I remind myself that everything is just fine, and decide to take a shower.

It isn't until I'm making myself a sandwich in David's kitchen—which is now stocked with actual food—that I see it. My breath rushes out and my heart stops beating. Because sitting out on the kitchen counter is a note.

David left me a fucking note.

It all hits me at once.

Everything is *not* fine. Things are *not* normal. Everything *has* changed between David and me, and now, not only won't David talk to me, but it seems he can't even be in my presence.

Suddenly I recall the last time David disappeared from my life without explanation. After the night I first met Brian—the night I thought, for one blissful moment, that David might see me as something more than just his friend's little sister. He and Sammy had gotten into a fight after that, one of the only fistfights of their twenty-year friendship. Sammy came home with a bruised jaw, and David stayed away from our house for the longest time I could ever remember. When he showed up a few weeks later with a fading black eye, I was already dating Brian, and while that brief moment—when David had stared at my lips outside that party—still held a part of me hostage, to him it was obviously long forgotten. Or so I'd believed.

But…what if this is his M.O.? What if I didn't imagine that almost-kiss, and David's subsequent disappearance from our house had nothing to do with his fight with Sammy at all? Maybe that's just what David does after a hookup—or *almost hookup*—he makes himself scarce. It certainly fits with his reputation when it comes to girls.

I don't bother to read David's note, instead crumpling it into a ball and tossing it where it belongs. Then I take out the trash and toss it down the chute so I can't be tempted to retrieve it later. Because it doesn't matter which words he chose to send the message. I received it loud and clear.

David and I—we don't share some inexplicable connection. He doesn't care about *me*. What he cares about is his friendship with my brother—the same way Brian, at the end of the day, cared about his "freedom."

I swipe violently at my cheeks, angry at my tears, at Brian, and at David…but mostly I'm angry at myself. Because of all people, I should know better.

I email Dr. Schall to set up a time to talk, and then call my brother and his girlfriend, Rory. She's the person I wish I could talk about David with the most. After two years, she has become like a sister, and with everything we have in common, I just know she'd get what I'm feeling. But if I told her what happened last night, she'd either tell Sammy, or she wouldn't; and if not, she'd have to lie to him. And I don't want to put Rory in the middle of everything.

I end up inviting Lani, Elise, and Toni over, and we binge-watch bad reality TV and order pizza. They offer to stay over, but I feel guilty inviting overnight guests to an apartment that isn't mine, and anyway, David will need to come home to sleep at some point.

But he doesn't.

Long after the girls leave, I still can't bring myself to climb into David's bed. I don't know how I can lay on the pillow that smells like him, or slide between the sheets that smell like us. I take a double dose of my anti-anxiety meds—the dose prescribed to help me sleep—and I'm still on the couch when my Kindle starts to blur. I don't even care about getting a sore neck as I give in and let myself drift off to sleep.

* * *

My dreams are beautifully vivid and perfectly meaningless, and I'm in such a deep sleep that I only vaguely register the creak of the front door, or the muffled rush of the shower running, and when a warm set of knuckles strokes along my cheek, I'm only half-awakened.

I think I hear my name. Or not my name. *Bea*. But only David calls me that, and I don't remember where he is, or why, but I do know he's not here. A sigh, and then I'm being hoisted into strong arms, and my own come up to automatically wrap around the neck of whatever figment my mind has conjured up. But his scent wraps around me like a blanket of David and whiskey, and I let it comfort me. I'm too lost in my own subconscious to deny myself this small solace, and I rest my face in the crook of his neck, inhaling more of him, relishing the scrape of his stubble against my cheek.

Vaguely I marvel at how well my mind seems to have memorized every detail of David, and I wonder how often it will let me indulge in him.

In my dream I'm carried to his bedroom, and I will him to make some kind of move—any move. But he just lays me on the bed and folds his large body around me from behind, nuzzling into my hair. "I'm sorry, Bea," he whispers. "I fucked up. I *always* fuck up."

I try to get my vocal cords to work, but nothing happens. All I manage to do is gently snuggle back into him.

His arms tighten around me. "I'm sorry."

The next thing I'm aware of is the bright room, and the fact that I am not waking up on the couch I fell asleep on. It's morning and I'm in David's bed, but I'm once again alone.

At least he doesn't leave a note.

Chapter Nineteen

David

I walk into the frat house after my last class and head straight down to Reeve's basement bedroom. It's the only one down here, and it's more like a small studio apartment than a bedroom—at least three times the size of most of the others, with half a kitchen and its own bathroom. But Reeve chose it for the same reason the rest of the guys didn't—it's secluded as fuck.

It also happens to be right off the basement gym, and that's where I find him tonight, getting ready to lift weights. I usually spot for him, which works out, since we both prefer to work out in the evenings. Or we did, before I turned out to be an epic pussy and started doing my workouts in the morning just to have an excuse to avoid Beth. But I need to avoid her in the evenings, too, so Reeve and I take turns spotting and lifting, working ourselves past the point of exhaustion, both running from different versions of the same thing, and neither ever getting very far.

But I don't know how to face her. Not after what I did.

Beth might think it was just a drunken hookup between friends…but what kind of *friend* takes advantage of a girl when she's been drinking—and his best friend's kid sister, at that? Even if I wasn't exactly in my right mind, either. But that's the problem—because even *in* my right mind, as guilty as I feel over it…I still fucking *want* her.

And that's my burden alone. Because *wanting* isn't the issue—
I've always *wanted* her. It's this precarious living arrangement that
tempted me beyond my restraint, and since Beth's safety is paramount,
I have to find some way to make it work. So that's what I've been trying to do. By keeping my distance. By leaving before she wakes up in
the morning, and staying out until I know she's probably asleep. And
by enlisting the pledges as my surrogate *bodyguards*.

In fact, right now, Rectum Ralph should be walking her home
from class, or to the student health center to volunteer. Or not so much
walking her as *following from a reasonable distance*, if you want to get
into semantics.

Reeve and I finish lifting and head into his room where I pour
myself a double of Jack and down it in one quick swallow before pour-
ing another. I power on Reeve's laptop and sign into my document
cloud, opening the play I finished writing down here these past couple
nights—the one I'm submitting to the theater department. The one
all about forbidden fruit and addiction and fucking disaster—that, if
selected out of hundreds, will earn me a significant grant, and the opportunity to actually have it *produced*. It's a pipe dream, but as I read
over the words I wrote just last night, it's one that feels just a bit closer.

I email it to my Playwriting professor with a strange reluctance. It
somehow feels a little too personal.

I force the thought away, and check my phone for an update from
Rectum, but I know it's still too early. Beth would have just gotten
out of class a few minutes ago. So I take another swig of my whiskey
and crack open a window before lighting a cigarette. These past few
nights, Reeve and I have spent less time with the rest of the guys and
more of it drinking alone down here like a couple of alcoholic recluses.
Reeve spends his time drawing angrily in that sketchbook he never
lets anyone see, and I've been furiously typing away as if finishing my
play would somehow get Beth out of my system.

It didn't. And I just can't deal with the guys right now. I can't listen to them talk their big game about pussy, and girls that mean nothing to them, and their pointless, easy bullshit. Not with everything on the line right now—my friendship with Cap, and Beth, my fucking sanity—all of it in danger of crumbling into fucking pieces.

Fucking *shit*. Why did I have to go and *do* this? 'The fuck is *wrong* with me?

For the first time in my defiant, rebellious life, I realize my father was fucking right about me, and it makes me sick to my stomach. Because this is who I am—the guy who always insists on crossing every goddamned line anyone has ever drawn in front of him, as if they only even exist as some kind of test. A way to prove they don't apply to me. Because they *don't*. They never have.

Except this one.

This *one* line applied—the only one I ever respected. And it wasn't an accident, either—it was conscious, and deliberate. I knew crossing that line would end my friendship with Cap, and even if that was something I was willing to sacrifice, which it wasn't—*isn't*, I silently correct myself—it's not like I'd get to keep Beth in my life if I had a falling out with her brother. He was the only reason I ever saw her in the first place. Before she got to campus this fall, anyway.

Cap's position is clear—has been for years—and now I'm lying to my oldest friend, not only about Beth being in physical danger with Brody, or emotional danger with Falco, but I'm lying about her being *safe* with *me*. Because after what happened last week, I can't continue to pretend that she is. At least not to myself.

Reeve's phone buzzes with a message, and his mouth twitches as he reads the screen—something he's been doing more and more of lately, I've noticed.

"Is that Lani again?"

"Fuck off," Reeve replies automatically, and I shake my head at him.

Reeve tosses his beer bottle in the trash and pops open a new one.

"I'm gonna go up and watch the game, " he murmurs as he takes a generous sip. "You should come up. For a while, at least. Bogart was talking shit about us blowing them off."

We roll our eyes almost in unison. But I get it. Not living in the frat house isn't a big deal as long as I still spend most of my free time here, like the other brothers who live in the dorms or off campus do—and like I did freshman and sophomore year. And even if I was here more this past weekend than I have been since Beth first started staying with me, I've been hiding down here with weights, and whiskey, and words, and I know I've been neglecting my brothers. But my head has just been all kinds of fucked up, and it's becoming too much damned work to play the easygoing version of myself they've all come to expect. All except Reeve, anyway.

I blow out a long-winded sigh, wondering if this is how Reeve feels all the time. I still don't know much about his ex, but I know she did a fucking number on him, and a part of me admires him for not bothering to pretend otherwise.

Pretending is fucking exhausting.

"Yeah. I feel you, brother," I mutter, no more enthused than he is. I shove a hand through my hair, wanting to tear it right out of my damned head. Because I don't know what the fuck else to do anymore. This hiding bullshit obviously isn't working for me. *Nothing* seems to be fucking working. Being close to Beth didn't work, and being away from her is working even less, and these past few nights, if I didn't at least have those few dark hours before dawn to feel her in my arms, I might genuinely lose my damned mind. "I'm just going to finish my cigarette first." Reeve's room is one of the only ones in the house that is smoker-friendly.

My phone buzzes, and I eagerly open Rectum Ralph's text, ready to feel that subtle sense of relief as I read his update on Beth. Because it's supposed tell me either that she's home safe at my place, or that he's waiting outside while she volunteers at the new student chatline.

But it doesn't. My heart freezes before scrambling like a fighter jet as I read Rectum's message. Because the fucker's fucking *lost* her.

Lost. Her. Like she's a fucking puppy who broke away from her leash.

I have him on the phone a second later, and his bullshit excuse does not calm me one iota. Like I give a fuck how sure he'd been that she was heading to the student health center. Like his worthless fucking *certainty* is a good enough reason to follow farther behind than usual, only to lose her when she changed directions. *Fucking moron.*

I order Rectum Ralph to go check the student health center just in case, spitting out enough expletives to fill a fucking sonnet, letting it all out on him so I don't unload on Beth. Because she's my next text.

Where are you?

I stare at the screen, and wait, clutching my phone so hard I'm lucky it doesn't crumble in my hand. But I don't have fucking time for this shit, so I do the unthinkable, and call her. It rings until voicemail, and my stomach bottoms out. Something's not right. We're strictly-*text* people, so she knows if I'm calling, I have to have good reason, and whatever fucked-up state our friendship may be in right now, she'd never blow me off like that.

Right?

For a split second, I entertain the possibility that she might be mad at me for *not calling*, or something. But it's not like that with Beth and me. It never has been. We go days, weeks, sometimes even months without connecting, and it never means we're any less...well, whatever we are.

But then again, I've never been inside her before, either.

Fuck, what have I done?

I know I've taken the coward's way out by hiding down here these past few nights, but now that we know what happens when we get too close, surely Beth understands why it's best that I stay away, doesn't she? At least for now, while the memory of her naked body, of the way she moaned my name, is still so fucking fresh.

I force that, too, out of my mind.

I knew what this was. Even as I gave in to the temptation I'd been fighting for what felt like millennia, even as I grasped onto the alcohol as an excuse to let myself break, I knew it wasn't real. That it was just a stolen hour gifted by Beth's whim and her libido, and most definitely by that fucking dance at Hot Box.

I knew better than to get that fucking close to her.

But it won't happen again, and at least that's one thing I know Beth is on the same fucking page about. Because her "I know" came faster than I could get even my words out—faster than I could get to the part about it being a one-time thing—about it not changing anything between us.

Because, *fuck*, was it reckless. If Cap ever found out—ever even *suspected*—he would be done with me. And the truth is, I don't know what that version of my world even looks like.

My father barely speaks to me these days—has barely spoken to me ever since he failed to force me into a business major so I could "become a productive member of society and someday support a family," and though my mother still calls every few weeks to *check in*, it's all surface-level bullshit. She follows my dad's lead; she always has, whether she agrees with him or not. In fact, I wonder if she even has her own opinions anymore, or if years of deferring to those of someone else has trained them away.

But the fact remains that Cap, Tuck…Beth—they're all I've really got. Sure, I've got Reeve, and the rest of the brothers, I guess, but it's different.

But I can't even worry about fucking Cap right now—not when Beth is fucking *missing*.

I try calling her again. Nothing.

Shit.

I call Toni next, thinking she might know where Beth is, or could at least go up and knock on my door to see if she's there. But she doesn't fucking answer, either. Then I try Lani, but she's at Campus West, and hasn't seen Beth since class this morning. I try the line for the front desk of my building, but Barney, our doorman, says he hasn't seen her, either. He reports back five minutes later that there was no answer at my door. Fucking *shit*!

I grab Reeve's beer from him just as he's about to tilt it to his mouth. Thank fuck he's only had the one. "You're driving."

He blinks at me for a beat before he registers the panic in my eyes, and I watch his own shift from surprise to purpose with one sharp nod.

We fly up the basement stairs and throw open the door at the top. I need my apartment keys. They're in my jacket. *Where the fuck did I toss that thing?*

"Where's the fire, March?" Steven-fucking-Bogart calls from the couch. "Pussy emergency? You and your boyfriend finally spend so much time down there that your dick's demanding you go find a female to stick it in?" He guffaws like he's made some genius quip, and, as always, Sal, his trusty fucking sidekick, follows.

"I'm around the block," Reeve murmurs, ignoring Steven. "I'll pull around," and he's through the front door.

I grab my jacket from the arm of the sofa, ready to wait outside for Reeve, but on second thought, I pause. He's going to be a minute, anyway.

"You hear from Liz?" I ask Steven. And not just because I'm still desperate to somehow convince her to cooperate with the detectives— even if that's still truer than ever. But because as douchey as Steven can get when he drinks, he's still my boy—my fraternity brother—and he does sincerely care about Liz. He's not one to admit it, of course, and if it ever comes up, his default mode is to cover it up with dirty jokes and sexual innuendo. But he's chased her since freshman year, and they've gotten pretty close, so no one was surprised that her attack hit him hard.

He looks back to the Jets game. "Nah." But I don't miss the strain in his shoulders.

So Liz isn't talking to him, either. That's got to hit hard, too, but no way would Bogart admit he was hurt by it, any more than he'd admit he's worried about Liz.

I should say something comforting, or encouraging, but I can't. I can't even imagine how he feels, knowing how scared she must have been—that he wasn't there to help her. If anything like that ever happened to Bea—

I'm out the door without another word, jogging to the curb to look for Reeve's car, which by some miracle is just swerving over to let me in.

Chapter Twenty

David

Reeve and I spend the better part of two hours searching every spot on campus I've ever known Beth to step foot in. And come up fucking empty.

In the end, I do nothing but sit on this sadistic fucking couch, rubbing my throbbing temples, staring at my phone on the coffee table in front of me. It comes to life every now and then, taunting me with hope, only to flash with the name of someone other than the person I'm worried nauseous over right now.

I haven't fucking moved since I got home almost thirty minutes ago, and the only thing keeping me somewhat sane is knowing that that piece of shit Brody hasn't been around. There's no way Beth would keep it from me if he were back on campus, even if she *was* mad at me.

My phone lights and vibrates, and I barely cast the screen a perfunctory glance when her name stabs me in the chest with a *Pulp Fiction*-level shot of adrenaline.

At least she's returning my missed calls.

"Where the fuck are you?" I roar in greeting. But even as I silently warn myself to dial it back, there's another voice, a darker one, reminding me she's the one who's out of line. Yet a-fucking-gain.

"Whoa," she breathes. Like I've caught her off guard—like I'm fucking *overreacting*.

"Damn it, Beth! *Where?*"

"I'm walking home from the rec center with Toni! Fucking *God*!" she snaps back, her voice an octave higher than a moment ago.

But I don't give a fuck about her attitude, and the tension in my neck and shoulders gradually loosens in relief. "The fuck were you doing at the rec center?" I ask, light-years more calm.

It seems to take Beth aback for a moment. "Are you seriously shouting at me right now? For *what*? And what *are* you—my fucking keeper?" she demands angrily.

I don't point out that I am *not*, in fact, *shouting at her right now*. Because now that I know she's fine—that she's on her way home, and not walking around alone in the dark—the urgency gripping my stomach relaxes its hold. "We'll talk about it when you get home," I promise her.

Fuck my fucking life.

I still haven't moved an inch when Beth waltzes into my apartment like she doesn't have a care in the world, tosses her bags on the floor and her keys in the bowl on the kitchen island, and helps herself to a bottle of water from the fridge—all without so much as fucking acknowledging me. So I continue to fucking sit here, elbows resting on my knees, eyes following her intently around the room.

"Beth." My voice is low.

I frown as I notice not only her school bag, but the small sports duffel carelessly dropped just inside the door. The sight of it ignites images of her packing her things that night after Hot Box, reminding me how few cards I actually hold in this whole situation.

"Where were you?" I ask again.

Beth's eyes flare, but she chews the inside of her cheek, holding back whatever it is she really wants to say, keeping up the casual act just to piss me off. Or to challenge me. Like we're locked in some game of *giving-a-fuck* chicken, and neither of us wants to blink first. "I told you. I was at the rec center," she says carefully, like I'm fucking obtuse.

I suck in a deep breath, my nostrils flaring with my long exhale as I try to beat her at her own game. *Calm and casual.* "With Toni…"

"Why does that matter?" she asks, trying to bait me.

"Did you walk there with Toni, too?" Even tone. Standard volume. *So far, so good.*

"Why don't you ask one of your fucking spies?" Beth crosses her arms over her chest obstinately.

I would if you hadn't fucking lost him! I want to shout. "That's not what they are." *Keep it the fuck together, March.*

Beth takes several steps toward me. "Is that why they follow me all around campus? And insert themselves into my conversations?" she huffs. But I know the *conversation* she's talking about. Rectum Ralph reported it to me on Friday right after it happened.

I stand from the couch. "You mean, when your piece-of-shit ex-boyfriend had the balls to shout at you in the middle of Standman quad? That *conversation?*"

This isn't about jealousy. Having Beth under me may have been some next-level shit, but that doesn't mean I want Beth for myself. At least not in any way other than the way I've *always* wanted her. And it isn't about fear, either. My stomach may roll at the thought of Falco telling her about the night he broke up with her—about the part I played—and the truth is, lately I've been wondering if I shouldn't just tell her everything myself. But I can't afford a distraction right now.

Because this matters. Beth's safety *matters*. *She* matters.

And that's all this is. It doesn't mean something more now because I've been inside her, and pretending otherwise is just high school bullshit. So why is Beth acting like she doesn't give a fuck about me one way or the other? To fucking prove something? Well, all she's proven is that this little casual act of hers is starting to piss me off.

"So he did tell you," Beth mutters coolly.

"Of course he fucking told me!" I growl.

Beth advances another few steps, and the closer she gets, the less control I have over any of this. "But he's not a fucking spy, right?" she retorts.

I glower at her. When will she get it through her pretty blond head? Brody could *hurt* her! And Falco could—well, he could hurt her, too. Maybe even worse. My gut rolls with panic. How can I just stand here and watch it happen all over again?

"You know what, kid?" I default to my unaffected tone, despite just having told myself how pointless and immature it is. "I'm not the one that ran straight from another man's bed into the arms of her ex."

Beth's mouth drops open before she clamps it shut, but her eyes are on fire with righteous indignation. Finally—*something*.

I keep up the detached act if only because it seems to make a dent in her armor. "You know, I'd love to know why *I'm* the one lucky enough to be the target of your wrath yet a-fucking-gain, when I've done nothing but go out of my way to look out for you. Meanwhile, Falco treats you like you're fucking disposable, disappears for three years, then calls you a goddamned *slut*, and you're all, 'forgiveness' and 'friendship' and motherfucking rainbows." I cock my head at her. "I'm starting to think you're doing it just to fuck with me. Either that, or you're just so goddamned stubborn that you're determined to let someone who has repeatedly fucked you over be a part of your life no matter what they do." I raise my eyebrows, as if to say, *your move*.

But the explosion I expect—that I'm fucking desperate for at this point—doesn't come. Beth eyes me thoughtfully with that same deep blue gaze that always sees too damned much, and I get the eerie feeling that she's got some ace up her sleeve. But all she says is, "*I'm* the stubborn one? Really, David?"

I shrug. "You know what they say about shoes fitting."

Beth's calm is no longer an act, but there's nothing casual about it—in fact, she's deathly serious. "I'd rather give someone a chance who may not deserve it than block people from my life who might not deserve *that*, either."

I blink at her. *Has she lost her goddamned mind?* "You're telling me you think Falco might not deser—"

"I'm not fucking talking about Brian!" Beth's patience goes up in smoke.

Fucking finally! But if she doesn't mean Falco, then—

"I'm talking about *you*, David," she says sharply. Her glare is brutal and unforgiving.

"'The fuck are you talking about, Beth?'"

She bites her lips, and I can't help but recall how sweet they tasted—how they ruined my favorite dessert for life—and I think of how incredible she must taste in other places. *Fuck me*, my mouth starts to water, and I have to swallow before I start drooling like a fucking hound.

But Beth's hesitation fuels my curiosity. "How am I stubborn, exactly?"

She meets my gaze dead-on. "Have you met your birth parents yet, David?"

Her question washes over me in a surreal wave of shock—at the subject, at the fact that after years of never mentioning it, she's bringing it up for the second time in as many fucking weeks. And at its possible relevance to Brian fucking Falco.

"As smooth as you are at changing the subject, I'm not quite as dense as you seem to think."

I glare at her.

"Maybe I am stubborn, David," she murmurs, a little defeated, a little resigned. "But you are, too. And like I said, I'd rather be the girl who gives people chances and gets screwed over, than the guy who doesn't care enough to let anyone in—who refuses to give people a chance just to punish them for a choice they made two decades ago!"

Shit. I don't know what to say. The thing is, Beth is right. Of course she's fucking right. And who the hell am I to judge her?

I suck in a deep breath and take a seat on the evil fucking couch, sagging under the weight of her accusation—of its accuracy, and what it cost me. Because I *was* too stubborn to reach out to my birth parents. *At first*. Until the night I snuck Beth into a nightclub in Puerto Rico, and she called me out on my bullshit. I'd said I wasn't brave enough—she said I just didn't really want it. She has no idea how right she was...*is*.

"I did." My voice is so low that, if not for her soft gasp in the otherwise silent room, I'd think she hadn't heard me. "Give them a chance."

"You...you met them?" Beth whispers tentatively as she takes a few hesitant steps toward me.

I nod. "Well, I met *her*. Turns out *he* was only ever in the picture for the one night." I resist the impulse to throw on a smirk and make light of it all. I think Beth has always seen through my bullshit anyway.

Beth closes the rest of the distance between us, and she shouldn't. She really fucking shouldn't. "When?" she asks gently, completely at odds with her tone of just moments ago.

"Few years ago," I murmur. She's close enough now that I can touch her, and I do. It's not even a conscious choice.

I reach for her hips, my thumbs slowly brushing back and forth, just under the hem of her shirt. I pull her even closer, guiding her between my open legs, looking up at her from my seated position. She doesn't resist. She should resist. Because I'm not sure I can.

"Well, what's she like?" Beth's hopeful eyes are wide with interest, and I don't want to crush her, but I'm surprised to find that for entirely selfish reasons, I do want to tell her about Delia.

But first things first.

I pull Beth down to my lap, needing to feel more of her—though I'm careful to position her so her sweet, round little ass doesn't meet the proof of how she affects me. But—inexplicably natural as it may feel—sitting like this, touching like this, it's not something we do, and Beth's eyes and mouth go adorably round as she gasps her surprise.

The sound instantly resonates low in my belly, shooting straight to my dick.

In a small act of mercy, Beth doesn't resist or pull away. Instead, her hands come up to brace against my shoulders, and just the sensation of her touch, even through my T-shirt, has me dying to feel her everywhere.

"So you want to hear about Delia?" I mean to sound teasing, but my husky tone makes it hard to pull off.

Beth nods a little uncertainly, and a loose lock of gold falls in front of the deep blue still waters of her eyes.

I tuck it neatly behind her ear, but not before stroking the soft strands with my thumb. "Okay. But first I want to know what you were doing at the rec center tonight."

Beth's eyes narrow slightly at my manipulation, but she gives in with a resigned sigh. "I signed up to take a dance class, okay? With Toni. It's not a big deal—just for fun, you know?"

A dance class? Well, that was definitely not on my list of explanations for her disappearance, or imagined worst-case scenarios. My mouth twists into a smile. "That's great, Bea." And I mean it. "As long as you don't walk there alone—at least at night, and at least for now." I mean that, too, and I hold my breath, needing her to agree—to give me this. Some goddamned peace of mind. Because she's driving me crazy. Or I'm driving myself crazy.

Beth rolls her eyes. "I thought we already talked about this."

She tries to turn away but I grip her jaw, forcing eye contact. "So did I," I grit out, my blood humming with frustration. "Did you even read my fucking note?"

"No," she snaps back, yanking her face from my grasp, and she takes advantage of my moment of surprise, pushing off of my lap and putting a few inches of space between us.

I turn to face her on the couch. "*No?*"

"*No*," she huffs again.

I raise my eyebrows, silently demanding an explanation.

But her eyes—those vast, expressive oceans that both hide and reveal so much—hold fierce. "I figured whatever you had to tell me you could do it in person when you saw me," she says carefully. She pauses to let me feel the full weight of her implication, and I do. And it pummels me right in the chest. "I assumed it was just a list of *safety rules*, anyway," she grumbles.

I barely manage to mask my wince. Not only do I feel like a bag of shit for spending the past few nights hiding from her in my frat house basement like a fucking loser, and even worse at hearing her call me out on it, but on top of everything, she's fucking *right*. That note *was* mostly a list of rules. Well, that, and a reminder of what she already knew—already agreed to the night before. That as amazing as it was, it couldn't change anything, and wouldn't happen again.

But even as I think it, my dick twitches just inches from Beth's perfect ass, precariously taunting me with the temptation of more.

"My dad used to do that," Beth murmurs. "To my mom." Her thin brows pinch together in thought, and I can't help but think how adorable she looks like that. Still, I want so much to run the pad of my thumb over every frown line—to iron them out until her beautiful skin is free of them completely. "He'd get mad at her for some reason or another, and give her the silent treatment," Beth continues. "For days, sometimes weeks. And these stupid fucking notes were the only way he'd communicate with her at all. Like he couldn't even stand to look at her, let alone talk to her."

I grab Beth's wrist to get her attention, scooting automatically closer to her. Her eyes collide with mine—innocence, desire, and fear clashing with guilt, raging lust, and fear of something else entirely. "That's not what that was about, Bea. I'm not like him," I swear to her—to myself.

Her frown lines deepen. "I know that," she whispers, and I believe her. I think she knows it with more certainty than I do.

I shake my head in self-condemnation. "Fuck, Bea. You're right. That note *sucked. I* suck." I rake my fingers through my hair, more frustrated with myself, with this situation—with my fucking *life*—than she knows.

"You slept with me, and then you disappeared." She lays it all out for me in stark, bitter truths.

"I was avoiding you," I admit.

Her full lower lip trembles ever so slightly, and before I realize what I'm doing, I run the pad of my thumb from one corner to the other. They're so impossibly soft, and I can't help picturing them sliding over the skin of another part of my body—the part that doesn't seem to remember how we got ourselves into this clusterfuck of a situation in the first place.

I take her chin and lift it to guide her gaze back to mine. "Not because I didn't want to talk to you," I assure her with more fervor than the moment probably calls for. "I just…" I brush another lock of gold out of her face. "I didn't know what to say, Bea. I pussied the fuck out." I blow out a long breath as if to punctuate my confession.

Beth isn't satisfied. "Why? You should be a pro at the whole friends-with-benefits thing, shouldn't you?"

But the girls I've fucked around with—they were always more *benefits* than friends, and not knowing what to say, I simply stare at her.

"You know what, David?" Beth takes a deep breath, then squares her shoulders as if steeling herself, and it takes me off guard. "I could sit here and pretend it was just a drunken mistake—and maybe it was. But I made a decision, and I'm responsible for that. And the truth is, until I saw your stupid fucking note, I didn't regret it, David. In fact, I…" she trails off and looks away, her cheeks heating in a gorgeous blush that sweeps down her delicate throat and over her cleavage before disappearing beneath the neckline of her shirt.

But I finally know what those gorgeous tits look like bare and flushed, and my dick throbs violently at the memory.

"I liked it," she says with far less confidence.

But her admission has the opposite effect on my own confidence, and fuck me and my precarious self-restraint. My knuckles find her jaw, and they stroke her soft skin, following the path of her blush down the column of her neck. I picture the way that neck arched in ecstasy, her mouth gasping my fucking name as her fingernails clawed at my back.

She *liked* it? *Bullshit.* She fucking *loved* it.

"So, do you regret it now?" I ask, feeling her out, my voice low, and more hoarse than I intend.

"What does it matter?" she retorts, but the light shake to her voice gives her away. "When *you* obviously do."

I have to clench my jaw to suppress my smirk—this girl lives to challenge me. "Do I?"

Beth's shrug is heavy and forced. "You know what they say about shoes fitting." She uses my own line against me, and I blink at her for a moment before I grind my teeth in agitation.

"Do you really believe that?" I ask, but at the same time I wonder how she can be so blind, I remember that I'm probably to blame for it. I'm the one who's been avoiding her, after all.

Another forced shrug. "Do I really believe that? Of course I do. What else is there to believe, David? I woke up that morning alone, thinking everything was normal, that nothing had changed..." She glares at me. "But it did, didn't it? Or you would've sent me a text instead of leaving that note. And you wouldn't suddenly start staying out until all hours, doing God only knows what with God knows who. But I suppose I should thank you for at least washing off whatever skank you spent the night with before coming to bed."

It takes me a moment to account for her bitterness, but when I finally recognize it as jealousy, I'm almost ashamed by how gratifying I find it. "So you've noticed I've been showering at night, then?" I call her out. "Because you always seem to be in such a deep sleep..."

Beth bristles in her seat, but she doesn't back down, and it only eggs me on.

My knuckles dance over the skin of her shoulder, and I lean in closer to watch as they leave a trail of goose bumps in their wake. Beth holds her breath as I murmur low in her ear. "So, you think I'm showering at night to wash *whatever skank I spent the night with* off my body before I scoop you off of this couch—the one you know full well I would never let you sleep on—and carry you to bed?"

She swallows audibly, but doesn't answer.

"Hmm?" I ask. "Before I wrap myself around you for the night? Or are we pretending we haven't noticed that, too?"

Beth shakes her head slowly, uncertainly.

I lean in even closer—close enough that her scent invades and intoxicates my senses—and then I tell her the truth. "What if I told you I started showering at night to give my dick some relief before I climb into bed with its most dangerous fucking temptation?"

Beth goes stone-still, but her sharp breath echoes between us. My pulse accelerates and my jeans feel somehow even tighter. I've always gotten a thrill out of shocking her—my innocent little rebel. But never have I crossed the line like this—so far past its limits I'd need satellite photos to make it out.

"Huh, Bea? What then?" Her skin flushes under my touch, which continues its path down along her arm. "You're not a kid anymore, right? Or so you keep telling me. And you grew up around guys—you know how this works. Don't you?"

Beth's swallow is so loud I'd swear you could hear it out in the hall. Her eyes flash to my lap for barely a microsecond, but you don't miss something like that, and fuck if it doesn't tempt me even more. "I'm pretty sure you can figure out what I do in there, huh, Bea?" I tease. "How else do you think I make it through the night without losing my mind? And even then, these past few mornings I've suffered such brutal fucking morning wood I've had to take a shower first thing after waking up, too." I give her yet another confession that colors her blush a shade deeper. "So, since apparently we're just putting it all out there, you might as well consider that my reaction to what happened between us—"

"You mean, your *pussying out*?" Beth may have been taken aback by my crude confession, but she sure as hell isn't backing down, and I have to suppress a pleased smirk.

"Yeah, that," I allow myself a small smile. After all these years, admitting my attraction sets off a surreal mix of both relief and anxiety. "What about anything I've ever said or done to you would make you think that was about *regret*? *Huh*, Bea? Did you even consider that it was actually about the exact fucking *opposite*?"

Her lips part, and, as if determined to prove my words, I kiss her. I kiss her hard. I kiss her to shock her. I kiss her to show her how much I fucking want her.

Beth moans, and it vibrates down my throat and lower. *Fuck*, I need to be inside her.

I pull back again and stare down at her. "What the fuck are we doing, Bea?" I ask desperately.

She blinks up at me, and for the first time I see how completely helpless she is. That she is just as much a slave to whatever the fuck this attraction is between us as I am.

"If you tell me to stop, I will," I promise her.

But she doesn't. She was the one who suggested *friends with benefits*, after all, and she doesn't say a damned thing. But her eyes—they're practically fucking screaming for me to do the exact opposite of *stop*.

"Please tell me to stop." It's a plea. Because I already know if someone is going to end this insanity, it isn't going to be me. My palm slides up her rib cage, edging along the underside of her breast, fingers shaking like a fucking junkie with the need to touch her everywhere. "Tell me to stop, Bea."

Her pulse races under my touch, her chest rising and falling faster and faster as her lips part either to give me what I'm asking for, or to give me what I *want*. "I...I *can't*."

Fuck. My mouth consumes hers, wishing more than anything I could truly show her just how much I want her. But Beth and me— even if we *could* have the *friends with benefits* arrangement she hinted at—we'd never be just the two of us. Cap will always be there, between us. And I wouldn't want to come between them anymore than I could bear to lose either of them.

What the hell am I doing?

I pull back again, and take a deep breath. Because our reality hasn't changed, and neither has mine. I don't want a girlfriend. I'm not looking for a relationship. And I don't know how to do casual with a girl who's as close as family, even if she happens to be the sexiest, most beautiful creature I've ever come across.

"Bea..." I wait for her to blink herself out of her daze. God I wish her lips weren't so red and swollen right now. I wish I didn't know I made them that way. I wish it didn't feel so fucking satisfying to leave my mark on her.

I blow out a shaky exhale. "We can't do this. You know that, right?"

Beth frowns, and it scrapes at something inside my chest.

I shake my head. "I'm not going to pretend I don't want to— obviously that ship has sailed. But you've been through enough with guys, Bea, and that whole *friends-with-benefits* thing always ends up being more complicated—"

"You think I couldn't handle it?"

I shove my hand through my hair in exasperation. The last thing I need is for her to see this as a challenge. Because I'll cave. I'm already close to caving.

"Because I'm not the one who left a note on the kitchen counter and then went into fucking *hiding*."

Touché.

Beth glowers at me. "And you really presume a lot, David, you know that? You think because I fucked you, that suddenly I want to get married or something?" She lets out a soft, humorless laugh. "The *last* thing I need is a damned *boyfriend*." She says the last word with such distaste. "I've been there and done that, and I have no intention of putting anyone's needs above my own right now. In fact, aren't you the one who's been telling me my whole life to do what *I* want to do?"

That does sound like me. But she's forgetting one major factor. "It's more complicated than that, Bea. You know it is. Cap—"

"Is my brother." She cuts me right off. "And he has nothing whatsoever to do with my sex life. It's none of his fucking business, David. And frankly, it isn't *yours*, either."

The fuck it isn't! My jaw clenches tight to keep the words locked in. Because rationally I know I have no right to them. I glare at her—at her heated stare, her harsh breaths, her full, parted lips. I picture the way she looked beneath me, moaning and writhing against me, her perfectly tight pussy squeezing my dick like it was created for me and me alone. I want her so much that even as I articulate the reasons I can't have her, it's hard to remember why they take priority over the chance at experiencing that all over again.

"But despite how you see me, I'm not a little girl, and I have my own needs. And if you want to let my brother dictate your sex life, that's *your* problem. But then you need to stay out of my way, David. Stop freaking out every time I talk to my ex, or dance with a guy at a club, and stop fucking kissing me!"

I lean in even closer, my hand cupping her jaw. "I think I've more than proven I don't see you as *a little girl*," I say meaningfully. Her stern glare falters, but only for a moment. "You want Falco?" I ask with exponentially less confidence. *Déjà vu* unsettles my stomach, and vaguely I can't believe I'm back in this same fucking situation all these years later. Or maybe I've just been here all along, and how fucking depressing is *that*?

Beth swallows anxiously, clearly still affected by me. "No, David," she breathes. "I told you. I don't want a relationship at all. I just want to enjoy college and have a good time. And like I said, what happened the other night…I liked it. But if you can't handle it with—"

"*Liked it*, huh?" I cut her off. Because she can downplay it all she wants, but I was there, and I have more than enough experience to know that that was not *adequate* sex. That was fucking *mind-blowing*.

Beth's blush deepens and my jeans feel so tight it's painful.

"Is that why you screamed my name so loud you probably woke the neighbors? Huh, Bea? Or why I still have marks on my back shaped suspiciously like your nails?"

Beth pouts, but her eyes are smiling. "You do not," she mutters—too goddamned adorable.

I do. I raise my eyebrows smugly, daring her to make me prove it.

But she doesn't. I haven't agreed to her terms, after all. Because I can read between the lines. I know Beth, and I know what she's doing hinting at *friends-with-benefits*—where she's going with all this *I liked it*, but *if you're going to let my brother dictate your sex life, if you can't handle it,* bullshit.

I know what Beth is demanding of me. She's issuing a challenge— *man up*, or *back off*.

But all I've ever done with this girl is *back off*. And now I'm supposed to just watch her flirt with Bogart, or be with Falco, or whatever guy she finds next? Because there *will* be another guy. There will *always* be another guy. They will flock to her for her beautiful face and tempting body, and they will stay for her smartass mouth and generous heart. Better guys than Brian-fucking-Falco. Guys that went to business school, and have high-paying salaries, and can buy her a pretty mansion like the one she grew up in.

Guys who are willing to make her promises. Guys capable of keeping them.

And I will have to stand by, and watch it all happen.

Well, *fuck that*.

I'm not agreeing to Beth's fucking terms, period. Having her once was not fucking enough. And I wasn't even fully sober, or in my right mind, for that matter. I didn't have the chance to fully appreciate the experience—to savor it. Brody could get arrested any day, and then Beth will move back to her dorm, and I'll go back to just being her friend. So if Beth wants this, too, why *shouldn't* I agree?

But I have my own terms.

My fingers trace the delicate bumps and grooves of her collarbone, teasing the goose bumps they elicit. "You're right," I murmur, and Beth's eyes grow impossibly wider. "It isn't Cap's business."

"No?" she breathes.

I shake my head. *No*. It isn't, but Cap doesn't agree, at least not where I'm concerned, and I'm still not willing to openly fight him on it if it means I risk losing my oldest friend. No matter how incredible Beth's body felt, or how sweet her lips taste. "But he still can't know." It's a stipulation, and I wonder when the hell this became a negotiation.

Beth blinks at me.

"He wouldn't forgive me," I remind her.

For a moment she looks like she wants to argue, but thinks better of it. She may not approve of Cap's line in the sand, but she can't deny it was drawn a long time ago, even if she doesn't know just how clearly.

"Like I said, it's none of his business," Beth says softly in agreement.

"Just while you're staying here, yeah? We can't let things get out of hand and risk getting caught…" And I can't risk either of us getting attached.

Her mouth parts, but no words come out. She nods slowly instead.

And just like that, we have a fucking deal. *Friends with benefits. No hiding like a fucking pussy. No telling Cap. Expires when she moves out.*

Yeah, I'm on fucking board. And right now, with her beautiful ocean blues glazed with desire, and my dick just about ready to burst through my jeans, I don't even feel guilty about it.

My hand slides up to fist the pretty blond knot in her hair, and I tilt her face up to mine so my lips can seal our fate. There's nothing unsure about them as they cover Beth's, and the moment her sweet taste infiltrates my senses, I'm fucking done for.

I don't stop for air until she's breathless, and I pull her gently by that silky, golden knot, guiding her back flat down onto the couch as I climb over her.

"So, *friends with benefits*, eh?" The needy rasp in my voice makes it hard to sound light and playful. "What kind of *benefits*?"

Beth breathes out a short laugh. "I think I already thoroughly demonstrated what kind of *benefits*, David," she counters, her mouth slightly turned up at one corner, its corresponding dimple peeking out as she tries to fight that mischievous little smirk that always manages to hit me right in the chest.

I grin wolfishly. "My favorite kind, then." My mouth crashes back to hers, and I run my hands over every inch of her enticing silhouette, taking full advantage of their newly upgraded security clearance. They travel every weaving, winding path of her body from her chest to her ass and every place in between, claiming every hill and valley, every groove and contour—exploring the tantalizing, forbidden curves I've just risked my oldest friendship for a taste of. And *my fuck* are they worth it.

Beth's legs open to cradle my hips between her thighs, and her hands delve into the hair at my nape, grasping it hard enough to sting. I feel it right in my throbbing cock, which grinds against her of its own volition.

Fuck, she kisses like everyone should. Wild, unbridled—no thought, all feeling. Suddenly the need to feel her skin-to-skin becomes desperate and urgent, and I'm peeling her top—and its built-in sports bra—up and over her head barely a second after my own shirt hits the floor.

Her breasts are absolutely magnificent, and they keep my hands and mouth busy for several minutes, before my lips close around her nipple, drawing a moan that has my dick demanding *out*. Beth seems to be having the same thought, because her hands go to my belt buckle, slipping just barely beneath the waistline of my jeans and brushing teasingly back and forth. But instead of taking the hint, I reach for her waistline instead, and it isn't until I get her fully naked and take almost a full minute to admire the utter perfection of her body that I come back to my own.

She watches with rapt interest as I finish undressing, and blushes again when I smirk at her. God, I love the way her body gives me a response even when her words don't.

Beth's deep blue eyes travel my body shamelessly before returning to mine, and the fire they meet me with emboldens me. My mouth takes hers violently, desperately, and her hands find my hair again— something I'm learning is a major fucking turn-on—as she wraps her legs around me. My throbbing hard-on slides against the softness between her legs, and we gasp together at the sensation.

Fuck. She is fucking killing me. I need to grab a condom, and quick. But fuck would I give anything to feel her bare.

I pull away and sit back, pulling her with me. "I need to get a condom. But first do something for me?"

Beth nods without hesitation, and I can't help but grin at her eagerness. It's just so goddamned sexy.

I lean back against the couch, guiding Beth to straddle my lap, my hard cock caught between our bodies. We both look down at where I strain against her belly.

"*Fuck* that's hot," I rasp at the sight of it. I swallow past the sudden dryness in my throat. This is too much. *She's* too much.

Beth licks her lips, and they're so close to mine, I kiss them. I suck her bottom lip between my own, pulling gently, and when she sighs into my mouth, I lose it. I grab her hips and guide her over me, but she takes the cue, and we kiss and kiss like we know this whole thing could end tomorrow—and it could—as she slides her center up and down over me.

Every nerve in my body screams for me to enter hers, and it would be so easy to just slip inside her, and I need to get there before I lose it all over her stomach like a fucking virgin.

Beth moves over me, slow but firm, and with the encouragement of my grip on the perfect handfuls of her ass, she creates a rhythm in time with our frenzied mouths, until my fingers tighten to halt her movements.

Beth looks quizzically down at me, but when she tries to climb off my lap, my arm shoots around her back to hold her against me.

I press a hard kiss to her lips, if for no other reason than I can. "Don't move," I say hoarsely, and then, keeping her flush against me, I lean over to the side table and open the drawer. I pull out the small wooden box, which Beth eyes with bemusement.

"Now don't judge me for this," I warn her. I open the box and get a condom, but Beth grabs the box from me before I can shove it back in the drawer.

Predictably, she bursts out laughing. "*Brother March's Emergency Condom Supply?*"

I fake a scowl. "Housewarming gift from Bogart," I explain.

Beth tries with limited success to stifle her laughter. "Steven thinks you need an *emergency condom supply? In your living room?*" She lets out one more giggle before quickly calming, as if considering something she doesn't actually find all that funny after all, and even though I shouldn't—because it shouldn't matter to my *friend with benefits*—I reassure her anyway.

"Well, yesterday I would have just called him an idiot, but for the first time I'm starting to see some wisdom in the idea."

Beth giggles, and all is right again. But as much as I enjoy the sound of her laugh, it's her moans I'm after right now, and I rock against her to make the point. Her eyes drain of mirth, and fill with unmitigated desire. She watches with fascination as I roll the condom down my length.

"If you're not sure, tell me now," I say, my voice low but serious.

Beth blinks at me. "I'm sure," she breathes, and the words sound utterly beautiful to my ears.

I cup her face and bring it close. "If you become less sure, or change your mind, you tell me. No matter what, or when. Clear?" I would never forgive myself if there was even a moment of this she regretted.

Beth smiles a soft, unfamiliar smile I don't understand, but for the briefest moment it's mirrored in her gaze, and it sends a surge of the strangest mix of calming warmth and thrill through my chest at the same time—and it fucking terrifies me. But she nods, and my dick throbs, reminding me of its impatience, and when Beth's teeth bite down on that plump bottom lip of hers, again, I just can't not kiss her.

For all of her inexperience, Beth kisses me back with all the passion and skill of fucking Aphrodite, and I wonder if Falco really was her one and only. But I banish the thought forcibly and fast. It doesn't matter anyway. Now, or ever.

Still, when my hand moves between us and between her legs, and I finally slip a finger inside her, I'm startled by how tight she is. If I didn't already know better, I'd suspect she was a virgin, which on its own would freak me the fuck out, but if it meant Falco had never been inside her...fuck, I'd take it.

Beth breathes hard, grinding onto my hand, barely able to keep up with her own kisses by the time I pull my hand away, and she groans in protest until I pull her flush against me. She gasps as my cock lines up with her center. I love her reactions. I love that they're so fucking real, just so fucking *her*.

I kiss my way along her jaw, down her throat, and across every bump and groove of her delicate collarbone, before pulling her soft earlobe between my lips. My condom is soaked, and again I curse the necessity of them. Feeling her skin to skin was of another fucking world entirely, and to experience that *inside her*...well, it will have to stay exclusive fantasy material, in any case. Because I know they *are* a necessity, one I've never neglected even once, and certainly wouldn't start with the one girl who actually fucking matters to me.

I stroke myself a few times, my free had cupping her cheek. "Your move, beautiful girl," I challenge her. And she is. So goddamned beautiful.

Beth licks her bottom lip before nervously pulling it between her teeth. "I've never...I..." she trails off, gaze locked on my very ready dick.

I clutch her chin and point it back at mine. "My eyes are up here," I smirk.

Beth playfully slaps my chest. I grab her wrists to stop her, giving a firm squeeze before I reach for her sides, digging in my fingers where I know she's unbearably ticklish. Beth jerks on my lap, and my hands shoot down to her hips to stop her before I fucking embarrass myself.

I've never had this before. I've had friends with benefits, technically; only I was never actually all that close of a friend to any of them. I didn't know them the way I do Beth—they didn't know me. Neither of us were at ease enough to be playing and laughing during foreplay. In fact, laughter is just about the last thing I'd have thought I'd want to hear before sex. But instead of being a turn-off, I just want her even more. I want to fucking own her. To tease her and play with her and make her smile and laugh only to drown it all in her moans before she screams my name.

"You've never what, Bea?" I ask softly.

"Been on top," she murmurs quietly. "I don't know how—I only...I—"

I shush her with a kiss she seems all too eager for, and it makes my dick jump between us. Beth's hips rock subtly and unconsciously in response, and fuck if that doesn't start the cycle over again.

I pull away, breathless. "Your body knows how, Bea," I exhale against her lips. "You're already doing it. We just need to get me inside you."

Beth nods. I grip myself at the base, holding myself steady as I lift her over me. Beth meets my gaze as if looking for something, but all I have to offer is encouragement and, well, fucking desperation at this point, but she bites her lip with concentration as she moves her hips into place. I lower her over me, slowly, filling her tight heat in progressive, long strokes until I bottom out inside her, her knees braced on either side of my hips, her hands clutching my shoulders for dear life.

I guide her hips over me. "See?" I rasp out, "just like dancing."

'The fuck. Did I. Just say?

But Beth's eyelids hang low, her lashes casting shadows over those gorgeous, needy blues, her teeth threatening to tear through that fucking lip, so I kiss it. She releases it only for me to catch it between mine, and then I'm licking and sucking at the perfect bow of her mouth, as I raise and lower her over my raging hard-on.

It feels too good. It looks too good. It's all just too motherfucking *good*.

Her perfect round tits fill my vision, and I make a beeline for her small, pink nipples, my mouth and tongue working her breasts until she's meeting me thrust for thrust, fighting to hold back her sweet little sighs, and I feel compelled to pull back and watch her as she lets herself go.

Her eyes are closed, her lips parted, and she grinds her hips into mine at the same moment I pump them—and my throbbing, swollen cock—up hard inside her, over and over, faster and deeper each time.

I drop my forehead down to Beth's, bringing my hand to her jaw, stroking her cheek with my thumb before sliding my hand down to the base of her throat. I wrap my palm around the back of her neck, pressing my thumb to her pulse so I can feel everything she can. Her heart beats a rhythm like a hip-hop song, fast and violent, echoing mine as I fuck her to its beat from below.

"How is this fair, huh?" I growl right into her ear. "How am I supposed to keep my hands off this tempting fucking body?"

I could come right now. I have to fight not to, and vaguely I wonder what it is that's making this so goddamned incredible. There isn't anything exceptional about the act itself, or our position, but there *is* something exceptional about the way Beth looks in it—the way she fucking feels—and I realize it must be the forbidden aspect of it all.

Yes. That's what this is. Cap declaring her off limits. Years of pent-up attraction and frustration. Star-crossed lust. Like the thirteen-year-old brats Shakespeare wrote about all those years ago, who probably wouldn't have had to fucking kill themselves if their families' feud didn't heighten the excitement of it all—who probably would have just hooked up a few times instead, before losing interest and moving on with their long, boring lives.

This arrangement with Beth is actually probably a good thing. A *smart* one. One that will make everything easier in the long run. We can get the *benefits* out of our system now, and then move on as the *friends* we're meant to be.

"*David*," she breathes, and I almost blow right there.

I need to hear more of it, and I reach between us with my free hand and rub her right above where I penetrate her, and even though I meant to please *her*, feeling myself pumping inside her has me dangerously close.

"How am I supposed to stay the fuck away when you ride my dick like you fucking *own* it?" I grit out between hard thrusts.

Beth lets out a breathy moan, and suddenly I'm a man with only one urgent and desperate mission—feeling the most incredible pussy I've ever experienced coming around me.

I rub small circles at her center, gripping her hip with my free hand to yank her down onto me faster and faster, until she's holding her breath between erratic bursts of exhales, her brows pinched together in some kind of carnal concentration as her body grips and chokes my cock like it's trying to keep me inside—to suck me even deeper.

My eyes roll back in agonizing pleasure a split second before I feel Beth explode around me just as surely as "David!" rips from her swollen lips.

It's nothing short of a miracle—mixed with sheer determination and will—when I manage to hold out through those suffocating spasms and cum-coaxing moans.

Because I'm not ready for this to be over yet—even for a moment. I need *more* of her. I need more *from* her. Namely, more orgasms, more moaning, more of my fucking name. And I'm feeling particularly greedy when it comes to those needs right now.

I keep myself buried deep, holding Beth painstakingly still until it's safe, and then I fold an arm around her back, the other gripping her sweet ass as I stand and take her with me. Her legs wrap around me all on their own, her ankles locking at the base of my spine, and, with a sick kind of pride, I want to tell her it's because she knows it's where they belong.

For now, I remind myself as my mouth takes hers in brutal kisses, my tongue pausing its onslaught just long enough to whisper how incredible she feels as I blindly stagger us to the bedroom.

As we fall to the bed in a mess of lips and limbs, and sounds that blend together in chords of unabashed pleasure, all thought shuts down entirely. I focus instead on sensation. And on my mission—which has recently become drawing as many moans as I possibly can from her.

Game fucking on.

Chapter Twenty-one

David

It isn't until hours later, when I have her held up in my arms, naked, sated, and sleepy enough that I'm not even sure she's still awake, that we start talking about anything other than sex. Not that I mind, it being one of my favorite subjects and all. Beth is inexperienced, but curious, and every orgasm she has seems to fuel that curiosity as much as satisfy it.

But you won't hear me complaining. Not after the most intense climax of my life, a refractory period barely long enough to change condoms, and a fucking mind-blowing encore.

But it's *this* that's most novel to me. The lying in bed together. The cuddling. Touching her, holding her, not as any kind of foreplay, but *just because*.

The most post-hookup contact I've ever had with a chick is crashing at her place, and even that's rare, and usually unintentional. I'm not some kind of manwhore or anything, but I'm a single, red-blooded, relatively good-looking guy who's never been in a relationship. Who's never even *considered* one. Relationships are for guys who want marriage and a mortgage and a nine-to-five. Not a guy who has no idea where he'll be when he graduates less than two years from now. So one-night stands and the occasional fuck-buddy has been it for me. And though this thing with Beth isn't really anything more than the latter, she's the first girl I've been with whose company I not only still want after sex, but want *just as much*.

I trace the outline of her earlobe with the tip of my nose from where I spoon behind her, marveling at the baby-softness of it. I can't see her face, but I'm too preoccupied with this small area of territory—from her ear down to her shoulder, and every inch of neck and jaw in between—to even lean over to check if her eyes are closed or not. I'm quiet when I ask her about her dance class—the one she took at the student rec center tonight—just in case, half expecting her not to answer.

But her soft, angelic voice is just as low when she does, whispering how Toni mentioned it to her a few weeks ago, how dancing at Hot Box reminded her how much she loved it, and gave her the courage to take Toni up on her offer. And then, even more softly and as though as an afterthought, she adds, "and you weren't here anymore, anyway…"

I bite back the reassurances and the apologies. I've already given her the latter, and the former could confuse things. They could be read as promises. And that's not what this is.

But Beth continues on, murmuring something about choreography that goes over my head, but her jaw stretches in a smile, and I scrape my midnight stubble along the back of it, happy enough that she seems to be. Beth isn't quiet—to people who actually know her, anyway—but she isn't especially talkative either. So when she goes on like this about something, I know it's something she's genuinely excited about.

I brush the long mess of blond hair—which came out of its knot at some point during our hours-long fuck-fest—over to her left shoulder, uncovering more soft skin to busy myself with as I listen to her talk. I like her like this. Open and chatty. Other than a few hums and maybe a grunt, I contribute nothing to the conversation as I skim my lips along the delicate tendons that run from the back of her neck to the tip of her right shoulder.

Every touch seems to encourage her, though—which is fine with me because I sure as fuck like touching her—and she detours into the Student Help Chat, and how well it's all going, never once reminding me of the fact that the entire thing was her idea. She talks about it like it's just a student program she's volunteering for, too focused on the people it's helping to give a fuck about something as trivial as credit. But she's the one who suggested an updated alternative to the help line during, like, the first week of classes, and if I didn't happen to remember her mentioning it to me at the time, I doubt I would ever even know about it.

"There's this one girl I chatted with—or guy, I don't actually know—but I think I really helped her, you know?" she says with such hopeful empathy my chest aches a little. But at the same time I can't help the way it swells with affection and pride for this girl who's been through hell, and who has come out the other end better than the rest of us. Because she *is* better than the rest of us.

"Of course you did, Bea," I mutter against her warm skin, still not willing to pull my lips away.

"You never told me about your birth mom," Beth murmurs after another minute, taking me by surprise even though I've been waiting for it. There wasn't a part of me that thought she'd let it go. I'm not sure I'd even want her to.

I grin against her shoulder as bittersweet memories—far too few—float around the edge of my consciousness, keeping the pictures out of focus, but letting in the sentiments. Laughter, jokes, shock and awe, and blinding brightness, even in the wake of utter bleakness. That's what thoughts of Delia are.

That's what Delia was.

And aside from telling Cap and Tuck about her existence, and my parents, obviously, I have never spoken of her to another living person.

But then, Beth is the first person I told she existed at all, and even as I consider her brother and Tucker, and even Reeve…I don't think there's anyone I trust more. Maybe it's because of her unquestionable compassion, and the fact that I can't see her face. Or maybe it's just because I promised I would. And so I do. I tell her all of it.

Well, not *all* of it. I leave the man who raised me out of it. Because a man doesn't have to get physical to hurt his kid, and that door only leads to anger and resentment, and I don't want to feel that right now. I don't want to invite negativity into this bed with us, into this apartment. So I skip the part where I worked up the nerve to come to my dad with the request, and how he used it to force me into a PSAT study course I'd been avoiding. I also skip the six months I had to study my way into earning the right to reach out to my own birth mother, and the way my dad held her information hostage as if my PSAT scores were its ransom.

But I do tell her vaguely about coming around to the idea of meeting my birth parents, and I wonder if she realizes how much of a role she played in it—that night when our families were on vacation, when she was really still just a child. When she'd called me *brave*, and for some unimaginable reason I gave her my deepest, darkest confession on why I wasn't. And she called me out on that, too.

I murmur soft and low, right behind her ear, my head resting on my pillow, hers resting on my arm. I liked her lying in my bed, but I like her lying on a part of *me* even more—it helps relax me, making it easier to go there. So I do.

I tell her how I went back and forth on whether or not I really wanted to know their story. *My* story. If I wanted to know *them*. "In my mind, all the possibilities I pictured left a fuck of a lot to be desired, you know?" *Junkies. Fourteen-year-old rednecks. Perfectly normal douche bags who just didn't want to keep their kid.* "And I pictured *a lot* of possibilities."

Beth breathes out a small laugh. "Writer's imagination."

I chuckle into her hair. "Yeah, maybe," I admit.

I tell her about how I worked up the nerve to tell my parents what I'd finally decided I wanted. I was just about to turn sixteen at the time, and, well, they were the ones with the information.

I skip over the time I lost because of my dad.

I jump instead to meeting Delia for the first time.

"That's when I found out the guy who knocked her up was never in the picture." He was her high school boyfriend, supposedly loved her, but when he found out she was pregnant, he offered to pay to terminate it—*me*—and when she wouldn't go through with it, he terminated their relationship instead.

Beth's spine tenses and if it wasn't pressed right up against my chest, I might miss it.

So it was just Delia, some lady from Queens who'd gotten knocked up and fucked over at eighteen, the latter all for refusing to end my life before it began. Since I'd learned I'd been adopted, I'd always presumed the choice was to keep me or give me away. I'd never questioned my life itself. It's funny—I'd never thought much about abortion before that afternoon at all. I just figured, chick's body, her choice—while taking every precaution known to man to make sure I never put a girl in the position to make said choice, other than abstinence, of course.

I brush my fingers lightly over Beth's stomach, loving the way the tight little muscles of her flat belly react to my touch. Her skin against mine is warm and soothing, and every touch keeps me grounded as I talk.

I tell her Delia's dad had died when she was young, and her mother was on hospice care. She had no extended family or anyone who could help her, and she could barely take care of her mother, let alone a baby.

That was it. All I knew about Delia's life prior to my being adopted at six days old. The rest of my story belongs to the people who raised me, and Delia's belonged to her. And it isn't a bad story. Or it wasn't. Her mom died a year after I was born, but then she managed to work her way through college and law school, and by the time I met her, she was a happily overworked immigration lawyer living in Brooklyn.

Delia never had any other kids. It turned out, she realized during college she was exclusively attracted to chicks. "She smiled like you do," I tell Beth. "With her eyes and her cheeks." Though she didn't have Beth's sweet lips.

Delia met her longtime girlfriend, Rose, during law school, and though they talked about adopting, themselves, for a while, once they were a little older and more financially stable, the timing never quite worked out.

Then she got sick.

"I bet she's really beautiful," Beth murmurs softly.

I blow out a heavy breath, wondering how she could possibly know that. "Yeah," I confirm.

And Delia knew it, too. It was hilarious. We'd go out to lunch and shit like that, and men and women alike would stare and smile. Delia wasn't above a little shameless flirtation if it worked to her advantage, either. Like to get better service from that bored waiter at the diner by her office—she'd just conveniently leave out the fact that she was gay for that one.

"She was like you in that way, too, actually," I admit to Beth. "Didn't need or wear much makeup. Just blessed by nature or God or whatever—in totally different ways, though." Delia was vaguely exotic, with dark hair and olive skin. Beth is more angelic—demure, but somehow in the most sexy way.

Beth tenses subtly, and if I didn't have my jaw pressed against her shoulder I might not have sensed it. "Is *different* a good thing or a bad thing?" she breathes.

I chuckle lightly and press my growing erection more firmly against the curve of her ass. Beth stiffens even more. "Well, I definitely didn't want to fuck my birth mother, Bea."

A laugh bursts from Beth's closed lips and I burrow my grin into the crook of her neck, tightening my arm around her waist. "Well, that is a relief to know," she teases.

"Yeah, keep wiggling your ass like that," I warn against her skin, "and I'll need my own *relief* in a second."

"*Again?*" she mock-chides.

I rock against her to make my point. I'm not there yet, but I could be in a microsecond. "Maybe we shouldn't talk about this now," I suggest. "My birth mother and you naked in bed aren't two things I want connected in my memory."

Beth twists suddenly under my arm, turning to face me without losing an inch of closeness, and it's impressive. And I sure as fuck appreciate it. But it's her eyes that have my full focus right now. This close, I have no power against them whatsoever.

"Please, David," she whispers earnestly, and I can't deny her now any more than I could when we were kids, and she would look up at me with those same big, blue eyes and ask me to sneak her ice cream, or to convince Cap to let her play with us. "Tell me more," she implores.

So I do. I tell her stories about the Delia I got to know over the next few months, and every smile I draw from Beth feels like a badge of honor or something. Like a prize I've earned—one I can actually be proud of.

Her thin brows pinch together in thought and she starts chewing on her bottom lip, so I free it with the pad of my thumb. I raise my eyebrows, giving her a look that demands she spit out whatever's bugging her.

Beth shrugs in my arms. "I would love to meet her sometime, you know? You could bring her to one of my parents' brunches."

I smile wistfully. I never even considered bringing Delia around my family or friends—or in this case, my friends who *are* my family. But now, imagining the scenario in a completely abstract, *what-if* kind of way…it fills me with a strange sense of warmth.

But it's quickly doused by reality, and for the first time since I started talking about her, the rare but familiar sting of grief pierces my chest and burns behind my nose.

"She really would have liked you," I murmur to Beth, tracing the small, barely noticeable freckles that dot her nose.

It's true, of course. Delia would have loved her. She admired honesty and good times, and Beth is the epitome of both.

Beth frowns, not surprisingly catching on to my use of the past tense.

"Cancer," I confirm.

Beth swallows thickly, and my fingers graze south to her pretty neck to trace it. "When?"

"She was diagnosed a few months after I met her. She died a couple of months after that."

Beth's eyes widen in shock, but she tries to compose herself. I don't blame her. It's a lot of information at once. "Which was…when?" She keeps her voice level.

My lips twitch in a smile. She's searching for context. To pin down this major life event of mine very few people ever knew about. "She died the summer before my junior year."

Beth frowns even more deeply. She knows what she was distracted with that summer, and I can't blame her for it—being wrapped up in her new relationship with her first boyfriend. I didn't want her to know then, anyway—I didn't want anyone to know. It was nobody's fucking business. Cap and Tucker only found out because my mom called them, and she only did that because it happened to be the one period in Cap's and my lifelong friendship that we weren't speaking. I never actually found out what my mom told them or didn't tell them. All I know is when I walked into the funeral home, they were both there in black suits, with minimal questions, and rock-solid support. Cap and I never talked about our fight again, but I've got the foreboding sense that, all these years later, it's going to resurface—and soon. With a fucking vengeance.

"I'm so sorry," Beth says, and it's not the same platitude people offer when they don't know what else to say. Beth's eyes beam with emotion—actual, genuine sorrow—for my loss.

But I want her smile back, not her fucking *sorrow*, and I want to remember the fun memories of Delia, not the end. Not right now. I don't want to think about visiting her in that bright, sterile place, hearing worse news after bad, watching her waste away to nothing in a matter of months. Even with cancer, you always think there'll be time. Maybe not years and years, but some time to fight, or at least *process*.

But Delia didn't get to fight, and I had very little time to process fucking anything. She got an inoperable diagnosis and a terminal prognosis, and she didn't discuss the details with some kid she was just starting to get to know. But after a few weeks of what had to have been the most aggressive chemo sessions ever administered, she and Rose informed me that they'd decided to prioritize Delia's quality of life over suffering more physical torment on the off chance it actually prolonged her life, if only marginally.

I remember wanting to jump out of my own body with how badly I wanted to try to talk her out of it. To fight for survival at any cost. But I was selfishly motivated, I knew even then. I'd just wanted more time with her—to get to know her better, slowly and organically, like we had since we'd first met.

I stuck around, because I did want to know her as much as I could, and she seemed to enjoy my company. It seemed to distract her. Even if it often seemed as if she was the one distracting *me*—with her inexplicable cheer and hopefulness, random stories, and borderline inappropriate jokes about the cute nurses. Where I felt robbed by the time we'd lose, Delia was only ever grateful for the time we were given.

I saw her about a week before she died, both of us high on the weed I'd baked into brownies to help with her nausea. Of course, Delia's high was complemented by a pain management cocktail dripping into her veins from a bag on a stand next to the hospital bed, all of which had been brought into her living room.

Beth thoughtfully listens to the rest, her head bowed in concentration as her fingers absently stroke comfort through my skin and straight into my chest, completely unaware that she's doing either.

It isn't until her touch falters that I notice the way she's chewing the inside of her swollen bottom lip.

"What is it?" I prompt her, but she only shrugs.

Beth traces the outline of my pectoral muscles, ducking her blond head under my chin, either to get a closer look, or to hide. "Do you hate him for it?" she finally breathes against me. "Your birth father? For wanting to…*terminate?*" It's as if she can barely bring herself to say the word. Her hands stop touching me as her arms wrap around her middle instead, as if she suddenly needs protection, and my arms fold tightly around her, pulling her more firmly into me as if I can somehow shield her from whatever is haunting her.

"No, Bea," I tell her honestly. "I don't."

Beth pulls back to meet my eyes without meaning to, but it's too late, her heart is in her gaze, and right now it is hurting.

Beth takes her refuge in the crook of my neck, and I let her, stroking her hair gently—trying to soothe her the way she did me just moments ago.

"No?" she challenges softly. "If he'd had his way you wouldn't exist. *You,* David." She swallows down some unfathomable emotion that takes me by surprise. "What about Delia? What if she'd listened to him and had the abortion—if you lost out on your chance to *exist*? What then?" she chokes out.

I press a kiss to the side of her head, inhaling deeply, letting her scent relax me. "Then she would have chosen the life she wanted. That's all any of us can ever do. I guess, for Delia, that didn't include a baby, but it did a pregnancy. And if it didn't…then what could anyone do but trust that she made the best decision for herself, at the time, for the life she knew she wanted?" I shrug.

I hadn't expected Beth to have such a strong reaction to my words, but it's there in her deep exhale, her renewed grip on me, and in her glassy ocean-blues. It's as if I've just issued some kind of pardon or something.

I wonder if I've hit on an issue she just cares deeply about, or if perhaps she knows someone close to her who's had to make that impossible choice. My thoughts flip like a Rolodex to Lani, Rory, Carl, even Toni—but I stop myself. It isn't my business. That's the whole fucking point, isn't it?

Beth and I don't talk anymore after that, and sex is the furthest thing from my mind when she eventually drifts off to sleep, still wrapped around me, her head tucked securely under my chin. It isn't until she rolls onto her back in her sleep that I see the trail of dried tears running down both cheeks, and I spend the rest of the night wide awake, desperately wondering at them.

Chapter Twenty-two

David

"You coming over to watch the Jets lose? Bogart got a keg, so I'm sure he invited half the fucking campus," Reeve grumbles. At first glance you'd wonder why he pledged a fraternity at all, until you remember that it's the only thing that keeps him even remotely social. Well, that, and of course there's the fact that he's a legacy, and his father is apparently a lot like mine when it comes to wanting his son to follow in his footsteps.

I shrug. "I'll see what Beth wants to do when she gets home," I murmur.

Reeve chews the inside of his cheek as if he's trying to fight a smirk. "*Home?* You two officially shacked up now?"

I roll my eyes. "Fuck off." I may talk to Reeve more than most, but that still isn't much when it comes to the really personal shit—and especially when it comes to Beth. All he knows is that he's barely seen me since the night we'd scoured the fucking campus for her.

Reeve is fully aware of the reason Beth is staying with me, but it hasn't stopped his annoying fucking observations, implying there's more to it—more to *us*. And while recent events may have proven him right, that doesn't mean I'm anywhere near ready to cop to it.

Reeve snorts, but though he doesn't say anything more, he hasn't let his little comment go.

"Dude, quit fucking smirking," I say in exasperation, failing miserably at my attempt to pull off a foreboding look to intimidate him off this line of questioning. Not that Reeve would buy it, anyway.

His lips twitch once more before he schools them back into his default inscrutable frown—the one I've heard girls describe as "broody," for which I've thoroughly enjoyed busting his balls. But his eyes still accuse me, and it's fucking irritating.

"She's like a sister," I repeat for the umpteenth time, cringing inwardly even as I say it.

He scoffs. "Didn't realize you were into incest. A little taboo, even for you, no?"

"Huh?" I stare at him. *What the fuck?*

He lifts his shoulder in a shrug. "You know, because you clearly want to fuck her, and all," he deadpans. "Or you already have."

And now I want to fucking pummel him.

Reeve splays his palm in surrender, even as he breaks out into an equally rare burst of laughter, and still it takes me another beat to realize he's just fucking with me.

I suck in a long drag of nicotine in an attempt to regain control of myself, turning toward the cracked window to blow it all away, like the smoke can somehow take with it all this goddamned stress. Because this shit isn't me. This hair-trigger anger, and jealousy, and indignation. These fucking *feelings* in general. It's all completely out of character, which is exactly why Reeve finds it so fucking entertaining. Because I am the laid-back guy. The one who gives zero fucks—who lets the background noise bounce right off without a backward glance.

Except when it comes to Beth-fucking-Caplan. My perpetual fucking *exception*.

But I'm not the only one with a weakness. "You still talking to Lani, huh?" I smirk, which wipes the amusement right off his face. *Score.*

Reeve shrugs. "Maybe."

But as much as I want to break his balls about it, Reeve hasn't been into a girl since he's been here. In fact, I don't think he's been into a girl since the ex I never met fucked him up in ways he's never confided, and if he's carrying a torch for Lani, I don't want to be the one to stamp it out. So, instead, I encourage him. "You should take her out."

Reeve laughs humorlessly, like the idea of taking a girl on a date is absurd. And maybe it is. I don't think I've ever taken a girl on a real date, either.

"She loves the wings at Toolies, you know. Lani's not high maintenance."

This time Reeve's laugh is sincere. "No shit." He smiles a rare, genuine smile. "That chick is a lot of fucking things, but high maintenance is *not* one of them."

I don't know what to say to that, and I feel like I'm missing some inside joke between the two of them, so I just suck in another drag of nicotine. I'm still thrown off by what he said about Beth—why it pissed me off so much when he referenced me fucking her. I *am* fucking her. *Friends with benefits*—that's all this is…right?

Reeve eventually finishes his drink. He grabs his jacket and reminds me to come by the house to watch the game before turning to the door.

"So, just theoretically speaking…" I stop him.

His eyebrows raise in question.

"Let's say my friend likes this girl…" My nerves lose their shit at the thought of talking about Beth with him—with anyone. But I can't exactly call Cap or Tuck on this, and I'm at a fucking loss at this point.

Reeve doesn't smirk this time. There's no pretense about the existence of my "friend," and the reality is I just admitted to him I like Beth. Actually, it's the first time I've really admitted it to myself. Because *wanting* her is one thing, but *liking* her, in a way that has nothing to do with friendship…that's fucking terrifying.

"What would you say if he grew up with this girl, and they're practically related?" My nonchalant tone belies nothing, but then, I hadn't meant it to.

Reeve sighs. "I'd say, *practically related* isn't *related*," he says meaningfully. "It's not like you share blood. But be careful. You can't go there for a quick fuck, man." He glares at me, and even pretenses of pretenses have vanished into thin air, and I'm too stunned that I'm actually having this conversation to fully process, let alone respond. "Trust me, March. You've got a lot to lose. Only risk it if it's really worth it."

But Beth is worth anything.

Is she worth my relationship with Cap? Is she worth risking the only real "family" I've got? That is what it has always boiled down to. And for the first time, I think this thing with Beth and me...well, maybe it *is* worth risking a decade and a half of friendship, for the chance at a lifetime—a future—of something *more*.

An image of Beth's beautiful heart-shaped face floats through my mind, her ethereal ocean blue eyes wide open with promises she's never actually offered me, and I remember, I've chosen her over Cap before. Years ago. When it counted, when it mattered—when she *needed* me—I chose her.

But even as I think it, I know I'm bullshitting myself. Because *that* was different.

This isn't about choosing *her*, but *myself*.

But then again...I am a selfish fucking bastard.

Chapter Twenty-three

Beth

I wake up the same way I have every morning since last weekend, wrapped up in all things David. His scent, his arms, his warmth. Never has it been harder to force myself out of bed.

Still in his sleep, he holds me like I'm valuable to him—precious. I try not to let myself grow accustomed to it, but it feels so good. Comforting. But then, David has always been a comfort to me when he could.

In fact, I dreamed of one of those times last night. When he first learned the truth about our families. That his dad may be a dick, but mine...mine could be a *monster*. It was the night David first gave me my new nickname, *Bea*, and I can't deny that his presence made the memory that much less awful.

I was nine when our families went to Vermont for a ski weekend, and Sammy and David were caught up in a basketball game in the gym, leaving me forgotten and bored on the sidelines. At some point David tapped out and told Sammy he'd take me to get ice cream, which he did. He didn't mention he also planned on sneaking us into the movie the resort was showing without tickets, but I didn't complain. As always, I was eager to follow his lead, trusting him implicitly, excited for a bit of adventure. Only, the movie ran past my curfew, and we lost track of time, and though he rushed us through the hotel like two bats right out of hell, the ominous, familiar sounds of doom hit us before we even reached our destination.

The memory is so vivid, my subconscious just having relived every awful moment of it—and every impossibly not-so-awful moment…

The sound of raised voices from the room I'd been sharing with Sammy and David, and my stunned fear as they reverberated from the barely ajar door. David's confusion, which quickly morphed to shock, and—most unwelcome—pity.

But it all registered at once, and I felt nothing in that moment other than sheer terror as I froze outside our door.

A loud crash preluded my father's vicious, accusatory voice as he laid into my brother, demanding he tell him where I was, and my mother's high-pitched pleas—never for herself, always for Sammy. And Sammy's progressively more defiant, smartass replies.

I remember how, for a moment, I thought David might go inside to back up his friend against my own father, and my heart stopped beating. But he must have seen something on my face, because he grabbed my hand instead, and rushed me down the hall and through a door.

One of the two lightbulbs was out in the small room fitted with two vending machines and an ice dispenser, and the dimness made it easier to hide. I didn't dare meet David's eyes. He didn't dare say a word. I backed against the far wall and leaned against it for support. I swore I could still hear my dad, could feel the vibrations of his fury in the walls, could smell the vodka fumes through the vents. I stared down at my camouflage Uggs—I'd refused to buy the pink sparkly ones the rest of the girls always wore—until David took a sudden step toward me.

"Bits…" he said hesitantly, looking down at me from his height advantage with concern and pity, and I hated it.

There was a small nook between the last vending machine and the wall, and I tucked myself into the corner of the room, folding my knees into my chest and wrapping my arms around them as if I could hold myself together that way.

I knew it was my fault. My father was mad because I was late. And I also knew I was an awful sister. That my father might hit Sammy again. Or my mom.

But I also knew the damage was already done. That once my father's switch had flipped, there was no shutting him down. Not until he either wore himself out, or did something violent enough to shock himself out of it. It wasn't like I could just walk into the room and say, "here I am!" and all would have been forgiven. Even at nine, I had enough experience to know my father would have just found something else to be angry about. He'd have just blamed Sammy or my mom, or both of them, for wherever I was, whoever I was with, and for every second I was late. And if it wasn't me, it would have been something my mom had said at dinner, or something Sammy had done a month ago. And the truth is, I know not one of them would have wanted David to witness it, anyway. We did have our pride, after all. Or *they* did, at least.

Not that I even had a conscious choice in that moment. My response to my dad's rare but brutal alcoholic rages had been conditioned since before conscious memory, and it wasn't the first time I'd found myself waiting it out in a dark corner somewhere.

David surprised me when he sat down beside me, squeezing his lanky frame between me and the vending machine. His arm came around my shoulders and he sighed. "Bits," he said again, waiting for me to meet his eyes. They were more serious than I'd ever seen them. "Does that happen a lot?" he asked.

I shook my head, *no*. I was so distressed at the time that it didn't occur to me to question how quickly and accurately he'd pegged the situation.

"But it does happen?"

I forcibly swallowed down the denial, and finally nodded.

David's jaw clenched. "To you?"

Another head shake, and it seemed to ease his tension one iota.

He jerked his chin in the direction of our hotel room. "To them?"

In his eyes I could already see him make the connection to my mom's familiar bruises, to his best friend's—to Sammy's broken arm we both now knew didn't happen playing football.

I nodded again.

David's arm tightened around me, and my head dropped onto his shoulder. We sat like that for a while, and I was grateful he didn't ask any more questions.

"Why do you still call me *Bits*?" I asked after a while.

David frowned. "What else would I call you?"

I didn't reply.

"Everyone still calls you Bits. Cap…Tuck…"

"It's a baby nickname," I murmured. For some reason, David was the last person I wanted seeing me as a baby.

"And *Dave* is so mature?" He scoffed.

"It's better than *Bits*."

He eyed me curiously. "You want a new nickname?"

I didn't. I just didn't want *him* to call me *Bits*.

"Hmm…" He looked me up and down, as if searching for something about me that might be worthy of inspiring a name.

I remember thinking he'd find nothing. That there was nothing interesting about me. And I'd been right.

"Okay, kid, I'll call you *B*…"

But I was so thrilled to shed my childish nickname—at least to him—that I didn't even mind that he couldn't come up with anything other than the first letter of my name. It wasn't until a few years later, when he happened to write it in a text, that I even knew it wasn't actually *B*, but *Bea*. But I suppose it's the same difference.

"What's wrong with *Dave*?" I asked him.

David smiled. "It's fine," he shrugged, "you know, for now. But it doesn't exactly scream big, powerful man, or look good printed on a book cover, now does it?"

I laughed. *Laughed*. Considering what sent us into that room, it was pretty extraordinary. "*David* does," I reminded him.

He smirked, arching his brow in that way he'd tried and failed to teach me how to do. "You wanna call me *David*?"

I shrugged. I did. I wanted to call him something no one else did, even if it was just his full name. I wanted to have a piece of him that was just mine.

So I did. From that moment on, I only ever called him David. And I was either *Bea*, *Beth*, or *kid*. He never called me *Bits* again.

David did keep a cautious eye on my father after that, until his final alcoholic rampage left my mother with a broken nose, and—when Sammy had had enough and finally hit him back—left me without a father for more than five years.

That was the first time I realized that the power of David's arms went way beyond the physical, and waking up surrounded by them has only reinforced that truth.

No wonder it's so hard to get out of bed.

But we do, like every morning, and we take turns showering, like every morning.

Depending on our class schedules for the day, I walk to class either with David or Toni, or on one occasion, with Ralph, whom—like the rest of my pledge-bodyguards—I no longer make walk a distance behind me.

I know I should tell David about Brody being back on campus, but after his overreaction to not knowing where I was last week, I don't exactly expect him to be reasonable about this particular development.

But Brody hasn't so much as looked my way, and since David basically has me monitored by a not-so-secret service of his own design, anyway, it's not like his knowing about it would make any practical difference.

Still, I feel guilty, and I know I need to tell him. And I *have* tried. It just never seems like a good time.

Surely not when his lips are on my neck the moment I walk in the door. Or when I wake up in those magical arms, to his signature smirk and ready hard-on—and, once, to a strange, pensive stare that barely lingered long enough for me to fully open my eyes. I don't want to bring up freaking Brody of all people when David is touching me, or making me laugh, or even simply comforting me with his presence. And it definitely isn't a good time after Sammy calls or texts one of us when we're together, and we spend at least the next hour or so drowning in guilt and not quite meeting each other's gazes.

But I do have to tell David, and soon. Before one of his pledges notices Brody around campus and recognizes him. I'm lucky it hasn't happened already.

Today I leave first, and Toni and I make our way to class, chatting excitedly about the new contemporary dance class she talked me into signing up for back when I still believed David would be avoiding me indefinitely. I say good-bye to her and wait to meet Lani outside the student union.

My cell phone buzzes and Sammy's name flashes across the screen, surprising me. My brother and I text pretty frequently, but he always makes sure to call at least once a week. I think he needs to hear my voice—as if he'd be able to hear it if I'd relapsed into depression or something. And who knows? Maybe he could. But we spoke just yesterday, and I can't remember the last time he called me two days in a row.

"Hello?" I answer.

"Hey, Bits." It's his forced-casual tone and it gets my guard up.

"What's wrong?" I ask instantly.

I can feel my brother roll his eyes. "Shit, kid. You always go there, don't you?"

I ignore his patronizing tone. "Is Rory okay?"

Sammy blows out a long-winded sigh. "Yeah, Bits. Everything's fine—relax."

I hate when he tells me to relax, and he knows it. I let out an exaggerated huff to mimic his sigh. "Well you're not exactly *Chatty Cathy*, Sammy, and we just spoke yesterday…"

When he tells me he wants to come visit next weekend while Rory is visiting her mom, panic edges its way in. He's still doing his casual act, and I want so much to buy it, but it's my nature to worry, and I can't help but wonder why *now*? Why so suddenly? If Sammy found out about me and David, he would be upset with me for being dishonest, surely, but my fear isn't for my relationship with my brother. It's for David's. But, selfishly, what I'm most afraid of is knowing it would cut short my time with David—time that could already end at any moment.

Sammy says he'll take the Long Island Railroad into town Friday night—that David will pick him up from the station. I can't begin to think about where the hell my brother is even going to sleep—or where *I* am, for that matter, since it certainly can't be in David's bed with him—and I'm about to text Lani to hurry up before she makes me late to Psych 101, when over on the far corner of the promenade, my eye catches the back of an unmistakable mahogany head of hair.

Even more than fifty yards away, I recognize the tension in David's shoulders, and when he turns a little to his left, he reveals not just the stress in his features, but the person they're directed at.

He leans into Liz, apparently murmuring something into her ear. Liz shakes her head at him, and throws a glance over her shoulder like she expects someone to jump out at her at any moment. My heart breaks a little more for her, but shamefully stronger is my desperate curiosity—my jealousy—over whatever the hell could have David so obviously and uncharacteristically aggravated, and what it could possibly have to do with Liz.

I know he's hooked up with her in the past, but I can't imagine he would do that now. Still, I can't fathom what else could be between them that might explain the intimate exchange.

And, of course, I don't *know* he wouldn't do that now. We haven't actually talked about it.

Liz stomps away from David, who rakes his hand through his hair in a familiar gesture of frustration, and I watch, frozen, as he shakes his head, checks his phone, and walks off in the direction of the communications building.

"Who are we staring at?" Lani interrupts my daze, but thankfully she doesn't share my finely tuned David-radar, because she just stares blindly into the crowd before I admonish her for being late, yet again, and hustle her toward class.

* * *

I'm still on edge hours later when Professor Bowman ends her lecture and dismisses us. I pack up my tablet and stare at my phone, opening my long-running text conversation with David, and my thumbs hover uselessly over the touch-screen keyboard, just as they have all day. I want so much to tell him about Sammy's sudden upcoming visit—to ask him what we're going to do. But I can't escape the image of him leaning so intimately down to Liz, whispering in her ear, and it paralyzes my fingers.

The worst part is the realization that all these years later, nothing has changed. I still harbor unfathomable jealousy over David March, and despite the fact that I'm sleeping with him, I still have no right to it. And while I managed to get it through my head long ago, I still can't seem to get it through my thick, pathetic heart that David isn't mine. That he isn't *going* to be mine.

My classmates file around me and toward the exit as I give up yet again, tossing my phone into my bag, and even Professor Bowman has left by the time I get myself together.

Just as I'm slipping on my jacket, I hear my name. And it chills my blood.

"Beth," a familiar voice calls from behind me.

I whip around to find Brody pushing his way around the two girls whose leisurely pace is blocking his path down the narrow aisle—the only two other students left in the lecture hall. His brow is furrowed with what appears to be a threatening mix of agitation and indignation, and my pulse runs frantic as it urges my body to do the same.

I knew Brody was back in class, of course, but he has been for over a week, and considering he hasn't so much as glanced my way, I figured his attention was elsewhere. Like on his well-deserved, impending arrest, for example.

But my fight-or-flight instincts are well-honed, and in one more heartbeat I'm through the door.

But so is Brody.

"Hey!" he shouts, and I pick up my pace even more.

The hall is far more deserted than it would have been just a few minutes ago, most everyone having already made it to their next destination before the next block of classes starts. There are just a few disinterested stragglers with buds in their ears and their eyes on their phones, but I suspect they are the reason Brody refrains from giving chase in earnest, and I'm infinitely grateful for them as I speed up into a jog.

But his long legs must cover twice the distance of mine, because he gains on me easily with every last stride. "*Damn it*, Beth! Will you fucking *stop*?" he growls, gritting his words through his teeth in a way that reminds me so much of my father at his worst that it makes my stomach roll with an eerie blend of *déjà vu* and dread.

I break into a sprint toward the exit like a madwoman. I can't imagine what the hell Brody could possibly want with me, but I have zero interest in finding out.

Rationally I know he probably isn't planning to attack me in the corridor of the Bio-Psych Building, where potential witnesses are likely to pass by. But I doubt Liz expected to be attacked wherever she'd been that night, either, and not knowing where that even was, or exactly what went down, just makes the whole thing that much more terrifying.

But unlike most gossip on campus, the details of Liz's assault never made it past the police—and whoever else Liz herself might have told—and as Rill Rock U's policy is not to comment or report on any ongoing criminal investigation involving a student, most people don't even know who Brody is, let alone what he did.

My heart races in terror as Brody's heavy, foreboding steps echo from not far enough behind me, and I grab for the door and fling myself through it just as he reaches—or grabs—for me, his fingertips grazing my wrist with the near-miss. My heart jumps into my throat as if it means to escape my body, and in this moment I can't even blame it.

Brody follows me outside, but pauses on the small stoop as I flee in the direction of the student union, gasping hungrily for the breath that panic and exertion stole away. I hug my arms around myself, slowing only to a brisk power-walk as I risk a quick glance over my shoulder. The ice-cold glower in Brody's narrowed eyes sends a shiver down my spine.

What the hell does he want *from me? To* defend *himself? What he did* was indefensible*!*

What he was accused of, a small voice corrects internally. But how can I doubt Liz? If she said it happened, I have to believe it did...don't I?

The only people around are those who don't have class right now and don't happen to be eating lunch, and while that's fewer people than any other time during the day, it's still busier than the empty halls of an academic building while class is in session. But barely moments later, hard, running footfalls pound in the distance behind me, and I don't even look to check if it's him, I just take off.

I risk a peek over my shoulder, but I don't see Brody at all.

"*Oh*," I gasp as I smack right into a stranger's broad chest, bouncing back and tripping over the backpack at his feet. I'm caught from behind only at the last second by a pair of unyielding hands on my waist, and I spin on my heels to face my savior, my attacker, or both, only to find the man who caught me is none of the above.

"Bethy? Are you okay?" Brian asks, his blond brows pinched together in concern.

I'm not okay, and I try to step back from him, but my foot catches on that stupid fucking backpack again, and I stumble before Brian's grip tightens to steady me. "What are you doing here?" I ask a little hysterically, even as my paranoid gaze darts around to recognize the broad-chested roadblock as Brian's teammate—the goalie whose name I can't remember—smoking a cigarette. *Should college athletes be smoking?*

Brian steps closer, still not releasing me, and I don't have the energy to fight him as he insists on eye contact. He must see my fear because he looks around as if for an obvious threat, frowning when none emerges. "Let me get you something to eat, okay, Bethy?" Brian finally releases me only to slide an arm around my shoulders, and I almost let him guide me inside the student union. Almost.

I twist from his hold without warning as the imminent danger subsides and I start to come back to my senses. In my peripheral line of sight, I catch the runner I thought was Brody practically screech to a halt a few feet away, and I recognize Dicknose—my very first pledge-bodyguard. Idly I think I could have used him several minutes ago, but now I don't even acknowledge his presence.

"I'm not hungry," I tell Brian. I mean to sound firm, but my voice trembles, and when my hands do the same, I fold my arms in front of me to hide them.

Brian's frown deepens. "Some coffee, then. Come on, Bethy, you're obviously upset—"

"*Beth*," I correct him, and suddenly that desperate fear of moments ago mutates into another familiar emotion—*anger*. "I've told you, Brian!"

"Will you *relax?*"

Ugh!

"I will *not* fucking *relax*," I reply. "As you pointed out, I'm *upset*," I remind him. "And the last thing I fucking need is my *ex* trying to take advantage of that right now."

Brian's eyes narrow only vaguely as he tries to keep his face straight. "You're still mad?"

I shake my head, never even blinking. "No, Brian. I'm still *done*."

Chapter Twenty-four

Beth

I fought the urge to run back to David's apartment and hide from the rest of the day, because even stronger was an answering determination to make it through unscathed. To refuse to let a couple of assholes materially affect my life, in any way whatsoever.

A year ago it would have been Dr. Schall's gentle, encouraging voice in my head, talking me through. But not today. Today it was my own voice, and it turns out mine isn't all that gentle. My inner strength sounds a lot like a snarky bitch, and I actually kind of like her.

But the truth is, more than Brody or Brian, it's David who's had my head spinning circles all day, and his curious interaction with Liz. And while a few weeks ago I would have just let it go, I'm not sure I have it in me anymore. Not when I've spent the better part of the day picturing the arms I woke up in wrapped around *her*, and the mouth that drives me utterly mad pressed against her lips.

It just doesn't make any sense—*David* doesn't make any sense.

I'd been under the impression Liz had barely spoken to him since the assault, and before that *he* was the one barely speaking to *her*. And that was *what*? A *microsecond* after he introduced her as his *friend*? From his sister sorority? I was like a "sister" to him not that long ago, too, and I can't help but think of how quickly and completely he disappeared on me after we first slept together, and that was while we were living in the same apartment. I wonder just what I'd have to do for him to do it again. All Liz did was make fun of my name.

I haven't spoken to David since this morning, except to answer his text asking when I'd be home, but he still has an hour left of class, so I have time to prepare myself.

Or so I thought.

I've barely hung up my jacket when David walks into the apartment, and I whirl around to face him, a pitiful deer in headlights. But only for a moment, as my own voice inwardly reminds me— ironically, in *David's* own words—not to *be a pussy*.

I square my shoulders, subtly lifting my chin, our gazes locked in place. But the sexy, fun, easygoing guy of the past week is nowhere to be found in his hard, inscrutable gaze, and I blink at him, my stare wavering just long enough for David to break it.

He turns from me wordlessly, chucking his leather jacket on the back of a counter stool like always, but this time I don't pick it up and put it away for him.

It's crazy how you don't really register some things until you miss them, like the fact that David hasn't walked in the door all week without making some excuse to touch me, and, missing it, my skin is positively aching for a caress, a shoulder rub, even a playful tickle. Something to connect me to him in a physical way.

David gets a beer from the fridge, not bothering to offer me one. He always offers me one, even if I rarely accept. He pops the top and chugs half the thing in a couple of gulps, and I just stand here and stare at him at a loss as he ignores me, giving his phone his full attention instead. *Has he ever done that before?*

I swallow anxiously, ready to just go hide in the bedroom and pretend to study while I overanalyze every last breath David has taken since this morning.

But I don't want to. I don't want to guess. Because the fact that he suddenly seems to have lost all interest in me the same day he was whispering sweet nothings in Liz's ear can't be a coincidence, and while David may not owe me anything just because of the *benefits*, if we really are such good *friends*, then surely the *friendly* thing to do is just to ask him.

"What's with you and Liz?" I ask with no preamble whatsoever. Inwardly I wince, but outwardly I never falter.

David slowly lifts his chin to meet my gaze, his giving nothing away. "'The fuck are you talking about?" he says after a beat. His eyebrows are slightly raised, like I'm boring him or something, and it stabs at my chest.

But I don't back down. I step into the kitchen, refusing to let either of us use the breakfast bar as a trench for cover. If I'm not hiding, he isn't either. "Liz," I repeat. "What's your deal?"

He arches a brow, like he doesn't get what this is about, and that stings even more. I've known David to be a lot of things, but a liar has never been one of them. At least not to his friends. Unless that's not what I really am, either. Maybe guys like David aren't really capable of having female friends at all, considering he seems to sleep with all of them.

But I saw his exchange with Liz today with my own eyes, even if I couldn't hear what was said, and there was nothing casual, or even *friendly,* about it. David continues to look at me as if he has no idea what I'm even talking about, and resentment rises hot in my belly. But I keep my calm.

"I just don't get you, David," I admit. "One minute you say you and Liz are friends, then she pisses you off, and you ice her out without a second thought. Or *worse* than ice her out. Because you weren't even cold to her. You were just... *nothing*. Like you didn't even care one way or the other."

David's mask of indifference slips as confusion knits his brow in earnest. He shrugs. "I didn't," he deadpans, and I don't doubt it. That's what scares me.

I swallow hard. "And yet there you were just hours ago, whispering to her like—" I cut myself off. Like *what*? Like they were *lovers* or something? *David and Liz*? It would almost be laughable—if the image of them together and laughter weren't entirely mutually exclusive, that is.

David's hazel eyes flash first with incredulity, then with understanding before his mask slides hastily back in place. But it's too late. I see through it—through *him*—just like I saw him with Liz earlier, something he obviously now realizes.

"Whispering to her like *what*, Beth?" David pushes, but he doesn't give me time to answer. "Like you and Falco outside the Stu-U this afternoon? Huh? Despite how many times I've told you he's bad fucking news?"

"Is that what you'll do to *me* if I don't listen?" The fear slips from my mouth before my brain can send it the signal to keep shut. "What happens when *I* piss you off, David? Will you just ice me out?? Avoid me like you did after you first got drunk and fucked me? Not care one way or the other?" Inwardly I choke on the words, but I keep my posture defiant and my chin high. "Is that what you're doing now?"

David glares at me as if I've somehow completely stunned him.

I don't know what kind of reaction I expected, but this isn't it. "Not care…about *you*…" David breathes, trailing off in what I first think is thought, but then realize is, in fact, disbelief. His eyes flare and his cheeks flush with indignation, and even though I've never wanted his anger, after just imagining his cold indifference, I'll take it. I'll take any emotion I can get as long as it proves he gives a shit about me, and how pathetic is that?

David takes a hostile step toward me, but I don't feel threatened. With David, the danger has only ever been to my heart and my innocence, and I can't remember a time when I wouldn't have willingly given him both. Even now, Liz or no Liz.

"You think you haven't pissed me off *enough* already?" he growls.

"What—the mother*fuck*—about any and every goddamned thing I've done since you got to fucking campus, exactly, would you say indicates my ability to *not* fucking care about you, huh?" He pauses to heave in a heavy but sharp breath.

"David—" I try to interrupt, but he isn't having it.

"*Huh?* Was it following you around so much I got called your damned *bodyguard*? Or giving you my lit notes—shit I never even shared with my critique partners? Sending pledges to watch out for you? Lying to my best goddamned friend, for you? Moving you into my *place*? To my"—he sucks in another sharp breath, meaningfully locking our gazes—"my fucking bed."

David's glare strikes me silent, fixing me with things it's never held before—or I've never noticed. Hunger, and possession, and, yes, a caring affection...but also a kind of helplessness. And how can I blame him for it? I know exactly how it feels.

David stalks closer, his mask vanished and all pretenses gone, and for the first time, he looks down at me with an intensity that shakes my very core, and makes me question everything I've always thought I knew about him—about *us*. "I *could* wash my hands of Liz, because I *didn't* care about her. It sounds fucked up, because we were friends—or we are—but...I just didn't." He blows out a slow, calming exhale and I'm glad for it. We need more *slow*, more *calming exhales*. "*You're* not *her*, okay? I don't just get to *wash my fucking hands* of you and walk away. Even if you already *do* piss me off half the damned time! I don't *get* to not fucking care! Trust me, if I could, I fucking *would*!"

I gape at him, shocked silent and not quite following, but utterly riveted. It's more emotion than I've ever seen out of David, all bursting from him at once like a pressure cooker, and I can't look away. I don't think I even blink.

"It's imprinted into every goddamned day of my life, every fucking *thought*—caring about you more than I should. Going to my best friend's house to play ball, and constantly wondering if his sister is home, what you're fucking doing, or pushing him to include you just for the fucking chance to be around you."

His next pause for breath is defeated, and it scrapes inside my chest. "Every guy's dream…" Even David's sarcastic tone is more resigned than bitter. "Constantly thinking about another guy's girl. Seeing you with him at school. At parties…" He's talking about Brian. "At your fucking house. A place that used to be a second home to me."

My eyes blur softly, and for the first time I imagine it all through David's eyes—what it must have been like for him. I know how it felt to see him with girls, and never once did I imagine that that devastating jealousy and heartache could have been reciprocated.

"Every time I see you with him all I can think of is the state he fucking left you in when he…" He shoves his fingers through his thick, dark locks, and I want so much to do the same. "You know…and hearing him call you that that night, Bea," David growls, but grits his teeth instead of finishing the sentence.

"I didn't *forgive* him," I blurt out.

"Forgive. Give another chance. Whatever." David gestures dismissively.

"I *forgave* him a long time ago, David, I told you that," I remind him, but I hold my fingers to his lips when he tries to interrupt. "But there's no more chances."

David's brow furrows, and he looks a little lost. His gorgeous hazel eyes shine with olive and honey, and for the first time, I find the courage to do what he's just done. Tell the truth.

"When Brian dumped me…the 'state I was in'…" I use David's own words, swallowing thickly. But he knows I don't talk about this, and he listens, silent. "I will never be that girl again, okay, David?"

He stares, not quite believing, not quite understanding—which is fair, considering I've explained nothing.

I suck in a deep, courage-mustering breath. "You know I was…" How do you describe depression to someone who's never experienced it? "Sad. But not just sad…"

David takes the last step between us, backing me into the counter, as if his physical support could steady my emotions. And strangely, in some ways, it does. And suddenly, I *want* him to understand. I'm not worried about him thinking me fragile, because I don't *feel* fragile. If David thinks that what I've been through makes me weak, then that's his problem. Because, ironically, in this moment, as I try to explain the worst of my demons, I've never felt stronger.

"I felt…*empty*." I tell him. "And it wasn't just because of Brian. I'd felt like that on some level or another for as long as I could remember. What happened with Brian, it just exacerbated everything—made it all come into the light at once. Or drown out the light."

"You *are* the light," David says softly, and it draws a small smile from me.

"But I didn't feel like it, David," I tell him. "I felt like emptiness and darkness were all there was. And a week after the breakup, I started taking my mom's Klonopin."

David scowls, not judging, but scolding.

"Not taking them," I amend. "But *taking* them—stealing them—one by one. I put them in a little jewelry box I hid under my mattress." I've never told anyone that before.

"Why?"

"Just in case," I admit. I notice the tension grow in his neck, his shoulders, but, still, I continue. "It wasn't even a conscious choice at first. I just wanted to have them. Like a Plan B. A way out."

"A way out of what?" David still doesn't get it. And why would he?

"Life."

His frown is deeper than I've ever seen it, and I give him a moment. "What was your Plan B?" He already suspects, because his tone is almost accusing, but mostly it's apprehensive.

"To take them. All of them. At the same time."

David pales, his hands gripping the counter on either side of me until his knuckles turn white. "You didn't." But he knows I did. And his gorgeous face grows pale as my silence confirms it.

"Why?" he demands, and I'm shocked to find his eyes wet. There are no tears, just a shimmer I've never seen on them before, and it takes me aback.

"It seemed like the best option at the time."

David retracts and slams his palm into the countertop. "The best *option?*" he snarls.

"I know it wasn't *now*. But I didn't have my meds then, David, and when things were bad, they felt like they would never get better—like *I* would never get better. Like I would just keep slugging along in misery indefinitely, dragging everyone down around me."

David's head shakes in denial through my every word.

"Once I made the decision to do it, I felt, like, *unburdened*. It was the happiest I'd felt in as long as I was able to remember at the time."

He swallows audibly, his mouth a thin line, his jaw clenched, as if he takes personal offense to what I'm saying. And maybe he does. But it wasn't about him. It wasn't even about Brian. It wasn't about anyone but me. "I planned it for a night Sammy and my mom would be out. You were all at Cooper's party after the last day of school. I looked forward to that day like you look forward to spring break after a brutal week of finals," I admit, "only times a thousand."

My hand comes up to brush his jaw, wanting to relieve some of the tension I caused. But it does nothing. Still, he turns into my touch.

"But Sammy came home early and found me, and thwarted all my careful planning." I smile, but David doesn't like my joke, and his glare wipes it off my face. "I didn't do it for attention, David. Waking up in that hospital room was the worst disappointment I've ever felt."

David grimaces, gritting his teeth like he's angry with me.

"But it made me get help. And it wasn't easy, I admit. But I'm me again. I'm a better me than I ever was even before. And I'm stronger for it, okay?"

That seems to ease his distress marginally.

"I'm not going to fall for Brian's bullshit, or give him any more chances. I ran into him today—literally—and he caught me. That was all. I told him after Hot Box that I was done. I gave him a chance—*at friendship*—and he blew that when he called me a slut in a club. End of story."

For several moments, David just stares down at me. "I was trying to get information about the Brody investigation," he murmurs finally. "From Liz. That's why I was whispering to her today. I didn't think she'd tell me anything if anyone could overhear."

"And did she?"

His jaw locks. "No."

I sigh. I don't know if I'm disappointed or relieved. Of course I want Brody arrested so he can't hurt Liz, or me, or anyone else again. But if that means David and I are done…my heart aches and my eyes sting at just the thought. I look away.

David's hands ascend to my shoulders. "You'll never do that shit again, Bea," he says without warning, softly yet sternly.

I stare at him.

"Promise me."

I frown.

He gives me a gentle shake. "*Promise.* The pills, or anything else. No matter how bad you feel. You will never do that shit again, you hear me?"

His fervor stuns me for a moment.

"Promise!"

"Of course I won't!" I snap back. "I would never do something like that again."

David glares at me, and I know what he needs from me—after all, he's said it quite clearly.

"I promise, David," I breathe.

He sucks in a sharp breath, every bit of his hostility fading as his shoulders sag, drained. "I wish you'd never met him," he murmurs.

I shake my head. "I told you. It wasn't really about—"

"Yeah, I get all that," David interrupts. "But I still wish you'd never fucking met him."

My smile is small and wistful. Sometimes I wish that, too, but I've long since stopped begrudging any experience that has made me *me*.

"I should have stopped it." His voice is so low I think I must have misheard him.

"What?"

David's eyes dart between mine. "That night. I almost kissed you," he says out of nowhere. His voice is low and hoarse. As if his confession has been held back for so long that even his own vocal cords oppose its release.

I remember that night, of course—that moment. I've replayed it in my mind a thousand times. Maybe more. It was the first moment—until recently, the *only* moment—that I actually wondered if David could return my attraction.

"You probably don't remember."

"I remember, David."

He blinks at me for a beat before his Adam's apple rolls with his swallow. I want to kiss his neck, to trace the spot with my tongue, to taste his skin.

"I *wanted* to kiss you."

"W-why didn't you?"

He takes a deep breath. "Cap."

Of course. *Cap*. Sammy. My brother. Right. Because I'm just David's friend's little sister, and that is all I will ever be. I nod slowly, resolutely.

"I thought you didn't remember."

"How could I not remember?"

"Figured Falco took the spotlight that night."

But Brian has *never* overshadowed David. Brian was something different, something attainable, and affectionate, and real. But he never changed the fact that when David was around, he sucked all the air from the room, and kickstarted my heart into overdrive until all I could hear was the echo of that familiar beat, *Da-vid, Da-vid, Da-vid.*

"Like I said, I figured you were, you know, distracted. That's why I never said anything about it, or apologized or whatever."

Apologized. Right. Because he'd almost kissed his best friend's kid sister. That's the kind of thing you apologize for. A mistake. But he didn't make it. He may have *wanted* to kiss me, but he had no problem restraining himself as I remember it. "I wasn't distracted by Brian, David. I just…thought I imagined it, to be honest."

"You didn't," he breathes.

That's just fantastic fucking news. *Now.* "Well you're four years too late, David. I mean, it's great to know that you wanted to kiss me, but thought better of it. Really." Sarcasm surges in my tone just as anger blooms in my gut. Because why? *Why* is he telling me this *now*? To frustrate me? To hurt me? So I know that even now nothing has changed? "So you decided not to risk upsetting Sammy then, and you'll do the same thing now. Is that why you're telling me this? To remind me that this is all temporary? Because I assure you, I haven't fucking forgotten. And you know what? For all Brian's fucked-up moves, at least he had the balls to take a chance!" I turn away, ready to put some distance between us, but he's still caging me in, and he presses his body flush against mine to make his point—he's not ready to let me go.

"You think this is me not risking my friendship with Cap?" He grinds his hard-on into my hip for good measure, reminding me just how many lines we've crossed these past weeks.

"There's no risk if he never finds out," I counter.

David glares down at me, so close that I have to look up at him through my lashes to make eye contact.

"I did risk it," he finally grits out. "Now, and then, too." David is holding back, I know. I know him well enough to know he wants to growl and shout at me. But he knows he's in the wrong.

I laugh in his face. "You risked *what*? *Wanting* to kiss me, and then backing away like I was a walking STD the second my brother came outside? And then disappearing for weeks? I told you—I *remember*. You were so afraid of me—afraid of *us*—of pissing off my goddamned brother that you stayed away from our house for the longest time in the history of your friendship!"

I try to wrench from his grip but he only holds me tighter. But why? So he can convince me that Sammy is more important to him than I am? I already know that, and I don't even blame him for it. I would never have asked him to fuck over my brother for me. I just wish he'd taken a chance. That he'd at least *tried* talking to him.

David's fingers slide up my nape into my hair, and he tugs gently until he's lifting my gaze back to his. "I wasn't hiding from you. Not then."

I try to look down again, but he gives me a warning tug, and I lift my chin in defiance. "Then why were you gone?"

"He didn't want me around."

I frown at him. "Sammy?" And then I remember they got into a fight. I never did find out what it was about.

David nods once.

"He gave you a black eye," I recall. "You bruised his jaw." It was swollen for weeks.

David lets out a short, ironic laugh. "That black eye was his reminder that I was not good enough for his baby sister. And that if I ever suggested otherwise again, our fight would go way beyond a few thrown fists and a couple weeks of my not being welcome at your house."

"What?" It comes out a gasp.

David doesn't release my hair. His free hand cups my jaw, his thumb tracing the line of my cheek. "Funny thing is, I never said I was good enough for you. I've always known I'm not that. But I realized then that for you, I could try."

I stare at him, utterly captivated and equally confused. He realized *then*?

"I tried, Bea. I sat him down and told him I wanted to take you on a date. That I would never do anything to disrespect you. Cap knows me. Knew me better than anyone. I hoped he knew that whatever shit I'd done in the past when it came to girls, it would be different with you." His brow furrows. "Maybe it would've been better if he didn't know me at all."

David's gaze skates away from mine, hiding his hurt at being rejected by his own best friend. "He reminded me that I didn't know how to have a girlfriend. I think his exact words were that I didn't know how to *give a fuck*, and that even if I'd tried, I would fuck up and hurt you, and then we'd be done. You and me. Him and me. Our friendship would be over."

I gape up at him in disbelief.

David takes a deep breath. "Look, he was right, Bea. I wasn't good enough then, and I'm not good enough now."

I shake my head, denying his words. They're not true. They were never true. How could he possibly believe them?

"It's true, Bea. But don't ever think that I didn't try. I did. We may have just been kids, but I tried. Cap was clear as fuck, okay?"

I don't say anything. Everything in me is screaming for him to try *again*. Or better yet, to tell my brother to go fuck himself. But I can't ask him to do that. I knew that going into this. I just told myself that all I wanted was for him to try to talk to Sammy, and it turns out he did that a long time ago. Even if it doesn't change anything in the long-run, it makes my heart melt a little, and etches David a little more deeply into its chambers.

So I don't reply in words at all. Instead, I kiss him. I kiss him soft and hard, slow and fast, with shallow licks and deep plunges, until we're both completely breathless.

David seems all for the distraction. His lips conquer my skin from my mouth to my cleavage, removing articles of my clothing as he goes. I grab for the hem of his shirt and he tears it over his head in one swift motion while my fingers work on his belt and fly. And all the while we kiss and kiss. We kiss for every almost-kiss we never had. We kiss for every lost moment, and every single tomorrow we are destined to miss out on, until we're both worked up into a frenzy, and I'm perched on the countertop in nothing but my panties.

David looks down at them, running his finger along my center. "I want to kiss this," he rasps.

My eyes shoot open and I swallow anxiously. "I...I've never done that," I admit. It's not that I don't want him to; it's just inherently nerve-racking. It's almost more intimate than actual sex, the thought of him getting up close and personal with that most secret part of me.

David frowns. "Never?"

And I know what he's thinking. He's wondering why Brian never did it. But we were young and inexperienced—or I was, anyway—and I was nowhere near ready for that. And Brian never tried.

"Nope," I confirm.

David shakes his head to himself, silently admonishing Brian, muttering what sounds like "fucking idiot" under his breath.

His next move is sudden and purposeful as he guides me down onto the countertop. He grips the sides of my panties, slowly dragging them down, and I lift my hips to help him.

He is so turned on that I think he might just burst free of his boxer briefs. "Bea." He rips my attention from his erection with a wry smile. "Lay back and relax, but lean up on your elbows." His eyes flash with wicked intent. "I want you to watch me lick you."

I nearly lose it from his words alone, and he doesn't miss my reaction. But David's excitement is palpable, and I do as I'm told, eager to learn what has him so enthusiastic.

And I do. I learn slowly at first, then faster and louder, and then violently and explosively.

And then I learn again. I learn until I can't possibly stand another lesson, and even then, David doesn't stop.

I gasp for breath, prying my eyes open to find him watching me with untold satisfaction, despite the fact that I am the only one who's been satisfied.

David reluctantly lets me bring my legs together, running his hands over my outer thighs, even as renewed waves of pleasure pulse between them when he licks his lips and groans.

I giggle. "You really seemed to enjoy that…"

David smirks. He runs the pads of two fingers between my legs, tracing me all the way down and back again. "If I could survive on only *this* for the rest of my life—give up all other forms of sustenance and exist on a diet of just you—I would. And any man who wouldn't isn't a fucking man at all."

I don't miss the jab at Brian, and maybe he's right. Because while Brian may not have been interested in going down on me, he sure insisted on being on the receiving end.

I laugh again, but I'm surprised to find David's expression deathly sober. But he stays silent, and it's unnerving.

"What if you didn't go back to Standman?" he asks suddenly and tentatively.

I blink at him.

"When that fucker's arrested," he clarifies. But I don't know if he's just talking about me staying here indefinitely, or extending our *bene-fits*, or…something more.

"What are you talking about, David?" I ask, and David steps back to give me room to sit up.

His eyes wage an internal war. "I'm talking about trying," he says finally. "Risking it."

"As in…" I need him to be very, very clear.

David blows out a short breath. "As in doing what I should have done four fucking years ago, Beth, and taking you for my fucking self." His tone is inexplicably self-recriminating, but I can't dwell on it—not when he's saying what I think he's saying.

"Tell me, Bea," he demands. "The truth. Do you want to stay?" He doesn't just mean in his apartment, and David holds his breath as I nod hesitantly, fervently, terrified and thrilled and utterly disbelieving.

He exhales long and hard, nodding to himself, like he's trying to muster something he's not sure he has in him. "Okay," he says to himself. "Okay. I have to talk to Cap."

I gape at him. "You need to talk to *my brother?*" I glare at him, my words sharp with incredulity.

"Yeah, Beth. I do," he says matter of factly. Like *I'm* the crazy one; like I should know better. But I do know better. I know he's full of fucking shit, and in one fell swoop I've just exhausted my last ounce of patience.

"You're full of shit, David!"

He frowns. "Bea—"

"Don't *Bea* me! You *are*! You don't need to talk to my brother, you just need an excuse—to prove *you're* not the pussy. So you can blame Sammy for it not working out. You can be honest with me. Just admit you don't want the same things I do. Or…you don't want them *with me*."

I hold my breath, pressing my teeth together so hard my jaw aches, but it's the only way to keep my lip from trembling. It doesn't, however, stop the traitorous proof of my heartache from welling in my eyes. But I don't want David to placate me or let me down easy. I just want the truth I've always known, once and for all, from his own mouth. I want him to just admit that he doesn't return my feelings. That he never has, and never will. It's the only way I will ever be able to finally let go of him for good, and move on with my life.

But placate me, he does. He steps forward until he's close enough to comfort me, but I shake my head, rejecting his touch as he reaches for me, and he retracts his hand. I hate his flinch at my rejection.

It doesn't matter. David doesn't need to make contact to touch me, not with those hazel eyes doing his dirty work.

I look away, needing an escape. "Just like you *almost* kissed me all those years ago, but didn't, right?" I remind him. Now he can *almost* try to have a relationship, and use Sammy as the excuse.

David's brow furrows deeply, casting shadow over his gorgeous hazel eyes.

"He's coming for a visit this weekend, did he tell you? Maybe you can talk to him then." It's a sarcastic challenge I expect him to back down from.

But instead, David nods thoughtfully, and I blink at him.

My phone buzzes and I ignore it. David does the same when his chimes a moment later. But his doesn't stop, and finally he mutters a curse and grabs it from the pocket of his jeans, discarded on the kitchen floor.

He frowns as he reads through his messages, glancing up at me in a way that makes my pulse accelerate in anxiety. My phone rings again, and this time, I answer.

Sammy has his fake-calm voice on when he tells me he needs me to come to the city for a family dinner. That my parents have to talk to us and it can't wait, and immediately I think my father must have had a relapse.

My heart stops. *What if he's drinking again?*

My mother only took him back a few years ago, and he's been a new man since then. Well, not a new man, just the best version of himself, and no one has missed the one alcohol draws out of him.

Sammy tells me David will drive me, and by the time I look up at him, he's already dressed with his car keys in hand, and he's holding up my discarded clothing.

Chapter Twenty-five

Beth

Less than two hours later, I'm giving my name to the hostess at Smoked, one of my parents' favorite steakhouses on the Upper East Side that's not too far from my father's law firm. David swears he's as clueless as to what's going on as I am, and other than the sound of Spotify's old-school hip-hop selections, the car ride was mostly silent.

I try not to let my mind go wild with fears, old and new, as it tries to deduce what could possibly call for this emergency family dinner. But my gut swirls with dread, because one thing I know for sure is it can't be anything *good*.

I think of Grandma Mimi—who hasn't stopped popping into my thoughts since Sammy called—but I force them away yet again. I just spoke to her two days ago. She's fine. She has to be fine.

David sucks in a sudden sharp breath, and it draws my attention to my grasp on his hand—to how hard I'm squeezing it—and I hastily let go without meeting his eyes. But now, with nothing to hold on to, to help take some of this anxious energy off my hands—figuratively and literally—it flows back through me in reverse, running through my veins like a dangerous current.

We hand over our coats to be checked, but I hang on to my scarf, as if it can protect me from whatever it is I'm about to walk into—like it can hide me from whatever I'm about to learn.

David lingers uncomfortably behind me, even as we're led to the back of the dining room, down a familiar narrow hallway, and into the semi-private dining area.

There are only five tables back here, and only one of them is occupied.

My father sees me first. "Bitsy girl," he greets warmly, but uncertainly, and his gaze gets caught on David behind me before my parents exchange an uneasy glance. It unsettles my stomach.

"Come on, sit down," Sammy says before standing to give me a kiss on the cheek, lifting his chin to greet David.

"Where's Rory?" I ask him.

"Class," he says dismissively.

The tension in the room is thick and suffocating, and I find myself unwinding the scarf from my neck, as if it will help me breathe more easily. It doesn't.

"Maybe Dave should wait somewhere else? Or perhaps you have a friend you could visit nearby?" My father addresses David directly, more unsure than I've ever seen the man—a renowned, world-class attorney who can command an entire courtroom and hold nationally-aired press conferences.

Still, my jaw drops at his suggestion. "Wait somewhere else?" I ask, indignant on David's behalf. "What is he? My chauffeur?" Sammy didn't know David and I were even together when he asked him to drop everything and drive me the sixty miles into Manhattan. I could have easily taken the train.

But, of course, to them, I'm still the fragile little girl with the too-big feelings who did that one, awful, crazy thing three years ago, and, in their eyes, I'm not sure I will ever be anything else. I can't help but peek back at David, wondering for the first time since I confessed my suicide attempt to him mere hours ago, if I was wrong, after all—if it *did* make him see me as weak. Because no matter how far forward I move, or how great my strides, to my parents and Sammy it's all overshadowed by that one summer night I can't take back—that I don't *want* to take back, not now that I'm stronger for it.

"He may as well stay," Sammy murmurs with open spite, but it doesn't seem directed at David. "He's going to fucking find out, anyway."

My dad doesn't argue, but it's when my mom doesn't correct Sammy's language that I realize how serious whatever *this* is, and I robotically take the empty chair between my mother and Sammy, putting my brother between David and me.

My dad opens his mouth to talk, but my mother places her hand gently over his, and takes over for him, translating words he hasn't even said yet into her own more soothing, compassionate tongue. "Everything is okay, Bits. I don't want you to worry—"

"Then rushing me to the city for an emergency family meeting in the middle of the week probably wasn't the best plan," I tentatively point out.

Another unsettling glance is exchanged between my parents, but this time, Sammy, too, is complicit, and I frown at him, so nervous for the answer that I nearly tremble as I ask, "Is Grandma Mimi okay?" My voice shakes.

My dad's eyes go wide and my mom tilts her head to the side as they both answer in unison, "Of course!" and "Grandma Mimi is fine."

Relief washes over me, but it only leaves room for more questions. "Then what—"

"I was going to tell you this weekend, Bits," Sammy interrupts me. "That's part of why I'm coming, but…" he trails off, meeting my father's eyes—the mirror shade of his own—without explaining a damned thing.

"Everything is fine," my father takes Sammy's cue. "The family is fine. This is old news, and not something I ever thought I'd have to explain to my own *children*, but—"

Fortunately for us all, my mother takes over again. "Not long after

your father and I first got married, we went through a rough patch…"
My dad averts his gaze, but my mom continues. "And he had an affair
with a woman at his firm. It went on for barely weeks before he broke
it off and confessed everything to me, and we moved on…"

"When?" I ask.

My mom exhales a long-winded sigh. "It was over twenty years
ago, Bits. Before you and Sammy were even born."

But I don't miss the strain in my brother's jaw or the way he now refuses to meet my father's gaze. "How long before?" I sound like a mouse.

"It was a few months before I got pregnant with Sammy," my mom
replies, the small chink of hurt in her armor in no way mitigating her
strength.

It's Sammy who's most affected, even if most would probably miss
it, and I silently thank God—not for the first time—that he has Rory
in his life. My heart aches. It took Sammy and my dad so long to get
anywhere close to having a father-son relationship again, and now, old
family ghosts are resurfacing with a vengeance. And, between the two
of us, Sammy does always seem to take the brunt of them—being con-
ceived barely months after my father had been unfaithful, and then,
not nearly enough years later, taking beatings I would only ever watch
in horror.

And still, it's *my brother* who comforts *me*. He reaches up and
squeezes my shoulder, if just to remind me I'm not alone—that he's
always there. And he always is.

I catch David's worried gaze for a brief moment, but I don't hold
it long enough to even reassure him that I'm okay, too scared of being
suspected by Sammy. Our family has had enough scandal for one
night already, and I fear we're only just getting started.

And then, I wait for the rest. For the other shoe to drop. Because I
know they didn't summon me out here to tell me about an old affair.

"Anyway," my dad says hurriedly, as if he can't wait for this part
of the conversation to be over, and I can't blame him, "a reporter for

the *Herald* has been sniffing around, and called my assistant for a comment the other day. I wanted to tell you myself, Bitsy girl, but—"

"Sammy thought it might be better coming from him," my mom finishes for him.

I glance between all of them, even David, and I don't understand their anxiety. "Better coming from him? That an affair Dad had two decades ago might come out in some local paper?"

My father swallows audibly and my mom slips on her most sympathetic smile—the one I'm sure she learned from Dr. Schall. "Well, that's what we'd thought. But apparently your father's celebrity clients have raised his profile somewhat and…"

"The dipshit 'reporter' sold the story to Page Six. It prints Friday," Sammy blurts.

I gape at him. *Page Six.* As in, *The New York* fucking *Post*? I don't even have to articulate the question.

"Yeah, Bits," Sammy confirms, squeezing my shoulder again, but it isn't his touch I want right now. In fact, he's the one blocking me from the person whose touch I want most, in more ways than one, and, it turns out, he's been doing it for *years*. And why? Because he didn't trust David? *Bullshit.* He didn't trust *me*. And maybe he was right— maybe I *was* too naïve back then…but I'm an adult now, and what's changed? I'm still being babied by my family and denied the one guy I've always wanted by my brother. Because I may have dared David to talk to him about us this weekend, but there isn't a part of me that thought he'd actually do it.

And now we've got this bullshit to deal with.

I turn my attention back to my parents. "Well, that's just great. So the entire country will know about Dad's affair." Including everyone we know. I sigh deeply, waiting for the rest. Because I know there's more. Not that this doesn't suck enough already, and I know it will be mortifying when it comes out, but it can't be the reason they dragged me to the city on a weeknight.

"Yes, baby girl, they will," my mom admits. "And it will be embarrassing for a while, but we'll get through it."

I take her hand over the table, and nod. Of course we will. We always do.

The truth is I'm not even upset for myself. I'm upset for my mom. I'm upset for Sammy. I'm even upset for my dad. I'm upset that after all these years, and pain, and hard work, my family is going to suffer humiliation for a stupid mistake my father made before Sammy and I were even born.

I wait for them to tell me the rest, but they just stare at me as David watches the scene unfold before him like he's not sure he belongs. They all blink at me, exchanging glances as if they're the ones waiting for something. But for what? My mom, my dad, and Sammy all watch me carefully, warily.

"Well, what else?" I finally force out. "What aren't you telling me?" I steel myself for the answer.

Bemusement furrows all three sets of brows as they continue to stare, still glancing at one another, still waiting for something.

And it's then that I realize there *is* nothing else.

They're not waiting to divulge some final, devastating piece of information…they're waiting for me to *shatter*.

And, ironically, *that's* what fucking does it.

Not my father's ancient scandal, or our family's impending disgrace, but *this*. The way they're looking at me right now. Like I'm fragile—damaged. Even though this hasn't even got anything to *do* with me—even though it's *my mom* we should all be concerned for right now, it's me they expect to break.

After three years of therapy, despite the responsibility I've shown with my medication, with my *life*—good grades, volunteer work, all of it…All they see when they look at me is a fifteen-year-old girl in a hospital bed, small and pale, stomach pumped, whose biggest regret was waking up at all. Except my father, of course, who couldn't be bothered to visit his suicidal daughter in the hospital. After all, that was almost a year before he came back into our lives. Resentment flares in my chest, and my chair scrapes loudly against the floor as I back it away from the table to stand.

"Is this why we're here right now?" I demand to no one in particular. "You think what? I'm going to freak out or something? That the news of your old affair would send me into some kind of tailspin?" Vaguely I notice Sammy and my mom peek over at David, wondering if he knows even more about my history than they realized, but David gives nothing away.

"I'm nineteen. I manage to live my life every day without your help." I'm careful to meet each of their gazes—other than David's, anyway. "Did you even know I'm dancing again?" I point the question at my father. "And I volunteer at the student chatline helping other students who need it—"

"Actually the chatline was her idea in the first place," David interjects, and we all stare at him. "Just saying," he adds, shrugging like he doesn't have a care in the world.

"It was," I confirm. "My idea. And it's helping people—*I'm* helping people. And you guys…You interrupt my school week to tell me something you could have told me on the phone."

"Bits—" my mom starts.

"No! You had me thinking something was wrong with Grandma Mimi," I remind them. "I thought something terrible had happened."

"We were just worried, Bitsy girl," my dad defends, and I square off to face him head-on. Ever since he came back into our lives, he has done nothing but treat me like I might crumble at any moment. And pitiful me, I was so grateful to have him back that I accepted whatever I could get from him. But as I look at the man before me, in his designer suit and silk tie—a man I know truly does love me—I decide that it isn't enough. My father owed me more than just love. He *owes* me more.

"You have no right to suddenly play the role of overprotective dad after you took a five-fucking-year hiatus." He tries to cut me off, but I don't let him. "*No*. You were sober for most of that time, and definitely when I was in the hospital—when I could have *used* an overprotective dad," I remind him.

His jaw snaps shut.

"You know, through all your success and professional accolades, all I ever wanted was for you to just fucking *be* there. That's what being a man is, Dad. It's sticking the fuck around." My gaze can't help but detour to David—David, who has *always* been there.

I glance between my brother and mother. It's them I'm most disappointed in—they should know me better than that after all this time. "You really thought this was necessary?" But my voice isn't just hurt, it's *strong*. Because they can underestimate me all they want. It changes nothing.

I take a step back, and Sammy stands. But so does David, and I barely hear him tell Sammy, "She's got this," as I walk out.

I don't know how David stops any of them from chasing after me as if I were a wayward child or something, but he does, and I make my way to where we parked on Sixty-Third and Madison. The fall evening air chills my skin, and I rub my arms, wondering when I dropped my scarf.

But David rounds the corner minutes later, with my coat, purse, and, of course, my scarf, and he doesn't say a word as he wraps it around my shoulders and unlocks the car door.

The ride home from the city is as quiet as the ride in, but when David glances at me, he doesn't look like he's waiting for me to break. He looks like he's trying to figure me out or something. Or maybe like he's trying to figure *us* out.

But the evening has left me exhausted and drained, and we walk morosely into the apartment, leaving our coats slung over one of the breakfast bar stools. I go straight to the bedroom and flop back onto my pillow, and David follows close behind, pausing in the doorway to stare at me.

"It's going to be okay, Bea," David promises, and I nod. I know it is. I don't know *how*, but I know it *is*.

Sammy is still coming this weekend, figuring it best to be out of the city when the story breaks, and even if I'm still annoyed with him about tonight, I'm glad. But I can't help but think about my conversation with David before my family's interruption this evening.

The truth is I *want* to see David put his money where his mouth is, and *risk it*, as he put it. But Sammy is coming in two days, and as David continues to stare at me from too far away, I wonder where we will be come Monday. And I dread it.

Chapter Twenty-six

David

I'm not bugging out. I'm *not*.

Cap will be here in less than an hour, and at some point this weekend I'm going to tell him about Beth and me. But I'm not bugging out about it. I can't. I have to keep my shit together, or it will all come out wrong, and he won't understand.

But this time—*this* time it's too late. I *can't* walk away from her. Not now that I've tasted her in every way imaginable—now that I've become addicted to her company, to her goddamned smile.

So this weekend there's a good chance my longest friendship is going to end.

But seeing Beth stand up to her family—to her father—that way, witnessing her inner strength and her perseverance, especially after having just learned the truth of how *much* she's actually survived…It made my excuses seem weak. Worse than weak—*pitiful*.

But it was hearing what she said about what makes a man— how she rejected basically everything my father ever told me about success—that reinforces my resolve. It's the way she met my eyes without even realizing it when she talked about *sticking around*…

Somewhere inside my chest, that new, full, floaty sensation surges hard, before calming with a strange, mellow kind of high. Beth makes me feel such weird fucking shit.

Still, I may never be rich or powerful, but if there's one thing I know I can do for Bea, it's that. I can stick the fuck around. Always.

And the more I've thought about it these past couple days, the more I realize she's right. That *is* what fucking matters.

It's more than her father did, and it's more than fucking Falco did. But I can do that. For her, I can do better than that.

For her...I can be honest.

I swallow anxiously as I decide, finally, after all this time, to tell her the truth about my role in her breakup with Falco, and I silently admit to myself that it may not just be Cap I lose tonight.

I could lose fucking everything.

I blow out a long exhale. This is going to be a serious fucking night. Cap is heading straight to the BEG house for the party. Beth is going with Toni—and Rectum, whether she realizes that or not—and I'll meet them there. Reeve is out with Lani, believe it or fucking not, but Bogart promised to keep an eye on Beth until either Cap or I get there.

Because I have a late meeting with the head of the theater department to discuss my play. The one that has now become a finalist for the production grant. My head shakes automatically in denial like it has every time I've thought about it—like it can't process the reality. But at the same time, I have to admit, nothing would stick it to my father like proving to him that writing can have value. Not just academic value, like the scholarship I earned to come here, which he easily dismissed. But a production is a business, and a grant is real, green money.

Still, it isn't my father I want to win this grant for. It isn't him I want to impress. There's only one person I give a fuck about impressing—the girl it will earn me a real, genuine smile from, the kind that shows in her eyes and in her cheeks.

I can't stop thinking about Delia, and all that time I lost—some due to my own stubbornness, but much of it because of my father, and his stupid fucking quid pro quo about the PSATs, and all his crap about how meeting my birth mom would be a distraction, when really he just wanted to hold it over my head to ensure I studied the way *he* wanted me to. I knew Delia for barely a few months. But the reality is I would have had double that amount of time if I hadn't let someone who didn't give a fuck about what *I* wanted stand in my way. And I've been doing the same damned thing with Cap—letting him call the shots, and steal time from me I'll never get back. But when you never really know how much time you're going to get, any time at all is too much to ask.

If Beth can stand up to her parents, then I can stand up to my own fucking friend. I can stand up to *myself*—to every notion about my worth as a man my father worked so hard to beat into my brain to try and deter me from choosing the future I knew I wanted. It backfired on him, big-time, because instead of backing off, I embraced the picture he painted, accepting my role as the perpetual disappointment— a failure—even as I earned success after success in essay contests and scholarships and even fucking test scores. But I couldn't even see my own achievements, not with my father's disdain casting such a wide shadow over all of them.

And I know exactly what has opened my eyes, and it isn't my play being chosen as a finalist for the production grant. There's only one thing in my life that shines bright enough to vanquish that shadow.

Like she can read my thoughts, a text comes in from Beth at that very moment:

> At BEG safe and sound. Phone is going to die. Looking for a charger. Just want to tell you that I don't have to have read your play to know it's brilliant. Because you are. Brilliant. And you're going to nail the shit out of your meeting.

I grin. *Damn right I am.* And then I'm going to man the fuck up, go to that party, and take what's mine.

Okay, I'm bugging out.

Chapter Twenty-seven

Beth

The BEG party is loud, and everyone is drunk. Even I'm kind of tipsy. I've never been nervous to see my own brother before, but with everything going on—with our family, with David—I don't even know how to behave in front of him right now.

An incoming text from Lani shows a picture of Reeve's denim-clad ass, something she's a particular fan of, as he walks away to use the restroom on their "non-date." She complains about his attitude as much as she gushes over him, and God knows I can't read Reeve for my life, but I'm starting to suspect his interest in her is more than casual, considering she's just about the only girl I've ever even seen his attention on, let alone seen him talk to for more than five seconds.

Sammy texts me that his train was delayed, and he should be here soon, but my phone is dying, so I decide to go ask one of the pledges for a charger.

But first, I shoot off a quick text to David, wishing him luck at his meeting tonight. He didn't let me read his play, but I have no doubt it's brilliant, and I tell him so, sending the message a split second before my screen goes dark.

Shit.

I turn to see if I can find Dicknose or Rectum, and a tall, blond head stops me in my tracks.

What the hell is Brian doing here?

David made it pretty clear he wasn't welcome at his frat house. But he sees me, and he fixes his accusatory gaze on me as he approaches.

"Where's your boyfriend?" he asks coldly.

Huh? "What?"

"You and March. Don't lie to me."

"What are you talking about, Brian?"

"Well, I guess his plan finally worked out after all these years," he says cryptically.

I blink at him.

"Oh, didn't he tell you?" Brian says snidely. "He was the one who convinced me to break up with you before graduation." He throws it out there like it's the most nonchalant thing in the world.

"Who is?" I ask, because he's still not making sense.

"March. He kept going on and on about all the fun and girls I'd miss out on if I stayed with my little high school girlfriend, and he got in my head. And it looks like it all worked out for him, huh? I fucked up, and he's got you wrapped around his dick."

I slap him. Fast and hard, my own palm stinging with the contact that surprises me as much as him.

Brian's hand comes up to his reddened cheek, and we both stare in shock at what I just did.

At what he just confessed.

My eyes prick with moisture, but I refuse to let Brian-fucking-Falco see even one more of my tears.

Instead, I decide to reveal a truth of my own, grateful that no one else is in earshot. "You don't get to say anything about anything I do or don't do, or who I do it with, Brian."

He opens his mouth, but I cut him off.

"No. *Enough*. You are the guy who fucked me, and abandoned me."

"I loved you—"

"You *abandoned* me!"

Brian blinks at me.

"You left me alone, to deal with everything by myself."

"You think our breakup wasn't hard on me, too?"

I want to laugh, but I hold it in. "Not as hard as wondering what I did wrong—thinking there must be something wrong with me. Some reason why sex with me was the thing that sent you running."

Brian shuts up.

"Not as hard as finding out I was pregnant a month later."

His eyes go wide.

"As hard as calling and texting nonstop, *terrified*, not knowing what to do, only to be treated like I didn't even exist. Or as hard as picking up the phone to schedule a fucking abortion at fifteen years old, only to miscarry the day before the procedure, and blaming myself even for that. And *definitely* not as fucking hard as deciding to swallow a bottle of pills just to make it all go away. To make *myself* go away."

Brian stares, silent, not managing a single word.

What a fucking pussy. Why did I ever think this boy was worth my time?

I shake my head. "*That* is who you are, Brian. Not just my *ex*, not my *first love*, but *that*. A fucking *coward*—and that's being kind. There's no friendship for you and me. There's nothing." I say meaningfully, never blinking, making sure he hears me. "So just leave me the fuck alone."

I turn away from him, needing some distance, some privacy. I make my way down a hall and through the first door I can find, pleased to find it leads to the basement steps.

I rush through the basement gym and into Reeve's bedroom. I've only been here once before, but it seems the most remote place in this house to hide. At least until I can get my head together.

Fuck Brian. Even if what he said about David is true—and the merciless voice inside me makes sure I know it is—Brian didn't tell me about it now because he wanted to do the good, honest thing, not anymore than that's why I told him about the pregnancy, or about the choice that, in the end, I made for nothing. No, I told him those truths to hurt him, just as he did me.

Because if Brian was *good* and *honest*, he would have told me about David's role in our breakup three years ago. But Brian wanted to have his cake and eat it, too. Actually, *no*—Brian wanted to *fuck* his cake, store it in the freezer a few years, and then take it out and fuck it again when he was done fucking all the cupcakes and pies and goddamned soufflés he ditched the cake for in the first place.

Well, Brian can go fuck himself.

A door slams overhead, and anger colors my cheeks at the thought that he fucking followed me. But Steven staggers drunkenly down the steps instead, unknowingly making his way toward me.

"Well, hello there," he slurs as he lights up what is definitely not a cigarette.

"Hi, Steven."

"You don't smoke," he mumbles, and I laugh, confirming that, no, I don't smoke. I know Reeve is one of the only guys in the house that doesn't care if people smoke in his room, and I guess David isn't the only one who takes advantage of that.

"You're really pretty, do you know that?" Steven says out of nowhere, his words slow and exaggerated. "You know about the Hope Diamond?'

I laugh at his randomness—at his drunkenness. "Like the jewel?" I ask, but vaguely I think I've heard him mention it before, though I can't place the memory.

Steven grins, big and goofy. "Yeah. The diamond."

"Yeah, well, I got that from the name," I point out, and Steven's brows pinch together in confusion. "Hope *Diamond*," I nearly have to spell it out for him.

He snorts with recognition—finally—practically guffawing like an ape, and I laugh again at his reaction. He is a ridiculous drunk. Steven takes a pull on his joint, moving closer and gesturing to offer me a hit, and I back farther into the room. "No thanks," I murmur. I recognized the smell from the rare times it wafted from the distance at a party, or the even rarer times it clung to my brother's or David's clothes, but no one has ever smoked pot so brazenly in my presence—and I have certainly never tried it myself. And it's not even that I wouldn't necessarily, but I sure as hell wouldn't do it here, now, for the first time with Steven-freaking-Bogart.

Steven sucks down another huge hit just before he stumbles over his own feet, causing him to exhale hard, blowing that entire monstrous cloud of pot smoke smack into my face. I cough and cough, choking violently, my lungs rejecting their first taste of smoke, my hands coming up to wave it away from my face as fast as possible.

"Sorry, *shit*." Steven flaps his hands in front of me as I lean back against the windowsill to try and get my bearings.

I'm still coughing and Steven is still apologizing when I reopen my eyes.

Fuck. Smoking *hurts*. Why do people *do* this?

"Sorry. Shit, man," Steven slurs again, and I'm not sure I can stand another round of his apologies when I wave my hands again, only the smoke is gone, and now it's Steven I wish I could wave away.

I just wanted to find some place to get away for a few minutes, and to charge my damned phone. Was that really so much to ask?

"March wants to keep you all to himself, you know," Steven says, yet again, out of nowhere.

Wait, what?

"But I don't think that's fair."

"What?" I gasp out, my voice box hoarse from the smoke-assault.

He looks me up and down. "The Hope Diamond."

Huh? We're back on this now?

He takes a step toward me, and I want to take an answering one back, but there's nowhere to go. "Remember when you danced with me at Hot Box?"

I swallow audibly. I can still taste the smoke in my throat. I know Steven isn't a bad guy. That he's David's friend—his frat brother—and there's no logical reason to be afraid. But then, me and logic and a little alcohol—we don't mix well, and I can't tell my gut feelings from my anxious ones, or read whether Steven is just being a drunk douche bag, or something worse.

I skirt my way along the wall, but Steven follows me, like it's a game or something. But I'm not particularly comfortable around drunk men—especially one I've just remembered I don't actually know all that well—and my body language couldn't be more clear. Steven doesn't heed it, though, which gets my hackles up even more, and I cling desperately to one last hope that this is all a misunderstanding.

I hold up my hands and make my voice work. "No, thank you," I say pathetically. I don't even know what I'm refusing exactly, since he didn't actually offer me anything. Other than the weed, that is, and he managed to get that into my body anyway.

Steven's grin is still sloppy, but it is also decidedly menacing, and a shudder runs down my spine as he drops the joint on the floor and backs me into the corner. I push at his chest, but he doesn't budge.

"Stop it," I tell him, clear and firm.

"Come on, sexy. March doesn't have to know…" And then his lips attack.

I try to turn away—to pull back—but Steven's mouth chases my every move, his hips pinning mine to the wall to prevent my escape. His hands take liberties that make my blood freeze in my veins, touching parts of me that know they belong only to David—that only *want* David.

No, leave me alone!

"Stop!" I demand, but Steven swallows down my protests, grabbing me around my wrists when I go from shoving to hitting. "Please!"

His touch burns my skin in an entirely different way than David's does, every one of Steven's forceful kisses tasting like rancid pot and beer. I want to throw a real, closed-fist punch like Sammy taught me years ago, but I can't free my hands enough to even do that.

I am truly fucking helpless, and that's what stings most of all.

He's just too big, and it isn't until he stumbles again that I manage to push him away just enough to slip out from under his body. I move as fast as I can. Just as I'm at Reeve's bedroom door, the door overhead opens again, and heavy footsteps stamp downstairs, freezing at the bottom as I make eye contact with none other than fucking *Brody*.

My heart flies off at warp speed, and I look between him and Steven in panic as tears fill my eyes and cascade down my cheeks.

I don't know what to do!

I'm alone in an abandoned basement with a handsy asshole and an accused rapist, and they're both staring at me like I owe them something.

Suddenly, all the strength I've built over the years seems utterly useless. What good is it when my physical strength is nothing compared to these big men who don't seem to care what I want one way or another?

Violent terror stops my heart cold. *What good will it do when there are two of them?*

Brody slowly approaches, taking us in, eyes inscrutable as ever, giving nothing away. "Am I interrupting?" He seems no more or less irritable and agitated than usual. Is this his version of *casual*? My heart sinks into my stomach, as it rolls with terror.

Steven turns to Brody, smirking with sinister intent, mimicking Brody's threatening steps toward me as I try to inch myself away. "No, homie," Steven replies, "you're right on time."

Chapter Twenty-eight

David

I'm a mix of nerves and eagerness as I head toward the Arts Building. The feedback I got from my Playwriting professor has been encouraging, and while I don't want to get my hopes up for something that is still such a long shot, this could mean so much for my future. Either way, this meeting is a major opportunity—and one hard to come by. As it is, they've had to squeeze me in after a dress rehearsal for their current performance.

With Cap en route, it makes it harder to focus, but I re-read that text from Beth calling me fucking *brilliant*, and I'm more than ready to *nail* this meeting, just like she said.

I head west on Washington, and there she is once again—Liz, outside the Stu-U, having yet another smoke. She never smoked before Brody—or missed one of our parties, for that matter. I glance at my watch, knowing I should really head straight to the Arts Building.

I jog to catch up to her instead. "Liz."

She rolls her eyes. "Will you leave me alone?" she says, exasperated, and I hold up my palms in surrender.

"Just wanted to see how you're doing."

She glares at me. "No you don't. You just want to convince me to cooperate so they can charge him."

"That, too," I admit.

She drops her smoke to the ground and stubs it out with her boot. "Well, you can go fuck yourself." She turns away, but I follow, peeking again at the time and noting, with more than a little frustration, that I'm heading in the opposite fucking direction from the Arts Building.

"Liz, he should be in jail," I tell her again.

She laughs humorlessly. "You have no idea what you're talking about," she mutters.

"Then enlighten me."

She just shakes her head, and exasperation tenses my spine, but I don't let it show.

"Come on, Liz. I feel guilty, okay?"

That gives her pause, and she looks up at me, confused.

"I introduced you to the guy," I remind her sheepishly. "The night before it happened, remember? Friday night, at Toolies."

She frowns. "It happened Friday night."

What? That makes no sense.

Liz's eyes flash with something I don't quite make out, but it resembles fear, and she turns and resumes her pace.

But I keep up with her easily. "Friday?" I ask, but she says nothing. "After the bar?"

"No, later. On my way home," Liz says dismissively, quickening her pace.

I've already spoken to Kari Marx, Liz's SDT sister who saw Liz come home that night—well around four that morning, according to her. Beth and I left Toolies around one a.m., when Liz was still there, so Brody must have attacked her sometime between then and what? Three-thirty?

But a memory hits me like a ton of bricks—Brody smoking outside Standman, hours after the bar, when I walked Beth home just after three. Around the same time he would have been attacking Liz.

"Where did it happen?" I ask her.

She doesn't answer.

"*Liz.*"

"On Greek row," is all she gives me. It's vague, but it holds a world of meaning, because Greek row is on the opposite side of campus—almost an hour walk from Standman Hall, and with the Friday night traffic after the bars close down at two a.m., even by car it would likely take that long…

But Brody couldn't have been in two places at once.

"He wasn't on Greek row at that time, Liz," I say meaningfully, and she stops in her tracks.

Holy fucking shit.

"He was at Standman," I tell her. "I saw him."

But she just stands there, frozen and fearful, and I don't understand it.

Unless…"You wouldn't make that shit up, Liz…" *Would she?* *Fuck.*

"Fuck you!" she snarls at me, and then resumes her hostile, purposeful gait.

I grab her shoulder just firmly enough to get her attention, and she whirls around and jumps away, her back tight with terror, and it takes me aback. She's behaving like a cornered animal, and I show my palms again to remind her that I'm harmless. I'm a member of her fucking brother frat, for fuck sake.

For the first time, I wonder if her "attempted assault" was more than just an *attempt*, and guilt surges hard for grabbing her like that.

But I can't comprehend why she'd lie to the police about what happened any more than I could fathom why she wouldn't cooperate with them.

"What. The fuck. Is going on?" I demand.

Liz's eyes dart between mine as if searching for something. "You wouldn't understand," she breathes tremulously.

I take a slow, non-threatening step toward her. "Try me."

She shakes her head. "I can't." Her eyes fill with tears, and they unsettle me to no end. The last thing I wanted was to make her fucking *cry*.

I try another tactic. "Where did you go after you left the bar?"

She swallows thickly. "Greek row."

"To your house?"

She shakes her head.

"To mine?" We often hang out at each other's houses after the bars close and the parties end.

She stares at me for a beat before she nods slowly.

I frown. "Why?"

Her voice trembles. "That guy at the bar—Brody—he rejected me. I felt shitty. Steven always hit on me and gave me compliments." She shrugs, but it doesn't come easy—like her shoulders weren't built for the weight they now hold. "I thought it'd make me feel better."

"What?" *What is she saying?*

Liz's eyes suddenly fire with indignation. "I know my reputation, you know. What you guys say about me. And you know what? I didn't fucking *care*. I *don't* care. I was having fun. I'm young, and single, and you guys can all sleep around and use whoever the hell you want, and you're all *so fucking awesome*. But me? *I'm* a girl. So I'm *not* awesome—*I'm* a slut. But I was better than you assholes who were supposed to be my friends and your stupid double standards. Until…until he thought he could take what he wanted even though I didn't want to give it. Not that night, not to him." Each word brings more tears, until they finally spill over, rushing down her cheeks in dark, mascara-stained streams.

"But I knew. I knew my reputation, and what you guys say about me," she repeats. "And I knew none of you would believe me. *No one* would believe me. Especially not over one of *you*."

One of us?

A devastating whimper rips from her throat as she chokes back a sob. "You guys are our *brother frat*," she cries. "You were supposed to look out for us. For *me*. And, yeah, we had our fun but…" She deflates into a pitiful pile of betrayal and ruin. "You were supposed to be my friends…*Steven* was supposed to be my friend."

Bogart? The color drains from my face as the blood pumps too slowly from my chest.

"I wasn't even going to tell anyone. Especially since we'd hooked up before, and I knew he'd just deny it even happened. But Kari saw me come home, and it was obvious something had gone down." She shakes her head in self-reproach. "But I couldn't make myself say Steven's name. I just *couldn't*. I just blurted out the first name that came to mind—the guy that rejected me at the bar—Brody."

Fuck.

I take a determined step forward and Liz flinches before I remind myself to stop being a fucking idiot, and splay my palms yet again. I meet her eyes, making sure my words resonate. "I believe you."

Liz blinks at me for a beat, not quite processing—or believing.

"I. Believe. You." I repeat myself with utter clarity. "If you say it was Steven, I believe you. If you say he tried to force you, I believe you. If you say he *did* force you, I believe you. *We* will believe you."

Liz stares, stunned. "Do you really mean that?" she asks hesitantly, tears still falling, but slowing.

I lean down, bending at my knees so our gazes are locked and level. "If Steven fucking Bogart hurt a girl—one of our fucking *sisters*— then he's no brother of mine. Of *ours*."

"He did," she breathes so low I barely make it out. "Force me."

I swallow down my rage.

Liz bursts into a new kind of weeping, hugging her arms around herself as I watch her burden lift just marginally at admitting the shitty fucking truth. But I meant it. The BEG guys may have a rep for being a bunch of goofballs and players, but we have our lines, and Bogart has leapt so far over all of them I can't even fucking recognize him anymore.

"I will take care of this, Liz. I promise you. I will get the guys to back you up. But you have to call the police. You have to agree to give them a statement—to testify, whatever. Right fucking now. Please," I beg her.

"He's going to deny it." Her voice is tiny.

"Most rapists fucking deny it," I remind her, and I'm almost sure it's that—her hearing me refer to Bogart as exactly what he fucking is a *rapist*—that convinces her. She takes out her phone.

"I'm sorry, Liz. I really am. But I have to go deal with this, right now." I start to dig in my wallet for Detective Blunt's business card, but Liz waves me off, and I see his name already displayed on the screen of her phone.

"You're going to be okay?' I ask her, even though I know it's a stupid question. I know it's a dick move—that I just forced Liz to open up and I'm leaving her alone outside the Stu-U in barely dried tears, but I have no other choice right now.

But Liz smiles with untold gratitude I'm not sure I deserve, and nods.

"Tell them to come to the BEG house. That he's there right now, okay?" I'm already walking backward as I talk, but I'm not headed toward the Arts Building. I'm rushing my ass to Greek row.

I know missing my meeting will almost definitely take my play out of the running for the grant, but I don't give a fuck about plays or production grants or sticking it to my old man right now. Not when the fucker who assaulted Liz is the very same "brother" I asked to keep an eye on Beth tonight.

Chapter Twenty-nine

Beth

"Yeah," Steven slurs again to Brody, "*right* on fuckin' time."

They both approach the corner I'm trapped in like a pathetic fucking rabbit, their steps slow—and Steven's sloppy—like they're stalking prey. I don't know if they planned this—or *how*—or if it's just a tragic twist of fate that put me alone in a basement with two scumbags at a frat party. Terror combines with the alcohol I've had tonight, making it hard to focus, as does the blur of tears.

"Leave me alone!" I say far more weakly than I intend. I swipe at my eyes, determined to fight, and refusing to give either of them yet another edge—even if it is a hopeless cause.

My eyes dart between the two of them, but Steven is closer, and he takes full advantage the moment my gaze swings to Brody.

He's back on me in a blink, and I shove frantically at his weight, begging and crying, cursing my own powerlessness.

And then suddenly I'm free.

It takes me a moment to catch my breath, to get my bearings, and then finally I register that Brody's hit Steven—that they're *fighting*, and that Brody is most definitely winning. My mind can't make sense of it—two men with more in common than they even realize going at it like lions fighting over a kill. And I'm the kill.

But they're between me and the only path to the exit, and I can do nothing but flatten myself against the wall, frozen in terror as the room echoes with angry grunts and muttered expletives. Brody is fearsome, possessed with a violence I wouldn't have believed him capable of during the short time we were friends, but seeing it now, he looks every bit the monster he's been accused of being.

The door overhead bursts open again, and for a horrible second I worry I'm so desperate that I've started seeing things.

But he's real, and I cry out with relief as David emerges. He's backlit from the bright room above, but just his posture—the familiar shape of him—gives him away, and he doesn't waste a single moment before he races down the stairs.

But David's sudden appearance momentarily distracts Brody, and Steven takes full advantage, decking him hard in the jaw. I just want out of here, but David rushes straight for the action, and all I can do is desperately scream for them all to *fucking stop*.

But they don't, and to my utter astonishment, I realize David isn't even fighting Brody. Instead, he helps him up, and hits *Steven*—hard enough to knock him out with a single punch.

Everything stops.

The action. The shouting. My breathing. Finally David looks at me—at the tear in my shirt I didn't even notice until now, at my disheveled hair—and his face crumbles to pieces. His piercing hazel eyes drown in an inexplicable mixture of devastation and regret, and undoubtedly unearned guilt.

Even though Brody is standing right there and the danger isn't over, even though I still don't understand what's happening, I run straight to David, needing the magical comfort of his arms more than ever.

David presses his forehead to mine, taking my face in his hands. He doesn't speak, but his gaze says more than words ever could, and, as if he can't help himself, his lips seek out mine.

He kisses me so softly, so sweetly, with such impossible tenderness, that I'm barely aware of yet another person joining the fray.

That is, until my brother's voice rips me from my daze.

"What the fuck?" Sammy roars, his eyes darting frantically around the scene in front of him, as if trying to make sense of puzzle pieces that just don't fit together. Or trying to, anyway, because he can't seem to get past the sight of me in David's arms, his mouth too close to mine, and before I can even speak, David pushes me behind him on instinct, as if he means to protect me from my own brother.

He stares at Sammy, unsure of what to do.

And then he says something I never thought I'd hear. "I was going to tell you this weekend, Cap. Beth and me…" he grits out a tense breath. "We're…together."

My brother's eyes go wide with indignant disbelief. "You're *together?*" He's barely able to get out the word as he steps toward us.

David simply nods.

Sammy's eyes narrow, his jaw clenched in a quiet fury I've never before seen directed at his oldest friend. "You're *fucking* my *baby sister?*" he growls.

I want to defend David—to tell Sammy he never did anything I didn't want, to remind my brother I'm not a fucking *baby* anymore—but I can't force out a single word.

David squares his stance, as if offended by my brother's crude assessment. "It's not fucking like that."

Brody stands in the corner, within kicking distance of a still-unconscious Steven, and even now, I can't help but blush. But something about having both David and my brother here with me, about David's lack of concern at Brody's presence—and about the way he reacted to him versus Steven, makes Brody's threat seem less imminent, and I trust David's judgment implicitly.

Wham!

Sammy's fist makes contact with David's cheek, and his head

swings sideways, but he takes the punch in stride. He doesn't hit back—he doesn't even raise his arms to defend himself—and I fling myself between them before Sammy can strike again.

"Stop it!" I cry. "Fucking *stop* it!"

I don't know how I expected my brother to react to David and me—I suppose a part of me hoped that now that he had Rory, he might understand. At the very worst, I thought he might voice his disapproval—maybe say something obnoxious or offensive. At no point did I consider he'd behave, quite literally, like a sixteen-year-old with anger issues he's supposed to have sorted out.

And never did I imagine him looking at me with such incredible disdain. It slices me open in ways Sammy never has before. He's the one who helps heal me, not the one who hurts, and that makes his bitter glare cut even deeper.

"What the *fuck*, Bits?" my brother spits out. "Have you lost your damned *mind*?"

David steps forward as if to defend me. "Don't fucking say that to her," he says pointedly.

My brother's nostrils flare, but there's a flash of remorse, as if he regrets at least his choice of words.

I want to diffuse the situation, but I don't know how. I don't know how to make Sammy okay with David and me, and I'm still half in shock from his reaction. Part of me wonders if David was right to keep us from Sammy in the first place, and I'm starting to regret all but daring him to out us.

And the worst part is I have no idea what happens now.

I wish I could tell David that I understand why he made the choice he did four years ago—that I forgive him for it. The truth is, selfishly, I never really grasped just what David had to lose, and just how close he must have come to losing it. And in this moment, when he's finally risked it all...I can't help but wonder if it's really worth it. If *I'm* worth it.

My brother looks to David. "You're a fucking dead man."

"I won't give her up," he replies, and I gape at him.

"You motherfucking *will*," Sammy says fervently.

But David keeps his calm, shaking his head matter-of-factly. Where I am unsure, David is adamant—his words, his stance, his expression, all utterly clear—leaving no question as to whether or not *he* thinks I'm worth it. And that means everything to me.

David looks meaningfully at his oldest friend. "I won't. I can't."

Sammy looks to me, as if I might contradict David, but *I* won't. *I* can't.

My brother shakes his head with a look of disgust that shatters my heart, turning his back on us both.

But before he can turn to leave, he catches sight of Brody skulking against the wall, and stops short. A flash of recognition strains Sammy's features before it's replaced by confusion. But it doesn't make any sense.

"What the fuck are *you* doing here?" he asks Brody, suddenly sounding more drained than angry.

Brody shrugs, vaguely sheepish. "Just wanted to talk to her a minute."

Huh?

"We agreed you'd wait."

David looks between them, as lost as I am. "What the fuck is going on?" he demands.

"Family fucking business!" Sammy shouts in his face, and David bites back a retort.

"He *is* family!" I remind my brother, whose gaze swings to mine.

"Is he now?" he deadpans.

I glare at him, shaking my own head in disappointment at how he's treating someone who is supposed to be one of his closest friends.

"Some shit went down," Brody says simply.

Some shit *went down? Like him being a fucking* rapist? *What the fucking hell is happening here?*

The last of my patience finally implodes. "Will someone tell me what the hell is going on!" I yell like the petulant child I keep claiming not to be.

All eyes turn to me—David's unknowing, Sammy's uncertain, and Brody's...

Holy shit. My heart freezes inside my chest.

Brody's eyes...they match my brother's identically. As in, not just their expression—though even that is unmistakably similar. But their shade—*our* shade—their shape...it's absolutely uncanny, and I can't fathom how I didn't see it sooner.

I gape between the both of them, trying to work out the incomprehensible.

But Sammy must see my shock. "Dad's affair," he says hesitantly. "The woman got pregnant."

Pregnant.

I look to Brody. "Your mom?" I gasp. I can't believe what I'm asking him.

He nods.

My dad. His mom. Pregnant.

"But—" My mouth slams shut. But, *what?* But *he's a rapist?* That doesn't change the fact that if what they're telling me is true, Brody is my *half-brother*.

David's touch on my shoulder makes Sammy's nostrils flare, but it soothes me immeasurably, and I meet his gaze. He shakes his head. "It wasn't him, Bea."

I blink at him.

"Liz just spat out his name. She didn't think anyone would believe Bogart had to force her. And it wasn't an *attempted* anything, either."

Steven lays still on the ground, whether from alcohol, his joint, or a well-deserved concussion, and guilt seizes my throat as I process all of it. That Brody, my apparent half-brother, wasn't stalking me or chasing me for some sinister reason. He just wanted to talk to me, probably to tell me the same thing David just did—that he's innocent. But not only wouldn't I give him the benefit of the doubt, I wouldn't even hear him out. I befriended him, and then turned my back on him at the first sign of trouble. Even if that particular sign was a fairly extreme one.

But Brody doesn't look at me with resentment. In fact, he looks like he's the guilty one.

"I'm sorry, I..." My voice shakes. "I thought—"

Brody shakes his head fervently. "Not your fault."

Isn't it, though? I believed this horrible thing about him after not even hearing it from his accuser, but from a third-hand rumor. My stomach sinks.

"I should've—"

But Brody cuts me off. "I just found out about you after my mom died—and when I found out you'd be going here...Then when I saw you—"

"*Stalked* her," David corrects him, firming his grip on my shoulder.

Brody doesn't respond, but he nods subtly as if to acknowledge it. "And when Sam found me." He looks to my brother. *His* brother. "But the timing..."

"I was going to tell you this weekend," Sammy murmurs.

"I agreed to wait until you guys could talk." Brody gestures to Sammy and me. "But I just wanted to get to know you, and then suddenly I'm being called in for questioning about some fucking assault on some chick I met for five fucking minutes..."

And I wouldn't give him the time of day.

"Well, she wouldn't talk to the cops to clear my name *or* to help them railroad me, as much as they wanted her to do the fucking latter. But I figured you'd heard when the DNA ruled me out, since you'd obviously heard when she accused me—within, like, minutes."

But I didn't hear. No one did. Liz wasn't talking to anyone about it one way or the other. "I didn't."

Brody nods and smiles a little sadly. "Figured."

Right. Considering I ran away from him like I was being freaking hunted.

"I'm sorry," I say again.

Brody shakes his head. "It's cool, Beth," he says nonchalantly, but how could it be?

"Really, I—"

"Hey." He cuts me off, and waits for me to meet his serious gaze. "We're cool."

The door overhead flings open to a chorus of drunken laughter and footsteps tramping unevenly down the stairs.

"Maybe we should take this somewhere else," David mutters. "We can go talk at our place."

Neither David nor I realize his mistake before Sammy's fury returns with a vengeance. "*Our* place?" he practically snarls. "'The fuck is even happening right now!"

I know my brother, and he has had enough, which he confirms by muttering something to himself and stomping up the stairs, pushing unceremoniously around the newcomers—two of David's frat brothers whose names I can't remember.

I don't know what I expected, but it wasn't this. Sammy has never turned his back on me in all my life. My eyes sting viciously, and it takes all of my willpower to keep them dry. I know I will never lose Sammy in the literal sense, but that doesn't mean I can't break us.

And what about David? They've been friends for almost twenty years. *Brothers*, themselves.

I may have just gained a brother I never even knew about—not that I can even begin to process *that* right now. But I fear I may have lost the one I've known all my life—at least as I've known him—*and* essentially lost David the very same thing.

But as David pulls me into his arms and presses a tender kiss to my forehead, I feed off his calm. Even in this sea of chaos, he is my anchor. And just the comfort of his proximity reminds me we've all been through worse—that we'll get through this, too.

We have to.

Chapter Thirty

David

I brush my lips over the soft skin of Beth's forehead, promising her things I can't articulate right now. I don't know what will happen with me and Cap, with her and Cap, but I know that as long as she wants me, I will be here. I will stick the fuck around.

I want to get her the hell out of this basement, but I know our night isn't over yet, and the sound of police sirens progressively growing in volume as they approach the house confirms it. *At least Liz fucking came through.*

I meet Brody's gaze over Beth's head, stroking my fingers soothingly through her tangled hair. "Liz told me the truth. It was Bogart who attacked her." I gesture with my chin to the pile of garbage at Brody's feet—my soon-to-be *former* frat brother. "She called them," I say of the cops, who we can now hear entering from the main floor.

It still doesn't make fucking sense. Brody—the creepy stalker who lurks in alleyways—is innocent. Not just innocent, but Beth and Cap's fucking half-*brother*. And Bogart—all-around good-time guy, and our chapter's fucking *president*—is about to be fucking arrested. He's the last person I would have suspected of fucking assault.

Except…as I let my mind go there, little things he's said and done over the years shift in context and meaning, and I become sick to my stomach. And then I remember the rip in Beth's shirt, the knots I'm painstakingly finger-combing from her golden locks, and my eyes fix on Bogart.

My jaw clenches and my arm tightens around Beth.

"Don't do it, man," Brody mutters. "Trust me." He gives Steven a not-so-subtle kick. "He's not fucking worth it."

He slides his gaze to Beth before meaningfully meeting mine.

"But she is."

* * *

There's something unburdening about the worst actually happening, only to realize it wasn't the worst at all.

Cap won't take Beth's calls or mine, and he didn't show up at our place after walking out of my frat house. And I won't pretend it doesn't sting in every way I always imagined it would. But...I have Beth in my arms, and for the first time, I know without a single doubt that if it were reversed—if I had Cap and lost *Beth*—that would be the true *worst*.

After we got home and she told me what Falco told her tonight, about my role in her worst heartache—especially now that I understand just how bad it was—I worried I might lose them both. But this fucking girl...she listened to my explanation, but she didn't need it. She just gave me the benefit of the doubt, just like that—something neither Cap nor my father has never given me.

I don't sleep. I just hold her, looking down at her blurred features, which are too close to my own to clearly make out, and I can't help but think she looks even more beautiful from right here. So many things in this life, even the things that appear the most beautiful— *especially* the most beautiful—fall apart when viewed up close. They reveal flaws and imperfections, hidden truths that change your entire perception of them.

But not *this* thing—this *girl*. Her flaws contribute as much to her perfection as her beauty does. It all works together to make her absolutely perfect, and now that everything between us is all out in the open, I finally let myself admit I never stood a chance against her at all.

When it comes to girls I've never much entertained feelings other than physical attraction, and mild affection at best. When you've been called worthless enough times by the man who raised you, you start to believe it's true. You stop looking at girls like Beth Caplan as attainable, and you sure as fuck don't see yourself as worthy of them.

But fuck that. Fuck them all. Because there's nothing *mild* about the torrent of emotion raging inside me as I look down at Bea, and I realize that with her by my side, reminding me of myself in my darker moments, we can have any fucking future we want.

Beth's eyes blink open, still evaded by sleep just like me, and she looks up at me with concern. I press a kiss to her lips to reassure her, but it's *her* eyes that comfort *me*. They are deep blue oceans, and I've been wading in their undertow for years, slowly drawn in until they finally caught me in their riptide. And when her lips part and she sucks in a harsh breath, like I affect her just as much, I start to think drowning wouldn't be so bad.

Epilogue

Beth

Eight months later

David climbs out of my parent's pool—the same pool he first learned to dive in—and shakes the water from his hair. The sun refracts off his tanned, wet, summer skin, droplets sliding tauntingly down his perfectly defined abs, and I feel it in the deepest part of me. But then, he's had me drooling over him for years, so why should anything change now that he's mine?

"Oh, come on, man! Pussying out?" Sammy calls from the water as he chucks the waterproof football at David's back, landing a perfect spiral as Tucker laughs endlessly.

"Just need to kiss my girl," David smirks, and Sammy grimaces and makes exaggerated vomiting sounds. That only makes Tucker laugh even harder.

Brody lounges in the chaise beside mine, averting his gaze at David's words, and I can't help but blush. It's still so hard to process the fact that we're related—that he's my *half-brother*—but every time I catch his familiar, deep blue gaze, it becomes somehow more real. And getting to know him better has helped, too, of course.

True to his word, David jogs over and steals a quick, chaste kiss before diving back into the pool. Rory swims over to Sammy to distract him, which works like a charm. He puts her on his shoulders and Tucker grabs Carl for a chicken fight.

"We got winner, Bea!" David calls from the pool just as Rory and Carl go down in unison, and I burst into laughter. "Or loser," David amends.

My parents sip sparkling water under the umbrella by the built-in bar, watching the fun, but more than satisfied with each other's company. Things were awkward between my dad and me for a while, but those things I said at dinner that night—I meant them. Only I didn't exactly have all the information. It turns out my father did come to the hospital after my suicide attempt. He rushed there, in fact, and didn't leave for days. But my mother thought it best that I didn't see him, and my psychiatrist at the time agreed. And they were probably right—I was certainly dealing with more than enough already.

Still, that didn't change the fact that my father and I had unresolved issues. When he came back into our lives, I forgave him without question—for everything he'd done before he left, for leaving, for staying gone—all of it. But my father still owed a debt of apology, and I knew he'd already paid it to my mother and Sammy but I was so desperate to get him back that I never demanded payment of my own. Until recently, anyway. But now that the Band-Aid has been ripped off, we've finally begun to heal our relationship in earnest, and it feels good.

It took David and Sammy a long talk and a lot of time before they were right again, too, but with every month that passes, I think Sammy is starting to accept that we are for real.

I think I am, too.

I'm still anxious about it. It'd be impossible not to be after all this time, and especially after my last experience with a relationship. But David is always eager to ease my insecurities, and I love that he indulges me.

Later that night, when I'm alone with David in my childhood bed, I get to thinking about the past. About the first time he told Sammy he had feelings for me, and I decide to ask him about it.

"What if you did kiss me the night I met Brian?" I ask. "Would you have broken my heart? If we started...you know?"

"Started going out?"

I shrug and nod at the same time, noncommittal, worried I'm being too presumptuous, assuming we'd have been in a relationship if Sammy had given his approval back then.

David sucks in a deep breath, but his eyes—seas of gray and green and brown—never leave mine. They are my crystal balls, but instead of looking into the future, I'm searching for a past that should have been mine. That could have been, if my brother hadn't rejected one of his closest friends.

"I was a real dick in high school, Bea." He lets out a short, ironic laugh. "I'm still a dick."

He is, sometimes. But never to me.

David sighs. "I really didn't care about anything. I fucked around a lot. I acted exactly the way Cap said I would."

I just stare at him, because he's giving me the reality but that's not what I'm looking for, and I will the crystal balls to show me the alternate life instead.

And then they grow serious and somber, and the clouds dissipate like magic, and they are utterly clear as they reveal my answer. "But no. If things had been different, if I had you...I wouldn't have done any of that shit. I wouldn't have had to."

I frown. "What do you mean *had* to?"

His full, kissable lips twitch. "I did that shit 'cause I felt bored and trapped, Bea." He lifts one shoulder in a half-shrug. "I never feel that way when I'm with you."

I smile wistfully for the young girl I used to be, and for my perfectly happy, giddy present-day self.

"I love you," David whispers suddenly, and I gape at him. He's never said that before.

"What?" I breathe.

"I *love* you," David repeats more insistently. "I'm *in* love with you."

Anxiety floors my pulse. "How?"

"*How?*" he repeats, incredulous.

"How do you know?" Because his confession summons one of my greatest fears. How can he possibly *know* that? How can he be sure the feeling he thinks is love isn't distorted by the affection of having been like family our whole lives? How does he know with any certainty that it's really even the romantic kind? What if his emotional vision is just blurred by our mutual attraction? Or *something*? *Something* to explain away what he's just proclaimed. *Twice*.

Because David March is not *in love* with me. It's just not possible.

His brow furrows so deep it casts his dark-hazel eyes in shadow, and he blinks at me.

"How do you know?" I ask again through trembling lips, much softer this time. "How do *I* know?" That's what I want to know more than anything. How *do* I know? How do I know what's real? How do I know if what I feel for him is love, or just another manifestation of my crush?

David's frown deepens even more. "Are you asking me how you know my feelings? Or your own?"

"Both," I admit.

He stares at me for a beat.

"It's just—David...I've always—"

He cuts me off, his frown imploding into a mask of determination. "You've always *what*?" he demands, but it's rhetorical. Not that he gives me an opportunity to respond. "Thought about me way too much, or stared at me too long, or felt it in your chest every time I walked into a fucking room?" His eyes rake my body and his mouth pulls into a vaguely wolfish grin. "Or pictured me naked more times than you could count."

A blush heats my cheeks, creeping downward over every exposed inch of me David's eyes just helped themselves to.

"Because I'm fucking familiar." His knuckles follow their path, barely grazing my skin, leaving goose bumps in their wake. "Do you know why I call you *Bea*?" he asks out of nowhere, and I blink at him.

"Because I asked you to stop calling me *Bits*?"

A smile tugs at the corner of his mouth. "But why *Bea*?"

I shrug. "I thought it was *B* at first—as in the first letter of *Beth*..."

David chews his lip to bite back an amused smile. "Nope. *B-e-a*..." He whispers a kiss just under my ear before breathing, "as in *b-e-a*-utiful..."

I slap playfully at his chest. "Stop it," I laugh.

But his eyes are deathly serious. "Stop what? You asked me to pick a new nickname for you on the spot, and even in that shitty moment, all I could think of was how beautiful you were."

I stare up at him, stunned.

"I *know*, beautiful girl, because I've *always* known," he says, answering my original question. "Even when I wasn't conscious of it. I know because I was willing to sacrifice the kind of love you think I'm mistaking for *love*—my friendship with your brother—in case you've forgotten. I know because not only would I do anything for you, Bea, but because I couldn't stand to see any other man in my place. Not now, not ever." He tucks my hair behind my ear, hazel eyes imploring me to hear him. "I know, because *I know*."

Wow.

"So the question is, *Bea*," he emphasizes my nickname, stressing its origin, and I melt. "Do *you* know?"

"Do I know if I love you?" My heart swells so epically it's as if it's trying to tell him itself.

David smiles. "Do you know that I love *you*?" he corrects me, like it's not as important for him to know how I feel as it is for him to make sure I know how he feels. And if that's not love, I don't know what is.

I nod.

David exhales his relief and brushes his lips over mine.

"And I also know that I've loved you since I first saw you."

David laughs. "I was like five."

I smile. "Exactly."

The End.

Acknowledgments

Above all, I always have to thank the incredible readers who have come along for the Something More ride, and who continue to show these characters and their stories nothing but love. Your support means everything to me, and you keep me going in those inevitable moments of self-doubt.

A gazillion thank you's to my amazing editor at Forever, Amy Pierpont, for her infinite patience, understanding, and support, and for making this story the very best it could be. Thank you for always showing these characters so much love! And to Madeleine Colavita for all of her help along the way.

Infinite thanks to my incredible agent, Erica Silverman, at Trident Media Group for believing in this series from the very start, for believing in *me*, and for always being in my corner, especially when times are tough.

To Amy Briggs, for taking the time to beta read for me, even while in the midst of a cross-country move, all while writing at least thirty different books herself (that may be an exaggeration, but if so, only slightly). Thank you for your invaluable feedback and reassurance, and, perhaps most of all, for always being there with a hilarious meme or rant, and your inexplicable sixth sense for knowing exactly when I need them.

Tali Alexander, Stevie J. Cole, Amanda Renee, Z.B. Heller, JC

Santo, Veronica Larsen, Danielle Jamie, my Fictionally Yours girls, my War Cry ladies, and all of the wonderful author friends I've been lucky to make during this journey—you guys both keep me sane, and make me crazy in the best possible ways. I love you all.

To the book bloggers and their blogs, big and small, whose support for this series seems to know no bounds, and who continue to devote so much time and effort for the simple love of literature; I am in awe of you. Bianca, Jordan, Sasha, Candi, Roxie, Michelle, Jen, Samantha, MyMy, Jenny Rose, Jezabell, Kristin and Amber, Stacy, Helene, and so, so many more I couldn't possibly name all of you. It astounds me every day how much time, work, and passion you put into your love of books, and I appreciate you more than you will ever know.

To my "Chosen Chicks": Amy, Angelica, Bianca, Candi, Cat, Georgie, Jen, Joli, Jordan, Kaitie, MeShelly, MyMy, Renery, Sanci, Sasha, Taylr, and Taylor, for your endless support, and to Christina Santos and Heather Brown for helping me with all things social media.

To my Pearl Girls, for keeping my reader group fun and exciting, and, of course, inappropriate, and for your constant love and support.

Thank you to the entire book community, for all of the heart you show every day, both for the books you love and the authors who write them. To everyone who takes time out of their busy day to post reviews, share book news, engage on social media, attend signings, etc., your passion for our characters and their stories is what gives authors the fuel to keep going.

As always, I have to give a special shout-out to my family.

To my sister, Becky, and sisters-in-law, Drew and Gabi, and Eden, for your endless encouragement and (presumably) unconditional love. To my brothers, Matthew and Elan and Jesse, and cousin-brothers, Nuriel, Leor, and Etan, for just being awesome, even if you're not exactly in the romance target market.

To my mom, Margo, to whom this book is dedicated (and it releases in the U.S. on her birthday!) for always encouraging me to keep writing, and who has always been my most vocal fan, beta reader, and cheerleader. Thank you for always being ready for Grandma-duty when life throws me curveballs. To my Aba, Jay, who adores my books, but loves my Facebook rants even more. And who can read *me* like a book—even when I wish he couldn't. To Lana and Mike, my second pair of parents, who are always on-call for Baba/Dyeda duty, words of wisdom, and unconditional support. You are even more valued and appreciated than you know, and none of my books could have been published without you. To my other second-mom/Aunt Michele, and Dod David, who were happy to take on the role of home-base when the rest of the family matriarchs booked it to SoFlo (not that I can blame them). Thank you for always being there. To Grandma Beverly and Grandpa George for a lifetime of invaluable advice, and for always setting the right example. *The Beverly way*, or no way at all!

To my husband and best friend, Roman, who has stepped up in ways neither of us ever imagined when life and deadlines ganged up on me, picking up my slack and carrying it with pride on his already over-burdened shoulders. He also happens to be the world's best father to my babies. You will always put both the "Roman" and the "antics" in *Romantic*, and I will always love you for it.

And lastly, thank you to said babies, for keeping me constantly entertained, and my heart always full.

About the Author

Danielle Pearl is the best-selling author of the Something More series.

She lives in New Jersey with her three delicious children and ever-supportive husband, who—luckily—doesn't mind sharing her with an array of fictional men.

She did a brief stint at Boston University and worked in marketing before publishing her debut novel, *Normal*. She writes mature Young Adult and New Adult Contemporary Romance.

You can learn more at:

DaniellePearl.com

Instagram @daniellepearlauthor

Twitter @danipearlauthor

Facebook.com/daniellepearlauthor